ONE B...
AT ...

CW00727681

BY
MEREDITH WEBBER

P.S. YOU'RE
A DADDY!

BY
DIANNE DRAKE

MILLS
BOON
&

Meredith Webber says of herself, 'Once I read an article which suggested that Mills & Boon were looking for new Medical Romance™ authors. I had one of those "I can do that" moments, and gave it a try. What began as a challenge has become an obsession—though I do temper the "butt on seat" career of writing with dirty but healthy outdoor pursuits, fossicking through the Australian Outback in search of gold or opals. Having had some success in all of these endeavours, I now consider I've found the perfect lifestyle.'

Now that her children have left home, **Dianne Drake** is finally finding the time to do some of the things she adores—gardening, cooking, reading, shopping for antiques. Her absolute passion in life, however, is adopting abandoned and abused animals. Right now Dianne and her husband Joel have a little menagerie of three dogs and two cats, but that's always subject to change. A former symphony orchestra member, Dianne now attends the symphony as a spectator several times a month and, when time permits, takes in an occasional football, basketball or hockey game.

ONE BABY STEP AT A TIME

BY
MEREDITH WEBBER

First published in Great Britain 2013
by Mills & Boon, an imprint of Harlequin (UK) Limited.
Harlequin (UK) Limited, Eton House, 18-24 Paradise Road,
Richmond, Surrey TW9 1SR

© Meredith Webber 2013

ISBN: 978 0 263 89892 7

Harlequin (UK) policy is to use papers that are natural, renewable and recyclable products and made from wood grown in sustainable forests. The logging and manufacturing process conform to the legal environmental regulations of the country of origin.

Printed and bound in Spain
by Blackprint CPI, Barcelona

Dear Reader

I realised recently that in my long and varied career as a medical writer I hadn't ever written a 'friends to lovers' story, yet I know this happens in real life.

Any number of disparate bits of information come together to make a book—or one of my books, anyway—and for this one I remembered a plane trip where I sat next to a member of the Elite Mine Rescue team on the first leg of his journey to the USA to help rescue some trapped miners. I was fascinated by his stories, but more intrigued by his enthusiasm for what was obviously a very dangerous profession—and they *are* professionals, all of them. Why this memory surfaced for this book I'm not sure, but there it was, all ready to use.

Then there was the child. Children have been fairly prevalent in my books. The powerful bond between a parent and a child, to me, can mirror the bond of love slowly and hesitantly growing between a man and a woman, a hero and a heroine—and, of course, a child can bring problems in its wake...big problems! But I loved Steffi from the moment that she appeared on the scene, rather unexpectedly even for me, so I hope you love her too.

All the best

Meredith

CHAPTER ONE

HE HADN'T EXPECTED it to feel so strange, walking into the ER at Willowby Hospital. After all, he'd been here often enough as a child—broken arm, a badly sprained ankle and, on one memorable occasion, suffering hypothermia after he'd been trapped down a well. Bill's fault, that! Bill crying pitiably at the top because her cat had fallen in—Bill going all girlie on him!

Whillimina Florence de Groote—his friend Bill!

Finally producing a daughter after six sons, Bill's mother had named her after both grandmothers, thinking it a nice feminine name, but from before she could talk, Bill had decided she was one of the boys and early on had insisted her name was Bill.

So Bill she'd stayed.

Lost in the past, he was startled when the woman who'd met him at the door—Lesley?—spoke.

'I'll introduce you to our senior nursing staff, and you'll meet the rest as you move around.'

But once again he was distracted, for there she was!

The wild, vivid, red hair, ruthlessly tamed for her work shift, burst like tendrils of flame from beneath her white cap, bringing smudges of colour to the sterility of the room.

'Bill!'

His delighted cry echoed around the still-quiet space and as he strode towards her, Lesley—he was sure it was Lesley—bleating, 'Oh, you know Bill?' as she followed him.

He watched as disbelief chased surprise across Bill's face, then delight dawned in a smile that made the brightly lit room seem even brighter.

'No one told me!' she said, abandoning the patient she'd been shepherding towards a cubicle to give him an all-enveloping hug. 'You didn't tell me you were coming,' she added, with a punch on his shoulder. 'But I'm so glad! Gran will be so happy. But what are you doing here? I'm working. Did you just call in to say hello?'

He grinned at her, the pleasure of seeing her again, from hearing the rush of words that was pure Bill, warming him right through.

'I'm working too,' he said, and saw shock dawn on her face.

'Working?'

He nodded.

'Here?'

He nodded again, still smiling broadly because he'd never seen Bill flabbergasted before, but flabbergasted she truly was.

'You've got a patient, I'll explain later,' he said, delighted that he could keep her guessing a while longer.

That drew a scowl but she did return to her patient, fully focussed on work once again, leaving Nick with a strange sense of… Well, he wasn't sure what it was— surely not *rightness* about returning home?

No, he was being fanciful. It was probably nothing more than the pleasure of seeing Bill again.

'You know Bill?' Lesley had been hovering behind him during the exchange.

'You could say that,' he replied, still smiling because somehow seeing Bill had made this decision to come home seem comfortable—even inevitable—for all he'd been thrown into work before he'd had time to settle in because of some emergency in the senior ER registrar's family.

Four hours later he'd had plenty of opportunities to see his old friend in action, her seniority evident in the way she designated duties and handled patients, always busy yet always calm and smiling.

Always attracting his attention whenever she was in sight, but that was nothing more than his natural delight in seeing her again. That she felt the same he had no doubt, for she'd flash a smile at him as their paths crossed.

Until now, when she was coming towards him with determination in her easy, long-legged stride, another scowl on her face.

'Tearoom *now*, Dr Grant!' she ordered, and he fell in obediently behind her, knowing he'd have a lot of explaining to do but pleased to have an opportunity to sit and talk to her in this small lull.

Had she ordered everyone out, that the area was empty? he wondered, as he followed her into the messy room. He wouldn't have put it past her, but right now he didn't care. All he wanted to do was give her a proper hug, to reaffirm he really *was* home again.

He caught her in his arms and swung her round, not easily as she was nearly as tall as he was—and only for a moment as she pushed away and glared at him.

'And what's all this about?' she demanded. 'Creeping into town without a word to anyone? And don't tell me Gran knows because I saw her yesterday and you know she can't keep a secret.'

He grinned at the red-headed termagant who'd bossed him around all his young life.

'Neither can you,' he reminded her, 'and I wanted it all settled before I told Gran. In the end, the job came up sooner than I expected so there was no time to tell anyone.'

Gold-brown eyes narrowed suspiciously.

'*What* is all settled?'

'The contract—twelve months with an option to extend.'

And now Bill was hugging him!

'Oh, Nick, Gran will be so happy. She never says anything but since that fall a month ago she's been feeling fragile and I think that makes her miss you more than ever. I can hear it in her voice when she talks about you.'

And you? Nick found himself wanting to ask, although why he wasn't sure. He and Bill had kept in close touch over the years, with regular emails and infrequent phone calls, very occasionally catching up in person when they'd both happened to be in the same city at the same time. It was what friends did so, yes, he did want her to be happy he was home…

'Sit, I'll make coffee,' Bill was saying, so he set the thought aside and sat, happy to watch her move around the little room, totally at home, composed—beautiful really, his Bill, although he'd probably always been too close to her to see it.

* * *

Bill shook her head as she set the kettle to boil, disbelief that Nick was actually here still rattling her thoughts. Her first glimpse of him had made her heart thud in her chest—just one big, heavy thud as she'd taken in the sight of the tall, lean man with a few threads of grey in the softly curling brown hair that had been the bane of his younger life. The black-rimmed glasses hid eyes she knew were grey-blue and gave him a serious look.

Her Nick, all grown up and devastatingly handsome now, she realised as she stepped back from their friendship and looked at him as a man.

They'd met in kindergarten class at Willowby West Primary School, a friendship begun when she had punched the boy who'd called Nick Four-Eyes. She'd dragged him home with her that afternoon, made him phone his gran to say where he was, then ordered a couple of her brothers to teach him how to fight.

And so the bond had been forged—a bond that had survived years of separation, though they'd always kept in touch and shared with each other what was happening in their lives.

Was there any tougher glue than friendship?

She found the tin of biscuits and put it on the table in front of him then brought their coffees over, setting them both down before plopping into the battered lounge chair opposite him, unable to stop staring at him and slightly embarrassed that he seemed to be equally focussed on her.

'Well?' she finally asked, mainly to break a silence that was becoming uncomfortable.

'It's been too long since we've seen each other,' he said. 'You've changed somehow.'

'It's been five years and then only for an hour at Sydney airport. Anyway, I never change, you should know that,' she teased. 'I was a skinny kid with wild red hair who grew into a skinny adult with wild red hair. But you, who knew you'd get so handsome?'

It was a weird conversation to be having with Nick—strained somehow. Although they'd gone in different directions after high school, he to Sydney to study medicine, she choosing Townsville for her nursing training, on other occasions when they'd caught up with each other, even briefly, they'd fallen back into their old patterns of friendship as if they'd never been parted.

Yet tonight was different.

'Will you stay with Gran?'

Gran was Nick's relation, not hers, but Bill was in the habit of calling in a couple of times a week, taking Gran shopping or getting library books for her.

With Nick here, Gran wouldn't need her…

'No, I spoke to Bob when the idea of the contract first came up. He offered me one of the penthouses at the new marina development he's just completed.'

'The sod!' Bill muttered, thinking of her eldest brother, the developer in the family. 'So *he* knew you were coming and said not a word to me! What's more, all I've got is a one-bedroomed apartment on the sixth floor in that building, and I bet he's giving you family discount as well.'

Nick smiled.

'But I am family, aren't I?' he retorted. 'I'm your seventh brother. Isn't that what you've always said?'

It was, of course, but it wasn't their relationship that was disturbing Bill right now, though what it was she couldn't pinpoint.

'It'll be a bit weird working with you,' she said, fairly hesitantly because that didn't seem to be what it was either.

Nick smiled and her heart gave another of those strange thuds.

'You only think that because you're used to being the one bossing me around and in the ER a doctor trumps a nurse.'

She rose to the challenge in his words.

'Oh, yeah? Says who?'

He didn't answer, just picked up his coffee, his smile still lingering about his lips, showing in fine lines down his cheeks and a crinkle at the corner of his eyes.

It was because she hadn't seen him for so long she had to keep staring at him, she was telling herself when the smile turned into a grimace.

'Aaargh! You call this coffee? You haven't heard of coffee machines? How backward *is* this place?'

Bill laughed.

'Not too backward these days but budget cuts are everywhere. You want fancy coffee you'll have to provide the machine and the beans, and everyone will use both and one night a junkie will steal the machine and you'll be back to instant.'

'I'll get a small one and lock it in my locker and it will be for my exclusive use,' Nick growled, sounding so like the old Nick of her childhood that Bill felt warmth spread through her.

This was going to be all right—wasn't it?

Bill was pondering this when Lesley burst through the door.

'Critical emergency on the way in, Dr Grant. Can you take the call from the ambulance?'

* * *

Forty minutes later Nick was ready—well, as ready as he would ever be. Although the town had grown, Willowby Hospital was still little more than a large country health centre. No specialist resuscitation area here, no emergency trauma surgeon on standby, just him and whatever nurses could be spared from the usual stream of patients on a Sunday night.

Him and Bill!

Right now she was setting up a series of trays on trolleys, IV and blood-drawing supplies, chest tubes, ventilator, defibrillator, medications, and was checking the supply of oxygen, the suction tubes, not fussing but moving with swift confidence and precision. Just watching her gave him added confidence about whatever lay ahead.

'The baler they spoke of—it's one of those things that rolls hay into huge round bales?' he asked, and she looked up from what she was doing to nod.

'Though what the lad was doing, putting his arm anywhere near the machine, is beyond me,' she said, before adding thoughtfully, 'I suppose if the string got caught you might think you could pull it loose and give it a tug. I've always thought night-harvesting had an element of danger because, unless you're used to night shifts, your mind might not be as sharp as it should be.'

Images of the damage such a machine could do to a human arm and shoulder flashed through Nick's mind, and he had to agree with Bill's opinion, but further speculation was brought to an end by the arrival of the ambulance and their patient, unstable from blood loss, his right arm loosely wrapped in now-bloody dressings, a tourniquet having been unable to stop the bleeding completely.

Nick listened as the paramedic explained what had been done so far—the patient intubated, fluid running into him, morphine to ease the pain, conscious but not really with them, so shocked it was clear the first-response team doubted he could be saved.

Hypovolaemic shock from loss of blood. The young man's heart would be racing, his hands and feet cold and clammy, his pulse weak—

'All we need to do is stabilise him enough for him to be airlifted down to Brisbane,' Bill reminded Nick, as if she'd heard the same thing in the paramedic's tone and had the same symptoms racing through *her* head.

So it began, the flurry of activity to keep the young man alive long enough for surgeons down south to save him. The paramedics had fluid flowing into him through his radial artery but he needed more.

While Bill hooked the patient up to the hospital's oxygen supply and monitors, taking blood to send to the lab for typing, Nick prepared to put a catheter into the left subclavian vein, anaesthetising the site, then advancing a needle carefully down beneath the clavicle, a guide wire following it when blood flowed freely into the needle's syringe.

Removing the needle, he made a small incision, his hands working mechanically while his mind raced ahead. Once the catheter, guided by the wire, was in place and more fluid was flowing in, he could examine the torn arm and shoulder in order to find the source of the blood loss.

'The tourniquet is holding back blood loss from the brachial artery,' Bill said, making Nick wonder if their childhood ability to follow each other's thoughts was still alive and well.

He looked across to where she was gently probing the damaged arm, flushing debris and carefully tweezing out bits of dirt and straw—the work a surgical assistant would be doing in a major trauma centre.

'I've been releasing the tourniquet and can see where the artery is damaged but he's so shocked I doubt that's the only source of blood loss.'

They were definitely following each other's thoughts!

He moved round the table, leaving another nurse to control the fluid while a third watched the monitors. He'd have liked to have an anaesthetist present, but that, too, was for city trauma centres, so he used a nerve block to anaesthetise the arm before examining it.

'There,' Bill said, passing him a loupe so he could see the torn artery more clearly.

Two tiny sutures and the tear was closed, but the nurse watching the monitors reported falling blood pressure.

Drastically falling blood pressure...

'V-tach,' the nurse said quietly.

The words were barely spoken before Bill had the defibrillator pushed up against the trolley and was already attaching leads to the paddles. Nick set the voltage, gave the order to clear, placed the paddles above and below the heart and watched as the patient's body jerked on the table.

He looked at the monitor and saw the nurse shake her head.

He upped the voltage, cleared again and felt the tension in the room as the body jerked and stilled, then the green line on the monitor showed the heartbeat had stabilised.

A release of held breath, nothing more than a sigh, but he knew everyone had been willing the lad to live.

For now!

'He's had three litres of fluid—he's definitely losing blood somewhere else,' he muttered, then turned to Bill. 'We need full blood—has he been cross-matched?'

'It's on its way,' she said quietly, then nodded towards the door where a young man in a white coat had appeared, stethoscope around his neck and, thank heavens, two blood packs in his hands.

'Rob Darwin, I'm one of two doctors on duty upstairs but Bill said you needed help down here, and when Bill calls, I obey. Her slightest wish is my command.'

He was joking, teasing Bill, but Nick had no time for jokes.

'Get that blood into him—it's warmed?'

Rob nodded and took up a position at the head of the table, fiddling with the fluid lines as he prepared to give the patient the transfusion.

'The bleeding has to be internal, but how? Where?'

Nick was talking to himself as he looked at the swollen, badly dislocated shoulder, picturing how the machine must have caught the arm and twisted it, trying to imagine where internal damage would have occurred.

'A tear to the axillary artery?' Bill suggested quietly, looking up from where she was putting clean dressings on the damaged arm.

'That or the subclavian,' Nick agreed. 'I'm going to have to go in and have a look.'

He glanced up at Rob.

'You okay with anaesthesia?'

Rob grinned.

'I haven't been here long but as Bill told me soon after I arrived, country doctors do the lot,' he said. 'How long would you want him out to it?'

'Hopefully twenty minutes, but double it—make it forty to be on the safe side. He's due to be flown out if we can get him stable.'

'The plane will wait,' Rob assured him, already checking the available drugs and drawing up what he'd need.

Bill prepared the area beneath where the young man's shoulder should be, quickly shaving the hair and swabbing antiseptic all around then stepping back as Nick made the incision.

'We know it's in the armpit—it should be right there,' Nick grumbled, but the muscle had been torn so badly it was hard to see where the armpit should have been.

A fresh flush of blood as Bill moved the lad's scapula revealed the tear, blood pulsing from it into the surrounding tissues.

'The pressure must have been enormous,' he murmured. 'It looks as if it's been ripped apart. I'll have to cut off the torn ends and sew it back together. The vascular surgeons in Brisbane can do the fancy stuff.'

Bill watched in utter amazement as the man she'd known so well as a boy—her first best friend—calmly performed life-saving microscopic surgery on their patient. But the whole shift had been one surprise after another, beginning with Nick walking into the ER as if he belonged there.

'Another suture!'

He snapped the order, making her realise he'd already asked while she'd been reliving the shock of his arrival. Her mind back in gear, she worked with him, actually thrilled to be seeing him in action—seeing just how good an emergency doctor he'd turned out to be.

Not that she'd ever doubted it. Nick had always been able to do anything, and even excel at it, once he'd set his mind to it.

Her friend Nick…

CHAPTER TWO

THE PATIENT WAS finally wheeled away, heading for an airlift to Brisbane and the experts who might or might not save his life and, with even more luck, his arm. Bill slid down the wall and slumped to the floor of the trauma room, oblivious to the mess of packaging, blood, swabs and tubing that littered the floor.

'Not bad for a first night on duty?' she said to Nick, smiling up at the man who leant against the wall across from her. 'Think you'll enjoy work back in the old home town?'

His face was drawn, the stress of the two-hour fight to keep the youngster alive imprinted clearly on his features, yet he found the shadow of a smile.

'Anything you can do I can do better,' he teased, using a phrase that had been bandied back and forth between them a thousand times in their youth.

A young nurse poked her head into the room.

'Want me to clean up?' she asked.

Bill shook her head.

'I'm off duty, I'll do it in a minute.'

She turned back to Nick to find him studying her, a strange expression on his face.

'What?' she asked, disturbed not by him looking at her but by her reaction to it—to him, the new him.

'Rob Darwin? Love interest?' he asked.

'As if!' Bill snorted. 'Not that he's not a nice young man, and not that he wouldn't like there to be something, but...'

She hesitated, finding her reluctance to date hard to put into words.

'No spark?'

Nick had found the words for her.

'None at all,' she said, 'and it seems a waste of my time and unfair to him just to date for the sake of dating.'

'Very noble of you,' he teased, then he smiled again.

This smile was better than the first one, and her reaction more intense.

Weird when this was Nick, but she didn't have time to consider it as he was speaking again and, anyway, maybe the reactions were nothing more than tiredness and the aftermath of stress.

'There must have been a spark with Nigel,' he was saying. 'What really happened there? You could have married him, the Great God of Surgery, and been taken away from all this. You could be down in the city, doing social stuff, running fundraising balls, lunching for good causes, decked out in designer gear instead of bloody scrubs.'

'Now, there would be a fate worse than death!'

The words were lightly spoken but pain pierced her heart as she remembered it had been that same 'Great God' who'd ordered her to have an abortion a month before their wedding because he didn't want people thinking they'd got married because she was pregnant.

She breathed deeply, aware that too much bitterness still leaked into her veins when she thought of that disastrous time.

The realisation that the man she'd loved had been nothing more than a shallow, social-climbing pretender had rocked her self-confidence and made her question her judgement about people, particularly men. The miscarriage two months later had exacerbated her loss of self-worth and it had taken years, back here in Willowby with her family and friends, to rebuild it.

Although now she'd grown a thicker skin and heavier armour to shield her fragile heart…

Nick heard the change in her voice and wondered how much damage her broken engagement had done to her trust—to Bill herself, given she was the most trusting person he had ever known. It worried him that he didn't know the background to the break-up—didn't know a lot of things about his friend.

His best friend!

What did the kids call it these days? BFF? Best friends for ever?

'Anyway,' she was saying, while his mind had drifted back to the past, 'if we're going to talk of what *might* have happened in our lives, *you* could have married Seraphina or whatever she called herself when *she* fell pregnant, and gone swanning off to New York to live off her earnings as a top supermodel.'

That was better, more like old times, Bill taking the fight to him!

'Serena,' Nick corrected. 'You're muddling her up with Delphina, who was the one before, and, anyway, I did offer to marry Serena but she wanted none of it, not me, not a child and definitely not marriage.'

Silence fell, the ghosts of dead children lying between them among the empty packaging and blood.

Bill reacted first, pushing herself up off the floor, stripping off her soiled apron and flinging it into a bin, then bending to begin collecting the rubbish off the floor.

'I'll do that.'

The young wardsman who appeared, mop and bucket in hand, waved her away and although she picked up a few more bits of rubbish, she was happy to leave him to it, following Nick out of the trauma room to find the big open area of the ER eerily quiet at six on a Monday morning.

'Everyone's sleeping in,' Andy, the duty ER manager, told them. Newly arrived on shift, he was spic and span, his face alert, his smile bright. 'Go home, both of you.'

'Got to dictate some notes on that last case,' Nick said.

'And I'm having a shower then heading for beach,' Bill told them. 'I need some sea air to clear my head before I can think about sleeping.'

Would she go to Woodchoppers? Nick wondered, not wanting to ask in front of Andy but aware he'd like to join Bill at the beach. Weird name for a beach, but it had been their favourite swimming beach growing up, Bill and her six brothers declaring it their personal fiefdom, keeping it free of any less desirable elements, particularly those pushing drugs to impressionable teenagers.

Whillimina de Groote and her brothers! They'd become the family he'd never had. Bill dragging him to her home after his first day at school, insisting her brothers teach the five-year-old Nick how to defend himself.

They'd taught him a lot after that…

* * *

Bill stood under the shower, the water so hot that steam
was fogging the cubicle, but no amount of heat or water
could wash away the uneasiness that lingered over her
reaction to Nick.

To Nick as a *man*!

How pathetic!

She'd known him for close to thirty years, considered him her best friend in all the world, so why, now,
would she be reacting to him as a man?

Maybe it was nothing more than the stress and tiredness engendered by their battle to save the teenager's
life.

She could only hope…

Accepting that the hot water wasn't helping, she
turned off the taps, dried herself hurriedly, rubbed at
the tangled mess of red curls that topped her head and
fell down past her shoulders, then pulled on an old bikini she kept in her locker, covered it with a volumi-
nous T-shirt, grabbed her handbag and hurried out the
staff exit, not wanting to bump into Nick before she'd
had a good run on the beach and a swim in the limpid,
tropical waters to clear her head.

Not before she happened to be on duty with him
again, in fact, and if she spoke to the ER secretary who
drew up the rosters, total avoidance might be possible.

Well, not total. He was back to see his gran, so they'd
undoubtedly run into each other at Gran's house…

But at least he'd come home.

She pulled up in the small parking area at Wood-
choppers Beach and slogged across the sand dunes, glad
the effort of crossing them made the beach the least used
of the beaches around Willowby. Pulling off her T-shirt

and dropping it on the sand, she began to run, slowly at first then, as her muscles warmed, sprinting faster and faster—short sprints then slow jogs, alternating the two, feeling the blood surge through her body, bringing it to life in a most satisfactory manner.

Two more lengths of the beach and then she'd swim.

'You shouldn't come here on your own—you never know who might be around.'

Nick's appearance startled her.

'Obviously!' she snapped at him.

But as he ignored her comment and fell into stride beside her, she knew all the good of her run had vanished, and with it her peace of mind.

It's only Nick, she told herself, but that didn't seem to stop the awareness that prickled in her skin all down one side—the side closest to her jogging companion.

Veering away from him, she headed for the water and dived from ankle depth into the clear, green-blue sea, surfacing to breathe then diving again to porpoise along parallel to the beach, relishing the silken kiss of the water against her skin.

Had she always been this gorgeous?

Long, lean, and tanned in a way redheads weren't supposed to tan?

Nick watched as she dived and surfaced in the water, only to dive again, her limbs flashing in the sunlight, her hair trailing behind her—a mermaid at play.

Was it because she'd always been a friend that he'd never seen her as a woman? Not that he could afford to see her that way now—they were friends! There'd be plenty of interesting and intelligent, even beautiful, women here in Willowby. It was only a matter of connecting up with some of them, and the thoughts he found himself having about Bill would disappear.

For all she joked about having escaped a fate worse than death when she'd dumped Nigel, she was the kind of woman who should be married—married with a tribe of red-headed kids clustered around her—because she'd always been a mother hen, adopting not only him but any fellow pupil in danger of being bullied or excluded from one of the childhood gangs.

He stripped down to his jocks and dived into the water, surfacing a little distance from her, uncertain enough about the strange reactions of the night to not want to be too close.

'Race you to the rocks,' she challenged, and started immediately, but his longer strokes and stronger kick soon had him catching up, so they swam together towards the smooth, rounded rocks that jutted into the water at the end of the bay until they were close enough for him to swim away, beating her by a body length.

Strange reactions or not, he wasn't going to let her beat him!

'Oh, that was good,' she said, coming up out of the water, her hair streaming down her back. 'I find it's so much easier to sleep during the day if I have a run and a swim before I go home.'

She looked at him for a moment, her golden-brown eyes assessing.

'*And* a hearty breakfast at the surf club back at the main beach. You up for that, or has your body become a temple so you can't eat delicious crispy bacon, and beef sausages, and fried tomatoes, and all the other things that are loaded with cholesterol and fat?'

Nick shook his head in disbelief.

'So you still eat like a navvy and stay as slim as a whip. Some metabolism you de Grootes inherited.'

'Not all of us,' Bill told him, smiling as she waded in front of him back to the beach. 'Bob's developed a most unsightly paunch, and Joel's heading in the same direction. Too many business lunches and not enough exercise, that's the problem with those two.'

Nick watched the way her butt moved as she walked in front of him and tried to think of Bill's brothers rather than how those twin globes would fit into his hands.

'Have you already moved into the apartment?'

She threw the question over her shoulder but it brushed right past him, his attention snaffled by the way the woman in front of him moved, and how her breasts hung low as she bent to retrieve her T-shirt from the sand, the bikini she wore barely covering her nipples.

'Nick?'

Had she caught him watching her as she turned, her eyebrows raised as she waited for a reply?

What had she asked?

Had he moved in…?

'If you call dumping a couple of suitcases in the bedroom and unpacking my wash bag as moving in, then yes,' he responded, hoping the gap between the question and the answer hadn't been too long. 'It's fully furnished so all I had to bring were clothes and personal stuff. I'd hardly begun to unpack when the hospital phoned to ask if I could work last night.'

Bill didn't respond, so disturbed was she by the sight of Nick's lean, toned body that casual conversation was beyond her. He'd shrugged as he'd mentioned unpacking, an unfortunate movement as it had drawn her attention back to his chest, with its flat wedges of pectoral muscles and clearly defined six-pack.

She wanted to ask if he'd been working out, but that would give away the fact she'd noticed and the way she was feeling it was better if the question went unasked.

She climbed the first dune and raced down the other side then up the next, aware he was pacing himself to stay beside her—aware of *him*!

It was bad enough that he was living in the same building, so now she'd have to avoid seeing him out of work hours as well as at work, without him suspecting she might see him as other than a friend.

A passing fancy, surely?

But her reactions to him were forgotten as she topped the last dune.

'What is *that*?'

The words burst from her lips as she saw the racing-green sports car, hood down, cream leather seats, sleek lines shouting speed and, yes, seduction.

'My car?' His voice was quiet but she heard the pride in it.

'Well, *that* will get you noticed in Willowby,' she muttered, aware of just who would notice it first—the constant stream of beautiful women who used Willowby as a jumping-off place for reef adventures. True, they worked, if you could call hostessing on luxury yachts or on the six-star island resorts working, but since the mining boom had led to the town becoming one of the wealthiest per capita in the country, the place had been swamped by women, and men if she was honest, look-ing to separate some of that money from those who had it.

'Gets me noticed most places,' Nick replied, and the smile on his face made her stomach clench.

That's why he'd bought it! She knew that much immediately, remembering the email he'd sent her many years ago when he'd returned from his first stint with the army reserve, serving overseas. He'd helped to put back together young men blown apart by bombs in wars that ordinary people didn't understand.

He'd come home, he'd said, with one aim—to live for the day. He'd promised himself a beautiful car, the best of clothes and as many beautiful women as cared to play with him. 'I'm honest with them, Bill,' he'd said in the email. 'I tell them all it's not for ever, that marriage isn't in my long-term plans. You'd be surprised how many women are happy with that—even agreeing that it's not for them either. Things are different now.'

Were they? Bill hadn't been able to answer that question then and couldn't now. For herself, she knew she wanted marriage, and children too, but not without love and so far, apart from that one disastrous experience, love hadn't come along.

'Ride with me,' Nick suggested. 'I'll drop you back at your old bomb after breakfast.'

'Ride in that thing? The town might have grown, Nick, but at heart it's still the same old Willowby. I only need to be spotted by one of the local gossips and my reputation would be ruined. Did you see the de Groote girl, they'd be saying, running around in a fast car with a fast man? You, of course, will be forgiven. About you they'll say, hasn't he done well for himself, that grandson of old Mrs Grant? And such a kind boy, coming home to be with his gran now she's getting on.'

Nick laughed and headed for his car.

'Okay, but I won't offer to race you to the surf club,' he teased. 'Too unfair.'

Bill climbed into her battered old four-wheel drive, the vehicle her father had bought her new when she'd passed her driving test. She patted the dash to reassure the car she wasn't put off by its shabby appearance, or influenced by the shining beauty of Nick's vehicle, but it was she who needed reassurance as her folly in suggesting he breakfast with her finally struck home. Even with her sea-drenched curls, and the tatty old T-shirt, she'd always felt quite at home at the surf club, but these days many of the beautiful people breakfasted there as well—

Whoa! Surely she wasn't concerned that Nick would compare her to some of the other women and find her wanting?

Of course she wasn't!

Then why was she wondering if there might not be a long shift somewhere in the mess of clothes, books and papers in the back seat of the car—wondering if there might be a slightly melted tube of lip gloss in the glove box?

Hopeless, that's what she was.

He'd selected a table that looked out from a covered deck over the town's main beach and the placid tropical waters. Bill slipped into a chair beside him, so she, too, could look out to sea. Far out on the horizon they could see the shapes of the islands that dotted the coastline—tourist havens on Australia's biggest natural wonder, the Great Barrier Reef.

'I've ordered the big breakfast for both of us,' Nick

informed her. 'Anything you don't want, I'll eat. And coffee—double-shot latte still your drug of choice?'

'It is, and thanks,' Bill replied, telling herself at the same time that a nice normal breakfast with Nick should banish all the silly stuff that had been going on in her head.

Especially as Nick was wasting no time checking out the talent, with his eyes on a group of three long-haired blondes, laughing and joking on the other side of the wide deck.

'The town's scenery's improved,' he joked.

'It's the money that's being splashed around,' Bill reminded him, deciding to take his comment seriously. 'Money attracts money but it also attracts the kind of people who like to have it—like to spend it. The problem is that while the miners and the people who work in mining support services are all earning big money, the price of housing goes up, rents go up, and the ordinary people of the town, especially those who don't own their own houses, are stuck with costs they can't afford.'

Nick smiled.

'Still a worry-wart,' he teased.

'Well, someone has to worry about it. Nurses at the hospital don't get paid more than their counterparts in other places in the state, yet accommodation costs in town are enormous. Fortunately the hospital has re-alised it has a problem and has built some small rental apartments in the grounds, but you spread that problem out across the town—the check-out staff at supermarkets, the workers in government offices, the council truck drivers—all the locals suffer.'

She stopped, partly because she was aware she'd mounted her soap-box and really shouldn't be boring

Nick with the problem but also because the blondes appeared to have noticed him—new talent in town?—and were sending welcoming smiles his way.

'Maybe they saw the car when you drove in,' Bill muttered.

'Ouch! And anyway the car park's out the back. No, it's my good looks that have got their attention—see, one of them is coming over.'

One of them *was* coming over. The leggiest one, with the longest, shiniest, blondest, dead-straight hair!

'Aren't you Nick Grant?' she asked, and as Nick nodded, she held out her hand.

'I told the girls it was you. You used to go out with Serena Snow, didn't you?'

Again Nick had to agree, and the leggy blonde introduced herself.

'I'm Amy Wentworth. I met you a couple of times at parties back then. What are you doing up in this neck of the woods? Holidaying? Off to the reef for a few days' R and R?'

So far she'd totally ignored Bill—not that it mattered, Bill told herself.

She studied the woman while Nick explained he was working here, living in the new apartment building at the marina but with no elaboration on why. Amy raised her eyebrows.

'Can't imagine you in a hick town like this. Oh, I know there's a lot of money around, but what do you *do* when you're not working?'

Nick grinned at her.

'I'll be doing pretty much what I did when I wasn't working in Sydney.'

Amy drifted away but Bill wasn't going to let him get away with that tantalising reply.

'Which was?' she asked.

'What which was?'

'The "pretty much what you did in Sydney" bit of that conversation.'

'Ah, but I told you years ago,' he reminded her. 'I had a good time and I intend to do just that up here. You don't need nightclubs and friends with yachts on the harbour to have a good time.'

'We've got a nightclub and a two of my brothers have yachts, or big motor launches,' Bill said defensively, and Nick laughed.

'Exactly, although I think the nightclub crowd are a bit young for me, but you can have a good time wherever you are. In fact, I'm off for three days next week and think I might pop across to one of the island resorts—do a bit of diving and fishing and...'

'Meeting beautiful women,' Bill finished for him.

Again Nick smiled, although this time it was a little forced because in the back of his mind he'd had another reason for returning to Willowby, one that was becoming important to him.

'That too, of course,' he answered glibly. 'Want to come?'

CHAPTER THREE

SHE DIDN'T REPLY, studying him intently for a moment instead, and he knew that look. Undoubtedly she'd picked up something from his tone.

'Did it hurt you?' she asked.

Yep, he'd been right about the look and although he knew full well what she meant by the question, he wasn't going to cede ground to her by admitting it.

'Did what hurt me?'

'You know full well what I mean,' she said crossly. 'Serena saying no to your proposal.'

His turn to study her. The problem with friendship— a strong and enduring friendship like the one they shared—was that you couldn't lie to the other party. Oh, you could fudge around a bit and dodge answering, but you couldn't right out lie.

He turned his gaze from Bill's too-perceptive eyes and looked out over the beach and island-strewn sea.

The truth!

'More than I could have imagined,' he admitted, and turned back so, now it was out, he could meet the gold-brown eyes fastened so steadfastly on his face. 'I don't think it was Serena's rejection so much. I liked her well enough. For all her self-focus she was fun to be with and happy that we more or less lived separate lives—both of us working long hours at different times—so I can't see why it wouldn't have worked.'

Bill's small, rather shocked 'Oh' broke into his thoughts but now he'd started he wanted to finish what he'd been saying.

'You know how I feel about the "l" word, Bill, so I can't say I loved her, but what had…not excited but certainly intrigued me was the idea of having a family—a wife and child—people who belonged, not to me but with me, if you know what I mean.'

The disbelief on Bill's face was so easy to read he had to laugh.

'Yes, yes, I know I said it would never happen, but finding out Serena was pregnant, well, it kind of changed something inside me, as if a wire that had been shorted out was suddenly reconnected and family stopped being in front of going down mines, abduction by aliens and the bogeyman in my fears.'

He paused, marshalling his thoughts.

'In part, it's why I came home—came back to the only family I've ever known: Gran and you de Grootes.'

'Looking for a family of your own?' Bill asked.

Again he paused, but honesty won out.

'Yes, I think so—I think it's what I need, Bill. What I really want.'

'Oh, Nick,' Bill said softly, and she covered his hand with hers as she had so often in the past. Though he'd reciprocated often enough, when some fool of a youth had hurt her in some way or when her pet hamster had died.

The strange thing was that this time it felt different. Nice, but different.

'I also need to sleep,' he said, regaining control over

some erratic emotions and reclaiming his hand at the same time. 'Then this afternoon I must go over and see Gran. You want to come?'

Fool! Wasn't he going for distance here until he'd sorted out his reactions to his old friend?

'No, I saw her yesterday—well, the day before now—although,' Bill said firmly, 'that brings me to another issue. I had an email from you only last week—you answered the one I sent to say she was looking a whole lot better—and there wasn't a word about coming here to work. And if you were talking to Bob and pinching the best apartment in his building then you must have been fairly certain then.'

Nick laughed again—the disjointed sentence was sheer Bill, words tumbling over each other to get said, especially when she was angry with him.

'One,' he said, holding up his hand and pointing to his first finger, 'I wanted to surprise Gran and if I told you…'

He let the sentence hang but had the satisfaction of seeing a faint blush colour her cheeks. As honest as the day was long, Bill would be the first to admit she found it almost impossible to keep a secret.

'And two…' he pointed to his next finger '…I wasn't sure you were even here. In that email you'd said you had time off and were going to Townsville to talk to someone about some course.'

She nodded.

'The mine rescue people, about a new course. It *was* to be this week and next, but was cancelled. Pity really because it was going to be on flooded underground rescues and I haven't done that yet.'

'Mine rescue—flooded underground mines?' He

could hear his voice rising but couldn't stop it. 'What do you mean, you haven't done that yet? What on earth are you doing, getting involved with mine rescue, and what are your brothers doing, letting you do it?'

Her laugh made the sun seem brighter.

'Oh, Nick, you sound just like Bob, but Danny and Pete are already in the elite mine rescue squad and they've encouraged me to get involved. I'm not up to their standard yet—not flying off to foreign parts to help out—but I can hold my own as part of the local team when the experts are away, especially with my nursing and paramedic experience.'

Nick didn't know why he was surprised, but just the thought of mine rescue made him shudder. Danny, the second of the de Groote boys, had taken him and Bill down a mine when they'd been in their early teens, and though Bill had revelled in the darkness and gloom, he had hated every minute of the musty smell and the idea of being over a mile beneath the mountain.

Had been afraid every minute of it, to be honest, but he hadn't mentioned that part to his fearless friend.

Though Bill was terrified of snakes, so—

'I'm heading home to bed,' she said, cutting into his thoughts and sounding so casually at ease she obviously wasn't feeling any of the strangeness he was. 'I guess I'll be seeing you around.'

She stood up, paused, then dropped a light kiss on the top of his head.

'Nice to have you back, curly,' she added lightly, before weaving her way between the tables and disappearing round the corner of the deck.

He couldn't help but turn and watch her go.

* * *

Bill pondered Nick's startling revelation that he'd discovered he wanted a family. Was that why he'd come home? Did he see Willowby as the place to raise this family?

They were unanswerable questions so she moved on to considering the uneasiness the subject had caused in her insides when it was nothing at all to do with her.

Although hadn't that been *her* dream? The memory of her delight in finding she was pregnant made her stomach tighten.

Enough!

No melancholy!

And anyway, wasn't there enough to occupy her brain with Nick's sudden reappearance?

She drove home slowly and carefully, aware she was tired, but her mind now snagged on the unexpectedness of the situation—on Nick.

But thinking about it, she could see it was only natural that Nick *would* want a family for all he'd spent his youth mocking the institution. She'd always known his mockery was to cover the hurt of his own parents' behaviour, jaunting around the world, crewing on luxury yachts, visiting exotic places, their son left with his grandmother not, as they'd said, so he'd have stability but because it had made it easier for them to continue to enjoy their lifestyle.

They'd eventually drowned at sea when their own, much smaller yacht was caught up in a typhoon, but their deaths had had little effect on Nick because Gran had given him more than stability, she'd given him love—unquestioning and all-encompassing love.

So, while Nick's admission was surprising, it was

her own reaction to it that needed more consideration.
As did her reaction to the sight of his bare chest, and
the way his muscled thighs had matched her strides on
the beach, or the strange feelings seeing him had pro-
duced, not in her heart where their friendship lived, but
along her nerves and—

No, she wasn't going there!

Surprise—that's what had caused the weird reactions.

She stopped at the control panel to the underground
parking area to press in the security code then drove in
as the big door opened. She parked and made her way
to the lift, the exhaustion that followed a busy night on
duty fast catching up with her.

Exiting on the sixth floor, she headed down the corri-
dor to her apartment, an end one with a view out to sea, a
really special place to live for all she'd complained about
its size. Two floors above her the two penthouses spread
across the top level—big four-bedroom homes, each
with three bathrooms, wide decks taking in the view out
over the Coral Sea, and a smaller deck on the western
side, looking back towards the green-clad mountains.

Bill smiled to herself, pleased that even in choosing accommodation that might only be for a year, Nick
was following his avowed intention to have nothing
but the best!

It had to be tiredness, Nick decided as he drove home,
that had weakened him to the extent he'd admitted his
disappointment over Serena and the baby to Bill. Normally he'd have teased her about being nosy, or asked a
question about her own love life to divert her attention
from the fact he hadn't answered, but, no, he'd heard

himself bleating out his pathetic reaction, even feel-ing remembered pain for the loss of a dream—a fam-ily of his own.

But he *hadn't* lost the dream, he reminded himself. Wasn't that why he was here? He'd been drawn back by Gran, of course, but also by the feeling that in Willowby he might find the woman who would help the dream come true. A family woman and, yes, his thinking had been that Bill would know someone who'd be just right for him—Bill or someone in *her* family. They were into family in a big way, the de Grootes.

And hadn't he always turned to Bill when he had a problem, or needed help?

Letting himself into the penthouse, he set aside his tumbling thoughts and sighed with pleasure. The fa-miliar view out across the island-dotted sea still took his breath away. And tired though he was, a part of him wanting nothing more than to slip into bed, he had to walk out onto the balcony and breathe in the fresh sea air.

He was home.

Second night on duty. No life-threatening emergencies and he'd heard from the hospital in Brisbane that his patient from the previous night was doing well.

'It has to be the night for the bizarre,' Bill said, slumping down beside him in the tea room during a lull in proceedings. 'I suppose dog bites are common enough, but the bite usually doesn't come with a cou-ple of dog teeth in the wounds. The dog must have been a hundred and five for its teeth to have come out so easily.'

Nick shook his head.

'I can't believe I nearly missed the second one. It was weird enough discovering one tooth in a puncture wound, but it was only when you were putting on the dressing that I realised I hadn't probed the second hole and, sure enough, another tooth.'

'Perhaps someone wrenched the dog off and that's why it lost the teeth.'

Nick considered this for a moment.

'No, there'd have been tearing around the wounds and there was no sign of that—just bite holes and teeth.'

'From an ancient dog or one with a gum problem.'

'And the kid with his head stuck in the bars of his cot,' Nick recalled. 'You'd have thought his father would have had a hacksaw to cut through a bar and release him instead of taking the cot to pieces to bring it in for us to do it.'

'It did look funny.' Bill smiled at the memory of the two parents arriving with the side of the cot held between them, and the grandmother carrying the perfectly contented baby, which had been looking around with wide-eyed curiosity and doubtless wondering about all the fuss.

'Cute baby, though,' Bill added, although she knew she should dodge baby conversations altogether because even after more than a year it hurt to see other people's babies.

'Very cute,' Nick agreed, rising to his feet as his pager buzzed.

'Drunk in cubicle three,' the duty manager told Bill as she returned to work. 'There's a nurse in there with Nick but they might need more help.'

Bill closed her eyes for a moment. Babies were upsetting enough, but if there was one thing she hated, it was handling drunks. They came in all shapes and sizes, and varied from angry and abusive, through straight obstreperous, to wildly happy, laughing hilariously as they threw up on your uniform and shoes.

'Obstreperous,' Nick said under his breath as Bill entered the cubicle. 'He's had a fall, I'd say into a bougainvillea as he has multiple abrasions, a dislocated finger and some very nasty thorns sticking out of his legs.'

The man in question was insisting he was perfectly all right, if Bill was translating his drunk speech correctly, but whenever he moved on the examination table the thorns dug in and he'd yelp with pain.

'I'm going to give him a local anaesthetic then fix the finger,' Nick continued. 'If you two can hold him still for a minute, I'd be grateful.'

The finger joint went back into place, and the young nurse cleaned and bandaged the man's hand so the finger would be supported while the joint healed.

'We'll start on the thorns,' Nick told Bill, but it was easier said than done when the man kept insisting he was fine and trying to climb off the table.

'Who brought him in?' Nick asked the young nurse.

'His wife. She's out in the waiting area.'

'Could you ask her to come in?' Nick smiled as he made the request and Bill couldn't help but notice the nurse's blush.

Still winning women over wherever he goes, she thought, but though she'd thought it a thousand times before, this time it didn't prompt a smile.

'Being a nuisance, is he?' the woman who entered demanded, before turning to her husband. 'Now, listen, you, sit still and let the doctor do his job or I'll take you

home and throw you back into the bougainvillea myself, and don't think I wouldn't do it.'

The man on the table quietened immediately and
looking from him, a bulky six-footer, to the small slim
wife, Bill had to smile.

'Thank you, madam.' Nick gave the wife a small
bow. 'It's good to know who's the boss in the house-
hold.'

She smiled at Nick.

'It probably wouldn't work if he was a habitual
drunk, but as it is, he can't hold his grog so mostly he
doesn't drink, but we've just had our first grandchild
and he went out with his mates to wet the baby's head—
they insisted, and now look at him. Fine example for
the kid he'll be!'

She spoke fondly and even smiled at her husband,
settling into a chair beside the wall to make sure he
behaved.

Bill worked beside Nick, swabbing each scratch and
wound as he pulled out the thorns.

'I can do this,' she said to him, but he shrugged away
her offer and continued working until they had the now
sleeping drunk patched up and able to be released to
his wife.

'Just watch the wounds in case they begin to fester.
There's no point starting antibiotics if he doesn't need
them, but come back or go to see your own GP if they
worry him,' Nick told her as he helped her take the man
out to the waiting room where an aide would help her
out to the car.

'Babies do keep cropping up,' he said to Bill as she
came out of the cubicle, a bag of debris in her hand.

I'm glad he said that, Bill decided, setting aside her

own feelings and thinking just of Nick. It must mean he's over or getting over the loss of what he'd thought would be his very own family.

'Some nights are like that,' she reminded him. 'I'd far prefer a run of babies, as long as they're not too sick, to a run of drunks.'

'Hear, hear!'

This from the nurse who had followed Bill out of the cubicle, although she'd spoken to Nick rather than Bill. The nurse was from an agency—distinctive in the agency uniform—someone Bill didn't know. But studying her now, as the nurse continued to chat to Nick, Bill realised she was exactly his type—tall, curvy, blonde.

And, no, that wasn't a stab of jealousy. Her and Nick's friendship had survived a long stream of blondes, some, like Serena, Bill had seen in photos, and some she'd only heard about through emails and texts.

The agency nurse was now suggesting she and Nick have a coffee and as the ER was virtually deserted, it was only natural he should accept, although he did turn his head to ask, 'Want another coffee, Bill?'

Bill shook her head and headed off to dispose of the rubbish, hearing the agency nurse question the name Bill and Nick explaining.

This had to stop! she told herself as she hurled the bag of rubbish down the chute. Her friendship with Nick had survived because neither of them had ever had the slightest interest in the other in a romantic way. Growing up, she'd have as soon considered falling in love with one of her brothers.

It had to be that she hadn't seen him for so long that she was suddenly seeing him as a man.

Reacting to him as a man!

When *had* she last seen him?

He'd been in New York, proposing to Serena, when she'd broken off her engagement to Nigel, and although Nick had promised faithfully he'd be home for her wedding, once that was off, he'd headed for foreign parts, doing his bit for the army once again.

Oh!

It all fell into place now. There'd been no mention of a second deployment overseas prior to all that happening, but obviously he'd been sufficiently upset to want to get as far away as possible from everyone and everything.

Poor Nick!

Nick chatted to the nurse—Amanda—and wondered why Bill hadn't joined them.

Not that it mattered. Amanda was amusing and obviously happy to keep both sides of the conversation going so he could brood a little over the reactions he was feeling towards Bill.

Physical reactions!

Disturbing, because at the same time it felt a little like incest—this was Bill, his friend…

'So, you'll come?' he heard Amanda ask.

Unwilling to admit he had no idea what she was talking about, he said, 'Of course!'

'Great. The boat will leave from the City Marina, gangway four, at ten.'

'Ten today?' Dead giveaway, that question, but it had just burst out.

'No, Saturday, silly,' Amanda said, giggling and cuffing him lightly on the arm, moving close enough on the settee for him to know he should have been following the conversation.

Oh, well, some time between now and Saturday he'd have to sort out an excuse. Except going out on a boat with Amanda, and presumably her friends, might get his mind off Bill.

And wasn't he here to meet women—maybe the one woman with whom he could plan his family?

The shift ended and he was pleased to see Bill's ageing car still in the car park. He wouldn't be tempted to follow her to the beach, which was good as he didn't think his libido could handle the sight of her in a bikini again. Not just yet, anyway.

Perhaps after Saturday...

Tired enough to sleep without the swim and run on the beach, he drove to his apartment, pulling up at the security panel at the entrance to the building's basement, staring in shock at what looked like a derelict's collection of junk on the footpath beside the big doors.

Except it wasn't a derelict but Serena rising from the pile of belongings. Serena with a doll in her arms.

Obviously he was losing his mind—hallucinating...

What drugs had he handled during the night?

Shock had him riveted to his seat as the mirage that possibly *was* Serena walked towards the car. Now he could hear the words she was saying clearly enough, he just couldn't make sense of them.

'Came in on an early flight, no one answering the bell, thought you'd be home eventually, and as you'd never walk if you can drive, I thought this was the best place to catch you, but now you're here I really need to hand Steffi and all her gear over, and I'm terribly sorry to do this, Nick, I really am, and I know you're going to be mad as hell, and I'll explain when we get to your apartment, but we'll have to hurry because I'm booked to fly out again at midday to catch the evening flight to New York.'

New York!

It was in New York he'd last seen Serena, heard her tell him she didn't want a baby, yet here she was, not with a doll but a baby in her arms...

He leapt out of the car, straight over the door, looming over her.

'What will you explain?' he roared.

Then a voice behind him said, 'Hush, Nick, you'll upset the baby.'

Bill!

Unable to get into the car park with him blocking the road, she must have pulled up behind him and got out to see what was happening.

'You must be Serena,' she added politely, and he remembered sending Bill a glamour shot of Serena some years before. 'You don't know me but I'm Nick's friend Bill. We grew up together and now we both live in this apartment block my brother built. And as our cars are blocking the entrance, what if we put all the gear into my car and you and the baby get in with Nick and we'll get the stuff up to his apartment and the two of you can take it from there?'

Nick watched in total bemusement as Bill efficiently loaded what looked like a truckload of baby paraphernalia into her car and Serena, plus baby, slid into his.

'Drive through!' Bill ordered, and he recovered sufficient composure to do as she told him, sliding the car into his parking space and watching as Bill stopped beside the lift and unloaded Serena's belongings.

But Serena was flying to New York this evening—

so why had she flown a couple of thousand miles north to leave the stuff here?

And the baby?

No, he couldn't think about the baby.

By now Serena had joined Bill at the lift and together they were stacking the gear inside, Bill's voice echoed around the basement—Bill's voice finally bringing him out of his daze.

'You're saying this little girl is Nick's baby?' Bill's outrage was clear and the words sank through his bewildered brain.

This is where you get out of the car and demand an explanation, Nick told himself, but his legs had turned to jelly.

He had a child.

A daughter!

Nick saw Bill take the baby and turn his way. She obviously felt it was time he emerged from his car and took control of the situation.

Would his legs work?

Of course they would.

He had a child—

He leapt out of the car.

'This is *my* baby?' he demanded, coming close to Serena and echoing Bill's words. 'You didn't have an abortion and you didn't bother telling me? Why would you do that? And now what? You've decided kids are more trouble than they're worth and you want to hand her over, as if she's a bit of furniture you no longer need?'

Bill had moved a little away, cradling the little head protectively against her chest, one hand over the baby's other ear so it couldn't hear him yelling at its mother.

'Look,' Serena muttered, holding up her hand as if

she needed to ward off further attack. 'I know this is inconvenient, Nick. When I had the baby Mum looked after her, with nannies to help out, but Mum's just got married again and I've got this huge offer for a special show in New York and Mum had a nanny lined up—Mum always vetted the nannies—but the nanny walked out and so I thought, well, it's not as if you haven't got family up there—with Gran and all those de Grootes you talk about all the time—you'll find someone to take care of her.

'She's a good little thing and she's used to strangers minding her and she's been to day care as well. I've brought all her things and the last nanny wrote down her schedule so I'm sure with a bit of help you can sort things out.'

At least Serena was right about family. At last count Bill had about twenty-two nieces and nephews, so someone in the family would be happy to take care of one more baby.

The thought brought anger in its train—a hot, deep, burning fury!

'I can't believe that even you—' he began, before Bill arrived and put her hand on his chest, pushing him back a step.

'You cannot murder her here—not in front of Steffi,' she said firmly. 'Besides, don't you think it's time you met your family?'

Bill's smile was forced but it worked, dousing his anger just a little, and when she put the little curly-haired girl into his arms it disappeared altogether.

Bill said, 'Steffi, meet your daddy.'

And Nick understood that love wasn't something you could explain or analyse, it was something you felt…

CHAPTER FOUR

Now HE TOOK control of the situation, ordering—yes, it definitely was an order—the two women to take the stuff up to his apartment.

'And you'll be?' Serena demanded huffily.

'Coming in the next lift—I'm certainly not going to overload it with a baby in my arms.'

And with that he turned his back on them and looked down at the warm scrap of humanity snuggled against his chest.

He had a baby!

Or did he?

Serena had been adamant about the abortion, so was this little girl really his?

He held her out and had to smile. A fluff of soft brown curls, wide blue eyes—Gran's eyes—and a dimple, now she smiled at him, in her left cheek, just where his annoying dimple was.

His heart jolted in his chest then hammered furiously and he held the baby close again because he knew he was shaking with the sheer enormity of this revelation.

He pressed kisses on her head and murmured nothings until his heart resumed its normal beat and he felt confident enough to hold her out again and look into her face.

'Hi, there,' he said softly. 'I'm your dad!'

Serious eyes studied him, taking him in.

Judging him?

No smile, but who could blame her?

'We'll be all right,' he assured her, and hugged her closer.

The lift returned and he got in, taking it to the top floor and striding out, ready to face whatever lay ahead, but knowing, already, that the baby was here to stay.

Bill had heard the word 'besotted', and probably even used it herself to describe a teenager's crush, but she'd never seen besotting happen—not as quickly and completely as it must have happened for Nick to walk into the apartment looking as he did.

Oh, dear, she thought, absolutely thrilled for Nick but worried over what might lie ahead.

She'd helped Serena take all Steffi's belongings up to Nick's penthouse, mentally listing all the things he'd need if he intended keeping the baby here—a cot to begin with and probably a playpen so she'd be safe if he was called to the phone.

Baby bath?

'Bill?'

Nick's voice brought her out of her mental listing.

'I asked if you'd mind taking Steffi down to your place for half an hour while I have a talk to Serena?'

Bill smiled as she took the baby, although the smile was forced.

But this was for Nick and she was pleased he didn't want the little one to hear her parents yelling at each

other, because some yelling was sure to happen, although as ever when she held a baby she had very mixed
emotions—reminders of what might have been.

Could babies feel doubt and uncertainty churning in
the breast that held them?

Just in case they could, she pulled herself together
and made a special effort, smiling at the little girl and
talking gently.

'So, Steffi,' she said as they went down to her apartment, 'you're, what? Nearly a year old? Ten months?
You're gorgeous, do you know that?'

The little girl smiled and that was it for Bill as well—
besotted!

Oh, dear.

Falling in love with this particular baby would *not* be
a good idea. This was Nick's family, not hers.

She'd expected Nick to phone so the knock on the door
when she'd just got Steffi to sleep on cushions on the
floor surprised her.

'I had to phone Bob to find out where you lived,'
Nick said, running his hand distractedly through his
hair. 'You've no idea, Bill, you just won't believe it.
Where is she? Steffi?'

Bill led him inside, pointed to the sleeping child, then
took him through to the kitchen for coffee.

'Sit,' she ordered, 'and drink this before we start.'

She handed him a fresh coffee, made one for herself,
then sat opposite him at the breakfast bar.

'So?'

Nick was still shaking his head, and she understood
the depth of his disbelief when he began.

'Having told me she'd have the abortion, she goes

to stay with Alex, the Russian photographer who worships the ground she walks on, and he throws up his hands in horror, not at her destroying a human life but because this is the photographic opportunity of a lifetime, something he's always dreamt of doing, and here's his favourite subject, his muse, presenting him with the opportunity!'

'What is?' Bill asked, totally bewildered.

'Well you might ask,' Nick growled. 'A coffee-table book detailing nine months of pregnancy—well, seven and a half months, in actual fact. Nude photos of Serena in all poses, in all lights, the bulge growing ever larger. Imagine how Steffi's going to feel about *that* when she's growing up.'

Bill had to laugh.

'Right now I think you have more to worry about than what Steffi's going to think as a teenager. Why didn't Serena tell you she'd changed her mind and was going ahead? You'd offered to marry her—you wanted a family.'

Nick groaned.

'Yes, I had and, yes, I did, but she really didn't want to be married, and apparently my talk of family had frightened her because it was the last thing *she* wanted. A family would tie her down and she needed to be free to pursue her career. I know that makes hers sound cold and uncaring, but she isn't really, she's just got the most total self-focus of anyone I've ever met.'

'So what was she thinking, going ahead with the pregnancy?' Bill demanded, wondering where uncaring finished and self-focus began.

'Oh, that's easy. You have to remember that Serena thinks differently to ninety-nine per cent of the human race and it turned out she knew this wonderful couple in New York who wanted to adopt so she knew the child would go to a good home, and she could keep in touch as a kind of surrogate aunt.

'*Only* Serena could think something like that was okay. The woman has a warped mind—I always knew that, even when I was going out with her. Her career is the be-all and end-all of her life, and everything else, even romance, is incidental. I blame her mother, who had Serena appearing in ads from the time she was born, but as an adult Serena's had choices and the number-one choice has always been her career.'

The disbelief and despair in Nick's voice shocked Bill so much she came round to give him a hug.

'It's okay. For whatever reason, she did keep the child, and Steffi's here.'

'It's not okay!' Nick roared, then turned quickly to see if he'd woken his daughter, and quietened his voice when he added, 'The only reason she didn't give *my* daughter up for adoption—apparently that old goat Alex had intended putting his name down as the father for adoption purposes—was that he suddenly decided he could document the child's life as well, but, you know what, once she grew from a swaddled bundle to a chubby six-month-old, she *wasn't photogenic*!'

Nick was right, the behaviour of two so-called adults defied belief, and he had every right to the anger she could feel in the tight muscles and sinews of his body.

'So, Steffi's now surplus to requirements,' Bill muttered, as a murderous rage began to build inside *her*.

'Well, not entirely. I think Serena, in her own way, probably loves her, and Serena's mother was always around, but who knows what would have happened to

Steffi if that Amy woman hadn't seen us at breakfast yesterday and phoned Serena, whose pea-brain immediately came up with a solution to the dilemma of this offer in New York right when her mother's off on a honeymoon, and whatever nanny she had decided to leave at a moment's notice. Give Steffi to her daddy for a while!'

'For a while?' Bill repeated.

Nick looked at her and shook his head.

'Apparently we can "talk"—Serena waggled her fingers in that silly way to make the inverted commas—when she comes home. *I'll* say we'll talk!'

'Let's worry about that later,' Bill suggested, hearing the exhaustion beneath the anger in Nick's voice and hugging him again. 'Now, at least, Steffi's landed in a proper family, with you to love her, and Gran, and me, and twenty-two kind-of cousins, and a plethora of aunts and uncles. All we have to do is sort out how to manage.'

'Manage?' Nick repeated, looking up at her as she went back round the bar and resumed her stool, aware that hugging Nick was *not* a good idea, no matter how badly he had needed to be hugged.

'Nick, you have a baby and you work and the ER at the local hospital isn't the kind of place where you can take your baby to work.'

He turned to look at his sleeping child and the expression in his eyes caused a stab of pain in Bill's chest.

'I work nights,' he said softly. 'I don't suppose there's such a thing as night care.'

Bill saw the complexity—the enormity—of the situation dawn on his face so wasn't surprised when he turned to her, anguish in his voice.

'What will I do, Bill? How can I manage?'

With a great deal of difficulty, Bill thought, but she didn't say it. The poor man was bamboozled enough as it was.

'*We'll* manage,' she said firmly. 'Serena was right about one thing. While Gran might be a bit beyond minding a baby full time, you've a whole herd of de Grootes out there who'll be only too willing to help. But first you have to decide just what help you want.

'Full time, part time? I know you've just started a new job, but there's such a thing as paternity leave. We can make some temporary caring arrangements until the hospital replaces you, if you want to be a full-time dad for a while so you and Steffi can get to know each other. Then there are well-trained nannies you can get, even in Willowby, again either full time or part time, live-in or daily, and they can be contracted short or long term.'

He stared at her and she knew he hadn't taken in much of what she'd said, his mind still reeling from shock and disbelief.

'You're exhausted. Give me your keys then go into my bedroom and go to sleep. When Steffi wakes I'll take her back upstairs and get things set up for her there.'

Oh!

'You do intend she lives with you?'

That woke him out of his daze.

'Where else would she live?' he demanded.

'Good! Now go to bed?'

It had to be a measure of his shocked state that he obediently handed over his keys and went into her bedroom, shutting the door behind him, no doubt so she wouldn't see him slump onto the bed and bury his head in his hands as he tried to come to grips with this massive change in his life.

A measure of his state that he didn't argue that she, too, needed to sleep, but Bill knew it would be easier for the hospital to find another nurse to take her night shift tonight than it would be to find another doctor.

Bill looked towards the closed door. In her heart she knew she should be getting less involved with this child, not more, but Nick was in trouble and she'd reacted automatically—helping out in times of trouble was what they'd always done for each other.

Nick sat on Bill's bed, head bowed, his fingers running through his hair as if rubbing at his scalp might stimulate his thinking.

What thinking?

His brain was numb!

He had a daughter?

What was he going to do?

How could he look after her even for a short time?

What did he know about bringing up children?

He didn't even know her birthday...

He gave a despairing groan and slumped back on the bed, surprised to find that he might actually go to sleep.

His body handling stress by shutting down his mind, the doctor in him suggested as he drifted off.

He woke mid-afternoon to find a note from Bill beside the bed.

We're at your place, here's a key.

'*We're* at your place...' he read again, this time aloud, and felt dread and panic surging in his stomach.

What should he do?

What *could* he do?

But even as he asked himself the question he remembered the feel of that little body against his chest and he headed into Bill's bathroom, took a shower, used her far-from-adequate razor to scrape stubble from his cheeks, then, clad in a rather ragged towelling robe he found behind the bathroom door, he grabbed his dirty clothes, and the key, and headed up to his apartment.

Except it wasn't his apartment, it was a nursery school. Colourful toys and strange objects were strewn around the place, and in the midst of this chaos a small person stood, holding onto his glass-topped coffee table—he'd have to get rid of that—and waving a chubby hand in his direction.

'Hey,' he said quietly, squatting down—not easy to do decently in the robe—and moving carefully towards her. 'How are you, Steffi? How are you, little girl?'

Wide-set eyes studied him intently, the little face serious as she took in the stranger talking to her. Then one chubby hand reached out for his and as he took it he felt his heart breaking right in two. Suddenly she let go of the coffee table and with grin as wide as the universe she toddled towards him, her delight in her forward progress bringing a gurgle of laughter as well as the smile.

He caught her as she toppled, and sat on the floor with her in his arms, picking up a floppy doll and making it dance in front of her.

But she was more interested in him, probing at his glasses, studying his face again, touching his hair, his ear, his lips until he felt his chest would burst with the love blossoming inside it, and he knew tears were forming in his eyes.

Bill must have been watching from a distance because as Steffi's crawled off his knee to stand up at the glass table again to practise her walking, Bill came in and sat down on the sofa, waving her hand at the chaos around them.

'I'm sorry about all this,' she said, 'but you know the de Grootes, competitive to a man—or woman in this case. I phoned Bob's wife to ask about a cot and a high chair and next thing I knew every one of the sisters-in-law had turned up, all bringing something for Steffi. You should see the bedroom. As well as the cot you have chests of drawers, colourful mobiles, pictures on the wall, a change table and some kind of bin that wraps up dirty nappies. That is, of course, if you're going to use disposables, which are a lot more eco-friendly now.'

For about the fortieth time today Nick was dumbfounded.

'Disposable nappies? I have to make decisions about things like that?'

Bill laughed.

'About a lot of things, Daddio!' she teased. 'There's home-cooked or scientifically balanced bottled food, there are about ten different kinds of baby formula and you have to choose one, there's how early to start swimming lessons, there's day care or a nanny, which kindy to put her name down for, which school will she go to, how young's too young to have boyfriends—'

'Okay!' Nick said, and as he held his hand up to stop Bill's teasing, Steffi grabbed it as support and again walked towards him, collapsing happily into a giggling heap on his lap.

He was in love!

'From a purely practical point of view,' Bill continued, 'I've told the hospital I won't be in for a week and
can mind her while you're at work and when you're
sleeping during the day. She's so good about going
down for a nap—on the cushions at my place and in a
totally strange cot—I think she's used to being passed
around to different carers—but I think it would be best
if she gets settled into her bedroom so, if it's okay with
you, I'll sleep over here until you're sorted.'

'Okay with me? Until I'm sorted?'

Nick rested his chin on his daughter's curly hair and
looked up at his friend, and smiled.

'You realise that might be never,' he warned, 'the
sorted bit. And when did we ever have to ask about
staying over at each other's places?'

He looked around at all she'd achieved while he'd
slept, and added, 'Thank you, Bill, from the bottom
of my heart. I was in such a blind panic I had no idea
where to turn or what to do, and you've calmly worked
everything out—made it easy for me. I owe you, big
time!'

Bill smiled at him, but he thought he saw a hint of
sadness in the smile.

The broken engagement? Had *she* been looking forward to a baby of her own?

In which case was this fair, relying so much on her
to be Steffi's carer while he worked things out?

'Well, now you're up and about, I'll introduce you to
your new belongings—the physical ones.' Bill's voice
was carefully neutral, nothing to read there, so maybe
he'd imagined the sadness. 'You can bring Steffi,' Bill

continued, 'because learning to do things with her on one arm is all part of fatherhood training.'

Which was all very well but how did he stand up with a baby in his arms? What if he fell?

He solved this dilemma by putting Steffi on the floor, standing up then lifting her, although he knew full well he *could* have performed the feat with her still in his arms. In the kitchen he was introduced to bottles, formula, baby food in small jars, yoghurt in the refrigerator, a sterilising machine that would have held its own in a hospital, bibs, baby bowls, baby spoons, baby cereal.

He took it all in, realising it was far less complicated than it had seemed at first glance, but it was Bill's attitude that was bothering him. Nothing overt, nothing he could put a name to, but it seemed as if she was distancing herself from him.

From him or from Steffi?

The Bill he remembered had been passionate about small children, babysitting all through their teenage years, so while he wasn't actually doing her a favour by letting her mind Steffi while he got sorted, he'd have thought she wouldn't mind. And, after all, she'd suggested it!

But there was something off—something too matter-of-fact in all this—

'Are you listening?' the person he was worrying about demanded.

'Boiled water,' he repeated diligently, then had to admit, 'No, I wasn't. What do I do with boiled water?'

Bill frowned at him.

'According to the notes, you still have to boil the water to mix with her formula for her bottles and she has three a day, one before each nap and one before bed.

She's got to be, what, eleven months old, so I would have thought maybe by now ordinary water would do, but I've written Kirsten's number on the notes, she's Andre's wife and the most sensible of my sisters-in-law and won't talk on for ever if you ring to ask her something.'

Nick looked at the notes, then back at Bill, thinking of the expression he thought he'd seen on her face—thinking too that, with the other strange stuff happening when he was around Bill, he should be seeing less, not more of her.

'Are you sure you want to take this on?' he asked. 'After all, I *could* just tell the hospital I can't work for a while, they'd battle on, and once I've read the notes, how hard can it be?'

She shook her head.

'You'll soon find out. I'm going to have a sleep, but I'll be up before you go to work. You can organise whatever you like with the hospital once you've thought it through.'

She tapped the notes to remind him to read them, and departed, leaving his bunch of keys and taking the single spare he'd used when he'd come up from her apartment.

And, despite the warm body he held in his arms, the place felt cold now Bill had gone...

Exhaustion hit Bill as she left the apartment, tiredness so strong it sapped her energy and she barely made it home, throwing off her clothes and climbing into bed, unfortunately conscious enough to pick up the scent of Nick on her sheets.

Damn it all. She *had* to sleep!

But emotion churned inside her—an emotion she'd

never felt holding one of her nieces or nephews. This was a new emotion—a heart-rending sorrow that Steffi's mother hadn't really wanted her, while she, Bill, had so longed for the baby she'd conceived, her arms had ached for a year.

And were aching again...

Go to sleep, she ordered herself, and training held true. She fell asleep but dreamt of empty cots and abandoned babies and Nick with his daughter in his arms.

She woke, barely refreshed, at six, and knew she'd better get upstairs so Nick could go to work. Showering, she told herself that if anyone in the world deserved to have his own family it was Nick, and she should be glad for him—*was* glad for him!

Kind of.

'How do mothers know to do all this?' he demanded as she walked into his apartment. 'The notes say she has dinner at five-thirty, a little meat cut up fine with mashed vegetables. It doesn't say what kind of meat or how you can cook a piece of steak while holding a crying baby in your arms and not burn the child, and is she crying because she's hungry or she needs her mother or what? How do I know?'

'You don't,' Bill told him, taking Steffi in her arms and rocking her back and forth until the crying stopped. 'You have to guess, but didn't she have a nap?'

'Of course she had a nap. Bottle and a nap at three, the notes said, and we did that, although I had to put the bottle in the freezer to cool the boiled water before I could give it to her. I can see I'll have to boil water ahead.'

'So you read the notes?' Bill persisted, watching as Nick turned a very large piece of steak on a griddle pan.

'Of course!'

He was cranky and she had to hide a smile so she didn't make things worse.

'The bit that said when she had dinner and what she ate?'

'Of course!' Really cranky now.

'And it didn't occur to you to get it ready while she slept?'

He looked up from the steak, frowning, growling.

'I was busy on the computer.'

'Oh, yes?'

'Well, I obviously can't put a baby seat in my car, can I, so I had to do some research on the safest vehicles for kids to travel in. You've no idea.'

Bill grinned at him, reminded him to turn the steak, then went to the cupboard where one of her sisters-in-law had stacked bottles of additive- and colouring-free baby food. She set Steffi in the highchair, strapped her in, gave her a small plastic spoon to play with, and opened the jar.

'Here,' she said to Nick when she'd warmed the jar in some hot water. 'Feed her this. It won't hurt not to have fresh cooked every now and then, and later, when it's cooled, she can gnaw on a bit of that steak.'

Knowing she would definitely laugh if she watched him feed an infant for the first time, she left him to it, going into the bathroom to run a bath, which Steffi would certainly need.

She'd just set a small plastic duck floating in the water when Nick appeared, both he and Steffi liberally smeared with food.

'I'll get the hang of this!' he muttered as he handed

her over, and he was halfway out the door before he added, 'I have to shower. Did I thank you?'

He came back in, embraced them both, then to Bill's astonishment he kissed her, not on the cheek or forehead or even the top of her head, as he was wont to do, but on the lips—*full* on the lips!

'Beyond the call of duty, this, friend Bill,' he said, his voice husky with what couldn't possibly be tears.

Except he hadn't had much sleep, and he'd certainly had the most emotional day of his life, so perhaps…

CHAPTER FIVE

HE'D KISSED BILL on the lips—Bill, his friend, on the lips!

Nick stood under the shower, wondering why this one small incident from an unbelievably momentous day should be occupying his attention to the exclusion of all else.

Including the fact he had a daughter…

Because Bill's lips had felt so soft?

Tasted so sweet?

Or because when he'd tasted that sweetness, felt the softness, he'd also felt a stirring somewhere else?

No, it was because he was shocked and tired—not to mention emotionally exhausted—that kissing Bill had suddenly taken over his mind.

Or he was thinking of it to stop himself worrying over what would become of him and Steffi.

So why was a voice in the back of his head suggesting he kiss Bill again? Perhaps when he left for work, although what the voice was really suggesting was a proper kiss—an in-the-arms kiss, Bill's slim body pressed to his, her lips parting to his invading tongue—

'Out now!'

He spoke the order aloud, hoping to rein in his rampaging thoughts. Far better to think of Steffi and all the problems her arrival was going to cause in his life.

'She'll need some new clothes—just lightweight cotton tops and pants to suit this climate,' Bill said when he walked into the room she'd prepared for Steffi. The little girl was dressed in a long-sleeved pink and white striped suit that covered her from ankles to neck. 'Most of her clothes will be too heavy up here. We'll shop tomorrow, she and I.'

Bill handed him the baby and wandered off, muttering something about getting the bottle ready.

He wanted to follow her, to have a good look at her, although he knew *her* reaction to the kiss wouldn't be written on her face.

In fact, she probably hadn't reacted at all, thinking, if anything, that he'd just happened to miss her cheek.

Deciding to follow her to the kitchen anyway— maybe looking at her would sort out why he'd kissed her lips—he wandered out of the bedroom and stood in the hall, looking into the kitchen where Bill was shaking a bottle to mix the formula.

Her back was to him so he was able to study her— slim legs encased in black leggings, a loose white T-shirt hanging to her thighs, tangled red hair falling below her shoulders, the front bit of it bunched up on the top of her head.

Bill, as he'd seen her thousands of times—so how could he possibly have become attracted to her now?

And why?

Because he hadn't had a regular lover lately?

Lover?

How could he possibly even think that word about Bill?

Was it that insidious longing for a family that had started when Serena had first been pregnant that was making him look at Bill differently?

No, far too convenient an excuse.

Steffi made a gurgling noise and Bill turned, apparently startled to see him there as faint colour spread across her cheeks.

'Have you got time to give Steffi the bottle?' she asked, handing it to him, then, without waiting for a reply, adding, 'I'll get a bib.'

Bill fled, heading for Steffi's room, unable to believe Nick had caught her as she'd been staring vacantly out the kitchen window, thinking about a kiss.

Not just any kiss, but his, Nick's, kiss!

A lip-kiss of all things. Of course, he'd probably aimed for her cheek and she'd moved her head at just the wrong moment.

And although she knew full well he'd have only seen her back view when he'd come into the kitchen, she'd actually blushed—her cheeks burning—at being caught out.

But the kiss had affected her so strangely she hadn't been able to *not* think about it.

Which was crazy as his lips had barely brushed hers, yet she'd felt fire travel from that touch, right through her body, heating her flesh and sending her nerves into a quiver of excitement.

Tiredness, she told herself, and grabbed a bib from where she'd put them in a drawer, intending to hurry back to Nick despite legs heavy with reluctance.

This is totally insane—that was the next bit of information she offered her disordered brain and twitchy body. This is Nick we're talking about.

Nick!

'Bib!'

She handed it to him as he sat on the couch, show-ing the bottle to Steffi while he tried to work out how best to hold her.

'Like this,' she said, settling the infant in his arms and fixing the bib herself.

Now walk away.

She knew this last bit of advice offered by her few still-functioning brain cells was extremely sensible—even compelling—but how could she walk away from the sight in front of her? Steffi totally absorbed in suck-ing down her milk, but one hand clutching Nick's little finger and her eyes never moving from his face.

As for Nick, he simply sat, looking down at his daughter, the love he felt for her already written so clearly on his face it hurt Bill's heart to see it.

Rationally she knew that finding he had a daughter was the best thing that had ever happened to Nick, but what lay ahead? Could Steffi be the start of the family he wanted or would he grow to love her more and more then have her snatched away?

Knowing the pain of that kind of loss, Bill could only feel for him—worry for him—yet that was better, surely, than worrying about kisses?

No, one kiss, singular.

One kiss didn't count…

Nick arrived home after a distracted night on duty to a silent home. Tiptoeing, he made his way to Steffi's room but the cot was empty. He assumed Bill was sleeping in the next bedroom, although they hadn't discussed any arrangements—anything at all, really.

The door was open and tucked under a sheet was Bill, making little snuffling noises as she slept, and nestled in beside her was his daughter, also asleep, although an empty bottle on the bedside table suggested that at some time during the night she'd woken up hungry and had needed to be fed again.

Nick stood in the doorway and looked at the pair of them, and felt again an overwhelming surge of love.

For Steffi, of course...

He walked away quietly, into the kitchen, but he'd barely reached the door when he heard a gurgle of laughter. His daughter was awake.

Thinking he'd pick her up and let Bill sleep, he hurried back to the room, but the gurgle had woken Bill as well, and she was smiling tiredly as Steffi played peek-a-boo in the wild red hair.

'Bad night?' Nick asked, moving into the room to scoop Steffi into his arms.

'Not really,' Bill said, sitting up so he couldn't help but notice the minimal nightdress she was wearing, a fine cotton shift that barely covered her small but shapely breasts and clearly showed her body curving down to a tiny waist. 'She woke at three and didn't settle so in the end I gave her another bottle and brought her in with me. So much change and strangeness for the wee mite, I thought she probably needed cuddling, lots of cuddling.'

She grinned and added, 'Then, of course, I was so worried about rolling over and squashing her that I took ages to fall asleep myself. She'll need changing and you'll find clean clothes in the second drawer down in the dresser. I'll be out when I've woken up properly.'

'And put some clothes on,' he muttered to himself as he walked away.

Steffi looked up enquiringly at him and he gave her a reassuring smile, then his nose told him that she really did need changing and that fatherhood wasn't going to be all smiles and gurgling laughter.

Bill was in the kitchen when he'd undressed, cleaned and dressed his daughter again.

'Have you any idea how much excrement a child this size can produce?' he demanded, handing Steffi to Bill so he could have a proper wash himself.

'It's what they're good at, at this age,' Bill told him, as she settled Steffi in the high chair and started asking what she'd like for breakfast.

'Cereal and fruit?' Bill suggested.

Steffi banged her spoon on the tray and Bill grinned at her.

'I thought so,' she said, pulling the box of baby cereal and a small jar of puréed fruit from the cupboard. 'Now your dad's clean, he can feed you.'

'Oh, no!' Nick retorted. 'I did it last night. I'll make our breakfast—coffee and toast do you? I haven't shopped but Bob made sure there were some essentials here.'

Bill agreed that coffee and toast would be fine. She lifted the highchair close to the breakfast bar and perched on a stool so she could feed Steffi while they had breakfast.

Nick tried to focus on what he was doing, but making coffee and toast demanded little in the way of concentration so the domesticity of the situation attracted most of his attention. He watched Bill, noticed the way her lips parted slightly as she spooned food into Steffi's mouth, saw the concentration on Bill's face, but something else…

Concern?

Something more he couldn't understand?

'I know Serena said she was used to being cared for by strangers, but you'd think she must be missing if not her mother at least her grandmother.'

Bill's statement cut into his thoughts.

Had she been worrying about Steffi's well-being while he tried to guess at something deeper?

'You'd think so,' he agreed. 'So, what can we do?'

Bill frowned at him but he knew the frown was for her thoughts, not for him—at least, he hoped so.

'I think all we can do is give her lots and lots of physical love—cuddles, talking, kisses, songs—using her name and telling her we love her. I've no idea how much infants understand at different ages, but I don't know what else we can do.'

Nick felt his chest squeeze. Hadn't love always been Bill's answer to everything? Love for her friends, her pets, her family. The arguments they'd had over love—he claiming it was something poets and musicians made up to write about, she firm in her belief it made the world go round.

But now he'd felt this thing called love—for what else could the emotion he felt towards his daughter be?—he realised that while it might not make the world go round, it was probably all they could do to help Steffi feel secure—give her lots and lots of love.

Show her love with talk and cuddles.

But was it wrong of him to expect Bill to be doing this when Steffi wasn't Bill's child?

Was it something to do with *her* relationship to

Steffi that was causing the shadows he kept catching on Bill's face?

'Write a list of what you need at the supermarket and Steffi and I will go there after we've bought her some tropical clothes,' the woman he was worrying about said as she scraped the last of the cereal out of the bowl and spooned it into Steffi's mouth, neatly wiping off the excess with a small facecloth she'd had the foresight to have nearby.

He'd show her love and he'd learn to do all these things, Nick told himself, and concentrating on learning all he could about caring for his daughter would distract him from the wayward thoughts he was having about Bill.

'I could shop later when I've had a sleep,' he said, knowing he needed to start right now because his wayward thoughts were increasing despite the fact he and Bill must have breakfasted together like this—yes, a thousand times...

Except he hadn't felt his gut clench when she smiled at him—not once in those thousand times.

'I think for a few days at least your spare time should be spent with Steffi, so you learn the rhythms of her life and you get to know each other better. Write a list and we'll shop while you sleep, then this afternoon she'll be all yours.'

It made sense so he wrote a list—a good distraction—although if Bill was staying here he needed to consult her on what she liked to eat.

'Same as you, remember, steak and salad, lamb cutlets and salad, roast lamb—basic food. Put what you want in the way of snacks and drinks on the list, I'll do the rest. If I'm to be lolling around here for the week I might as well do the evening meal. We can gradually shift Steffi's evening meal a little later, and with you working nights you need to eat early so we can all eat together, which, the sensible Kirsten tells me, is a good habit to get into.'

Except it makes us seem like a family—the thing I wanted—but we're not, Nick thought as he left the room to find a pen and notepad, really leaving the room because the distraction of Bill's long, tanned legs tucked up on the stool was stronger than the distraction of learning to look after his daughter.

One week, that's all it would be, Bill promised herself as Nick left the room. Within a week she'd have settled Steffi into her new, if temporary home, found a decent, reliable nanny to give Nick back-up care when he was working and she could leave him to get to know his daughter on his own.

The 'if temporary' part worried her. It was all very well for Serena to tell Nick they'd 'talk' when she returned, but knowing Nick there was no way, now he knew about her, that he would give up his daughter.

No way he could, Bill suspected, remembering the besotted look on Nick's face.

She sighed and reminded herself that she needed to be careful too. Even more careful than Nick, for Steffi wasn't and never would be her daughter, so falling in love with the wee mite was just not on.

Detached—that's how she had to be. She could love Steffi as she loved her nieces and nephews, but stay detached...

She'd sent Nick off to have a sleep and was clearing up the kitchen when he reappeared, clad only in longish boxer shorts that he must wear as pyjamas. Her eyes were drawn inexorably towards his chest and were so focussed there she hadn't a clue what he was saying.

'I missed that,' she said, cursing inwardly because her voice came out all breathy.

'I was saying you can't take Steffi to the shops— no car seat.'

Desperate to distract herself from that chest, Bill lifted Steffi out of the highchair and set her on the floor, handing her a couple of wooden spoons and a saucepan to bang.

'I've got a car seat,' she responded, 'and whichever sister-in-law brought it insisted on installing it so she knew it was secure. She even adjusted the straps to fit Steffi. And there's a stroller in the car as well, so we're all set,' she said, skipping out of Steffi's reach as the toddler decided hitting legs was more fun than hitting a saucepan.

'You've thought of everything,' Nick grumbled as he turned back towards his bedroom, although he did relent, swinging back to smile and say, 'I have thanked you, haven't I?'

To Bill's dismay she felt a blush rising up her neck towards her cheeks as she remembered just how he'd thanked her. Thinking quickly, she bent down to lift Steffi in her arms to shield her so-transparent reaction from Nick.

'Of course you have,' she mumbled against Steffi's fluff of hair.

Now he'd never sleep because *now* he was remembering the kiss. Nick headed for his bedroom, muttering under his breath. Bad enough he'd had to fight the impulse to touch Bill—on the shoulder, knee, neck, cheek—all through breakfast, but by reminding him that he *had* thanked her, she'd reminded him of the kiss.

He couldn't do it—couldn't have her living here while this peculiar reaction to her was going on in his body.

Not that he could manage without her.

Although…?

Running through his roster in his head, he remembered he had three days off coming up soon.

When?

Five nights on then three off, wasn't that the system here at Willowby?

So two more nights on duty, and by the end of his three days off, the hospital human resources department should have found a locum to fill in for him. Two weeks, that's all he'd asked for.

He'd need to sleep for some time on the first of his days off, but he could sleep when Steffi slept. He'd show Bill over the next two afternoons how well he could manage his daughter so his friend wouldn't be worried when he told her he could cope without her.

And on that cheery note he fell asleep, only to dream of a long-legged, red-haired siren running through his life, always just ahead of him, taunting and tantalising him but never within reach.

Something really good was cooking when he woke up, and the aroma permeating the house was more than enough to tempt him out of bed.

'What *are* you cooking?' he demanded as he came into the kitchen, starving because he'd slept through lunch.

'Casserole for dinner,' Bill replied, 'but there's ham

in the fridge if you want to make a sandwich for a late lunch. I'm doing a big casserole of meat and veggies in the slow cooker so you can freeze it in meal-sized portions and always have something you can shove in the microwave when it's been a bad day.'

Nick was pulling butter and ham from the refrigerator as she finished talking and from where he was the words had an ominous sound.

'What kind of bad day?'

Bill turned from where she was adjusting knobs on the steriliser and smiled at him.

It had to be hunger that was making his heart miss a beat while a desire stronger than he'd ever felt before surged through his body.

Sure the state of his arousal would be obvious, he dumped the makings of his lunch on the table, mumbled, 'Tell me later—I should shower before I eat,' and fled the kitchen.

It had to be the dream, he decided as he stood under the shower that was not quite cold but definitely cool.

And if it wasn't the dream—if he was going to get an erection of mammoth proportions every time Bill smiled at him—then one of them had to go.

Now.

A not unhappy wail from Steffi's bedroom made him amend that to *soon*.

Very soon.

He dried himself, pulled on clothes then, thinking Bill would still be busy in the kitchen, went to retrieve his daughter from her cot.

She'd pulled herself up and was peering at him over the top, smilingly delighted with her achievement.

'Yes, you are a clever girl,' he assured her, lifting her

and holding her close, feeling again the somersault of love this small mortal had brought into his life.

And because, for at least the next few days, they both needed Bill, she would have to stay.

'So I'll have to keep my mind on you and the problems you're causing in my life, young lady,' he told Steffi as he put her on the change table and began the process of nappy-changing.

'Yuck!' he said, as he undid her nappy.

The word brought a crow of delight from his daughter, but as he cleaned up the little bottom he noticed redness.

Nappy rash.

He knew the words, but treatment?

With one hand on Steffi's tummy he surveyed the array of tubes and jars of cream on hand beside the change table.

'This thick stuff?' he wondered, waving the jar in front of the little girl.

Steffi gurgled her approval, but it was the 'Well done!' from the doorway that confirmed he'd chosen the correct remedy.

'I need to read the notes again,' he said as he smeared the white cream liberally all over Steffi's little bottom, but only part of his mind was on the job, the rest of it thinking about Bill—wondering why on earth, after all these years, he should suddenly be attracted to her.

He finished changing Steffi and, remembering she usually had a drink of water after her sleep, carried her into the kitchen where Bill had a covered container of boiled water ready for any occasion.

'I'll get the cup,' Bill offered, and she filled the little cup and screwed the lid on, handing it not to Nick but to Steffi, who grasped one of the handles and tried to manoeuvre the sipping part into her mouth.

'Can't quite manage it, kid?' Bill teased, and she held the cup so Steffi could suck from it.

They were close, so close, Nick holding the baby, Bill with one hand on Steffi's back, helping her to drink, then gold-brown eyes lifted and met his, and a heaviness in Nick's chest stopped his breathing.

It seemed their gazes held for minutes, although seconds seemed more likely, the spell broken when Bill smiled and said, rather breathlessly, 'Well, isn't this the silliest thing ever?'

And without waiting for an answer, she took Steffi from his arms, said, 'Get your lunch,' and disappeared with his daughter into the living room.

He made his sandwich and considered staying right there in the kitchen to eat it, but that would be even sillier than whatever was happening between them. Bill's statement had confirmed she, too, was feeling the attraction, so surely the best way to deal with it would be to talk about it.

Calmly and sensibly discuss it—maybe work out some rational reason why this should be happening between them now.

He took his sandwich into the living room, where Bill was lying on the floor, Steffi bouncing up and down on her stomach.

Nick sank into an armchair, took a bite of his sandwich, a sip of tea, then decided there was no time like the present to get it out into the open.

It?

Could something like the desire he was feeling for this woman be encompassed in a simple 'it'?

'It must be that we haven't seen much of each other over the last few years,' he said, then worried that perhaps she hadn't been talking about attraction earlier and he'd gone and made a fool of himself.

She peered at him around Steffi's head.

'You think?'

'Well, something's happened, hasn't it?' he grumbled. 'Come on, it's not like you not to be offering an opinion—several opinions, in fact.'

'About what?' she asked, all innocence, shifting so Steffi was now on the floor but remaining close to her so Steffi could play with her hair.

'You know damn well what.'

He was growling now, certain the woman was taunting him, stretched out so languidly on his floor, legs, hips, waist, breasts offered up to him, while the lips that had tasted so soft and sweet quivered with a little smile that was driving him to distraction.

He finished his sandwich, refusing to play her game, but when Steffi's attention was fully absorbed with a toy that made the most extraordinary noises when she pushed buttons and pulled on levers, Bill sat up, moving closer to him but stopping just short of resting her head on his knees, as she'd done countless times in the past when they had been no more than friends.

Which they were now, weren't they?

'Remember us sitting like this while we sorted out one or other of our love lives?' she asked, following his thoughts with such precision it was scary.

'Or sorting out the problems of the world,' he reminded her.

She nodded, then put her hand on his knee.

It was nothing more than a friendly gesture, yet his

skin beneath that hand burned as if she'd branded him. He wanted to lift it off so the pain would go away, and he wanted it to stay there—for ever…

Silence fell between them, although the bells and whistles continued to rattle around the room from Steffi's toy, and her giggles of delight distracted Nick so when Bill spoke he didn't catch what she was saying until she was well into her statement.

'—because your life is complicated enough as it is right now, what with Steffi, and Serena coming back to talk. We don't need to make it more complicated by having an affair.'

'Who mentioned an affair?' he demanded.

She grinned at him.

'Are you saying that isn't what your body wants?'

'Of course it is—no, of course it isn't. Why an affair anyway?'

'Well, I hardly think it could turn into a for-ever-and-ever thing, could it?'

She ran her finger over his lips, freezing his thoughts, although he'd have liked to ask why it couldn't be for ever and ever…

'Nick, the attraction is there,' she continued gently. 'It's inconvenient, nothing more than that. I'm saying I think we have to live with the inconvenience of it. We'll both be busy enough with work and caring for Steffi, and once you're sorted with a nanny I won't need to be living here so it will be easier. But your world has been turned upside down—mine too, to a lesser extent—so it's only natural that our bodies should be turning to each other for support.'

'It's not support my body wants from yours,' Nick

growled, taking that tantalising finger and sucking gently on it.

'Or mine from yours, to tell the truth,' Bill admitted, shivering a little as she removed her finger and leaned against his legs, resting her head on his knees, licking at his skin to get a taste of Nick—the kind of taste she'd never considered she could ever want.

'And you can stop that,' he told her, easing her away from his legs and settling on the floor to play with Steffi. 'Go and do whatever you have to do—we'll be right until dinner and bathtime. See you around five?'

So, that was it for the attraction conversation, Bill realised. She hauled herself off the floor, bent to kiss the top of Steffi's head as she said goodbye, and left the apartment.

But she couldn't shut the door on thoughts of Nick.

Nick as a man.

Nick as a desirable, sexy man who was stirring her body into an agony of wanting.

She pulled her mobile out of her pocket and phoned him.

'I suppose the alternative would be for us to have a quick, passionate fling and get it out of our systems then we could go back to where we were,' she said as soon as he answered.

'And just when could we conduct this fling?' he demanded. 'I can't even answer the phone without my daughter trying to wrestle it from me, and we'd no sooner get to the interesting part than she'd be yelling from her cot. *Coitus interruptus* at its best.'

'At least I wouldn't get pregnant,' Bill told him, chuckling at the image he'd described. 'But you're right, best we just ignore the whole thing and hope it will go away.'

'Like a really, really bad cold,' Nick grumped, then he disconnected the call.

CHAPTER SIX

BILL DID BUSY stuff to distract herself, washing, vacu-
uming, putting fresh sheets on the bed, and clearing
debris from the refrigerator as she'd be eating at Nick's
for this week at least.

Food, refrigerator, Nick's—

She grabbed her phone again and hit Nick's speed-
dial number.

'Not another suggestion about our sex lives?' he muttered as he answered.

'Of course not,' Bill told him. 'Something far more
important than sex. I don't know why I didn't think of
it earlier but, Nick, we haven't told Gran about Steffi,
and if we don't someone else is sure to now all the de
Grootes know, but what do we say?'

She heard Nick groan.

'Damn and blast—I should have gone over yesterday
but yesterday was a disaster from start to finish. Can
I borrow your car? I'll take her now. We'll have time
before dinner—but then there's her nap.'

'She'll sleep in the car and, yes, we'll go in my car.
I'll drive.'

'You'll come?'

Nick sounded so surprised Bill had to laugh.

'Didn't we always face Gran, or my parents for that matter, together when we were in trouble?'

'I'm not sure trouble quite covers this situation,' Nick replied, sounding so uneasy Bill felt a pang of sympathy for him.

Better that than lust, she realised as she told him to pull himself together, grab a brightly coloured bag off the chest of drawers—'It's got spare nappies, cream, clothes and baby wipes in it'—and meet her in the car park.

She brought her car close to the lift and had the back door open when Nick and Steffi emerged. Taking Steffi from him, she strapped her in, aware Nick was watching every move, learning all the time.

Aware too of Nick as a man—the impossible dream...

'I wondered when I was going to meet my great-granddaughter. Whillimina's family have been phoning all day,' Gran greeted them, then she lifted Steffi into her arms and smiled down at her. 'And don't bother telling me what it's all about,' she said, addressing both Nick and Bill. 'I'm too old to be bothered with details. I just need to know the little girl is being properly looked after, and that I get to see her at least once a week and mind her from time to time.'

'Oh, Gran,' Nick said, his voice so husky the words barely came out, then he hugged the woman who'd brought him up, his arms easily encompassing both her and his daughter. 'I'm sorry I didn't let you know about her earlier but it's all come as such a shock.'

Gran led them into the living room and waved for them to sit down. Steffi was playing with the glass beads around Gran's neck, apparently quite comfortable on the older woman's knee.

'I'm glad you're back, of course,' Gran said, 'but when you made the arrangements to return you didn't know about young Steffi here. Things will change, you know.'

'And how,' Nick told her, but Gran wasn't finished.

'Not just in adjusting to having a child, but now you know about Steffi you will have different priorities and I don't want you to feel you have to honour your contract in Willowby because of me. You were a good boy and you've grown into a fine man, and you keep in touch with me more than most young men would with their parents or grandparents, but you have to live your own life, remember.'

What was she saying?

Nick ran her words through his head, thinking he could ask Bill later what she'd thought of them, but Bill had excused herself to make some tea.

'Once I've sorted out the care arrangements, Steffi won't make too much difference in my life,' he told Gran, who smiled and raised her eyebrows.

'We'll see,' she said gently. 'We'll see.'

Bored with the beads, Steffi was trying to climb off Gran's knee so Nick rescued her and put her on the floor, pulling a stacking toy out of the bag Bill had obviously prepared for outings such as this.

'And Whillimina?' Gran asked, nodding her head towards the kitchen. 'I hear she's helping you take care of Steffi.'

'Only until the hospital can give me some time off and we get a nanny to look after her when I go back to work.'

It sounded like an excuse and he knew Gran would pick up on it.

'Is it fair on her, considering all that happened to her in the past?' Gran asked, right on cue.

All that's happened in the past?

Nick wanted to ask Gran what she meant, but Bill came through the door at that moment, carrying a tray with teapot, milk and sugar, cups and saucers and a plate of biscuits on it.

'Set it down on the sideboard where Steffi won't be able to reach it,' Gran said, removing a Dresden figurine from her great-granddaughter's hands.

Bill poured the tea and the rest of the visit was taken up with local gossip and general conversation.

'Do you think someone's told her about Serena and what happened that she was so incurious about how a baby lobbed into my life?' Nick asked Bill as they drove back towards the apartment.

Bill considered the matter for a while then shook her head.

'I doubt it. I didn't tell my lot much—just that you had a small child and needed stuff for her. Some of my sisters-in-law are probably dying to know, but most people would just shrug and accept it. I think with Gran she knows you'll talk about it when you're ready and she's willing to wait until then.'

'Talk about it when I'm ready?'

Nick's voice was so loud Steffi gave a little whimper then settled back into sleep.

'How can I ever be ready when I haven't a clue what's really going on?' Nick asked in a more subdued but still panicked tone. 'So I know about Steffi and she's here with me now, but what of the future? What will Serena's "talk" entail? I want to stay here, Bill, to work here, for at least for a year and probably longer. I'd actually been thinking for ever…'

His voice tailed off and he was silent for a moment, before he asked, 'Can we drive to the beach? Not Wood-choppers but Sunrise, where we can sit in the car and look out at the water.'

Bill understood exactly what he was asking—understood why as well. As teenagers they'd often sat on the headland at Sunrise Beach, looking out at the sea while they'd solved the problems of the world.

Or their love lives…

Bill parked the car in a corner of the car park and they sat in silence, Steffi asleep in her car seat.

'I came here to see Gran and be with her,' Nick finally said, 'but, in truth, the life I'd decided to lead was palling. You can have too much fun, you know.'

He sounded so serious Bill had to fight an urge to laugh, but instead turned towards him and took his hand.

'It was the family thing, I imagine,' she told him. 'Once you'd had that thought—seen the image of yourself as a family man in your head—it would have been hard to shift, and Willowby would have been a natural place for you to settle.'

He lifted her hand and dropped a light kiss on her fingers.

'I guess so, although at the time I didn't dwell on the family thing for long. Serena had squashed the idea so quickly and completely I thought I'd put it out of my head until quite recently when coming up here mainly for Gran made me think of it again.'

'You could never have put it out of your heart,' Bill

murmured. 'Not having had a real family of your own. Once the idea sneaked in it would have been hard to dislodge.'

He squeezed her fingers.

'I suppose you're right, but what next, Bill? What do I do? What do we do?'

Bill retrieved her hand before he could excite it—and her—further, though a light kiss and a hand squeeze was hardly erotic foreplay.

'*We* do nothing,' she said, 'not as a "we". But you look after Steffi with me or a nanny to help and you go to work and visit Gran and do all the things you intended doing when you came up here.'

'Except,' she added, remembering the leggy blondes at breakfast, 'the rushing out to the islands to have a wild old time on your days off. Later, when Steffi gets to know you and feels at home, you can have a social life again, though judging from my family's experiences late nights are severely limited by their children's habit of getting up at an unreasonably early hour in the morning.'

Thinking she'd handled the conversation quite well, for all the churning in her stomach as she'd denied the 'we', Bill sat back in her seat and looked out towards the islands, noticing how calm and clear the water was, thinking a swim might clear her head.

'So, that's me done,' Nick said. 'What about you?'

She turned towards him.

'Me?'

His eyes were shadowed, his mouth serious, and she wondered what on earth could be coming next.

'Gran asked if it was fair to you to have you minding Steffi. To quote Gran, "considering all that happened".'

He touched Bill's cheek and she felt the shiver of reaction—or possibly despair—rattle through her body.

'What happened? Is this to do with Nigel? With you calling off the wedding?'

His voice was deep with understanding, with sympathy—with love, the friendship-love they'd shared for ever—and Bill felt something crack inside her.

The lump in her throat was too big to swallow so she made do with a nod.

'Tell me.'

It wasn't an order, more a whispered plea, but suddenly the lump disappeared and she found she could talk about that time, about discovering she was pregnant a month before the wedding, Nigel's horrified reaction—'people will think that's why we married, we can't have that'. His demand she have an abortion, her realisation that he was a shallow, selfish, social-climbing toadie and calling off the wedding. Then—

'But what happened?' Nick asked, obviously enough as she certainly didn't have a baby now.

'I miscarried,' she said, and felt his arms close around her, drawing her to his chest, holding her tightly as he told her how sorry he was, how stupid she was not to have told him, how he'd have come to her, she should have known that.

When the hug turned from sympathy to something else she afterwards wasn't sure, but somehow they shifted their positions and Nick was kissing her full on the lips.

The sun was shining, the sea was calm, Steffi was asleep...

Bill kissed him back.

The world didn't come to an end.

Anything but!

In fact, as Bill responded, meeting the demands of Nick's lips with demands of her own, her body came to life in a way she'd never felt before. Heat surged through her, her blood on fire, while her breasts grew heavy with desire and the ache between her thighs made her twist in her seat as she tried to ease the longing.

'This is stupid.' she managed to mutter as Nick's hand left her cheek and roved across the skin on her neck, sliding down to cup one heavy breast. 'Idiocy!'

'I know,' he mumbled back, nuzzling now at the base of her neck and causing goose-bumps all down her spine.

But the kissing didn't stop, the desperation in it suggestive of a starving man needing to eat his fill in case the meal should be his last.

Bill's head tried to rationalise the situation—this was Nick, he was in trouble at the moment, shocked by the discovery he had a daughter, he needed comforting.

And she'd just told him what had happened—she was entitled to a little comfort herself.

But as the intensity of her response to Nick's kisses grew, she lost track of the excuses and gave herself up to the pleasure of kissing Nick and being kissed by him.

It wasn't Steffi waking up that stopped them but the arrival of another vehicle, a battered four-wheel drive, pulling up not at the other side of the car park, in spite of it being empty, but right beside them.

They broke apart, and seeing Nick's flushed face Bill knew she'd be fiery red herself. To hide her telltale cheeks, she turned in her seat, pretending she was checking Steffi, who still slept on, blithely unaware of the behaviour of her father and his best friend.

'And what are you doing here, Whillimina Florence? Not necking with some worthless boy, surely?'

Dirk, the youngest of her six brothers, a mad keen fisherman no doubt heading for the rocks below where they were parked.

'We're actually enjoying a few moments' peace and quiet while Steffi sleeps,' Nick responded, getting out of the car and coming around the hood to shake Dirk's hand—shielding Bill from him at the same time.

'Or we were until you arrived,' Nick added.

'Heard about the kid,' Dirk said, grinning at Nick and peering into the back of the vehicle to check his information was correct. 'Bet that's put a dampener on your social life.'

'Maybe it needed one,' Nick replied, and Bill knew he meant it, though she wondered, apart from his sudden longing for a family, if something more had happened to her friend.

Perhaps he'd really loved Serena and had been hurt by her refusal to marry him?

Oh, damn and blast. Surely not?

Although it would explain the passion of his kiss.

Rejected by the woman he adored, he'd taken off for overseas and now, back in Australia, had turned to the next one that came along, who just happened to be her, Bill…

She wanted to wail in protest and bang her head against the steering-wheel, then bang Nick's head against anything handy.

How stupid could one woman be? Kissing him back when she knew nothing could happen between them—knew, whatever had happened in the past between him and Serena, Serena would be back…

'Sorry, but I have to feed the kid then get to work,' Nick was saying to Dirk, 'but if I can organise Gran to sit with her for a few hours later in the week, I'd love to join you on the rocks. I'll give you a call.'

Organise Gran to sit with Steffi?

So Nick, too, had realised just how stupid the kiss had been, and he was already working out how to get *her* out of his life—well, possibly not right out but he was definitely figuring how to put distance between the two of them.

'Fishing with Dirk?' Bill asked when she'd said goodbye to her brother and Nick was back in the car.

He turned and smiled.

'Simple pleasures,' he said. That fitted with all the other stuff he'd said, but it also wiped away any memory of the kiss—drew a line under it without it being mentioned while telling her in no uncertain terms that there *was* a line, and it would not be crossed again.

Driving back to the apartment block, she wasn't sure whether to be glad or sorry. Common sense, of which she'd once had plenty, told her she was glad. She could count it as an aberration and tuck it away deep in her memory and with any luck forget it altogether.

That's likely, an errant voice in her head piped up, but she knew she had to ignore it.

Somehow he had to ease himself out of this situation without hurting Bill, Nick decided as she drove him towards the apartments. The hurt she'd already endured— hurt he'd known nothing about—was more than enough and Gran was right—how fair was it to expect Bill to take care of his child now he knew what she'd suffered?

As for that Nigel…

No, Nick told himself as he felt anger against the man building in his gut, forget the past and work out how to get through the next little while.

He had to get over the attraction business and definitely avoid physical contact because kissing her had made the situation worse. He had to forget the hunger he'd tasted on her lips, a hunger that had met and matched his own.

His future was too uncertain.

Well, not uncertain in one way. Steffi was his future and if he could just concentrate on that and ease Bill out of his life—or at least out of his apartment—as quickly as possible, then everything should be okay.

He glanced at her, and saw the little frown puckering the clear skin of her forehead and wanted more than anything to touch her, to assure her everything would be all right, but the kiss had made it impossible for him to touch her—possibly ever again. The kiss had shifted their relationship into a place where it couldn't be...

'If you cook a potato and mash it with some peas and a little gravy and carrot from the casserole in the slow cooker, I think Steffi will eat that for her dinner.'

Nick's turn to frown.

Was that all Bill had been frowning about?

Steffi's dinner?

Could she have shoved her emotional confession back into some box in her mind and switched back to practical Bill?

Could she have dismissed the *kiss* so easily?

They'd reached the entrance to the car park and she was leaning out to press the code that opened the big doors so he couldn't see her face, but even if he could see it, would he be able to read it?

The Bill he'd kissed, and who'd kissed him back with mind-blowing enthusiasm, was a Bill he didn't know at all.

'I'll drop you both off and be back in time for you to go to work,' she added as she pulled up next to the lift. 'I need to pop over and see Kirsten to ask her about nannies—she had one when she went back to work after her kids started school—just part time, some kind of share arrangement with another mother. I know there are a couple of agencies in town but she'll know which one is best.'

Nick took in the information, aware as he did so that Bill was intent on distancing herself from him, just as he'd intended doing from her. Yet somehow it aggravated him that she'd moved first.

Pathetic.

That's what he was.

'Well, go on, out you get, and don't forget your daughter,' Bill told him, back to her old bossy self, which aggravated Nick even more.

But he got out, unstrapped Steffi from her car seat—a feat in itself—and carried her and the colourful bag into the elevator, refusing to wave as Bill took off, tyres squealing on the concrete floor.

CHAPTER SEVEN

'HA! YOU WEAKENED,' Nick said to Bill when she turned up an hour before he was due to go to work. 'Bet you thought I couldn't do the bath myself.'

This, he'd decided as he'd fed and bathed his daughter, was how he was going to play things. As if nothing had ever happened between them.

The tightening of his body suggested it hadn't totally accepted this idea but he soldiered on.

'Nothing to it,' he said, pointing to where a pyjama-clad Steffi was playing with toys on the living-room floor.

'Until you need to shower yourself,' Bill said, smiling as Steffi noticed her and began to crawl towards her, gurgling a welcome.

'I did wonder about that and decided that's why you had the playpen thing. Pop her in there with some toys and shower quickly.'

'Well done, you,' Bill said, swinging Steffi up into her arms so Nick wasn't sure if her praise was for him or his daughter. 'But now I'm here I'll read her a story while you do whatever you have to do to get ready for work, okay?'

Bill turned back to face him as she added the last word, and he knew she was asking something else.

Like were things okay between them?

Or, dread thought, was it okay if they never mentioned the kiss?

'The casserole was fantastic,' he said by way of reply, 'but Bob didn't include containers for freezing things when he furnished this place so I've left it all in the pot.'

He decided that had answered the first possible question—a normal Nick-Bill conversation. The second question was unanswerable.

He showered, shaved and dressed for work, returning to the living room to find Steffi already asleep in Bill's arms.

'You want to pop her into bed?' Bill asked, and he bent and lifted his daughter, smelling the baby smell of her and feeling his heart swell again with love and pride.

Knowing that, whatever happened in the future, Steffi's welfare would come first.

He carried her into the bedroom and laid her down gently in her cot. Bill had followed him, carrying a small ornamental angel. She fiddled with it for a moment, plugging a lead from it into a power point then pressing one of the angel's wings.

'Intercom,' she explained. 'I put the receiver near my bed so I can hear her if she wakes in the night. Kirsten gave it to me this afternoon, along with some info about nannies. We can talk about that tomorrow.'

And with that she slipped away, leaving him watching his sleeping daughter, trying to take in the enormous changes that had happened in his life in three short days.

'Not that I regret them,' he told the sleeping Steffi, reaching down to pull a light sheet over her.

He called goodbye to Bill, who'd disappeared into the bedroom she was using, and left for work, hoping it would be a busy night so he didn't have time to think about Bill or bedrooms or anything other than work really.

Bill heard the door close behind him and came out of the bedroom, telling herself how pathetic she was, hiding away like that. Although she'd had a valid excuse, putting new batteries into the receiver of the intercom and setting it up on the table next to her bed.

In the kitchen she peered into the slow cooker, cursing herself for not slipping back down to her apartment before Nick left, to get some containers to freeze the leftovers.

Tomorrow would do.

Helping herself to a plateful, she sat down to eat it, wondering how long it would take to find a nanny and wondering if *not* living here with Nick would make things better or worse as far as the attraction went.

She'd barely finished her meal when her mobile trilled.

The hospital!

Nick?

Answer the damn thing, she told herself, and did so.

'Mass panic,' Angie, the triage sister, told her. 'I know you've got time off for some reason or other but we need anyone we can get. A backpackers' minibus overturned on the bypass, fourteen passengers and driver all with various injuries. The first admissions will be at the hospital in fifteen minutes. Can you come?'

Thank heaven she'd seen Kirsten just that afternoon was Bill's first thought.

'I'll be there, possibly not within fifteen minutes but as soon as I can get there,' she told Angie, then she phoned Kirsten, who'd offered to babysit any time, explaining, as she'd said it, that her two were off at her mother's place for a few days and being school holidays she was free herself.

She could also ask Kirsten to bring freezer containers...

'Kirsten's minding Steffi,' Bill said, finding Nick as soon as she walked into the ER, knowing if he saw her there before she explained, he'd panic.

He was bent over a stretcher, listening to the ambo explain the treatment that had already been given to the patient, but he nodded to show he'd heard Bill's words then smiled.

'Glad you're here,' he said briefly but with such genuine gratitude that Bill knew the situation was dire.

'Second ambulance two minutes out,' Angie said, when Bill approached the triage desk. 'I've more doctors coming in but no one to take this patient yet. Will you meet and assess? Nick can join you when and if he stabilises the young woman he's with now.'

Bill nodded, and grabbed a trolley, knowing the ambulance would have to turn around to return to the accident. They'd move the patient onto it, quickly transferring her to hospital monitoring equipment so the ambulance equipment would be free.

The patient was another young girl, blunt chest

trauma, intubated and with fluid flowing into her, but Bill could hear a wheezing noise and wondered if the oxygen she was getting was flowing out as quickly as it flowed in.

'Open pneumothorax,' the ambo said after they'd settled her on the trolley. He lifted the sheet that covered the young woman and pointed to a large sterile dressing on the left-hand side of her chest. 'Freak accident. She must have been holding her backpack on her knee when the bus tipped over and a weird silver thing went into her chest. We had to remove it to put the patch on her, but it's there near her legs somewhere in case the docs need to see what it is.'

He handed Bill the paperwork and took the empty stretcher back to his ambulance.

The 'weird silver thing' was of no importance to Bill or the young woman right now. The patch was acting as a flutter valve, one side open to allow air to escape, but the wound would have to be closed, and quickly. Were there surgeons coming in? Another nurse arrived and together they assessed the patient, knowing everything they did, even in an emergency, had to be checked and rechecked.

The young woman's breathing was slow and shallow and oxygen levels in her blood were veering towards dangerously low.

Thoracostomy!

Did every nurse's head have words rarely thought of just sitting there waiting to be thrown up when necessary?

'See if there's a doctor free,' Bill said to her assistant. 'She needs a drainage tube put into her chest to get rid of any fluid collecting in there, then the wound closed as soon as possible. But if we can get the drainage going she'll be more comfortable and hopefully her blood gases will improve.'

The nurse returned, almost inevitably, with Nick, but this was work and in a work situation personal issues were forgotten.

Bill explained while he examined the patient, then, taking care to keep away from the wound, anaesthetised a small area of her chest. Bill had the thoracostomy needle and drainage tube ready for him and within minutes the drain was in, fluid and blood flowing from it.

Lifting the sterile dressing, Nick examined the wound.

'She needs it closed,' he said, and turned to the young nurse. 'Can you find out how soon a surgeon will be here and where this lass is on the triage list? I can close it if no one else is available.'

Of course you could, Bill thought, again realising just how competent an ER doctor Nick was, but it was the realisation of why he was so good—his time with the army—that made her heart ache. That time must also have deepened his desire for a family. Well, now he had one—or part of one. With Serena's return he'd have the real thing, which was why she herself had to butt out right now.

Rob Darwin arrived before she had time to become melancholy over this decision—one, in fact, she'd already made.

'Two surgeons up in OR with the bus driver who looks like losing his leg, but if you're happy to do this, I'll assist,' he said to Nick.

Around them they could hear the noise of other nurses and doctors shouting for this or that, the chaos of a multiple casualty accident continuing, but within the cubicle everyone's concentration was on the patient, on closing the young woman's chest so her heart and lungs could function properly.

Nick worked with such precision, cutting more skin around the wound, cleaning the flap he'd need later to close the hole, clearing blood clots from deep inside, Rob holding back the skin while Bill irrigated the flesh beneath. Whatever had driven in had gone between ribs but had torn the cartilage connecting them.

Carefully Nick put the muscles and tissue back together again, stitching and stapling until finally the wound was sealed by the young woman's own skin, drawn tightly across her ribs.

'What did it?' he asked as he straightened up, leaving Bill to apply the dressing.

'Something silver—it should be by her legs,' Bill told him. 'The ambos think it was in her backpack, which she was holding on her knees.'

Nick felt beneath the sheet and found the small silver statue of a cat with its right paw raised.

'If it's a good luck charm, it didn't work, did it?' he said, returning it to its place beside the girl. 'That paw must have gone straight through her chest when the accident happened. Perhaps she had it in her hand at the time, showing it to someone.'

'Well, she's had some good luck landing in a hospital where an ER doctor can close her chest with a minimum of fuss,' Rob said, then he turned to Bill. 'Can I grab you a coffee?'

As soon as the words were out he must have realised his mistake and offered to get one for Nick as well, but as an approaching siren told them another patient was on the way, they both refused, and Rob went off to refresh himself before heading back into the fray.

'He's still hopeful of getting a date,' Nick said, his voice strained but that could be stress. 'Perhaps if you went out with him you'd find the spark.'

And put a distance between you and me, Bill thought, but didn't say it, knowing it was exactly what Nick was thinking.

'I think that's called using people and I'll deal with the stupid situation between us in my own way,' she snapped, then headed for the entrance to prepare for the next arrival, although as she watched the ambos unload the patient, she wondered if going out with Rob might not be a good idea.

Not all romances began with instant attraction.

And Rob was relatively new in town and lonely, and by going out with him she could introduce him to some other women and maybe he'd find someone who *did* feel a spark.

So, rather than using him, she'd be doing him a good turn and at the same time distancing herself from Nick .

By midnight all the patients had been stabilised, some flown south for further treatment, some hospitalised and the lucky few with minor injuries had been packed off to their hostel. Not wanting to keep Kirsten up later than necessary, Bill signed off and headed home.

'No trouble at all,' Kirsten said. 'She's a gorgeous little thing, isn't she? I've been watching her sleep. What's the story?'

Bill sighed.

'Who knows really? The bits I do know are so unbelievable I don't like to think about them. Briefly, Nick thought his girlfriend was having an abortion but she didn't and now there's Steffi, and right now her mother is in New York, which is why the baby's here with Nick, and after that—who knows?'

'Nick won't let her go,' Kirsten said, 'Steffi, I mean. Never having had a family, she must seem like a miracle for Nick.'

'Exactly,' Bill said, and must have sounded bleak for Kirsten put an arm around her shoulders.

'It *is* good, isn't it—for Nick, I mean?' she probed, and Bill assured her it was.

'I'm just overtired,' she said. 'How you manage kids and work I'll never know.'

She thought she'd sounded okay but the wondering look on Kirsten's face told her she'd failed.

'Well, look after yourself,' Kirsten said, giving Bill a hug. 'And if you need to talk to anyone, remember I'm not the family gossip.'

Bill had to smile for it was Bob's wife Jackie who claimed that title. Kirsten was the last person in the family to repeat anything told to her in confidence.

Nick found himself scowling at Rob Darwin every time they crossed paths that evening, but as the flow of ambulances was reduced to a trickle and the patients he was treating only had minor injuries, he had time to consider the situation more rationally. He knew he should be glad the man was interested in Bill because he himself certainly had no proprietorial rights on her, no claim at all, in fact.

And he definitely shouldn't be kissing her, for all his mind *and* body were obsessed by her.

Perhaps obsessed wasn't the word. Surely he couldn't be *obsessed*? Obsessed drew pictures of stalkers and serial killers in most people's minds—

'You all right?' his patient asked, and he knew he must have groaned.

'Fine, just a long night. And you'll be fine too. Just remember to check the coverings on the wounds every day and if you start getting some yellowish seepage, come back here or see a GP.'

'I'll definitely come back here,' the patient said, and for the first time Nick registered that she was a very attractive young woman. English, from her accent, and though her long blonde hair was matted with blood and her face streaked with grime, he knew she'd clean up into something special.

He smiled at her, hearing Bill's voice whispering *Cradle-snatcher* in his head.

'You do that if you need to,' he said in his most professional voice, knowing it was highly unlikely she'd be back while he was on duty. One more night then he could take some time off and sort out a workable arrangement for himself and Steffi.

The thought of her brought a half-smile to his face and he realised again that, whatever lay ahead, giving Steffi a stable, happy life had to be his number-one priority.

Once Bill shifted out, it would be easier to work out what to do next. Easier to stop thinking about her as well.

It had to be.

He looked around the ER. The place had gone from chaotic to all but empty, only one sad drunk sitting on a bench and Nick had been told the man was homeless and often spent the night in the ER.

Had *he* ever had a family?

Surely not, for wouldn't a family have kept him sane and safe and off the streets?

Although not all families worked…

'Mine will,' he muttered.

And was startled when a passing nurse said, 'Your what will what?'

He grinned at her.

'Sign of advancing age, talking out loud,' he said, then realised the nurse in question was Amanda, the woman who'd asked him to join her and her friends on a trip to the islands. 'Oh, by the way, I won't be able to make it at the weekend—unexpected complications.'

'Old friend Bill more than just an old friend?' Amanda asked, surprising Nick so much he had no time to retort before she added, 'Hospital gossip machines work just as well in the country as in the city, and everyone in the ER has seen the way you look at her.'

He had to quash this right now! More for Bill's sake than for his.

'I've known Bill since we started school together in the kindergarten class, what's more—' like some pathetic loser about to tell a lie, he found himself crossing his fingers behind his back '—the gossip I've heard links her with a certain other doctor—one who was in here earlier.'

He walked away before he got himself deeper into the mire, sorry he'd had to implicate Bill in a relationship that didn't exist but not wanting to explain his current situation.

Not that he could explain it because he had no idea exactly what it was—apart from a disaster.

Although Steffi wasn't a disaster and if he concentrated on getting life right for her, then everything else should fall into place.

Or so he hoped.

He arrived home to find his friend and his daughter both dressed for the beach.

'She loves the bath so much I thought I'd try her in the pool—there's a paddling pool beside the big pool and the water in it is quite warm. But I thought it best to go early before the sun gets too hot. Here, you can have a little play with her before you head to bed and I'll put the washing on.'

Bill handed Steffi to him and walked away, and though he wanted to watch, he didn't, turning his full attention on his daughter, who was gurgling with delight, hopefully because she was pleased to see him.

'We'll manage on our own, won't we?' he said, lifting her high into the air. 'Just one more night with Bill then it's you and me against the world, kid,' he added, while she laughed down into his face.

He hugged her close, reaffirming the fact that she was more important than anything else in the world right now, and getting their lives together sorted out had to be his first priority.

So why the hell, when Bill returned, did he suggest he grab a coffee and some toast and join them at the pool?

Because he wanted to see with his own eyes how his daughter took to the water?

Or he wanted to see Bill in a bikini again?

Ridiculous—that was tempting fate and the look Bill

gave him told him she thought so too, but he excused himself by deciding he didn't want to miss Steffi's first dip in a pool and hurried to fix some breakfast so he could join them.

Hell! She could do without seeing Nick with no shirt on. Didn't he realise they had to be seeing less of each other, not more?

Bill brooded on this as she and Steffi went down in the lift, exiting on the ground floor and walking out the back of the foyer to a beautifully landscaped recreation area. The two pools, formed so they looked like natural rock pools, were set in lush tropical vegetation. To one side was an outdoor barbeque and picnic space, tables and chairs set up beneath palm-fronded shelters.

On the other side was a long, narrow lap pool for serious swimmers, but for now all she and Steffi needed was the paddling pool.

Steffi saw the water and began to clap, making Bill realise she wasn't new to pools. Of course, her mother's New York apartment building could be modern enough to have one on site, probably on the roof.

Her mother.

Serena.

Just keep the beautiful blonde in the forefront of your mind when those abs come into view, Bill told herself, dropping their towels on a nearby chair, putting a little more sunscreen on Steffi's face then carrying her towards where the pool sloped from ankle depth to probably shoulder depth on Steffi.

The little girl paddled happily on the edge, splashing water up at Bill and chortling her delight.

'The notes said she's had swimming lessons.'

The abs had arrived, although right now they were decently covered by a T-shirt.

'I must have missed that part but lessons or not, you can't take your eyes off them for a minute around water,' Bill replied, then felt foolish and added, 'But of course you'd know that. I think child drownings are among the cruellest things we see in the ER.'

'Well, that's put a dampener on the fun, hasn't it, Steff?' Nick sat down in the water with his daughter and squirted water in his fists to make fountains.

She squealed with delight and once again he felt his heart fill with happiness. Whatever he had to sacrifice to give her the best possible life, he would. Not that resisting his attraction to Bill could be regarded as a sacrifice when they hadn't got past the kissing stage!

'One kiss does not a relationship make,' Bill said quietly, and he knew that once again their ability to follow each other's thoughts was in play.

'You are so right,' he told her. 'Now, how about you take over here while I swim about a hundred laps to convince my body of that?'

Bill laughed, which suggested that everything would be okay between them, but he knew it wouldn't—not unless they saw as little as possible of each other between now and when Serena returned. And, no, he told himself, he wasn't going to question the ethics of going back to Serena for the sake of his daughter—it was the right thing to do and he would do it.

Swim first, then sleep then one more night on duty, after which he'd get his new life organised...

How could so much have been organised while he slept?

Nick woke at two in the afternoon to find a note that

informed him his daughter was at playgroup, whatever that might be, and would be home at two-thirty. Two nannies were coming for interviews, Anna at four-thirty and Dolores at five-thirty.

Dolores? Who was called Dolores these days?

It had to be a measure of his overall confusion that he was spending precious brain power, limited right now, on an unknown person's name.

He showered, glanced around the apartment to make sure it was tidy then phoned Bob, who put him onto the right car dealer for the vehicle he'd decided would be safest for Steffi.

CHAPTER EIGHT

'AND JUST WHERE have you been?'

Bill was obviously angry when she greeted him just inside the door of the apartment when he returned at four twenty-five.

'I'm not late for the appointment,' he pointed out.

'No, but nervous would-be employees are usually early. Anna's sitting out on the deck with Steffi.'

Nick took in the faint flush of colour in Bill's cheeks and guessed the anger in her voice was more that of relief, the release of tension when someone had been worrying.

Over him, or the fact that he might miss the interview?

'I'd have phoned if I'd thought I'd be late,' he said, touching her gently on the forearm.

She stiffened immediately, then turned away, obviously not interested in the answer to her earlier question.

So he didn't tell her…

Why she'd let herself get all uptight over Nick being late, Bill didn't know. All she *did* know was that her relief at seeing him had prompted a surge of anger.

Stupidity, that's what it was!

She closed her eyes and prayed he'd like one of the

nannies enough to employ her and *she* could fade quietly into the background of his life.

This idea should have brought pleasure, but her visit to the playgroup with Steffi, seeing the other mothers and their children, watching Steffi's delight as she'd taken in the noise and colour, had brought back all the pain she'd suffered with the miscarriage, in her arms *and* in her heart.

'Plenty of small children around for you to play with,' she reminded herself, only to realise that since she'd come home after the miscarriage she'd deliberately avoided spending too much time with her smaller nieces and nephews. The older ones, yes, she regularly took them to the beach or went to watch their sporting fixtures.

But the infants—the toddlers…

'Would you two like tea or coffee?'

She called through the open door out to the deck, not venturing out because she didn't want to get involved.

Steffi looked up at her voice and left her hold on Nick's knee to stagger a couple of steps towards her, but Bill resolutely turned away.

Losing one child had been bad enough. To have this one worm her way any further into her heart then be lost to her—that would be too much.

She made the coffees, as requested, set the mugs on a tray, added biscuits and a fruit strap for Steffi and took the lot out on to the terrace.

'Aren't you joining us?' Nick asked.

Bill forced a smile as she replied.

'No, Anna and I had a good chat earlier.'

She fastened a bib around Steffi's neck and handed

her the treat, sitting her down on the tiled deck so she could eat it without smearing it all over the furniture.

'She seems a very placid child,' Anna said, and Bill found a better smile.

'She's the best,' she said, glad to be able to answer honestly. 'I suppose she's been used to so many different carers, she takes change for granted.'

Bill slipped away. While she'd been talking, Nick had leaned down and lifted Steffi onto his lap and the adoration on the little girl's face as she looked up at her father had nearly broken Bill's already badly damaged heart.

It's right they stay together, she told herself. It's how things should be.

But accepting the rightness of it did nothing to alleviate her pain.

Nick liked Anna and having read her references— all excellent—and seen her interacting with Steffi, he was certain she'd be the perfect nanny for his daughter. Because Bill had arranged another interviewee he would see her, too, but he felt more relaxed now he had at least one carer available.

'How do you see the hours working?' Anna asked. 'The agency explained you're a doctor who mainly does night duty, so would it be a live-in job?'

He studied the young woman, attractive enough, with a bright smile and a pleasant personality, then tried to picture her living with them—with him and Steffi—in the room Bill was using now—

'Look,' he said, feeling his way as another solution took vague form in his head. 'Originally, yes, I was employed to work in the ER and I told the hospital management that I'd be happy to do night shifts. Night shifts give you more time off—five nights on then three days off. In point of fact, it turns into four days off as they don't count the first day when you're supposed to catch up on the sleep you missed the previous night.'

Anna nodded but looked vaguely puzzled about where the conversation might be going.

'I should explain that I came back to Willowby largely to see more of my elderly grandmother, and the night shifts offered more opportunity to do things with her during the day. But now...'

Anna smiled.

'You're confused because you have to consider Steffi's needs as well, but in my opinion you'd still be better off doing night shifts. You get to see her in the morning when you come home, and in the afternoon. Depending on your timetable you could even eat dinner with her and put her to bed. Then on those days off you're all hers—or all hers and your grandmother's.'

'You're right,' Nick agreed, although in his gut he was still uncomfortable about the young woman sleeping here.

'How would you arrange your working hours if I stick to night duty?' he asked, throwing the onus of the decision back on her.

She considered it for a while, absentmindedly picking up another biscuit and eating it.

'I could start on the evening you begin duty and stay over for the five nights and days so you can sleep on your first day off. I'll be getting a meal for myself and Steffi so will do dinner for you each night, then when you're off duty I leave you in charge.'

It sounded okay but Nick still had misgivings.

'Is this the way nannying works? Do you not worry about living in a house with a man you barely know?

And doesn't if affect your social life? I mean, do you live at home or do you rent and if you rent, do you still have to pay rent if you're not there five nights a week?'

Anna smiled at him.

'Most employers don't give a damn about their nanny's social or financial life. In my case, I live with my partner—we've been together four years now. How I see it working is once Steffi's in bed and all my duties are done, with your permission and after you've met him, I'm sure my partner would be happy to visit.'

Uh-oh! Nick thought, imagining the two in the bedroom while Steffi screamed blue murder. Although wasn't there an intercom…?

'Not every night,' Anna continued, 'because he has his own interests, but occasionally he might bring over a DVD we can watch together. But that would only be with your permission. If you have any doubts, that's okay. You say the job's only temporary—that Steffi's mother is coming back—so I can survive a few weeks of not seeing my partner for five nights of the week.'

Nick felt reassured—mostly reassured. His sticking point still seemed to be the bedroom, which he now considered Bill's…

'You sound like a very sensible young woman and, being one, you probably realise the agency has sent two people for me to interview. I'll try to make up my mind by tomorrow morning and will be in touch either way.'

To Nick's surprise, because he'd been very impressed by Anna, Dolores won the nanny stakes hands down. An older woman, perhaps fifty, she was bright and vivacious and Steffi sank into her ample bosom and grabbed the chunky beads around her neck, obviously enamoured.

'No worry about the times you go or come, Doctor,' Dolores told him when he tried to explain the hours. 'I will be here for the little one. If you are here, I make myself scarce but can still make meals for you and her so you can spend more good time with her. She and I we do shopping, you write down what you like to eat. Money you pay for five nights I stay is more than enough for the week if you don't mind my living here even when not working. That way I can work a little bit—like a housekeeper as well as nanny. Nothing extra to pay.'

Nick knew he had to delve further and discovered Dolores's permanent home was with her son and his wife and family.

'This kind of job a nice holiday for me,' she told Nick. 'My grandchildren, five of them, and so wild, but being mother-in-law not my place to tell them how to behave so I have to keep mouth shut. I love them all, and they are good for me, but whew!'

She waved her hand in front of her face to indicate how tiring her grandchildren were.

Nick laughed, even more certain this woman would be the best possible nanny for his daughter.

He made arrangements about time and pay, aware he had to pay her through the agency. She played with Steffi for a while then carried her to the door, kissing both her cheeks before handing her back to Nick.

'I teach her a little Spanish,' she said. *'Adios, mi angelita.'*

Steffi waved a chubby hand, her gaze following Dolores as she headed for the lift.

'Well, kid?' Nick said to her, and Steffi crowed with delight.

Bill was in the kitchen, chopping vegetables, ap-

parently for Steffi's dinner as the pile was varied but
rather small.

'I thought we'd have grilled salmon and salad,' she
said, without looking up. 'I'll do a lamb cutlet for Steffi
but she can try the fish as well because she should be
eating fish and it's not mentioned in the notes about
what she eats and doesn't eat.'

Bill glanced up long enough to hand Steffi a piece
of broccoli then turned her attention back to what must
have been a really difficult carrot.

'So, she doesn't want to know about your new nanny,'
Nick said to Steffi, who was munching on the broccoli.

Bill glanced up again, anxiety and something he
couldn't read in her eyes.

'You've decided on one of those two?' she asked.
'There was one that will suit?'

Steffi slid out of his arms and crawled over to
where her saucepan and wooden spoons were left on
the floor, so Nick could turn his full attention on Bill,
who sounded even more anxious than she looked.

'They were both great but Dolores wins hands down.
She's older, which appeals to me, and she's obviously
very used to children, and there was something moth-
erly—or grandmotherly, I suppose—about her that won
Steffi over from the start.'

'That's good,' Bill muttered, and turned her attention back to the carrot, though she did glance up to ask,
'Do you want to eat early with Steffi? If so, it might be
an idea to turn on the barbeque to heat the grill plate.
It's always better to cook fishy things outside because
of the smell.'

Thus dismissed, Nick headed for the balcony, where
the beauty of the view struck him afresh. He walked

back inside, picked up his daughter, took Bill by the hand and led her outside.

'Isn't it great?' he said. 'And smell the sea.'

The sun was setting behind the building so the water was washed with pink and streaked with gold, the islands nothing more than purple lumps along the far horizon.

He put his arm around Bill's shoulders, as he must have done a thousand times in the past, and although she stiffened, he left it there.

'I thought you'd be pleased to be free of looking after me and Steffi,' he said quietly to his friend, resolutely ignoring the cries of his body that it wanted more than friendship.

'I would never want to be free of our friendship and I would hate to not be some small part of Steffi's life,' Bill said carefully, after a silence that had stretched too long.

Nick hugged her close, a friend hug.

'Daft woman!' he said. 'As if you'd ever be free of the two of us. You're our best friend, remember?'

Bill eased away from him, kissed Steffi's cheek and headed back indoors.

'Unfortunately, I do,' she said as she disappeared.

Nick set Steffi down with some toys Bill had left on the deck, and turned on the grill plate on the barbeque. He knew Bill was hurting, but why, he wasn't sure. There was the sudden eruption of attraction between them. It was mind-bogglingly strange, and with the advent of Steffi, definitely inconvenient, but they were both mature adults, they could resist attraction.

Couldn't they?

Of course they could, Bill probably better than him for she was a strong woman.

But there was something more, some pain he—
Steffi!

He'd been in New York when Bill had let him know
the wedding was off. So Steffi must be much the same
age as her child would have been and here he was, accepting her help, relying on her to look after Steffi when
every time she looked at the child she must feel pain
stabbing into her heart.

How stupid could one man be?

Not that there was much he could do about it now,
but Dolores was starting work in a couple of days…

They ate their early dinner on the deck, Steffi finding salmon very tasty.

'I'll clean up while you bath her and yourself,' Bill
said, and though Nick longed to talk to her, to say he
understood and to apologise for the pain he must unwit-
tingly have caused her, he knew now wasn't the time.
He'd be too rushed and, anyway, how could he put his
thoughts and emotions into words?

Bill watched the pair depart for the bathroom and
sighed. She stared at the after-dinner debris and sighed
again.

'Get a grip!' she finally muttered to herself, and she
stood up and began to stack the dishes on a tray.

It was great that Nick had found a good nanny, even
better that she could get out of his apartment. Then
this—surely you couldn't call it love-sickness—would
pass and her life would return to normal.

Or something approaching normal anyway…

She stacked the dishwasher, cleaned up the kitchen,
put away all Steffi's toys and seriously considered getting into bed and pulling the covers over her head, possibly for a year.

Although it would be better to do that in her own apartment, rather than Nick's.

And she certainly shouldn't be thinking bed and Nick in conjunction like that because it reminded her of all that could never be…

Giving up on the bed idea she went back out onto the deck. The lights from the marina at the base of the building lit up the neighbouring area, but the sea was a deep, dark navy and the distant islands nothing more than black shadows.

The familiar view, even seen from this height, soothed her troubled mind and eased the ever-present ache in her heart. She could almost smile at her stupidity because being attracted to one's unavailable best friend had to top the stupidity list.

'Steffi's asleep and I've set the baby monitor.'

Nick's voice came from behind her and she didn't turn, although when he slid his arms around her waist and held her lightly, she leaned back against him—yes, stupidity again but didn't she deserve *something*?

'I've been totally insensitive, letting you take over Steffi's care,' Nick said, his voice gruff as if this weird conversation he'd just begun was affecting him deeply. 'I didn't know what you'd been through but that's no excuse. I just let you step in without even considering how it would affect your life.'

Bill turned to face him, distancing herself by putting her hands on his shoulders and stepping back so she could look into his face.

'*What* are you talking about? I was happy to step in—in fact, I took it all on myself. You didn't have much say in it. So why are you wallowing in guilt?'

Nick studied her for a moment, as if trying to read

something in her face, and just standing there, looking at him looking at her, Bill knew it was more than attraction she was feeling for this man.

It was love.

'Steffi must be the same age as your baby would have been,' Nick said, pulling her close again into a warm hug—a *friendly* hug! 'It must hurt you just looking at her.'

Bill pushed away again and shook her head.

'And this is worrying you now when I'm about to be replaced?' she teased, then she became the hugger and Nick the huggee. 'Of course I look at Steffi and wonder what if, but having her to play with, to care for has been sheer joy, so enough of the guilt trip. Just get yourself off to work so you can afford to pay the nanny, not to mention kindergarten fees, swimming lessons, school fees…'

Nick stopped her teasing with his hand across her mouth and the kiss she pressed against his palm was as automatic as breathing.

The hand stayed there for an instant, then Nick turned and walked away, saying, over his shoulder, 'And that's a whole other problem, isn't it?' in a voice edged with what sounded like anger, although it could just as easily have been frustration.

Isn't it just, Bill sighed to herself.

CHAPTER NINE

DOLORES HAD FITTED so well into his and Steffi's life that Nick found himself, as his next days off drew close, wondering if he should consider some social activities. Amanda had mentioned a party and Bob had invited him to some big do at the yacht club. Bill, who hated boats because they moved so much, was unlikely to be there.

Bill.

She'd moved the few things she'd had with her out of his apartment on the day Dolores had moved in, and although Dolores obviously saw her—Miss Bill says this, Miss Bill says that, she would report to Nick in the evenings—Nick hadn't set eyes on her.

He knew from an occasional scribbled note on a patient chart that she must be working the day shift in the ER, but their paths hadn't crossed.

Should he call her?

He knew he should, if only to say thank you for all she'd done, but if he called, he couldn't trust himself not to ask to see her, and as she was obviously distancing herself from him, that would be unfair.

Although he *really* would like to know if she was finding this separation as difficult as he was. Did she think about him all the time, catch glimpses of someone she thought was him in the distance, only to be disappointed? Did she think about the kiss and find her body heating as she remembered?

Sitting at his desk in the little alcove he'd set up as a home office, he leaned his elbows on the desk and clasped his head in his hands.

And groaned!

'Dinner, Dr Nick,' Dolores called, and he pulled himself together and went through to the kitchen, where Steffi was already in her high chair, a lolly-pink bib around her neck, her chubby hands banging spoons on the tray.

'Nice bib, kid,' Nick said, and she crowed with delight.

'Miss Bill gave it to her.' Dolores straightened the bib, showing the giraffe appliquéd on it, then brushed her hand on Steffi's hair. 'Didn't she, sweetie?'

Dolores set a plate of meat and vegetables in front of Nick then sat down to feed Steffi. He'd learned by now that Dolores preferred to eat later but always made sure he and Steffi ate together.

The meal was delicious—all Dolores's meals were delicious—but this evening it failed to distract him from thoughts of Bill—Miss Bill, as Dolores insisted on calling her.

He'd thought, once their cohabitation had stopped, that the ache of desire that had been there in her presence would disappear, but, no, it simply grew stronger.

Work and Steffi, all he had to do was concentrate on those two things and surely, eventually, the attraction would die a natural death. People talked about unrequited love, but this was simply unfulfilled desire, a completely different animal.

'And we were at the mall so I didn't get the mail today.'

Dolores had finished feeding Steffi and was stacking dirty dishes in the dishwasher when Nick caught up with her conversation.

'If you don't want to collect it on your way to work,' Dolores continued, 'I will get it tomorrow.'

How could anyone be thinking of mail?

Nick smiled to himself at this totally inappropriate thought. He simply *had* to get his mind off Bill.

'I'll get it on my way out,' he assured Dolores, although it would mean stopping in the foyer on his way down to the basement car park.

It also meant he just happened to run into Rob Darwin, who was stepping into the lift as Nick exited.

They exchanged nothing more than courteous good evenings, but Nick knew someone in the building must have let Rob in and what were the chances that three people living here knew him?

Nick opened his mail box, emptied it, and tucked all the mail under his arm while he relocked the box. Given his mood, it was probably inevitable that the one piece of mail that slid to the floor was a postcard with a picture of the Statue of Liberty on it.

Refusing even to read it, Nick thrust it back in with the rest and went down to the basement.

Work didn't help. For a start he kept picturing Bill there, buzzing around with her quiet efficiency, always anticipating his needs when he had a tricky patient.

And when he wasn't picturing her there he was picturing her out with Rob Darwin, dining across a candlelit table from him, her hand touching his, just casually at first.

Would they park by Sunrise Beach on the way home?

His gut churned at the thought and by the end of his shift it took all his strength of mind to not knock on Bill's door when he got back to the apartment building the next morning, just to see how she looked...

And check whether Rob Darwin was there?

No!

He went directly to his apartment, showered, played with Steffi, ate the French toast Dolores cooked for him, and went to bed, certain that in sleep he'd lose the torment of his mind and body.

They were at Woodchoppers, Bill in a lime-green bikini, a colour that seemed incongruous until she slid into the water and the bikini apparently disappeared, melding in with the colour of the water so her sleek, slim body, rolling slowly over in the tiny waves, appeared naked.

Then he was in the water with her, both of them naked, swimming together in some way, bodies touching, arms pulling in unison through the water, Bill's body fitting into his, made to fit into his, her back moulded to his chest, the water cool, his blood on fire.

She turned and lay before him, offering herself up to him, but he didn't take her, simply looked, drinking in the riotous red hair, the pale pink of her lips, the tips of her breasts, as pink as her lips. He leaned closer to lick them, first one then the other, while she smiled to hide the trembling of her body.

Slim waist and flaring hips, more red curls, a nest that tempted his fingers, but he needed to know her better, to trace the contours of her body, feel the satin texture of her skin, kiss the little freckle just there at the base of her neck and now, a desire prolonged too long, taste again the sweetness of her lips.

Honeyed sweetness, moist warmth within, Bill no longer passive, stirring beneath him, raising her hips so her body slid against his—slid into place—to where it was made to be.

Drifting now, entwined, their bodies one, but the water failed to cool the fire that raced through his blood and burned along his nerves—the fire of need, of want—the urgency of desire.

He'd take her, she was his after all, part of him, the better part. They'd reached the rocks, soft rocks, and there he rolled her so she lay along his body, her breasts crushed against his chest, kissing him with a passion that told him the fire was in *her* blood as well, burning along *her* nerves...

He rolled her beneath him, touched her face, brushed back the burnished hair, smoothed his fingers over the lightly tanned skin that stretched across her cheekbones. Kissed her eyelids, kissed her nose, kissed the indentation beneath her pink ear, then lost himself once more as her lips parted, begging for a kiss.

For more than a kiss?

Of course for more. She was his, he was hers, it had to be—

Had he groaned aloud that he woke to the agonised sound reverberating around his bedroom?

That he woke up and sat, sweating, shivering, cursing now that he'd regressed to adolescence and the steamy dreams of youth, though Bill had never been part of those?

He clambered out of bed, aware he was alone from

the silence in the apartment, and headed for the shower, letting the water cascade over him, trusting it to wash away the memory.

Dreams faded, didn't they? Disappeared soon after waking, leaving nothing but ephemeral fragments too fine for memory to grasp?

Not this dream.

CHAPTER TEN

'YOU LOOK FANTASTIC!' Rob said when Bill collected him from his apartment near the hospital.

'Thank you,' she said, enjoying the compliment—stupidly pleased because, guessing her brother had also asked Nick, she'd made an extra effort, even straightening her hair so it hung like a shining dark red curtain down past her shoulders. 'But just remember I'm taking you there so you can meet some people outside the hospital circle. This is not a date.'

'Yes, ma'am.' Rob saluted as he said it, adding, with a wry smile, 'And I'll try to hide my broken heart.'

'Piffle,' Bill retorted, 'I bet you're so used to women falling at your feet, I'm nothing more than a novelty because I haven't.'

'Not *that* many women have fallen at my feet,' Rob argued, but he grinned as he said it and Bill had to hide a rueful sigh.

How simple it would have been to have fallen at Rob's feet—or even fallen just a little in love with him. How easy and uncomplicated. He was attractive, attentive, intelligent and had a good sense of humour—what more could a woman want?

But, no, she had to do the unthinkable, and for some

perverse reason fall in love with her totally unavailable best friend.

This time the sigh must have escaped for Rob, who'd been opening the car door for her, said, 'You're not regretting asking me to this do, are you? Do you not usually mix with the local social crowd?'

Bill slid in behind the wheel.

'As a lot of the local social crowd are related to me I can't avoid mixing with them, but as family, not at things like this. But, no, I don't regret asking you, it will be fun, beginning with the shock on my various sisters-in-laws' faces when I walk in with a handsome man who absolutely none of them know.'

Rob came round the car and sat beside her.

'Good,' he said. 'Let's both have fun!'

'Fun?' she muttered to herself ten minutes later.

Had she been out of her mind?

She didn't even have time to register her family's reactions to her presence, because the first person she sighted was Nick.

Nick, looking superb, in light-coloured slacks, a white open-necked shirt and a grey jacket that would probably exactly match his eyes.

Nick, talking to the leggy blonde they'd seen at breakfast that first morning—

Amy someone?

Nick, raising an eyebrow, nothing more, as he took in Rob by her side.

Glad she'd spent a fortnight's salary on the slinky white dress that showed off her curves as well as her tan, Bill led Rob into the throng, introducing him to friends and relations, assuring him he didn't need to remember names, finally finding Kirsten's sister, Sally, a stunning brunette, who was currently single, having recently discovered the man she'd thought she loved was married.

'Sally, this is Rob, a friend from the hospital. He's new in town so would you be a darling and look after him for me while I do the rounds of the brothers who are here? If I talk to one and not another, they get all precious.'

Sally whisked Rob off to get a drink, and Bill, aware she had to drive home—with or without Rob—took a glass of sparkling mineral water from a passing waiter and slid towards one of the open doors that led onto a narrow deck overlooking the boats in the yacht club marina.

Straight hair and a slinky dress hadn't cut it when it came to armour against Nick. Just seeing him had made her stomach somersault, leaving her so shaken it had taken all her strength to smile and nod and talk until she'd found an opportunity to hand Rob to someone else and escape while she collected her emotions.

She breathed deeply, taking in the salt-laden air, listening to the clinking of the ropes and fastenings on the boats as they moved in their moorings, gazing upwards at the star-filled sky.

Now think!

Obviously if she was going to have this kind of physical reaction every time she saw Nick, she had to take steps to *not* see him. They'd remained friends through long separations so if one or other of them left town, surely they could revert back to their platonic relationship?

She could get a job anywhere and maybe it was time to move on. She'd come home to lick her wounds after the Nigel debacle and the loss of the baby she'd never had, but she was fine and fit and strong once again.

Apart from a little heart-sickness, love-sickness, whatever—but work could cure that. Challenging work—something different, a foreign country, somewhere she'd be needed—

'I think your boyfriend's fallen hard for Sally—surely there was a less attractive woman you could have left him with?'

Nick was right behind her, so close she could feel the heat of him, smell his aftershave.

'He's just what Sally needs,' Bill answered, refusing to turn round because if hearing Nick's voice made her feel so uptight, then seeing him would probably paralyse her completely. 'He's nice and uncomplicated and funny and definitely not married.'

'I'm not married,' Nick said, his voice tight, strained, husky with emotion.

'No, but you have a family you can't betray so it's the same thing.'

Bill had done her best to keep *her* voice light and even, but the words had come out in a pathetic, wimpy kind of wail.

It was because he was so close—so close and yet not touching. Her nerve endings were reaching out towards him, straining against her skin so it was tight and hot—wanting to feel him, to be held, to lose herself in—

She stepped closer to the railing, hoping to break the bond that wasn't there.

Refocussed on her thoughts.

Maybe—

'Will you go back to live in Sydney?'

The 'when Serena returns' hung, unspoken, in the air.

Nick didn't reply, the silence stretching so long Bill wondered if he would, but when he did speak she knew it was something he'd been considering already.

'I want to stay here, Bill. I owe it to Gran, and also, now there's Steffi, I think I'd like her to grow up here. Serena has always worked out of Sydney, but these days she's in demand all over the world so I can't see why she couldn't be based here as well. She's Steffi's mother, Bill, for all her bizarre behaviour, and I'm sure, in her own way, Serena must love her daughter. Mother, father, child—that's a family, isn't it?'

'Exactly what you wanted,' Bill reminded him. 'But you should at least *try* to sound pleased about it.'

'How can I?' came the anguished cry, then his arms looped around her waist and he pulled her back so she was held against him, her body fitting his as neatly as two matching pieces of a puzzle. 'Damn it, Bill, how could this have happened? And why now, when it's impossible? Was life meant to be this way? One disaster after another?'

Bill rested her head against his shoulder and looked up at the sky.

Play it lightly, she told herself, although she knew the rapid beating of her heart beneath his hands would have already given her away.

'Melodrama, Dr Grant?' she teased. 'You can hardly label Steffi a disaster. More a miracle, and a delightful, gorgeous miracle at that. As for us, well, that would probably never have worked, even if we'd given in to the attraction. We know each other too well—there'd have been no mystery to keep the buzz alive.'

She was doing really well, she thought, until he lifted her hair and kissed the nape of her neck, sending a vio-

lent shudder of desire right through her body. And if her
heart had been racing earlier, it now went into overdrive,
hammering against her chest, while she could feel the
moisture of her need between her thighs.

'Say that again—the bit about it not working,' Nick
murmured against her skin, but Bill was beyond speech,
beyond thought or voluntary movement. She let Nick
hold her, let him kiss his way along her shoulder, let his
hands roam across her breasts, thumbs teasing at her
traitorously peaking nipples.

She grabbed the railing, no longer trusting her legs
to hold her up as her bones melted under the onslaught
of Nick's touch.

A sudden gust of wind, a louder rattle in the rigging
of the yachts and she came thudding down to earth.

'For heaven's sake, Nick, we're practically in public!'
she growled, trying to twist out of his grasp but only
succeeding in turning to face him.

'So, where can we be private? Your place?'

Now she pushed away, shaking her head, hoping like
hell she wasn't going to cry.

'You don't mean that, Nick, I'm sure you don't.
Mother, father, child—family, remember? If you were to
betray that then you're not the man I've always thought
you, and certainly not the man I love.'

She spun away, heading not back inside but down
the steps at the end of the balcony towards the marina
itself. The 'l' word had come out without censorship but
hopefully he'd take it as friend love not lover kind of
love. Rob would have to fend for himself because there
was no way she could go back inside and face family
and friends with any kind of composure.

The tears she refused to shed were banked up behind

her eyes and she knew from the heat in her cheeks that they'd be fiery red.

With anger, frustration or pain?

She had no idea. All she knew was that her feelings for Nick had strayed so far beyond the realms of friendship that she would *have* to get away.

Nick wanted to follow her but knew he couldn't. Knew also he'd have to stay out on the balcony a little longer while the raging desire in his body cooled and he could face the crowd with some semblance of control.

She was right, of course. Even thinking about the things he'd like to do with Bill was a betrayal of sorts, but how could he face Serena with the suggestion of family if he'd physically betrayed her?

He thumped his fist against the railing, which did nothing more than hurt his hand, and was relieved when he heard a voice behind him—Amy joining him on the balcony.

'I thought I'd lost you,' she said. 'Boy, it's a crush in there. You didn't say if you're interested in a trip to Hayman Island on your next days off. I'm working as a boat hostess out there now and can get you a good deal on accommodation, and there's a huge party for the launch of some new perfume going on all week.'

'Thanks, but, no, thanks,' Nick said, but inside his gloom lifted just a little as he realised how much one small person had changed his life. A couple of days on a tropical paradise had no appeal whatsoever when set against a couple of days playing with Steffi.

Perhaps he wouldn't always feel like this, but right now the more he got to know his daughter, the more fascinating he found her.

So fascinating he found himself explaining his refusal.

'Steffi's going to walk on her own any day now, and I'd hate to miss seeing her take off.'

Amy laughed and shook her head.

'I gathered when you were talking about her earlier that she'd won you over, but to hear Playboy Nick refusing a gala party to see a baby take her first steps, that beats everything.'

She studied him for a few moments before adding, 'So it means you and Serena will get back together?'

'I'm assuming so,' Nick replied, ignoring the cold lump that formed in his stomach as he spoke.

'Well, that *will* be interesting,' Amy said with a smile he couldn't quite fathom. He hadn't liked the emphasis on the 'will' either but she disappeared back into the party before he could ask what she meant.

But at least now he could leave without worrying he'd run into Bill either in the marina car park or the building basement. The less he saw of Bill the better.

'Oh, Doctor Nick, I was going to phone you but Miss Bill arrived with the spade just in time. The little one, she was making an awful noise with breathing but Miss Bill has her in the en suite and she's okay now.'

Bill arrived with a spade?

Nick was striding towards his bedroom but that bit of the garbled conversation kept repeating itself in his head.

He opened the door to a fog of steam, a bedraggled-looking Bill sitting on the lavatory seat with Steffi asleep on her knee.

No spade.

'Croup!' Bill said as Nick bent over his daughter, automatically feeling for a pulse, listening to her breathing. 'Dolores said she opened the air-conditioning vent in Steffi's room because she was restless when she went to bed. If she has a bit of a cold, the cool, dry air could have caused the croup.'

Bill was talking sense, he knew that, but his medical brain was telling him that sudden stridor in a child's breathing could be caused by an inhaled foreign object.

'She's breathing normally now.' Bill answered his doubts as he lifted Steffi into his arms and held her tightly against him. 'I think she can go back to bed. I asked Dolores to turn off the air-conditioning earlier and although humidifiers are rarely needed up here in the tropics, it might be advisable to have one on hand for those hot nights when Steffi might need air-conditioning in her room.'

Nick looked down at Bill, at the hair beginning to regain its curl, at the damp dress clinging to her figure...

No, he wouldn't look there.

'We never had it, did we?'

Bill met the question with a puzzled frown.

'Had what?'

'Air-conditioning, you dope.'

That won an almost normal Bill smile.

'Never knew it existed outside of supermarkets and shopping malls. Remember how packed the malls were on really hot days?'

'Malls, hospitals and court houses,' Nick recalled, while relief flooded through him that he and Bill hadn't lost their easy, casual friend-type conversation.

Relief that vanished when she stood up and he remembered his dream when the lime-green bikini had apparently disappeared. The white slinky dress was in danger of doing the same thing and in his mind he saw her standing there naked in front of him.

His heart stopped beating, his breathing arrested, the world stood still and silent as he simply gazed at the woman he couldn't have.

'Put Steffi to bed—or maybe into your bed,' she said, breaking the spell so his organs resumed their normal function. 'That way you'll hear her if her breathing becomes hoarse.'

She smiled at him then—a lovely, cheeky Bill grin—and added, 'I bet that's one you haven't thought about yet. Is the kid allowed to sleep in your bed from time to time?'

He hadn't, but neither had he ever thought he'd feel anything other than the love of friendship for Bill, although right now, in this steamy bathroom, he began to suspect that was exactly what had happened.

Escaping was the obvious thing to do and he had the perfect excuse—putting Steffi to bed. The steam had made her clothes damp and she'd need a dry nappy. He'd do that—change her—now...

'I can't get out with you blocking the doorway,' Bill complained, but a tremor in her voice suggested that she, too, was feeling the tug of desire that had come from nowhere to confuse them.

The tug of love?

Had she said 'love' earlier?

'Move!' she ordered, remaining where she was, not coming close enough to push him out the door.

Not wanting to touch him for fear of where it might lead?

He moved, carrying Steffi through to her bedroom,

assuring Dolores the little girl was all right, reassuring himself at the same time.

A small red plastic spade was lying on the floor beside Steffi's cot. Having dug with it himself when he'd taken his daughter to the beach, he now understood the earlier conversation.

Dolores, who followed him in, picked it up and set it in the box of toys.

'Miss Bill found it in the lift and knew it was Steffi's,' she explained, then she burst into tears, falling over herself as she apologised again and again.

'Dolores, I would have turned on the air-conditioning,' Nick said very firmly. 'No one is blaming you. Now, go and have a cup of tea or a drink of whatever you need. I'm home and I'll take care of her tonight so shift the monitor into my room and get a good night's sleep yourself.'

But Dolores didn't move, repeating all she'd said, apologising tearfully over and over again until Bill appeared, put her arm around the older woman's shoulder and led her away.

Steffi, woken by the noise or by having her clothes changed, looked up at Nick and smiled sleepily. His heart filled with joy and as he bent and kissed her belly button he knew she had to come first in his life, her welfare, her physical and emotional development the most important things in his life.

The thought brought pain but better he suffer than she grow up with parents fighting for her. Mother, father, child—a family...

Bill sat in the kitchen, pouring a little rum into the cup of hot chocolate she'd made for Dolores, pleased the woman was finally calming down. But much as she,

Bill, wanted to leave—to escape before she had to face Nick again—she couldn't leave an even half-hysterical woman on his hands.

His attention had to be focussed on Steffi.

'It was a natural thing to do and of course Nick isn't going to fire you. You're the best thing that's ever happened to him and his daughter,' Bill repeated for about the eleventh time.

Dolores looked at her, her eyes red from weeping, her normally olive skin blotchy with emotion.

'You think so, Miss Bill?'

'I know so,' Bill said, and she leaned over and kissed the older woman on the cheek. 'Nick and Steffi couldn't do without you.'

'And when his wife comes back? He showed me postcard from New York.'

'Heaven only knows what will happen,' Bill told her, 'but I can't imagine you won't be part of their lives.'

Dolores smiled and Bill knew she could finally escape. Nick would stay with Steffi wherever she was sleeping.

Nick...

CHAPTER ELEVEN

TEN DAYS LATER Nick flew to Sydney with Steffi, Dolores and all the baby paraphernalia he now counted as normal baggage. Much as he hoped he and Serena could make a life in Willowby, he knew it would be easier to talk to her in her own apartment.

She'd had two days to get over any jet-lag she might be suffering, and although she hadn't sounded delighted when he'd told her they were coming, she hadn't objected.

Surely that had to be a good sign.

And she wasn't stupid, so she'd understand his argument that she could really be based anywhere…

'You worried, Dr Nick?' Dolores asked, as he drove the hire car he'd organised from the airport to Double Bay.

'No, Dolores,' he replied, although his gut was churning and every imaginable disastrous scenario was racing through his head.

The only scenario he hadn't imagined was finding Alex at the apartment—Alex cooing over Steffi, who obviously remembered him, while Serena barely acknowledged her child.

'Alex is here because he wants to photograph Australia,' Serena explained, and while Nick thought that might be a tall order, he refrained from comment. 'I didn't know you'd bring your nanny, she'll have to share with Steffi. I think the building manager has roll-out beds available.'

Nick had already fitted five people into three bedrooms in his head and realised Serena was assuming he would share her bed.

But wasn't that why he'd come?

To build the family that he wanted?

Mothers and fathers did share beds...

'I can sleep on the couch,' he heard himself say, when Alex, carrying Steffi, had led Dolores off to show her the bedroom they would use.

Serena studied him, eyebrows raised.

'Do you hate me so much, Nick?'

He shrugged, feeling awkward and uneasy because he didn't fully understand the situation himself.

'I don't hate you at all,' he said—at least that much was true. 'Yes, I was angry and upset over your deception but how could I hate you when you've given me Steffi? However, we're virtually strangers to each other. Not counting your brief visit to Willowby it's been eighteen months since we've seen each other—longer than that since we've been together.'

She smiled now.

'I doubt we've forgotten how to make love,' she murmured, moving closer so he knew he should take hold of her, feel her body against his—feel excitement, even.

Except he couldn't.

'I think we need to talk first, to work out where we're going.'

The smile faded from her face and it was her turn

to shrug. With all the elegance of her trade she moved away, over to the marble coffee table in the centre of the living room, bending to pick up a packet of cigarettes.

'You're not going to smoke with Steffi in the apartment!'

The words burst from his lips and he knew he must have spoken far too loudly because Serena spun towards him, more shock than surprise on her face.

'So now you're the smoking police,' she said, her voice tight. 'I remember *you* used to have a cigarette from time to time.'

The sly smile that crept across her face told him she knew her words had struck home, because occasionally, when she'd had a cigarette after sex, he'd had a puff or two—sharing hers, thinking of it as another kind of shared act...

He forced himself to remain calm.

'I'm sorry I reacted badly but Steffi's had a bad attack of croup and I've been worried about her lungs. Can we sit outside while you smoke?'

Serena nodded and led the way out onto the balcony. From here he could see glimpses of the harbour, the sun glinting off the water.

'The view from my apartment in Willowby has more water, but the harbour view is always magnificent,' he conceded.

'So, you could get used to it again?' Serena asked. 'We'd need to move to a bigger apartment because the nanny should have her own room and we'll always need a spare for visitors.'

This was it! This was where he had to say something.

But what?

And how?

How!

The word appealed to him. He knew her life, he'd work into it that way.

'How are your bookings looking? Where do you go next? Will you be mainly overseas?'

Serena squinted through a trail of smoke that curled up from her lips—lips that would kiss Steffi tasting of tobacco.

If she ever kissed Steffi...

'And you're asking why?'

Yes, Serena wasn't stupid. Self-focussed but not stupid.

He'd come to talk, Nick reminded himself. So talk.

'I think, ideally, Steffi needs both her parents. I realise your career is very important to you and I think she'd learn to live with the fact that you're often away, as long as she has stability in the rest of her life, like myself and Dolores—or whatever nanny we might employ.'

That sounded good so far, he congratulated himself while he waited for a comment from Serena.

'And?'

That was it? A one-word prompt, giving no indication of what she was thinking or feeling?

'As you know, I returned to Willowby to be close to Gran, to whom I owe so much. I think it would be a great place to raise a child, or children, and I wondered whether it mattered to you where you were based. If you're mostly flying out to assignments around the world, you could just as easily fly from there, not right away as you've obviously got this Australian trip planned, but after that?'

He'd made a mess of it, he could feel it in his bones, although Serena's face showed no emotion whatsoever.

Neither did she respond, simply putting out one cigarette and taking another one out of the packet, holding it distractedly between her fingers.

'Well?' he finally asked, and hoped it hadn't sounded like a demand.

'You've obviously been thinking about this for some time,' she said, 'this fantasy of family. Yet you're not willing to share my bed.'

So that was what had upset her!

You could fix that by agreeing—would it be so hard? a voice in his head demanded.

The shiver that ran through his body—not distaste but definitely uneasiness—gave him the answer.

'I think we should look at where we're going before we leap into bed together,' he said. 'Sex rarely solves anything—in fact, it probably makes situations more complicated.'

'You've changed,' she said, and although he knew a lot of the change was to do not with Steffi but with his feelings for Bill, he had an easier answer.

'I think having a child changes everyone.'

'Maybe.'

Nick had to be satisfied with that enigmatic response because Alex joined them on the balcony, still carrying Steffi, who was playing with his beard.

'We could photograph the child in all the places we spoke of,' he said to Serena. 'Ayers Rock and White-haven Beach and in the snow.'

'No!'

Nick and Serena spoke together, Nick adding, 'Well, at least we agree on something,' although he guessed Serena's 'no' was for a different reason. She didn't want Steffi stealing her limelight.

'Okay,' Alex said, accepting the judgement and setting Steffi down on the floor. 'And don't you dare light that cigarette and breathe smoke all over the child,' he added to Serena, who, to Nick's surprise, obediently put the offending object back into its box.

'So, the Australian photography, that's one project you've got lined up?' he said to Serena, grasping Steffi's hand as she pulled herself up on a chair and stumbled towards him. 'What's next?'

But Serena didn't answer. Standing up, she stepped carefully over Steffi and headed inside, the slamming of a door suggesting she'd taken refuge in her bedroom.

'I keep telling her not to smoke at all,' Alex complained, 'but she says it's all that keeps her from eating and that way she stays slim.'

He shook his head and followed Serena indoors, knocking cautiously on her bedroom door.

Nick swung Steffi onto his knee.

'Not going too well, is it, kid?' he said, then he kissed her neck and delighted in her baby smell and her warm chuckles.

But not for long!

He had four days to work something out with Serena, and although his head told him Willowby was the ideal place for his family, his heart suggested that staying in Sydney might be easier for a whole lot of reasons—not because it was definitely Serena's preference but because of the distance from Bill.

Bill tried not to think about what was going on in Sydney. She told herself she hoped Nick could work it out, but in her heart of hearts she hoped he'd work it out so they stayed in Sydney. He could fly up to visit Gran…

So life went on—going to work, coming home, doing

everything she could to not think about Nick, although memories were everywhere, especially when she visited Gran, who talked so excitedly about Nick bringing Serena home to Willowby, about weddings and more babies, every word a drop of acid etching pain into Bill's heart.

Work provided, if not solace, a least a release from constantly thinking about Nick. It was impossible to let your thoughts drift in a busy ER.

'Bill, you're on the mine rescue team, aren't you?'

Angie had slid into the cubicle where Bill was dressing an elderly man's leg ulcer.

'Yes,' Bill replied, her mind on the job, thinking Angie might be asking because she was interested in joining the team.

'Then I'll take over there,' Angie said. 'There's an alert. An accident at Macaw.'

Bill's heart, which had stopped beating at the word 'alert', resumed when she heard Macaw mentioned. It was an underground mine and both her brothers now worked in open cuts.

As she left the cubicle the phone she carried in one pocket began to vibrate and she knew this would be the call asking her to report to Rescue Headquarters.

Her stomach clenched as she thought of what might have happened. All the mines had their own safety officers and trained rescue personnel, but the mine rescue team was called in for serious accidents—a roof collapse, miners trapped...

'It's what we've all trained for,' the team leader reminded the group as they kitted themselves out in overalls, breathing apparatus, hard hats with attached lights, and lethal-looking tools that could cut, or lever; with ropes and whistles and walkie talkies.

Emergency equipment was already being moved to the mine, including the huge jet engine that would pump inert gas in to smother explosive gases. She knew enough about underground mining to be aware of the safe-refuge chambers, where trapped miners could gather, and escape shafts equipped with ladders for them to escape. Gas was the big problem, gas that could explode into fire or poison people trapped beneath the earth.

'It's a rock fall, not a fire,' the team leader told them. 'And Macaw's got the latest in monitoring and communication equipment so by the time we get there they will know just how many and where the men are trapped.'

Bill thought of other mine disasters she'd read about or seen on TV and was glad about the communication because at least the men could talk to the outside world.

When the team arrived at the mine, the management had their rescue protocols under way and could tell them fourteen men were trapped, eleven in a safe-refuge chamber, only one miner that they knew of quite seriously injured.

'We've one team working on access to the chamber now, and another drilling a new ventilation shaft down to it. We think the other three men are further down that stope and we've men trying to get to them from an escape shaft.'

Knowing no one would have been allowed into the mine, even for a rescue mission, unless the air readings were good and the shafts secure, Bill felt a surge of hope that all the men would be rescued alive.

Maybe not today, but before too long.

* * *

In Sydney, Nick had renewed his conversation with Serena. Steffi was having a sleep and Alex had apparently calmed Serena down so she was willing to listen to him.

'We got on well before,' he reminded her. 'We really only broke up because your work took you away so often. I'm not asking you to stop work, only asking if you don't think, for Steffi's sake, we could make it work again.'

'In Willowby?' Serena demanded. 'I think not. I was only there for a few hours and the heat nearly killed me. Besides that, there's my social life. It's all right for you, you've friends up there, but all my friends are here or overseas.'

Nick wanted to point out that people's social lives changed as they grew older and had more responsibilities but knew that wouldn't cut any ice with Serena. They'd suited each other before because they'd matched—playboy and playgirl.

And he'd thought that life was fun?

'And Steffi?' he asked, as he'd yet to see any indication that Serena cared one jot for her child.

'She's my daughter.'

The shrug Serena gave as she answered made Nick want to shake her. She might not love her child but she was obviously willing to use her as a bargaining chip.

Or was she?

Was he just assuming that her blood tie was as strong as his?

'Do you want her?' he asked, and now Serena turned to face him.

'Why wouldn't I?' she demanded, and Nick threw up his hands in despair.

'I've no idea,' he said. 'Not about this, or you, or any-thing! According to what you told me earlier, you were willing to have her adopted as soon as she was born, then last month, when you had to fly to the States for work, you were apparently quite happy about dumping her on me, so what am I supposed to think?'

'You're supposed to understand I'm her mother,' Se-rena said, and Nick, his heart sinking, knew she saw Steffi as nothing more than a pawn in whatever game she was currently playing.

'And?' he prompted, not wanting to say too much, not wanting to let the anger building inside him loose anywhere near his daughter.

'That's all. You must realise that in family law dis-putes the judge almost always gives custody to the mother.'

'You're saying you want her?' Nick demanded, his stomach in knots at the thought of having a legal fight for his daughter. 'You want to be part of her life? Al-ways, or just until she gets in the way of your career?'

Serena lit another cigarette from the stub of the one she'd just finished, and blew a lazy plume of smoke into the air.

'What do *you* want, Nick?' she asked, and Nick, al-though now he was wondering about it himself, an-swered her.

'I want us to be a family,' he said. 'I think that's the least we can do for Steffi. She didn't ask to be here, but now she is, let's see if we can give her the best possible life, which, to me, means two parents.'

'I only ever had my mother, and you had no one but your grandmother,' Serena reminded him.

'And look at the mess we both made of things,' Nick

snapped. 'Why do you think I want two parents for Steffi?'

'I won't accept such nonsense. I'm successful, you're successful, but I get your point, I just don't get living in that God-awful place up north. If you want to play happy families with me and Steffi, you'll have to play here.'

It would be best to be here, Nick conceded in his heart. Far away from Bill and the threat to his equilibrium that she now represented.

'There's Gran…' he muttered, but so tentatively Serena had no trouble laughing off his feeble objection.

'You could fly up twice a month to visit her,' she said. 'Even take the child.'

The child?

Was he wrong to be thinking of Serena as the mother figure in his family if she didn't love Steffi?

'Do you love her?'

The question erupted out of him—far too loud and far too abrupt.

Serena smiled the serene smile he knew she practised so it matched her name.

'I'm her mother, aren't I?' she responded, telling him absolutely nothing.

He slept on the couch, took Steffi for walks around traffic-busy streets, talked to Alex and Dolores, his life in limbo.

Because he wouldn't share Serena's bed?

He'd asked himself the question, suggested perhaps everything would fall into place once he did, but something held him back—something more than a few errant kisses up in Willowby. It came down, he decided, to Serena's attitude towards Steffi. She showed no interest in her child, never stopping to play with her, to touch her, to hold her in her arms and cuddle her.

And slowly it began to seep into his family-obsessed brain that perhaps the mother, father, child scenario wasn't all that it was cracked up to be. Well, he'd always known that, known the divorce statistics and the prevalence of single-parent families, so why had it seemed so important to him?

'I've booked a table at Fiorenze for tonight,' Serena announced, coming out onto the deck where he was watching Alex and Steffi build a tower of blocks. 'Alex and I are off tomorrow, so this will be our last chance to talk.'

'Tomorrow?' Nick repeated, looking from Serena to Alex, who simply shrugged.

'Tomorrow!' Serena repeated.

Nick knew he must look as stunned as he felt. The previous talk had been of a departure ten days away.

'You mean we've got one whole day in which to work out the rest of our lives?' he demanded.

'And one night,' Serena added, smiling in such a way he knew she'd planned this carefully. A candlelit dinner at a place where they'd eaten often in the past, then home, slightly tipsy, to fall into bed together.

Maybe it would work…

He'd barely had the thought when she added, 'You're more than welcome to stay on here—it would give you time to find us a bigger apartment.'

Nick closed his eyes and counted to ten, determined not to explode in front of Steffi. He realised now that Serena's mind had been made up from the start, which was why she'd cut off any discussion about their future.

For some obscure reason—just to have a man around?—
she wanted him back and was happy to have 'the child',
as she called her daughter, included in the package. Tonight, in Serena's mind, he'd fall back into her bed and
the matter would be settled.

She'd disappeared before he'd regained enough control to follow her and insist they talk—off to buy a new
dress for tonight, according to Dolores.

He slumped down on the couch, knowing he'd been
too weak, too tentative, trying to do what was best for
everyone without upsetting any of the parties.

Well, maybe not best for everyone but best for Steffi.

Sick of the chaos in his head he flicked on the television and stared blankly at the screen, only slowly coming to the realisation that every channel was showing
the same thing—a mine, miners trapped, mine rescue
teams already on site. The disaster was here in Australia—Macaw.

Macaw was near Willowby…

CHAPTER TWELVE

'DOLORES, PACK UP all Steffi's things, we're going home,' he yelled, beginning to stuff his own gear into his bag then realising he'd need to book a flight.

Impossible. Every journalist in Australia was trying to get to Willowby—

'Dolores, can you drive? Have you got a licence?'

'Of course, Dr Nick, you know that, but why, what is wrong?'

'We'll have to drive, no chance of a flight. We'll take turns and stop overnight somewhere on the way—we have to think of Steffi.'

Serena arrived home as he was stacking all their gear in the hall.

'What's this?'

'I'm going home—there's trouble—I'm needed there.'

She looked at him for a long moment then said, 'It's that woman Bill, isn't it? It's always been Bill!'

And on that note she stormed away, slamming the bedroom door for must have been the twentieth time since his arrival.

It wasn't until he was out of the city, on the freeway, heading north, that he had time to consider what Serena has said.

It's always been Bill!

Had it?

No, he was certain that wasn't the case. Until he'd come back to Willowby he'd never thought of Bill as other than a friend.

So why had the attraction flared so quickly?

'I don't know,' he muttered, waking Dolores up from a light doze then being unable to explain exactly what it was he didn't know.

Because Bill had done some of her training at Macaw and knew it well, and possibly because, in the stressed situation, the recue organiser didn't realise she was a woman, she was one of the two chosen to go down the escape shaft to follow the miners through to where the three missing men might be trapped.

Excitement and trepidation churned inside her as she followed her partner down the ladder. Her brother Dan had told her that the ladders were checked every day so although this one seemed to move away from the wall a little, she kept faith in it.

'Two more levels to go,' the miner at the bottom of the shaft told her, and Bill touched him on the shoulder in thanks and sympathy, knowing how much he must want to be doing more to help his mates but sticking to his job in the whole operation right there at the bottom of the ladder.

The next shaft was darker and they turned on their lights so it glowed like a vertical tunnel with a train coming through. One more shaft and they were on the level of the fall, bright lights ahead showing them where the men were working.

'We've opened up a small passage over the top of

this fall,' one of the miners explained, 'but we can't get the communication probe through.'

He looked at Bill, the least bulky of the four people in the shaft.

'Reckon you can crawl up there and push it through.'

'I'll just drop this gear,' she said, and ignored the 'Crikey, it's a woman' comment from the second miner, leaving her partner to explain she was one of the top members of the mine rescue team. Clad just in her overalls and with a tiny mike attached to her shirt just below the collar, she was ready.

One of the men hoisted her up and she clambered into the small space the men had cleared, slowly edging her way forward, following the fine metal tube that was the probe, glad to see bolts in the stone above her that told her the roof of this part of the tunnel was safe.

The going was so slow she sometimes wondered if she was moving at all, but eventually she could see the end of the thin wire.

The probe had stuck on a rock that projected from the wall and she had to manoeuvre the tube around it, and keep feeding it forward. The opening she was in grew narrower and she knew she wouldn't be able to follow the probe, but a shout as she pushed it further and further told her it had reached the trapped men.

Berating himself all the way, Nick drove north. How stupid had be been to think a family could work without love? How stupid had Bill been, too, now he came to think about it!

Berating Bill for her stupidity was easier than thinking of her endangering herself in a mine accident, or trapped underground, or—

He'd think of numbers. He could reach Brisbane in ten hours, twelve allowing time to stop and rest and eat and let Steffi have a run around. Another ten—or twelve—and he'd be home.

He pressed the speed dial on his phone for the fortieth time and got the out-of-range message from Bill's mobile. He thought of phoning Bob but common sense told him it was better he didn't know what Bill was doing—not while he was driving.

Dolores drove as calmly and competently as she did everything else so he could sleep while she was at the wheel.

It was tempting to keep driving but, no, working in the ER he knew too well the risk of an accident when driving for too long. They'd stop, eat, sleep and go on refreshed. Tomorrow they'd be home.

Home!

He didn't dare dwell on Bill, on where she was or what she might be doing, he just knew he had to be there, to be close to wherever she was...

Bill could hear the excitement in the voices ahead of her, but although their words would be clear to those at the other end of the communication probe, they were jumbled coming through the rock to her.

She tried to work out differences in the voices, certain there were two, but three? She wasn't so sure.

'I'm coming out,' she said into her mike and, carefully, she began to edge backwards, knowing there would probably be other things she'd have to shove through to the men. Squirming backwards over stones wasn't fun, and it took far longer than she'd taken going in. Time ceased to exist but in the end she managed, knowing she was almost out when someone caught hold of her boots then guided her feet to footholds on the rocks.

'All three safe,' one of the miners told her. 'You did good,' adding, 'for a girl,' but smiling as he said it—the smile a bigger thank you than words could ever express.

She sat now, knowing the rule to rest when you could, while the men listened to the probe and began to plan the next move.

'How big is the gap, do you think?'

Her rescue partner came to sit beside her and Bill replayed her journey in her head.

'There's a rock jutting out from the wall that had stopped the probe and from what I could feel with my hand in that area, there's maybe a gap the size of a small water pipe. Once I got the probe through there, it wasn't impeded in any way. It reached the men about a metre past that small gap.'

'Small water pipe?'

He shaped his fingers to show her the circumference he was imagining and she agreed he'd got it right.

'Could it be widened?'

Bill closed her eyes and looked at a mental image of the rock jutting out in the light from her helmet, at the rocks around it, one exceedingly large one right at the top.

'Not without a great deal of trouble,' she replied.

'Well, we'll make do with what we've got,' her partner said. 'You willing to go back in?'

'Of course, but if you're getting pipe sent down, get that flexible stuff that will bend a bit around obstacles. I can use a guide wire to push it through, like the one the probe had.'

Technicalities kept them busy, messages going back and forth for hours until it was time for Bill to crawl back into the narrow space again, this time pushing the pipe in front of her, the pipe that might prove a lifeline for the miners if they were trapped there for much longer.

He *had* to know!

Having spent the night in a motel just north of Brisbane, they were on the road again at dawn, and Nick finally cracked and turned on the radio. He knew Dolores would have watched the drama on the television in her room at times during the night, but he'd been resolute in not watching anything that might stop him sleeping.

'It is bad, Dr Nick,' Dolores said. 'It is why we're going home?'

'Yes.'

One word was all he could manage, the news that rescuers had reached the eleven men in the safe refuge should have cheered him, but it had been followed by the information that members of the mine rescue squad were three levels underground, still trying to get to the other three men, and that had dried the saliva in his mouth, certain Bill was there—three levels underground...

Drive carefully and steadily, he told himself as he switched off the radio and turned Steffi's nursery rhymes back on, singing along to 'One little, two little, three little ogres' and wondering why nursery rhymes, like most fairy-tales, were unnecessarily grim.

Steffi, however, loved it, and after they'd done monsters and goblins he had to turn off the next song and keep singing, coming up with other creatures like bunyips and yetis that they could include in the song.

'Miss Bill, she sings this song too,' Dolores said, and Nick felt his stomach clench.

How stupid had he been to even consider Serena might want to be a mother to their child! Serena, who hadn't once cuddled her daughter, let alone sung her a song.

They stopped by a park and got out to let Steffi play awhile, Dolores buying sandwiches and fresh bottles of water, heating Steffi's bottle in a café across the road, promising Steffi a proper cooked meal once they reached home.

'No more of this bottled stuff,' she told the little girl, who didn't seem to mind what she ate any more than she objected to a two-thousand-kilometre car ride.

Dolores drove and he tried to sleep, but the closer they got to Willowby the more anxious he became. In the end he phoned Bob.

The tube was harder. It caught on things and bent the way she didn't want it to go, not that she could see where she *did* want it to go. She reached one arm as far forward as she could, scraping it, even through her overalls, against the jutting rock but needing to find the obstacle that lay ahead.

Loose dirt.

Dirt was easy.

Dig it out.

Glad she was wearing gloves, she dug and scraped, pulling the dirt back towards her body, tucking it under herself then digging and scraping again.

Behind her she could hear the anxiety building,

someone trying to push the tube further into her tunnel, although she wasn't ready for it.

She tried to explain the problem to the men back at the rock fall but as she had no earpiece she didn't know if she'd been heard. So she continued, digging, scraping, pulling back the dirt until finally the tube advanced, very slowly, guided by the wire and now her hand, which might be stuck in the hole for ever the way she was feeling now.

They were within four hours of home, late on the second day of their mammoth journey, when they heard that the eleven men, one seriously injured, would shortly be brought to the surface of the mine.

In an unemotional tone the reporter announced that rescue attempts were continuing for the three other miners.

'And that's all?' Nick demanded of the radio, because by now he knew, from Bob, that Bill was down that mine.

'She will be safe,' Dolores assured him. 'The one thing Bill is is sensible so she won't take any risks.'

'Oh, no?' Nick muttered, and drove on.

The tube went through.

Bill heard the shout of delight then felt it move beneath her as they tugged it further into their small area of dubious safety.

Now to get out so things could be fed through the tube. Water and eventually food going in, information about the situation in the tunnel coming out. The probe was good for communication but if the engineers in charge of the rescue needed a diagram of the area and some indication of the placement of the rock fall, the men could supply it.

She began to edge backwards, harder to do now because of the tube *and* the dirt she'd shifted back.

Harder to do because she was tired.

Nonsense! You've been a lot tireder than this on night duty and still kept focussed on your work.

She edged a little further, inching backwards, body cramped and aching, praying that any moment someone would grasp her boot and she'd know she'd made it.

Nick dropped Dolores at the apartment, carried up all their baggage, then, not bothering to return the hire car, drove straight to the mine.

Growing up in Willowby, with mines on the doorstep of the town, he knew exactly where Macaw was, and if he hadn't, the mass of emergency and private vehicles parked nearby would have told him. Daylight was fading as he pulled up outside the high wire fence but bright arc lights lit up the scene so it was like something out of a movie.

Or a nightmare.

Certain they wouldn't let him in, he stood by the gate and scoured the grim faces of the men by the site office for one he knew.

Dan de Groote!

He yelled the name and Dan turned, saw him waving from behind the fence and came towards him.

'Word was you were back in Sydney,' Dan said, looking none too happy to see him.

'I'm not, I'm here. Bill's down there, isn't she? Can I come in and wait?'

Dan waved his hand towards the crowds of people gathered outside the fence.

'I should let you in and not all of them—other relatives?'

'I *am* a doctor,' Nick reminded him. 'I could be helpful.'

Dan's glance towards the ambulances already within the perimeter fence told Nick what he was thinking, but in the end he nodded.

'Just wait there while I get you a tag and once you're in keep out of everyone's way, okay?'

Nick almost smiled because just so had Dan, the eldest of the boys, always treated him and Bill, letting them join in some wild game the 'big boys' were playing, as long as they kept out of the way.

She couldn't move.

The tube had somehow changed the dynamics of the little tunnel. The tube and the probe and the dirt.

Well, she had to move, to wiggle and wriggle and ease herself just a little, forget inches, they were old measurements, go for millimetres. A millimetre at a time—she could do it.

Tag hanging around his neck, Nick waited on the periphery of the crowd of sober, worried men near the mine office. Something had gone wrong, he could tell from their voices.

And now arrangements were being made for more men to go down below, Dan saying very loudly he was going, Nick, without thinking, stepping forward.

'I'll go with you.'

Dan threw him a hard look.

'You're claustrophobic, remember?' he said, 'besides not being trained. But you can make yourself useful as a doctor. We brought up the badly injured man first and the doctor we had here has gone with him to hospital. The rest of the eleven men we've rescued are coming up now. Go check them out.'

He pointed to where a large tent had been set up, close to where the ambulances were parked, and Nick, knowing Dan was right—an untrained person in this situation could bring risk to all the rescuers—went across to make himself useful.

'Someone else is trapped, one of the mine rescue people.'

He heard the whisper as he waited for his patients to arrive and knew, with cold certainty in his gut, that it was Bill.

And he hadn't told her he loved her.

Where that thought came from he had no idea, but he knew it was true. The mad dash from Sydney had been for love.

CHAPTER THIRTEEN

FINALLY ALL ELEVEN men were up, checked and reunited with their anxious families before being ferried to hospital for more comprehensive examinations and treatment.

Night had fallen, and an eerie silence hung over the complex. Nick edged his way back towards the site office where, he knew, the rescue was being co-ordinated, and found not Dan but Pete.

Nick heard an echo of Bill's voice—Dan and Pete, both members of the elite rescue team—the best of the best.

'I'm going down,' Pete said. 'Dan let me know you were here. You want to come?'

One look at Pete's face was enough to confirm that the rescuer in trouble was the boys' adored little sister, Bill.

And in bad trouble if Pete was here, too.

Nick didn't hesitate, taking the overalls Pete was holding and clambering into them as he followed the miner to an area behind the main buildings.

'You won't go soft on me?' Pete demanded as he handed Nick a helmet with a light attached. 'We're going down three levels.'

'I won't go soft on you,' Nick promised, and they started carefully down the ladder that led into what, to Nick, was like the very centre of the earth.

One shaft, another, then another, until finally voices and bright lights led them to where the fall blocked the three men from escape. In the bright lights three miners, stripped down to underwear, sweat gleaming from their skins, were carefully levering and shifting rocks from the base of the fall. A rescuer in full gear talked quietly to the trapped men through a communication probe, and a thinish, flexible tube that led up and over the rock fall told Nick exactly where Bill was trapped.

He couldn't think of how far underground he was, all he could do was concentrate on Bill, willing her free from her prison. Pete had joined the men digging while Dan and the second rescue team member talked about tubes and probes and the possibility that there'd been a slight movement in the rocks that had been enough to trap Bill in her narrow tunnel.

'Can you remove the tube?' Nick asked Dan, and they all stared at the dark hole above their heads, seeking inspiration. 'Would that help?'

'Who knows? The danger is that in moving it we might do more damage. She's okay, she's only about a metre from the trapped men, and although she must have lost her mike while she was wiggling around, she is talking to them and they're relaying information back to us. Apparently she had to dig away some dirt to get the tube through and she pushed it back underneath her as she dug. Now she's using her free hand to dig it out from underneath her and trying to edge backwards that way.'

Nick closed his eyes, trying to picture the situation,

shutting down the panic in his chest when he considered just who was stuck in that unbearable situation.

'Suction? Like a vacuum cleaner?' he said to Dan. 'Would it alter the dynamics and make things worse if we sucked some loose dirt and rubble away from up there?'

Dan considered the idea for a moment then walked away to talk to the men.

'We can't use the mine's ventilation suction,' Pete said, 'it'd be far too strong and could bring down more rock, but Nick's idea is worth a go—some kind of industrial vacuum cleaner that'll suck up dirt.'

The second rescuer sent a message to the operations room and within ten minutes a very clumsy-looking barrel vacuum cleaner was in Nick's hands.

But not for long!

'Sorry, mate,' Dan said, 'but you have to take a back seat on this one. We can't risk a further fall.'

The valiant little machine sucked, was emptied, sucked again, emptied again, until a yell of triumph went up from the man currently manning it—Bill's boots were in sight, edging gradually towards them.

He shouldn't be here.

He didn't belong.

But how could he be anywhere else?

Pete reached up as the boots came closer, talking to Bill now, easing her feet down onto footholds in the rocks, talking all the time. But it was Nick who pushed both Dan and Pete aside to catch her as she fell the last few feet to the ground, catch her and hold her, just hold her.

'You're the doc, you're supposed to be checking her

out,' Dan reminded him, but Nick's arms wouldn't un-clamp from around the woman he'd so nearly lost.

Eventually he climbed behind her up the first shaft, Bill recovering enough to tease him all the way about how at any moment the earth could come crashing down on them.

'Don't worry, when I heard about Macaw I thought it had,' he told her. 'I thought I'd lost you for ever without ever telling you I love you.'

'Telling me you love me?'

Bill's startled reply echoed down the shaft but hopefully they were far enough up for it not to have been heard by the men still working below.

'Of course I love you. According to Serena I always have, I just hadn't realised it.'

Bill had reached the next level and waited until he emerged when, ignoring the miner standing guard there, she turned to hug him hard.

'Serena?' she asked.

'We'll work it out,' he assured her.

'Steffi?'

'We'll work that out too.'

Nick eased his arms from around her and looked into her dirt- and blood-streaked face.

'Preferably above ground,' he reminded her, and she led him to the next shaft and began to climb.

'When did you get here?' she asked, and it took most of that climb to explain their mad drive north.

The third shaft was easier, the light from above re-assuring Nick that the real world still existed. But Bill was tiring fast, so he climbed closer to her, trying to take some of her weight off her arms and legs, half car-rying her when they finally reached the top and anxious helpers hauled out first Bill then helped him clamber up and stand upright.

Paramedics had already put Bill onto a stretcher and as they wheeled her to the makeshift emergency room, he walked beside her, holding her hand, not caring what anyone thought.

Apart from a multitude of scratches, torn nails and fingers from her digging, and red patches that would eventually be bruises, she was fine.

'Nothing a good hot shower won't cure,' he told her, when he'd finished what he'd tried to make a professional examination, although his heart went into overdrive when he remembered the danger she'd been in.

'Take me home,' she said quietly, and Nick was only too happy to oblige.

She was quiet in the car, sitting with one hand on his knee, and he knew the stress of her entrapment must be catching up with her.

Except that when she spoke, it was to ask what she'd asked earlier.

'Serena?'

He shrugged.

'I don't know,' he said, 'I really don't. All I know is that I'd be living a lie if I settled with her, loving you as I do. I had thought it was the right thing to do for Steffi, but now I realise it would be unfair to everyone. Somehow we've got to come to some agreement over Steffi without her becoming the rope in a tug-of-war. But all that can wait. You're safe and you probably need some sleep and I definitely need some sleep, and tomorrow, as the wise men say, is another day.'

'I think we might be at tomorrow already,' Bill reminded him, and she moved the hand that lay on his knee, giving him a little squeeze that brought him more joy, right then, than a kiss.

He took her back to her own apartment, where he helped her out of her clothes, showered her gently, applied antiseptic lotion to the scratches and put dressings on her hands, then slid a big T-shirt over her head and tucked her into bed.

'I'll take your spare key so Dolores can bring you some food,' he told her, bending to kiss her on the lips.

She slid her arms around his neck.

'You're not staying?' she whispered. 'I thought you'd wanted us to be here alone? That night at the yacht club?'

'No, I'm not staying and, yes, I do want us to be alone, but not now, not like this, my love,' he responded, kissing her again, but gently still. 'You need to sleep and then you need to think about where *you* want to go in this situation. It might be hard, Bill, if I have to fight Serena because there's no way I'm giving up Steffi. If that happens, you'll be caught in the crossfire.'

She cupped his face in her palms.

'And if I said I didn't care—that however bad things get they couldn't be worse than life without you?' she asked him. 'If I said I loved you?'

His heart was behaving badly again and it was only with a mammoth effort of will that he eased away from her, tucked the sheet around her and kissed her one more time, this time a goodnight kiss but not goodbye...

Bill woke, stiff and more than a little sore but with a sense of well-being in spite of her physical state. She examined her surroundings as she considered this state and slowly memory returned—Nick had kissed her goodnight—and she had to smile.

-Although…

Might have to fight Serena—you'll be caught in the crossfire—Steffi rope in tug-of-war…

Memories of before the kiss dampened the sense of well-being.

It was all very well being gung-ho about fighting side by side with Nick so he could keep Steffi, but what if they lost?

What would it do to Nick?

Thinking of that was bad enough, but she knew she was only throwing that around in her head to stop herself thinking of the big one.

What would it do to her?

Okay, so she already loved Steffi, but at a distance— a little closer than her nephews and nieces but still as an outsider in her heart. But if she married Nick—and that had seemed to be the gist of things last night—and having mother 'rights' so to speak, Bill knew damn well her love for the little girl would send its roots deep into her heart.

And *then* to lose her?

From being ready to leap out of bed, shower, and rush up to see Nick and Steffi, Bill indulged in a tiny whimper of self-pity and stuck her head under the pillow.

Two minutes later she realised just how pathetic her behaviour was. She didn't do the leap-from-bed thing but she did drag her body up and out into the shower, where all her scrapes were red and sore and her bruises coming out nicely.

She stood under the steaming water until it started to

get cold—Bob must have put in cheap water heaters—then she dried her herself, rubbed at her hair, carefully dressed herself—whimpering occasionally at the pain of movement or when she dragged clothing over an extra sore spot—then made her way up to Nick's apartment.

It was Nick she had to consider in this business—Nick her friend, Nick the man she loved and, if memory served correctly, Nick who loved her back.

Nick who'd overcome his very real claustrophobia to come down a mine to help rescue her.

And she was going to leave him to battle Serena on his own?

Not stand beside him because of some wimpish fear of being hurt?

She rang the bell of his apartment but when he appeared, Steffi in his arms, she felt again that dreaded fear of loss.

Nick looped his arm around her and drew her inside, scolding quietly all the time.

'You should have stayed in bed. Dolores is making some chicken soup for you. Have you had enough sleep? How are your cuts and scratches? I'll have to have a look, put something on them. Come and sit down.'

The words flowed over Bill like balm, but although they soothed it was the way Steffi's fingers caught at her hair that hurt more than scratches.

Bill eased away and sank down into an armchair, staring at a mess of Steffi's toys on the living-room floor. Nick set the little girl down and she toddled off into the kitchen.

'She's walking properly now,' Bill said, and the mix of happiness and dread made her voice crack.

Nick came and sat on the arm of her chair, tangling

his fingers in her still-damp hair the way his daughter had.

'Tell me,' he commanded, and somehow Bill did, pouring out her doubts and fears.

'It hurt so much, losing the baby, Nick,' she said, doing pathetic again, 'that now, twelve months later, I'm only barely over it. I just don't know if I could go through that again—if I'd find the courage a second time around.'

Nick lifted her out of the chair, and sat down in it with her on his knee.

'I can't pretend there's not a chance,' he told her, his lips pressing kisses on her neck by way of punctuation. 'But do we throw away the joy and happiness we could have now—right now—because of what might happen in the future?

'By some miracle we've found each other in a way we never expected to—we've loved each other for so long, but this love is different, special and all the more powerful because of the love that was already there. So it might not move mountains, but with you by my side— and now I've been down to Level Three in a mine—I'd give it a damn good try.'

He turned her enough to kiss her properly now and Bill felt all his conviction—and all his love, *their* love— in that long, deep, probing kiss.

Eventually, she kissed him back, telling him without words that she agreed.

Or thought she did.

A long time later he lifted his head and looked down into her face.

'I would understand if you decided to run for your

life—to head off to deepest, darkest somewhere to get away from this.'

The slight tremor in his voice told her he meant every word, and it was that tremor that restored her courage.

'When you've gone down to Level Three for me?' she teased softly, then *she* kissed *him*.

CHAPTER FOURTEEN

'So, what happened in Sydney?'

Such a simple question, Nick thought as Bill clambered off his lap and settled on the floor close to his legs, looking up at him with such trust and love and hope he found it hard to talk.

Let alone explain.

'I've no idea,' he admitted honestly. 'Well, to a certain extent I can describe the visit, but the underlying currents are beyond me.'

He hesitated.

How could he tell Bill about Serena's attitude without being disloyal to his daughter's mother or portraying her as cold and heartless, which he knew for a fact she wasn't?

'Start when you arrived,' Bill suggested, resting her head on his knee so she was no longer looking up at him.

Which somehow made it easier...

'It was weird, Bill. For a start, she barely acknowledged Steffi's existence. Alex was there and he was delighted to see Stef and she was obviously just as pleased to see him, but Serena...'

Another pause as he tried to recall their arrival, but

the days had blended into each other and the bit he had to get out wasn't getting any easier.

'I don't know why,' he said, still hesitant, 'but for some reason she had taken if for granted we'd get back together—physically. I think I might have told you that. It didn't make sense, especially when she didn't seem to care about Steffi at all and got downright angry when Alex suggested he photograph Steffi again.'

Having got that out, he lapsed into silence because he couldn't think of any more words to say.

Bill, resting against his legs, reached up one hand to grasp one of his and they sat in silence for a while until finally she stood up and perched on the arm of the chair.

'If you think back to when she was persuaded by Alex to keep the baby so he could photograph her, at that stage she was determined to give Steffi up for adoption as soon as she was born, so I would imagine, during her pregnancy, she was determined not to get emotionally attached to the child she was carrying.'

'Hmm,' was all Nick could add to that suggestion, although it did make a kind of sense. 'But after that, when she *did* keep Steffi?'

'Again it was for Alex. She's been his favourite model for ever, his muse, as you called her, and suddenly here's this interloper capturing his attention. You said she got angry when he wanted to photograph Steffi here—maybe it's nothing more than Serena's own insecurity. Maybe that's why she wanted you back again, so she'd have the security of someone special in her life. From what I've read of Alex, he's getting old, and a model's working life doesn't last for ever, so...'

Nick reached up so he could pull Bill's head down to his and kiss her.

'You realise you're making excuses for a woman you barely know, and what you do know about her must make your teeth itch.'

Bill grinned at him and he felt his heart swoop around his chest in a great burst of love.

'I'm not really. I've never understood other people's relationships and I don't try, but I would imagine there's huge insecurity in any model's life—are my looks going, am I getting fat, will I get the top jobs this year? Possibly having Steffi around only added to it. If you think about Serena's childhood, she barely stopped working to *be* a child, so she's probably at a loss as to what to do with one.'

'You're probably right,' he told her, and kissed her again, because not only was she beautiful, and bright, and a wonderful woman, but she was kind, and compassionate, and understanding—and he wanted to kiss her anyway.

'Do you think she'll fight for Steffi?'

So they were back there again—back in doubtful land, with Bill remembering the pain of loss.

'I can't promise that she won't,' he said.

Now, Bill thought to herself. Now's the time to commit to Nick.

'Of course you can't,' she said, 'but I can promise that, whatever happens, I'll be with you every step of the way—with both of you.'

Nick stood up and pulled her into his arms again, holding her close, not kissing her, just holding her, and Bill knew that everything would be all right. Somehow they would get through whatever the future might hold because their love was strong enough to—

Well, to move mountains!

'Marry me,' he whispered in her ear, just as Steffi came toddling back, her high-pitched 'Beee!' making them spring fairly guiltily apart.

The day, which had begun underground about a million years ago, was finally drawing to a close. With Steffi in bed, and Dolores visiting her family for the last few days of the leave Nick had taken, he and Bill were alone on the deck, lights out, looking out to sea, sipping hot chocolate with marshmallows in it because it had been that kind of day.

'You didn't answer my proposal,' Nick complained when, his drink finished, he set the cup down and took Bill's hand in both of his.

'What proposal?' she demanded, turning to face him. In the dim light reflecting up from the marina her hair was a dark cloud around her pale face, her eyes nothing more than deep shadows.

'My proposal in the living room'

'In the living room?'

He could practically hear the gears turning in her head and wondered how far he could push her before she exploded into anger.

'I asked you something,' he reminded her, telling himself that teasing her was only getting a little of his own back for his panicked agony of the rescue mission.

'You *did* not!'

Good, she was angry now and he loved an angry Bill. Once she'd let fly at him he could take her in his arms and feel the tension in her body then feel it ease as he held and kissed her, eventually feeling it turn to a different kind of tension…

And why the hell was he wasting time teasing her like this when he could be holding her, kissing her right now?

He stood up and pulled her out of the chair, wrapping his arms around her just as he'd known he would.

'I said, marry me, remember?' he whispered as he brushed the hair back from her ear to kiss her in the hollow just below it. 'Steffi came in and you didn't answer and now it's too late because I'm taking no answer as a yes and I'm going to kiss the breath out of you.'

'Starting here,' he added, his mouth taking possession of hers.

'Like this,' he murmured, sliding his tongue between her lips…

Random questions flashed through Bill's head. Was this okay? Hadn't it been too sudden? Was it just Steffi that had brought them together? This was Nick, but was this love?

She heard a faint moan and thought it might have been hers, then her mind went blank and she gave in to sensation—to the warmth in her blood, the fire along her nerves, the prickly expectation on her skin and the ache of desire deep within her body.

All this from a kiss?

All this and more because kissing Nick was like nothing she'd ever experienced before, like nothing anyone in the universe could possibly have experienced because otherwise they'd all be doing it right now…

'Bed?'

She heard the word but was still grasping for its meaning, too lost in sensation to be thinking straight.

Had she hesitated too long that Nick released his hold on her, just slightly, so he could look down into her face.

'Too soon?'

She smiled, and shrugged, and felt the heat that told her she was blushing like a schoolgirl.

'No—yes—oh, I don't know.'

'I do,' he whispered, and kissed her once again, so gently, so thoroughly, so beautifully she had an urge to cry—again! 'It's been a very long and enormously emotional day, one way and another, so for tonight we shall be abstinent. In fact, how soon can you organise a wedding? We could stay abstinent till then, get a few days off somewhere, with Dolores minding Steffi, and stay in bed the entire time, room service providing enough in the way of food to keep up our strength.'

Bill smiled at him—at her friend Nick, trying, as always, to do the right thing. She rested her hand on his cheek and said, 'Or we could go to bed tomorrow night...'

EPILOGUE

GIVEN THE SIZE of Bill's family, they'd decided to hold Steffi's second birthday party in a park. Balloons hung from trees, a marquee festooned with ribbons provided shade and shelter should it be necessary, and twenty-three small boys and girls, all dressed, more or less, as bears were rioting on the grass.

'Do we have to do this party thing every birthday?' Nick demanded, coming to sit beside his wife, who was settled on a folding chair in the shade of a tree, watching three of her brothers trying to organise a pin-the-tail-on-the-donkey game with very little success.

Katie, the eldest of the de Groote grandchildren, had adopted Steffi from their first meeting, and she was organising some of the smaller ones in some game that involved standing up then falling over, the little ones screaming with glee.

'I think every second year will be enough,' Bill told him, 'but then on the off years this one will probably need a party, so get used to it.'

Nick reached over to pat the very large bulge of his wife's stomach.

'If you got this guy out today or tomorrow then we

could combine the parties, considering Steffi's real birthday isn't until tomorrow.'

'Yes, but would it be fair?'

She was actually frowning over the fairness of combined birthday parties for her children and Nick felt again a gust of love so strong it nearly struck him down. He had thought that after a year of marriage this might stop happening, but although he loved Bill all the time—well ninety-nine point nine per cent of the time as she could still be aggravating—these gusts of love still came out of nowhere, leaving him shaken at the thought that this might never have happened—that they might never have got together in this way, just gone on being friends and lost the magical, rewarding, cosmic wonder that was their love.

Steffi, with Katie's help, was blowing out the candles on the bear birthday cake when Bill felt the first contraction.

Hmm, the doctor had said any day now, although she still had a fortnight to go.

Ignoring it, she helped cut the bear into small sections and handed around plates of gooey chocolate cake.

The second contraction suggested things might be getting serious. Could she really have the baby on Steffi's birthday?

This time last year she'd been preparing to get married—they'd decided their daughter's birthday was as good a day as any.

Preparing to marry Nick—her BFF.

It still seemed surreal, yet sometimes when she caught an unexpected glimpse of him and her insides turned upside down, she knew that it was real—somehow they'd moved from friends to lovers, from friendship to passion so hard and hot she could feel herself blushing right now as she thought about it.

She'd read somewhere once that love was all-encompassing, and as the third contraction tightened her belly, Bill looked around at all her family, at Gran, wearing bear ears on her head, various de Grootes in fancy dress, Steffi the cutest bear of all, theirs now Serena had agreed they have custody, Dolores, on standby for when Bill went into hospital. Yes, love *was* all-encompassing!

Nick came and stood beside her, his arm coming to rest around her shoulders.

'Not to worry you,' she said quietly, 'but you might drop me off at the hospital on your way back to the apartment.'

He turned to look at her, his face going pale under his tan.

'You're serious?'

She smiled and with difficulty got close enough to kiss him on the lips.

'Of course! I'm a nurse, remember, I know these things.'

'But shouldn't you be sitting—or lying down—or doing *something*?'

'I am, I'm counting the minutes between contractions and you've been to all the pre-natal classes, you know I can stand up and move around as much as I like all through the birth if I want to. Right now I want to watch everyone enjoying themselves, but you might speak to Dolores and tell her we'll need her to move in tonight.'

Nick stared at her.

'You're for real?'

She had to laugh.

'Nick, you knew this was coming. You said yourself

today or tomorrow would be good. Surely you're not going to go to pieces on me now?'

He wasn't, of course!

He was a doctor, he knew about this stuff, it was just that his brain had stopped working and his legs were none too steady, and he wasn't sure that he could handle having two children—could he love them equally, could he ever love another child as much as he loved Steffi?—and then there was Bill, and he didn't know that he could go through seeing her in pain like he'd seen other women during labour, and—

'Nick!'

Bill's voice brought him out of his funk.

Well, almost.

'Go and talk to Dolores, ask Kirsten if she'd mind organising the clean-up here at the park, then we'll put Steffi and all the presents in the car, you can drop me at the hospital, then when Dolores gets to the apartment you can come back to the hospital.'

He stared at her.

'And bring my bag—the one that's packed. We've been through this.'

Nick stared at her some more, saw her smile and knew she knew exactly what he was thinking.

She kissed him once again, although he felt the wince of pain she gave as another contraction grabbed her body.

'We'll be fine,' she promised him. 'You'll love this baby differently from Steffi but still love him just as much. Love is the one thing we've got plenty of. And I won't die in childbirth and you won't faint, watching it.'

She looked at him again and added, 'Now, was there anything else?'

He shook his head and took her in his arms.

'Except to tell you that I love you, Mrs Grant,' he said, his voice so husky he wondered if she'd heard the words.

'That's good,' Bill told him. 'Now go and talk to Kirsten and Dolores and find Steffi and the presents and—'

Nick cut off the instructions with another kiss and when Bill kissed him back he knew she was right, and that this new baby he and Bill had made would be every bit as special as Steffi, and—

Well, he couldn't really remember all the other things he'd been worrying about.

Stuart Alexander Grant, weighing in at a splendid three point eight kilos, arrived on his sister's birthday, much to everyone's delight. Holding him in his arms, looking down into his red, downy face, Nick felt again that rush of pure, unadulterated love he'd felt when he'd first held Steffi.

'We'll be right, mate,' he said to his son, then looked up into the radiance of Bill's smile, at Steffi cuddled up to Bill on the bed, her little fist holding tightly to Bill's curls, and he knew they'd all be right—his family!

* * * * *

P.S. YOU'RE
A DADDY!

BY
DIANNE DRAKE

To Doc Nona, with all my admiration.

First published in Great Britain 2013
by Mills & Boon, an imprint of Harlequin (UK) Limited.
Harlequin (UK) Limited, Eton House, 18-24 Paradise Road,
Richmond, Surrey TW9 1SR

© Dianne Despain 2013

ISBN: 978 0 263 89892 7

Printed and bound in Spain
by Blackprint CPI, Barcelona

Dear Reader

A few years ago I met an amazing woman—Nona—who travelled by horse through the mountain regions of the eastern United States. What fascinated me about her was not so much that she spent day after day on the trail, in the woods, in the mountains, and in areas so isolated the world had forgotten them—I was fascinated by the fact that she was a doctor who packed her medicine into her saddle bags and took it to the people who lived in those areas. People who wouldn't have it otherwise.

At the time I guess I didn't even know such areas existed in the United States, much less that the people from those places didn't have access to the same things I had. But Nona was diligent in what she referred to as her 'calling', and she took her skills and knowledge to people who didn't take for granted the conveniences of life most of us are accustomed to having.

I like writing about people who, like Nona, have a similar calling. People who don't practise 'convenient' medicine. That's why you see this recurring theme in so many of my books. There are dedicated, quiet people in this world who serve without accolade. I've met them in my travels, been befriended by them, seen them work under conditions I can't even begin to describe. They *do* have a calling—a higher calling, I believe. And it's because of them I bring you the story of Deanna and Beau, who wrestle with the life they had in New York, and the one they'll face together in a community one hundred miles from nowhere.

As always, wishing you health and happiness

Dianne

PS Check me out on Facebook at:
www.facebook.com/DianneDrakeAuthor

CHAPTER ONE

ONE SIGH SAID it all, and for Deanna Lambert that sigh filled an entire story—past, present and future. She stared at her face in the mirror for a full minute, unsure what the face staring back was telling her. Do it? Don't do it? Keep your fingers crossed and hope for the best?

"You're no help," she groused at her image, then pulled up her red tank top and finally assembled the courage to look at her belly yet again. She brushed away another tear. Ups and downs now. That's what her life was about, ups and downs. "I wish I knew what to do. Wish somebody would just say, Deanna, do this." But situations like hers didn't come with a set of instructions. Only regret. More regret than she knew what to do with. And pain. Dear God, the pain nearly crippled her.

Assessing her belly, Deanna's new daily routine, she splayed her fingers over the warm flesh, willing herself to feel the child just beneath her fingertips. It was silly of her, of course, but this baby was her only connection to Emily, and she wanted desperately to hold onto that connection, feel that connection the way she used to. Count on it.

She couldn't, though. Not any more. But this baby…

it was different. A hope she wasn't ready to accept. Permission to move on. A blessing ready to be claimed.

Another tear trickled down her cheek and she swatted at it with the back of her hand.

"Part of me wants to go and find him. He's your daddy." At least, biologically he was. "And maybe he would want to know about you." But the truth was, men who made sperm donations didn't want to know. It was an anonymous gesture, often for the money and sometimes out of generosity. Or ego. So which was it for Braxton Alexander? she wondered. The unbearable weight of not knowing was dragging her down. The unbearable weight of carrying her cousin's baby—a baby who would never see his or her mother—was dragging her down ever deeper.

"Resolve it immediately," Dr. Brewster, her obstetrician, had warned her. "Your blood pressure is borderline high, you're not getting enough sleep, you've lost three pounds. Regardless of whose baby you're carrying, you're that baby's lifeline. You've got to take better care of yourself. So figure out what you need to do, and do it."

Kindly old doctor. And he was right. She had to figure out what to do, and do it. "But darn," she murmured, as she backed away from the mirror and pulled down her top, "why couldn't somebody just tell me what it is I should do?"

She was in this alone. Carrying a mistaken baby—her cousin's child who, beyond a shadow of a doubt, was not the progeny of her cousin's husband. However a mistake like that could be made in this age of technological wizardry. *Oops, wrong sperm, Mrs. Braxton. We're terribly sorry.*

A mistake that had cost Emily her life, as it had turned out.

"It would have been good," she said to the baby. "Even if Alex didn't want you after he found out, Emily would have been the best mother anyone could have because she wanted you so badly." Even after three miscarriages and a stillbirth Emily had never lost hope. "And I would have helped you raise her." Deanna ran her hand over her red tank top to smooth the wrinkles but more to acknowledge the love she felt every time she touched her belly.

And she did love this child. She didn't feel equal to the task of motherhood, and hadn't ever even thought of herself in those terms, to be honest. But that didn't negate the feelings she had for Emily's baby. And those only grew stronger every day. Along with the irrational guilt. Survivor's guilt, she'd been told. "So, the question remains, should I tell your father about you, or let him exist as the anonymous donor he was?"

Stupid question. Anonymous donors wanted anonymity, presumably. But something was pulling her in a direction she knew she should resist. "OK, so maybe we could go there and simply watch him for a while, see what kind of man he is. What kind of genes you'll be getting from him. No harm in that, is there?"

No harm except the emotional one that kept her hanging onto something she didn't understand. Dr. Brewster was right. She had to resolve this. But by going all the way to Tennessee? Specifically, Sugar Creek? That's where the investigator she'd hired said he was living now. One law firm, a private investigator and some pretty formidable legal maneuvering had gained her a little information, more than most women had when they made their selections from the information inside the catalogs, and that should have been enough. But it wasn't.

And maybe that's because she really did want to know, or simply because hanging onto a man she should never, under any circumstances, meet meant putting off the inevitable—facing what happened next.

All she wanted to do was see him. Nothing else. And wasn't it her right to know more about the father of the baby she carried? OK, so maybe it wasn't. But she was…curious. What, specifically, she wanted to know about him, she had no clue.

She did want to stop hurting, though, and maybe that's what this near obsession was about. Losing his cousin, her best friend, had turned into a pain she didn't know how anybody could endure, and she was looking for anything to make it stop. Maybe that's what finding Dr. Braxton Alexander was about, at least in part. Something to keep her occupied until something else made sense.

"So, we go to Sugar Creek," she said to the baby, looking at the already packed bags by her front door. They'd been packed for days, and she'd gone this far several times before. Then stopped. But today was different. She could feel it in her resolve, in her heart and, yes, in her belly. Today she would carry those bags to the car, climb in and head south. All the way to Tennessee.

"But before we leave, I need to stop by the cemetery and tell Emily what we're going to do," she told the baby. "Emily," she whispered, as tears started welling again. "I really don't know what I'm doing, and I'm so scared…"

* * *

"Welcome to Sugar Creek, Tennessee," Deanna said on an ambivalent sigh. This was it. She'd done it. Well, part of it. She'd managed to get herself here. As far as the next part went, she had options and she wasn't ready to decide which one to choose. So for now she was here to work. At least, that's what she'd tell people. Reports to do, financial donor sources to track down, people to hire who would implement her programs. Her temporary lease here was for a month and she'd brought enough work with her to keep her busy for three, so the part about coming here to work wasn't a lie. Nurse researcher with plenty to do.

Now, stepping out of her car and raising her binoculars to look down the south face of the mountain at the lay of the little town, she noted how the quaint buildings stretched pleasantly up and down Sugar Creek Highway. There was an outcropping of foothills and more green trees than she'd ever seen in any one place in her life jutting out prominently in any direction she looked other than the main part of town itself.

"It's very pretty. And it's got a grocery store, café, general merchandise store, and beauty shop. I think we'll have a nice month here." With or without tracking down Braxton Alexander.

Even though she'd never lived in one, Deanna loved small towns, loved the whole countrified experience. As a nurse researcher, she'd devoted her entire career to finding ways to make healthcare better in areas where it wasn't easily accessed. Places like Sugar Creek, which sat in a beautiful, secluded valley a hundred miles from anywhere. It wasn't the beauty of such places that caught her attention when she took on new assignments but the seclusion, because her job was to bridge the medical gaps.

"But this town is one of the lucky ones," she said. "It has a doctor. Your daddy." Your daddy... Odd how that was so easy to say. "Judging from what I read about him, he's very good." And she'd read everything she could find. A few articles he'd written about general surgery, some accounts of awards he'd received. Nothing about why he'd given up a lucrative New York City surgery to isolate himself here. As a GP, no less.

Midday carried with it a cool June breeze, and a chill washed over Deanna as she lowered her binoculars and, once again, thought about what she was doing here. Chasing Braxton Alexander. This wasn't just a small change of direction for her. It was a total life-changer. She was having this man's baby—a baby she'd never planned on having—and sitting on a mountaintop hoping to catch a glimpse of him somewhere.

How much more perverse did life get than that? She tilted her face to the sky and, for the first time in weeks, actually felt a little bit of relaxation slide down over her.

"I'm pretty sure I'm glad we came here, but I suppose there's a lot still to be determined." She liked talking to the baby, particularly here. Possibly because she was so close to the daddy. Or maybe because she'd put physical distance between herself and everything that reminded her of Emily.

"Now we're going to have to figure out what we're going to do next...*for real*." She laid her hand on her belly. "So, here are our options. We can watch and keep quiet. Try finding a way to meet him. Or we can always play it by ear. See what happens. Hope for the best."

However it worked out, she had a whole month ahead of her to find the answer and act on it. Or not.

"She's making eyes at you, boss." Joey Santiago led the chestnut mare into the stall then took off her lead before he stepped out and latched the door behind him. Brushing his hands together to shake off the dust, he said, "They all do it. Big brown eyes, so many expectations. You've let them have their way with you once too often, and now you pay for it every time you come in here."

"Not pay for it, Joey. Enjoy it." Beau leaned over the Dutch door of the stall and gave the mare a couple of lumps of sugar, like he always did. It's what he'd done as a child every time he'd spent a few days or a few months here with his grandfather, and he'd continued doing it after he'd moved in for good when he'd been a teenager.

"And they love you for it."

"Horses don't love," Beau protested. "They merely get used to certain things." The way he had, growing up. "Come to expect them. Recognize them when they're being offered."

"You're wrong there, Beau. They love, just like we do. You can see it in their eyes."

Joey had been here for as long as Beau could remember, doing odd jobs, gardening, taking care of the few horses his grandfather always kept, and taking care of Beau's grandfather after his stroke. He was also part of the two-man team who had raised him when his dad had gone off on benders and wherever else it was the old man had gone to avoid life, responsibility and, most of all, fatherhood.

"Some of us don't love, though," Beau countered, still cringing over his marriage fiasco nearly two years later.

"You loved," Joey countered. "Just not wisely. But with a horse you don't have to worry about duplicitous intentions. A carrot and a few kind words will get you unconditional love for ever. And even if you don't yet have a taste for falling in love again, that's going to change. Just in your own time."

"Or in no time," Beau quipped, preferring not to think about Nancy. Two years later, he still did, though. It was inevitable, he supposed, because of the way she'd changed his life. But all this love talk made him nervous. He wanted to climb up on one of these horses and ride so hard it knocked the memories right out of him.

Joey, a stocky man with thick black hair, shook his head as he peeked over the half-door in the next stall at Nell, who was ready to give birth any time. "I watched you at the races last spring, in Kentucky. Watched you get so excited when Donder almost won the Derby. I saw love in your eyes for that horse, Beau. I know you're not dead in your emotions like you think you are. Just holding it back."

"Emotionally dead is easier."

"Or safer. But that's going to change. Mark my words, when the time's right to move on, nothing's going to hold you back."

"I've been ready to move on for two years." And everything was holding him back.

"And yet you haven't," Joey quipped. "Strange how that works, isn't it?"

Joey was right, of course. But Beau didn't have to admit that out loud because, in ways he didn't want to deal with, he was just fine being held back. It kept him away from the possibility that what he'd gone through once could happen again. Admitting you'd been so blind and, on top of that, so insanely stupid on so many levels… No, there would be no repeat acts for him, and the only way to guarantee that was to keep his distance. Big distance.

"What's strange is standing here talking to you about my love life when I've got fences to mend out on the back forty." Barring emergencies, no more patients for the day and no house calls for the evening. With any luck he'd be so worn out by nightfall that, for once, a good night's sleep—out there—would come easily. Then he'd get an early jump on it in the morning and be back here by noon to open the clinic. But he had to quit talking first. And quit moping as well.

"So which one you running away from? Thinking about that whole mess you had with your wife, or the problems you've got going with Brax?"

Leave it to Joey to turn one emotional train wreck into two. He loved the man, knew he only wanted to help. But, damn, not this way. "I've got no problems with the old man," Beau snapped. "Just a difference of medical opinion." Big difference of opinion.

Joey chuckled. "Your way, his way. Two stubborn men who don't want to budge. Glad the extent of my medical knowledge doesn't go beyond applying a bandage and some good, old-fashioned horse medicine."

True, they were alike in a few ways. Stubbornness for stubbornness, maybe they did match up, but only a little bit. "OK, so maybe we have *some* similarities. But the old man thinks he can practice medicine again, and I know he can't. It's time for him to retire."

"Two peas in a pod. Actually, let's make that two

peas in separate pods since you're not seeing eye to eye on pretty much anything right now."

It bothered Beau more than he let on. He liked being here, on Brax's land, close to nature, in a place where no one could touch him. It let him remember the best times of his life when he and his grandfather would go out to mend fences together then stay over for a camp-out.

He missed those uncomplicated days. Missed his once uncomplicated life. But the complications came from so many directions now—some of his doing, some from Brax's physical condition. Too many bitter pills to swallow.

"That's why I'm going out for the night. Brax and I need some space. There's too much conflict going on in the house and it's not good for him."

"Not good for you either."

"But I'm not trying to recover from a stroke."

"A little space might be good. I'll give you that. But what if Nell decides that tonight's her night? Or there's a medical emergency?"

"Call me." He patted the pocket of his chambray shirt, where his cellphone was tucked away. "Or come get me in the helicopter." Yes, Brax had a helicopter. A necessity in these spread-out parts for a GP who still made house calls. "And I'm fine to be out there by my-self, brooding about my life and all the things I can't fix, so quit worrying about me, OK?" Actually, he was looking forward to going up to his spot to contemplate his past, present, even his future. Because right now it was one big blur, and he wasn't sure about any of it.

"You up on the ridge all alone, your grandfather holed up in his study all alone… Like I said, different pods, same peas."

Beau chuckled, and patted Joey on the back. "Leave me the hell alone, will you? The last thing I need is all that perception hanging around me, making too much sense." The truth was, he was still in a wallowing mood, and he'd become damned good at it.

"You're not going to find a better view anywhere in Sugar Creek," Kelli Dawson said, as she pushed back the double doors and invited Deanna to step outside onto the porch to the see the view. Kelli was the rental agent, giving Deanna the grand tour of her home for the next month. "Hot tub in the left corner, porch swing in the right. And look at everything you can see from here."

It was breathtaking, Deanna did have to admit. And the photos Kelli had e-mailed didn't do this cabin justice. "But you're going to sell it?"

"I'm just the listing agent. My client wants to sell, but it's been on the market a year now and nobody's interested. Sugar Creek is a nice town, but it's small, too isolated. Our doctor here has to use a helicopter to make house calls."

Braxton Alexander was the doctor, but she needed to hear it acknowledged. "Your doctor is…?"

"Doc Brax. Wonderful man. Everybody loves him." That was encouraging. It was nice to know the baby's daddy was liked. "He's been an institution here for ever. Delivered most of the babies around here. Including me!"

No way…! According to the donor card, Braxton Alexander was thirty-six. Was she chasing after the wrong person? Wasting her time, not to mention her emotional investment, in the wrong place?

"And he's still delivering babies?"

"Not since his stroke. He recovered from it pretty well. Needs a cane sometimes to help him get around better. But I'd still let him be my doctor if he hadn't quit, because his mind's as sharp as ever. By the time my grandpa was Doc Brax's age, he was forgetful and he just seemed so withered up. But Doc Brax looks good for his age, and Joey, the man who runs Braxton Acres, says he'll be able to get rid of his cane any day now."

"How old is Doc Brax?"

"Seventy-five, I think. Could be seventy-six."

Not the baby's daddy, then, unless the sperm bank had got that wrong, too. "He's the only doctor in this area?"

"He was, until his grandson Braxton, known as Beau took over. Good doctor, but not friendly like his grandfather. People don't think he likes being back here… He used to be the town troublemaker when he was a kid. But he does what he's supposed to now, and he's as good as his grandfather, so the rest of it doesn't really matter." Her smile widened.

"Upstairs you'll find the game room and TV. Downstairs you'll find the laundry and a couple of extra bedrooms. And on this level…you've seen it all. The kitchen, the great room. Oh, and there's a whirlpool in the master suite."

"It's lovely," Deanna said absently, her mind still on the Braxton Alexander who'd fathered Emily's baby. Good doctor a plus, lacking in personality a minus. Troublemaker as a kid an even bigger minus! "I think everything will suit me just fine."

"You can call out for groceries, too. Number's by the phone. If you want to hole up for the entire month and never leave, you can. So, what was it you said you were going to do? Write a book?"

Sugar Creek, where everybody knew everybody else's business. That could work to her advantage, or against it. One way or the other, she was going to have to be very careful here, because her business was nobody else's. "Something like that."

"Well, if you find yourself craving company, my office is on the main street. Stop by any time. We can have lunch or I can show you around. There's not much to do here so it's always nice to make new friends."

She liked Kelli. Maybe under other circumstances they might have been friends. But she wasn't here about friendship, wasn't here to have lunches or insert herself into the local culture. This trip was only about finding out what kind of man had fathered Emily's baby, and once her curiosity was satisfied, she'd leave. Hopefully she would return to the larger apartment her own real estate agent was scouting for her right now. Another of those life changes happening too fast.

After hastily unpacking and tossing a few articles of clothing on the bed rather than hanging them, Deanna fixed herself a pitcher of lemonade and headed out to the porch swing. This was her next month: sitting, watching, hoping to learn. So why not start it now?

"They say your daddy isn't too personable," she said, laying her hand protectively over her belly as she lowered herself into the swing. "But that doesn't really matter, does it? Not to either of us. I want you and love you, so it's going to be fine even if he is an old grump." Although somehow she'd wanted him to be pleasant, and she was a little disappointed by the prospect that he wasn't. "So what else are we going to discover?"

The truth was, now that she was here, she was scared about it, and feeling more alone than she ever had in her life. "But we'll get through it," she said. "I always do." A fact that scared her even more because, for the first time since she'd agreed to carry this baby, she realized she didn't want to do it alone. But alone was what she was.

So very alone. And nothing could fix that. "So now I'm going to cry," she said as the tears welled in her eyes. "Damn the hormones." And the loneliness.

CHAPTER TWO

IT UNVEILED ITSELF before her eyes, almost in slow motion. Even from her mountaintop perch she saw the beginning of it, two cars climbing up the modestly steep highway leading into town, one in the front, one bringing up the rear at a safe distance.

Nothing out of the ordinary except the deer that darted out in front of the first car then paused in the middle of the road to stare at its would-be attacker, and run safely off to the other side. All this while the first car swerved to avoid it then jammed on its brakes, sending it into a fishtail that caused it to cut in and out, from lane to lane, over the center line, then whip back to the other side. Correcting and over-correcting to right itself.

That's when the full realization of what she was witnessing grabbed hold and propelled her off the swing and right up to the rail of the porch for a better look. And as that horrible realization sank in deeper, and the second car jammed on its brakes to avoid the veering of the first car, her hand crept to her pocket and her fingers wrapped around her cellphone as the second car braked too hard and skidded…and skidded…and skidded…

A sickening crunch of metal permeated the mountain air, one so hideous it caused a roost of black birds in a far-off tree to flee their sanctuary with great protest and screeching. Holding her breath, Deanna didn't divert her eyes from the road below as her fingers slid over the phone's smooth face. She glanced down just long enough to see the numbers to push, and pushed.

Then, as she looked back down the side of the mountain, the second car was flipping, side over side, repeatedly hitting the pavement. Its course to the edge of the road clear, the clutching in her heart turning to a stabbing pain. "Dear God," she murmured, as the emergency dispatcher came on.

"This is 911, what's your emergency?"

"No," Deanna cried in a strangled scream, hoping God or somebody would hear her and stop the second car's inevitable plummet over the side of the mountain.

"What's your emergency?" the dispatcher asked again, followed by, "Miss Lambert, are you all right? Please, can you hear me?"

Hearing her name snapped her back into the moment. "Yes, I'm here, and I'm watching a wreck in progress. Two cars..." She glanced left, to the semi heading down the mountain, its driver not yet able to see what was ahead. "And maybe a semi, if it doesn't get stopped in..." Her voice trailed off as she watched the second act unfold.

"Where, Miss Lambert?"

Again, hearing her name from the dispatcher jolted her. "It's a road I can see from my porch, but I don't know its name. I'm in my cabin..."

"Above the Clouds," the dispatcher supplied, then asked, "South porch?"

"Yes."

"Can you tell me, exactly, what kind of damage or injuries we might be looking at?"

Massive, devastating injuries, she thought. "Yes. One of the cars has just gone through the guardrail and over the edge. And the other…" She swallowed hard. "It hit the guardrail a few times and it's still trying to correct itself on the road… I think the truck coming from the other direction's going to hit it."

Whether or not the driver of the semi saw the impending disaster ahead, or simply assumed the car careening head first at him in his lane would move over, Deanna had no idea, but the excruciating squeal of the semi's brakes and the low wail of the truck's horn was what snapped her totally out of the surreal watching mode and into action.

"I know exactly where it is," the dispatcher said, "and I've sent out an alarm to the volunteer fire department. They'll be there as fast as they can."

How long would that be? In a study concerning rural emergency response times Deanna had conducted last year, she'd discovered that those waiting times could be fatally long—sometimes thirty minutes, up to an hour. And from what she'd just witnessed, there were people down below who needed help before that. "What about the local doctor?" she asked. "Can we call him?"

"He's out mending fences right now, but I'll give his grandpa a call and see what we can do to get him there. Kelli Dawson's my daughter, by the way. And I know this is probably not the best time to say this, but welcome to Sugar Creek, Miss Lambert."

She heard the cordial greeting, but it wasn't registering because… "Oh, my… No!" The semi didn't hit the oncoming car, as she'd thought it might, but in its attempt to do a hard brake, it jackknifed and turned over, sliding on its side along the road.

And the car swerved right into it, hit the back end of its trailer with full-on force, bringing both the truck and the car to a stop. "More casualties," she informed Kelli's mother. "Two cars and one semi now. Can't see how many people…" Wasn't sure she wanted to see how many people.

But after she'd clicked off from the dispatcher, curiosity got the better of her and she grabbed her binoculars, took a look. Nobody was moving. No one was trying to climb out of the carnage. No one was trying to climb up the side of the mountain from where they'd toppled off.

And there was no one there to help. That's what scared her the most. People down there needed help and she prayed they weren't past the point where help mattered.

Without a thought for anything else, Deanna grabbed her medical kit, one she carried out of habit more than necessity, and sprinted for her car. She backed it out and headed down the steep road, making sure not to speed lest she ended up like one of the cars below. At the turn-off to the highway, she slowed to let a minivan by, made a left-hand turn and headed for the crash site, hoping help would be there when she arrived.

But the minivan was the only car present, and the woman driving it was standing outside her vehicle, torn between running to look for victims and trying to subdue three small children in the rear of the van. Her cellphone was in her hand and she was physically standing in front of the van's door. Was she trying to block the view from her children? Deanna wondered about that as she pulled alongside the van, waved to the woman, then continued to drive into the heart of the scene.

It's what she would do, she realized. She would protect Emily's baby from seeing what she herself was about to confront. She absolutely understood that mothering priority. She wasn't sure she'd respond that way in a crisis out of a natural tendency but, looking at it from a purely practical point of view, there was no denying the minivan mom was doing what she had to do. Something Deanna hoped she would learn when she became a mom.

As Deanna brought her car to a stop, several hundred yards short of the crash site, her cellphone jingled before she had a chance to step out. "You're a nurse?" the deep voice practically shouted. He sounded winded.

"I am. And who are you?"

"Local doctor. Beau…"

She wasn't even going to ask how he knew who she was, that she was a nurse, her cellphone number… "Your ETA?"

"Five minutes, tops. But without supplies. You're on the site already?"

How did he know that? "Just got here. Don't know how many victims yet."

"OK, you go see what we've got and I'll keep the line open, Miss Lambert. And please start the assessments, establish the priority if you can, figure out what I need to do first, and I'll be there as fast as I can."

He knew her name, too. And trusted her to prioritize the scene? She hadn't done that in a while. Hadn't been in active practice for years. Maybe if she'd told him that, he wouldn't be so trusting of her.

Those were the thoughts that stayed with her for the

next seconds as she grabbed her medical bag, switched her phone to her earpiece, and headed straight for the first car. "I'm not sure we're cut out for small-town life," she whispered to Emily's baby as she went straight to the driver's-side window of the car that had hit the semi, and looked in.

"In case you're listening, Doctor, I have a red sedan embedded in the back of the semi's trailer. Inside, three people. Male, mid-twenties, driver. Female passenger, approximately same age. Both unconscious. Airbags not deployed. No seat belts. From what I can see, both have had head contact with the windshield, profuse cranial bleeding both victims. Not seeing movement of any kind. And back seat…"

She bent, took a closer look, and was hit with a cold chill. "Child, age approximately three. No child seat. No seat belt. And…" she pulled open the car door and kneeled inside "…he's conscious."

"Stay with the child, Miss Lambert. Do you hear me? Stay with the child. I'm a minute away."

Not that she would have left this little boy. "Hello," she said, crawling all the way in. Instinctively, she reached over the front seat, took the driver's pulse. Found nothing. "My name is Deanna," she said to the toddler. He was curled up in a ball on the floor, looking at her with huge blue eyes that registered shock and terror and total confusion. "Can you tell me your name?"

Crawling across the seat until she was above the little boy, she leaned forward until she could get a good positioning on the female passenger's neck and, again, felt no pulse. "Can you tell me where you hurt?" Were his parents both dead? Admittedly, she wasn't in the best position to make assessments on the couple, so she wasn't making any assumptions.

"No pulses detected," she said to the vague voice on the phone. "Nothing affirmative, though. I'm not at a good angle to tell."

"But you're in the car?" he asked.

"Yes, with the child."

"Is the car safe? No fuel leaking, nothing that looks like it's going to ignite? Not close to the edge of the road?"

"Front end's a mangled mess, but I'm safe." She was pleased he actually sounded concerned.

"No chances, Miss Lambert. You keep yourself safe. Do you hear me?"

Yes, she heard him. "I have every intention of doing just that, Doctor," she replied. To get Emily's baby safely into the world, she would take no risks.

"Is the child injured? Can you tell if he's hurt?"

"Can't tell yet. I'm trying to check, but it's cramped in here." Cramped, even without her baby bump. She wondered how, in months to come, she was going to maneuver *with* a baby bump. "We'll just have to wait and see how that works out," she said to Emily's baby.

"Yes, I suppose we will have to see how it works out. In the meantime, I'm coming up behind you, so hold tight."

Startled that she'd been caught talking to Emily's baby, she glanced over her shoulder to see exactly where he might be behind her and there he was, larger than life…a cowboy riding her way. Actually, galloping. On a horse. OK, so maybe not a *real* cowboy in the Western movie sense but he was certainly a doctor on a horse who gave her an unexpected chill. And he was also a big, imposing figure of a man. Jeans, T-shirt, boots. *Sexy.* "Other casualties?" he shouted, as he slid off the horse and ran straight towards her.

Deanna shook herself out of her observation, out of the pure fascination that was overrunning her, displacing the fugitive fantasy with the reality. "Um…don't know. We've got a car over the side, about two hundred yards back…" She pointed to the black skid marks snaking across the road for a hundred yard stretch. "And a truck. Don't know anything about the driver. Haven't had a chance to go over there to see him yet."

The doctor, Beau, crowded into the back seat of the car right behind her and nudged her forward most of the way to the opposite door then twisted around and proceeded to wedge himself between the back seat and the front. Doing his own assessments, as Deanna attempted to make herself more accessible to the boy, who'd curled even tighter into a ball.

After mere seconds he sucked in a sharp breath, which Deanna heard, and understood.

"How about we get the child out of here?" Beau asked. "There's nothing here he needs to see."

Even though she had been prepared to hear the words, the implication hit her hard. "Both of them?" she asked.

"Both of them." He began to back out of the car, pulling his massive form out of the too-small space. "How about you? Are you OK in there?"

"Don't have a choice," she said, as she began the struggle to lift the boy from the floor and at the same time assess him for injuries she might not have seen right off. The truth was, nothing about this was OK. But it wasn't about her feelings or memories. Or any inherent fears she might have for what this child was about to face.

"Then I'm going round to the truck. Janice Parsons, standing over at the minivan, said she'll look after the boy if we need her to, so shout if you need anything else, OK?"

If she needed anything else? She needed everything, including a way out of this. Her parents, Emily…it was all closing in around her. Smothering her. "Oh, and the dispatcher said she'd get the volunteer fire department out. But I don't know how long that's going to take."

"Too long," Beau shouted, his voice diminishing even before his words were all out. "Damn problem with all of this. It always takes too long!"

Deanna rose up and took a quick glance out the window, just enough to see him run behind the truck, and while she knew she wasn't alone here, that's how she felt. Amazing how twenty seconds crammed together in a car with him had bolstered her self-confidence.

"So, is your name Tommy?" she asked the child, as she gently moved in to take his pulse. Strong, a little too fast. But he was scared. "Or Billy?" She wiggled her hand from his and brushed long, curly blond locks from his forehead, then took a look into his eyes as best she could. Pupils equal and reactive. "Or Porcupine?" Counted his respirations—normal.

"Not Porcupine," he finally said.

She was so relieved to hear his voice. "If it's not Porcupine, is it…Bulldog?"

"Not Bulldog," he said, tears welling up in his eyes.

She began a gentle prodding of his limbs, no heightened pain sensitivity noted. Then his belly. Not rigid, no distension. "Kangaroo?" she asked, trying to move him slightly to his side to make sure nothing was sticking into him in any way, like shards of glass from the shattered windshield or objects that might have flown around the car. But he was clear of everything, and she was beginning to wonder if he'd been curled up on the floor of the car when this had happened. Maybe asleep?

He whimpered something Deanna didn't understand but which she took to be him asking for his mommy. Glancing over the seat to the lifeless form, she drew in a ragged breath. "Mommy needs to rest right now. So does Daddy. So I'm going to open this car then we'll get out very quietly so we won't disturb them. Will you help me do that, Kangaroo?"

"Not Kangaroo."

"Is it Hippopotamus?" she asked, as she pushed on the car door then climbed out. "Or Walrus?"

Leaning back in, she scooped the boy into her arms and lifted him away from the wreckage, taking great care to make sure his face was buried in her shoulder. What an awful thing, seeing your parents that way and having that memory linger as your last memory of them. Her parents had died this way, in a car wreck. But she hadn't been in the car, and her very last recollection of them was the hugs and kisses they had given her when they'd dropped her off at her aunt and uncle's house. Hugs, kisses, and I love yous shouted from the car window as they'd pulled away from the curb… "I personally like Cheetah, or Chimpanzee."

"It's Lucas," the child said, but so quietly it was more a muffled sob than a word.

Did he know? Did he have some innate feeling that he'd just become an orphan? She hadn't when it had happened to her. In fact, it had taken months to sink in, months in which she'd spent every minute she could with her face pressed to the window, watching for them to come back.

Deanna didn't know about Lucas, though. Didn't know if he had an innate feeling, or just plain knew, because she didn't know a thing about children. She'd never been around them except for a few mandatory clinical rotations through pediatrics, and she'd certainly never planned on having them herself. She'd never been struck with that maternal urge the way Emily had. While it had defined her cousin, it had eluded her. So motherhood had never been included in her life plan— a decision she'd been fine with.

Of course, Emily's baby changed all that. Still, she wasn't consumed with an innate sense of motherhood the way she'd expected to be, the way she'd seen it in so many other women she'd known. The way Janice Parsons was when she bundled Lucas into her arms so protectively the instant Deanna handed him over to her.

"I think he's OK," she said, a little envious of the way the boy went from her embrace to someone else's so easily. Hadn't she snuggled him the right way? "His name is Lucas, and I'll have the doctor do another exam on him as soon as he can. In the meantime, if you could…"

There was no sense in finishing the sentence. Janice's mothering instincts were on full alert as she turned Lucas away from the wreckage. All that natural tendency—a beautiful thing to see, really. "Don't give him anything to eat or drink," she said, taking one last look at the boy then at Janice, envying the way she exuded motherliness from every pore.

Would that ever be her?

That thought plagued her as she ran over to the edge

of the road where the guardrail was smashed and broken, then looked down. Thank God, the drop-off to the first ledged area was barely more than a hundred feet. Sure, it was a long distance if you were in the car going over it, but the distance was short enough that she was cautiously optimistic.

"Hello," she shouted. "Can anybody hear me?"

The response was one staccato honk, which came as pure relief. But also frustration, knowing she couldn't make that climb down. Thank heavens some kind of natural instinct had kicked in and kept her planted on *terra firma*, because her natural inclination would have had her over the side before she'd even given it a thought. She still wondered, though, if that instinct would be enough in the long term because, dear God, everything in her wanted her to go over that edge.

"Help's on the way," she shouted, actually taking a step backwards. "Please, don't move. And if you have a cellphone…" She called out her number and actually stood there for a second, waiting for a call back. Which didn't come. "I'm going to go get the doctor. We also have the fire department on the way. So don't give up. We're going to get you out of there in a few minutes."

"Truck driver's wedged," Beau said, the instant Deanna rounded the front of the truck. He was standing on the asphalt, looking through the windshield at the driver, who was stuck fast between the steering-wheel and the seat. "Internal injuries, some bleeding. Broken arm. Mangled leg…not sure if it can be saved. Head trauma but conscious. Strong possibility of hemorrhagic shock once we get him out. I can't do anything about it until we have more help.

"I'd stay in there with him but it's too tight and I

don't want to risk slipping or moving the wrong way and hurting him more than he already is."

"We've got survivors in the car that went over," she said, trying to sound positive.

"Were you able to get down there?" he asked, his eyes glued to what was visible of the man in the truck.

"No, but someone honked."

"So all we need is…"

"Everything," Deanna said. "All we need is everything." She studied the man next to her for a moment. Mid-thirties, but with some lines etched in his face. Dark brown hair, a bit over the collar and wavy. Brown eyes. The kinds of things that would have been included on the sperm-donor card—had there been a donor card. But in addition to the sperm switch, the donor card had gone missing.

What wouldn't have been described on that card, though, was the kindness she saw in his eyes. From that, she was drawn in immediately. Not that his good looks alone couldn't have done it but those were an added bonus, gave her some hope for the way Emily's child might look. "My name is Deanna Lambert. But I'm betting you already knew that, didn't you?"

He smiled, although he didn't even glance in her direction. "You're renting a cabin here for a month to do some medical writing. Live in New York City otherwise."

"And my zodiac sign?"

He chuckled. "Give me ten more minutes and I'll not only tell you your zodiac sign, I'll describe your high-school graduation in detail."

"That bad here?" she asked.

"Or good, depending on your point of view. The

people here describe it as caring and, for the most part, I think that's right." Finally, he glanced at her, but for only a second. "I'm Beau Alexander, by the way. Local and possibly temporary doctor, aspiring horse breeder, mender of fences."

She'd known who he was, but hearing the name—*from him*—still shocked her, made her reason for being here even more real. Scared her, too. Most of all it made her feel sad, thinking about the way such a happy pregnancy was turning out. "I think I may be renting the cabin above your ranch."

"Above the Clouds. Nice view. Been up there a couple of—"

His words were cut off by the ringing of Deanna's cellphone, and without thinking she clicked it on. Listened for a second. Drew in a deep breath. "It's the people in the car," she said to Beau.

"What?"

"I gave them my cellphone number in case they wanted to call me. So they're calling."

"Damn," he muttered, impressed with her resourcefulness. More than that, impressed with everything he'd seen of her so far. "Good thinking."

"Only thing that came to mind. So, do you want to do this?"

He shook his head. "Got to stay focused on the driver, and I have to go back into the truck as soon as the fire department shows up and can keep the door open for me." The distant wail of several sirens caused him to sigh in relief.

"They're at Turner's Points now...you can tell by the echo. Turner's is the first place in the canyon that catches the sound like that. And it means they'll be here in about five minutes." He ran up to the truck windshield and gave the man a thumbs-up then turned back to Deanna, who was already on her way back to the side of the road where the car had gone over.

"Deanna," he shouted to her, "direct the medical end of the rescue when they get here, because when I get back into the truck I'm not getting out until after my patient does." Meaning he was going to have to wedge himself into a damned uncomfortable spot practically underneath the man, and stay put. He had to brace the man's leg, hopefully apply some kind of a splint, before they could move him, and at the same time keep his fingers crossed that the driver would survive the efforts to cut him out of there.

He glanced back at her, watched the way she instructed the paramedics who'd just arrived. He observed her body language, her no-nonsense stance, and liked her instantly. He wished he could have someone like her working alongside him every day.

"Hire someone like Deanna," he grunted, more to himself than out loud as he hauled himself up the side of the truck after two firefighters had dismantled the door for him and tossed it down on the road like it weighed no more than a plastic water bottle.

"Couldn't hurt," he said under his breath as he reached the top then started to lower himself back inside. "Might even help."

Considering the way he and his grandfather were battling over how to run a medical practice, he was pretty sure that having someone capable like Deanna involved would be another of the old man's objections. But Beau had to have his say in the matter if he was going to stay here permanently. And having a nurse or a medical assistant seemed like a good idea.

He'd known her for only a few minutes yet he wanted Deanna. Snap judgment and right fit, he believed. But he'd heard she was only renting for a month, which meant she wasn't staying in Sugar Creek. So now the problem was that Deanna had become the only person who flitted across his mind's eye when he thought about hiring another staffer. And she was such a nice fit he wasn't sure how to alter that image.

"Well, Mack, this ought to be pretty easy, once I get you splinted up," he said, trying to sound optimistic in order to bolster the truck driver's spirits.

"Don't think it's going to be easy, Doc. But I'm willing to give it a try. Need to be home later…wife's having a few friends over for dinner. It's my granddaughter's fifth birthday. Don't want to miss that."

"Just one granddaughter?" Beau asked, looking through the windshield at Deanna, still admiring what he saw. Striking woman. Tall. Hair the color of honey. Very subdued, though. Here, in the middle of this accident, showing so much command, she had such a sense of calmness about her. It baffled him because, as experienced as he was as a surgeon, he was still feeling the adrenalin rush.

"Just the one." he said. "Got a grandson, though, who just turned two. You a family man, Doc? You got kids?"

"Nope. Had a wife for a while. It didn't work out. Glad now we didn't get around to having children because she was…" he did a quick visual assessment of Mack as he climbed past him then lowered himself to a position almost underneath him "…selfish. And that's being kind." Pulling a flashlight from his pocket, he looked at the man's leg for a second time. Definitely a fractured tibia. Not mangled but also not good.

"Married her for her looks, got what I deserved because when you got past the looks all that was there was pure, unadulterated selfishness." For all intents and purposes.

"That bad, eh, Doc?"

"Bad doesn't even begin to describe it," Beau said, shifting position but trying to keep well away from his patient. Outside, he could hear the noise level increasing, multiple voices shouting. "Next time..." He drew in a shuddering breath. "No next time. At least, not for a long, long time."

Mack chuckled then sucked in a sharp breath. "I got lucky the first time out," he said, his voice noticeably weaker than it had been even a minute before. "Married the perfect woman, had thirty-five good years so far. Hoping I'll have a few..." Another gasp for air. "A few more."

I hope so too, Beau said to himself as a blanket dropped down from the door opening.

"Cover you two up," the burly voice shouted. "Windshield's coming out next."

Seconds after that the windshield had gone, and Beau was amazed by the speed with which everything was happening. He'd never worked a rescue from this end of it, and he wondered how many times over the years his grandfather had been called on to do something like this. It was a side of Brax he'd never considered, and he felt embarrassed that he hadn't. "Need a splint in here," he called. "And MAST trousers."

"What can I do from out here?" Deanna yelled to him from just beyond the front of the truck. "I've got rescuers setting up to go over the side right now to help the people in the car, and I'm not needed there until they bring them up. So what can I do for you in the meantime?"

"Oxygen, IV set-up…fast fluids."

"Already got them set up."

"Possible field amp." No way he was going to say "amputation" where the patient could hear, but if internal injuries didn't turn into an issue, the mangled leg might. "You OK with that?" he asked.

"Sure, I'm OK. I'll get everything together," she said, turning and running back to the rescue truck.

"She's a pretty one, too, Doc," Mack said, his voice almost gone now. "Better watch out."

Mack was right. Deanna was already fascinating him way more than she should. "Look, Mack, this is going to be a little tricky because of the way you're wedged in. Your right leg is pretty bad, and you might have a fractured pelvis. Not sure what we're going to do about those yet because I think you could also have some internal bleeding going on because of the way the steering-wheel is shoved into your belly."

He glanced up as one of the medics fresh to the scene dangled into the door opening, endeavoring to take the driver's blood pressure. "Since you're pressed so tight against the wheel, it's serving as a pressure bandage of sorts, keeping the blood circulating to your vital organs. But once the wheel is removed, there's a good chance you're going to experience a major internal hemorrhage." A mild understatement as once he was unwedged, the fight would be on to save him.

"So there's going to be some surgery in your future as soon as we can get you to the hospital. Right now, because you're in shock, you're not feeling so much pain. But in another minute, when we make the big move to get you out of here…I'm not going to lie to you. It's going to hurt like hell. But that pretty nurse out there's got an IV with your name on it, and she's ready to get some painkillers into you. Are you with me so far?"

"Doesn't sound like a picnic, Doc. But I'm with you."

"Good, because it's going to happen pretty fast now." He watched Deanna direct the stretcher to just outside the truck then recheck the supplies laid out for this part of the rescue. Sill cool as the proverbial cucumber, she was the only one involved here who didn't seem frantic.

"Can I ask you one favor, Doc?"

"Sure. What is it?"

"Somewhere in the back I've got a birthday present for my granddaughter. However this turns out, would you see that she gets it?"

A lump formed in Beau's throat. "How about I save it for you to give to her?" he said. "And I'll tell her to save you some birthday cake."

"Appreciate it, Doc. Now, if you don't mind, I need to call my wife…"

"You talk while I splint your leg and get you ready to move." He didn't want to hear the conversation, it would be too personal.

So he bit his lower lip hard to create a distraction for himself and quickly splinted Mack's lower leg, trying to block out the way Mack was trying to be supportive to his wife even though he was the one in critical condition. Trying to block out thoughts of Nancy, who didn't have it in her to think of anyone but herself in a critical situation.

Pulling the last elastic bandage into place around

Mack's splint, Beau started to withdraw himself from the cab to allow the standby firefighters and medics their turn with him. "OK, let's get you out of here and on the next helicopter to the hospital. You with me?"

Mack's cellphone dropped to the floor, which was actually the passenger-side door, and as Beau twisted to grab it for him, he saw the wrapped birthday present and grabbed it as well. Something soft, a stuffed animal, he guessed.

"Deanna," he yelled, then tossed it out for her to catch. "Mack, cross your arms over your chest and let the medics do all the work. And, please, don't fight against them." After one last check to make sure Mack was as stable as possible, Beau unwedged himself all the way and practically poured out of the front of the truck, bouncing off the hood then hitting the ground with a thump, landing rather ungraciously on his bum right at Deanna's feet.

"You OK?" she asked, extending a hand to him to help him up.

"No, I'm not," he snapped, taking hold of her hand—such soft skin—and righting himself. "Sorry. I'm OK, but my patient…" He shrugged then looked back at the truck as the firefighters cut away large chunks of the truck to get at its driver.

"Look, Beau, I don't do this too often…patient care. Especially trauma and field rescue. But I understand the basics, we're as ready for him as we can be. So just tell me what I need to be doing."

He nodded. "What about the car that went over?"

"Both people inside are injured, one conscious, one not. Until the rescuers get into the car, we won't know any more."

"OK, then." He looked at the MAST trousers, which Deanna had laid out on the ground and opened up all the way. They were essentially the same as a blood-pressure cuff, with all the same sticky fasteners, gauges and tubes running in and out to blow them up. If knowing how to get them ready was what Deanna called the basics, she was greatly underestimating herself. "Let's do this."

Giving a nod to the rescuers in the truck, who were awaiting his direction, Beau stepped away from the trousers to allow the rescuers a clear path then turned to watch them cut away the steering-wheel and dashboard, almost in the blink of an eye.

In that same blink of an eye his patient ripped out the most blood-curdling scream imaginable. Beau drew in a shuddering breath and felt the squeeze of Deanna's hand on his arm. "I hate this," he whispered. "Damn, I hate this."

"I've got morphine ready."

Another awful scream and her squeeze tightened. "If he lives that long."

"He'll live that long." Deanna dropped to her knees as the firefighters ran forward and laid the driver directly atop the open trousers. Immediately she began to pull one of the legs over Mack's left leg, while Beau did the same with the right, and in a fraction of a second, they were both closing the fasteners.

There was another scream from Mack but this one weaker, and at the end of it he passed out. "Stay with us," Beau said, as he pumped pressure into the trousers. "You've got birthday cake to eat."

"Birthday cake?" Deanna asked, without diverting

her attention from the site she was cleaning on Mack's arm for an IV.

"His granddaughter's birthday. You're not bad for a writer, by the way. Pretty good skill sets in the field."

"Not bad for a writer who's putting an IV in someone who doesn't have a blood pressure," Deanna corrected, then smiled as she slid the needle into the vein near the crook of Mack's left arm.

"Do you like working trauma?" he asked, still astounded by her efficiency.

After she had taped the IV in place, she glanced over at Beau, who was listening to heart and breath sounds. "Don't dislike it. Not sure I'd want a steady diet of it, though." Returning her attention to her patient, she attached the IV tubing then hooked that to a bag of Ringer's, which would help replace fluid volume lost through bleeding. "And you?"

"Surgeon, by training. Country GP...by obligation. Maybe by choice, but I haven't made up my mind yet."

"Ah, two diverse worlds with just as diverse appeals." She signaled for the medic to hand her an oxygen mask then placed it on Mack's face.

"Maybe too diverse," he said, leaning over Mack to check his eyes for pupillary response. "Not sure where I fit yet."

"Which is why you're here?"

"I'm here because my grandfather isn't able to manage his practice any longer, and there's no one else to take care of his patients until I decide if I want to stay or bring somebody else in. He needed me, even though the old coot isn't about to admit it."

"Am I sensing family discord?"

"More like family stubbornness." He pushed himself away from Mack, then stood up and waved for the medics to take the man. "Not such an endearing trait, I've been told."

"So now what?" she asked, as she also stood, then stepped back. "An hour or so to the hospital? Will he be able to do that in his condition"

"Less, by helicopter."

"If you can get one. Airlift in areas such as this isn't always convenient when you need it."

"Unless you own a helicopter."

She arched her eyebrows. "I'm impressed."

"I was too when my grandfather bought it. Not so much now that I have to fly it."

"You fly?"

He shrugged. "Somebody has to. But normally I sit in the back with the patient and let Joey do the flying. He manages the ranch, tends the horses and my grandfather, flies the chopper." Something about her made him lose all caution, and just when he thought he'd perfected the fine art of keeping his privacy at all costs. Another pretty face, he decided. Like Mack had said—watch out!

"So we'll transport Mack to your helicopter, and…"

"And hope the people they're going to bring up from over the edge can make do with an hour's ride in the back of an ambulance."

"You really are deprived out here, aren't you?"

"Not deprived," he said, not so much offended by her remark as curious about it. "Slowed down, forced to be inventive."

"My mistake," she said, following Beau, who was running along behind the medics who were ready to load Mack into the back of an ambulance that would transport him to the Alexander landing strip.

"Logical conclusion. Look, you handle the rest of it. I've got to go." Which was exactly what he did. He climbed into the ambulance with Mack then watched Deanna until the doors shut on him. Even then, he stared through the tiny window until she was but a speck in the distance.

Deanna Lambert... Their paths had been meant to cross, he decided. He didn't know why, didn't even know what kind of medical writing she did. But it didn't matter. Something had just started, and while he didn't know what it was, he was anxious to find out.

CHAPTER THREE

"NICE VIEW OF my grandfather's ranch," Beau said, settling into the porch chair next to Deanna. He stretched out his long legs. "He used to hate it that someone up here could sit and watch what he was doing. But then he discovered the beauty of a good pair of binoculars and while I haven't seen him actually watching anybody up here, I think it gives him a certain sense of satisfaction knowing he can look up as well as they—or you—can look down."

"I don't blame him. I don't like being watched either. I spent a lot of my youth having people looking at me, trying to figure out what to do with me, and now I like to keep to myself."

"And yet you're a nurse?"

"Not in the sense most people would think of it but, yes, I'm a nurse." They were seated on the north porch this morning, watching the emerging new day and trying to forget all the haunting, hideous memories from yesterday.

Her parents had died in a car wreck. Then Emily had asked, *"Deanna, can I come stay with you for a few days? Alex and I had a fight and I may leave him for good."* Rainy day, emotions overpowering rational thought, horrible outcome. Deanna cringed, reliving it, not sure she ever wanted to get into another car. So she fixed her attention on the vast forest she could see from her porch. Concentrated on something pleasant, for herself but mostly for the baby. "This is lovely, though, isn't it? So many trees. Nature everywhere you look."

Beau chuckled. "Sounds like you've been cooped up too much."

"I get out, it's always about work, though. Never really have much time to relax and when I do, my view at home is the rooftop next door. From just the right position, which is my left shoulder pressed to the wall with my neck cranked to a forty-five-degree angle, I can look out of one of my windows and see part of the city skyline. But I usually come away with sore muscles if I do that so I keep my curtains closed."

Of course, when she returned, she would have a new apartment, something a little farther away from the city. Maybe in a suburb, with nice playgrounds and lots of children.

Beau chuckled. "I lived in a place like that once. In medical school. One room, with a bathroom so small you had to sidestep into the shower. There were two windows, total—one with a view of the street and one with a view of a flashing red neon sign: *'Ralph's Packaged Liquors'*. During the day, though, when it was turned off, from the right angle you could see a little park at the end of the block, with some trees. Sometimes I'd catch myself standing there, just staring at trees. I had all the trees in the world right here, never even saw them."

It was pleasant just relaxing, enjoying the morning. And it seemed so natural it nearly made her forget she was sitting here with the baby's father. Never mind that for the moment, she decided. She simply wanted to enjoy his company. Everything else could come later. "We all do that, I think. Take the easy, dependable things in our lives for granted. But I'm not taking this view for granted. It's spectacular. I could sit here for hours and just look at...*trees*."

"And I have an idea down there, somewhere amongst those trees, someone might be looking up here. Brax is too idle these days, doesn't have enough to keep him busy, and he got that little glint in his eyes when I told him I was going to drop in on you."

Impulsively, she waved in the direction of the Alexander ranch. "You should have brought him along."

"He's a stubborn old bastard. Fought the development up here when it happened, claimed it wouldn't be good for his patients. And as far as I know, he's never been up here."

"Then he's missing out, because the view of his ranch is stunning. Even though from here you look like ants." She shifted, tucked her feet up under her, thought she could get used to this. "So, any word from the hospital?"

"Mack, the truck driver, did well in surgery. They saved his leg, removed his spleen, took out part of his liver. Put him in traction for his pelvis. Tough road ahead for him, lots of rehab in his future, but he's got a good family, a huge family, actually, and they'll get him through it."

And all she had was this baby. Amazing, though, how the developing life inside her connected her to so much more than she could have ever expected. She and the baby might not be a large family but they'd be a good family. "Did he get any of that birthday cake?"

Beau chuckled. "Not yet. His family decided to put off the birthday celebration until he's able to eat solid food again."

"Good family," she said, truly glad for the man. "And the other couple? The ones who went over the edge?"

"Lucky all the way around for them. A few sprains, strains and bruises. Husband went home this morning, but they're keeping the wife an extra day because she had a slight concussion. And Lucas is fine, too. Social Services is looking for relatives who can take him in, but right now he's still with Janice Parsons, the mini-van driver you gave him to, and she's going to keep him until other arrangements are made. So, how are you doing? That was a lot of effort for your first day in Sugar Creek. You look tired."

"First day? More like first hour. And, yes, I'm tired. Didn't sleep much last night, which means I'm paying the price for it this morning." Stretching her back, she stifled a yawn. "But basically I'm OK. What brings you up here this early other than to see if I'm spying on your ranch? Don't you have patients to see?"

"I save my mornings for...well, I'll admit it. I spend time with my horses. Childhood passion I'm getting to indulge now that I've come back to Sugar Creek. So barring a heavy schedule or an emergency, I block out a couple of morning hours to spend time in the stables. And if there's nothing pressing for the next hour or so, I like to do physical work on the ranch. The medical practice comes first, of course, but I believe in balance in all things, and a good part of my balance is tied to the ranch. Oh, and I do house calls in the evenings."

"Seriously? You make house calls?"

"Comes with the job when your medical practice is

so spread out. It's necessary out here, and it gives me a chance to get off the ranch. It's especially nice if I can ride my horse."

"Tennessee cowboy doctor," she commented. The image of him on a horse was...nice. "In some parts of the medical world you'd be laughed at for your old-school ways."

"I have a surgical practice in New York and I can pretty well guarantee my patients there wouldn't care to see me ride up on my horse."

At his mention of New York a chill shot up her spine. That got her right back to his sperm donation—in a New York clinic—and the fact that she was carrying his baby. All of it a wet blanket effect that caused her to straighten up on the swing, kick off the casual stance and don the starched one. "Yet here you are in Sugar Creek, being a country GP. How is that working out for you?"

"Let's just say I'm still getting used to it. Still trying to get myself settled into it after almost a year. And still trying to figure out whether or not I'll succeed in it, as part of me is still city surgeon. But all that said, I do like the lifestyle I have here. I've never worked harder in my life, and never had such a sense of...freedom."

Was this a good idea? Sitting here, actually getting to know the baby's father—when her only intention had been to come here and observe from afar, maybe sample some of the local flavor and hope to pick up a few tidbits about him as she did. Never had she planned on...well, this!

Deanna, I don't know what to do. I just got a phone call from the clinic. The baby you're carrying isn't Alex's. There was a name mix-up. Similar names, I think.

Emily's words had started a nightmare that had ended right here in Sugar Creek, on the porch, sitting comfortably next to her. "Yet you don't know if you're staying or going?"

"I love it here. Always have. But loving it and settling down here are two different things and I'm not sure if I'm cut out to be a country doctor for the rest of my life. In fact, I'd never really thought much past New York until I got the call that Brax had had a stroke and I was needed home for a while." He shrugged. "You do what you have to do, and for now this is what I have to do."

"Well, New York certainly has its charms." Charms she loved probably as much as Beau did. So she could understand his conflict. Uprooting a life was never easy and most of the time it came with a lot of trepidation. She'd had her fair share of that, although not so much now that she was here, enjoying the cabin, enjoying the view. Even enjoying the company of Emily's baby's daddy.

"So does Sugar Creek. Different charms, though, depending on what you want from your life. But things change. People change. Life changes and you either stay even with it or you get left behind."

"But can you really ever get ahead of it?" That had never been the case for her, but her life was different now and she hoped that somehow, some way she could get ahead of it. Lead the situation rather than allowing the situation to lead her. That's what coming to Sugar Creek was really about. Her attempt to get ahead of it. Finding out everything she could about Emily's baby's father was what would help her do just that.

Getting to know Beau Alexander was where she had started. That push in the right direction.

"Better to spend your time trying than falling further and further behind, I suppose. So now all I have to do is convince myself that settling down here in Sugar Creek isn't the same thing as getting left behind, and I'll be good. Although a year into the quest and I'll have to admit that the things I want to keep ahead of are changing."

"Sounds to me like you're trying to reconcile yourself to staying."

He sighed heavily but it was a contented sigh, not one out of exasperation. "Maybe I am. Duty calls, you know. And it's a pretty strong call when there's no one else to take care of the people around here. Besides, I owe it to Brax to do the right thing for him. He was the stalwart force in my life when everything else was going to hell and for that reason the adjustments aren't as difficult as they might be otherwise."

"You call your grandfather by his name?"

"There weren't any women in our lives…not for very long anyway. So we never stood on formalities. Al was my dad. Brax my grandfather… We're both Braxton Beauregard Alexander. And I'm the ninth in line to get the name."

"Braxton Alexander," she said. Alexander Braxton— Braxton Alexander. Sure, there was an uncanny similarity of names, but mixing them up? *Having a baby this way was Emily's idea, not mine. So do any damned thing you want, Deanna. Keep it, get rid of it. It's not mine and I don't care.* Even now, remembering Alex's words chilled her to the bone.

"Look Deanna, I didn't come up here to bore you all the details of my family name or how I need to decide what I'm going to do with my life. When Brax heard there was a pretty young nurse staying in the cabin, he insisted I come and invite you to breakfast, so...consider yourself invited.

"And as I said, we don't stand on formality around here. You're welcome to wander down the mountain for any meal we put on the table. No invite necessary." He grinned. "Unlike back in New York, where you'd probably be admitted for a psych evaluation for showing up unannounced and without an invitation."

"My New York's not that rigid. But, then, I don't encompass much of New York in my interests or lifestyle so that pretty well limits me. That, or we just run in different circles."

"Funny. I didn't take you for the kind of person who would limit herself in anything."

"There are lots of different kinds of limits, Beau. I think I've chosen mine to fit what I need."

"But what about what you want?"

Deanna thought about that for a moment, pondered the many things she wanted but wouldn't allow herself to have. Ultimately, what you wanted hurt the most when you lost it and, in her experience, she always lost it. So why invest in her wants when the outcome was a given?

OK, so that was the dreary side of life showing itself, but in this case dreary was practical. It worked. And there was no need for him to know any of this because he was now, in some inexplicable fashion, tied up in her list of wants. She wanted to be around him, get to know him. Make sense of him so she could come to know Emily's baby in some way. "What I want? Right now, it's to get to work. It's not getting done with me sitting out here staring at the morning."

"All work, no play should make you hungry, so how about that breakfast invitation?"

She was hungry, she had to admit. But to insert herself into the heart of the Alexander clan? Although Beau's grandfather was family to this baby, too. But this was too much, too soon. "I, um…I appreciate the offer. But, like I said…"

"Your book awaits."

"No, not a book. More like a report. I'm a nurse researcher, and I work for a group of physicians who have a very specific vision about getting better healthcare to places that don't have it. You know, rural populations, isolated areas. So to that end I do the preliminary research, write the papers and journal articles that will bring in the financial donors for various projects. Sometimes I lecture, and every other semester I teach a class."

"Sounds complicated."

"Not really. Not when you know what you're doing."

"And you're pretty good?"

"I'm pretty good."

"Like the Ellerby Project in West Virginia, where you found funding for Dr. Louis Ellerby to start a clinic in an area that hasn't seen convenient healthcare in a century?"

"You've read about me?"

"About your work. Last night at the hospital, while I waiting for Mack to come out of surgery. Although I'll admit I did some internet searching on you and came up with…practically nothing."

That was a relief. She was still concerned, though, that he'd been digging around into her past, as bland as it was. Although turnabout was fair play, since she'd been digging into his past. "Just the way I like it." She was a little uncomfortable, though, knowing he was *looking* at her.

"Being in the background?"

"Not in the background. As often as not I get to implement one of my projects and see it come to life. But I don't like…fuss."

"Are you here in Sugar Creek to *fuss*? You know, find a problem with our healthcare and fix it?"

It hadn't occurred to her he might think that. Or that her presence here could look like she was on a project. "No, I'm here to… I just needed time away from the city. I've got some decisions to make about my future, sort of like what you're doing, and I'm in the middle of a move when I get back home. So, basically, I needed a break. Sugar Creek seems the perfect place for that and, as far as I can see, it's in good hands, medically speaking. You may be spread too thin, but compared to some of the places I've been…"

Suddenly, Beau sat bolt upright and twisted to face her. "Work for me," he interrupted, not sure why he'd just made the offer. "I know you didn't come here to work, and I'm not even sure why I'm asking. But I am. So, come and work for me, Deanna."

"What? I mean…I don't understand."

"You look for solutions, and I need to see if a nurse, or even a second doctor, would be my solution here. And I don't mean full time. Just spend a couple hours a day in the clinic to see some of the lesser cases. Maybe a house call or two. To see if my problem can be fixed."

"Your problem?"

"A grandfather who doesn't want anybody in the practice. He's old-school, a one-man show. And critical of how I'm running his practice. The thing is, for me to stay here I've got to find a way to appease him and still run things the way I need to, and right now I'm drowning. He says it's because I'm unfocused, but I say it's because we exist in two different medical worlds, and that the day of the solitary GP is over. Medicine has more, it's expanded since Brax was my age, and while in knowledge it hasn't left him behind, in practice it has.

"But I have to prove that to him, let him see something that makes him understand that I have to do things my way or I won't be able to stay here. Then Sugar Creek turns into one of those problems you're sent to solve."

"And with me working for you…"

"You'll see both sides, where he's wrong, where I'm wrong. That's what I need."

"Then you think he's entirely wrong and you're entirely right? Is that the premise I have to work with if I take this on?"

Of course he was right. But he just didn't know where he was wrong or else he'd fix it. "Let's just say Brax and I share a certain stubbornness, which is probably working against both of us."

"No probably about it. Too much ego hurts the practice."

He chuckled. "See, that's what I mean. We need that kind of observation. And I'm willing to pay for it. I read about this clinic you're trying to expand in Wyoming. It needs a small surgery. Work for me, and it's funded."

"Just like that? I give you a few hours and you give me a surgery?"

"And a new exam room. The article said you wanted to expand by adding one more exam room."

Well, one thing was certain. He was catching her attention with his offer. "You know how to make a hard-to-refuse offer, don't you?"

"Well, I thought about it, rejected it, thought about it again, and…" He shrugged. "Never hurts to try."

"I'm not even sure I've got time…"

"Make time," he said earnestly. "Whatever you can spare. Work any time you're able, fit it into your schedule, not mine."

"As tempting as this is, you have to know one thing. If I do this, and I'm not saying I will, but if I do I'll be fixing a professional problem," she warned. "Not a personal one between you and your grandfather. That's for you two to sort out."

But with the professional fix would come the personal fix, he hoped. He really did love the old guy, but loving him and trying to run his medical practice were two entirely different things. And their problems with the practice were beginning to affect their relationship.

"You're right. It is. But it's complicated, Deanna, because it's hard to separate one from the other. If we can get the problems with the practice sorted and come to some kind of understanding, I'm sure Brax and I will go back to normal. So, yes, all professional."

"Before I commit to anything, let me ask you one simple question. Do you want to stay here? You sound like someone who does, yet I'm sensing a streak of resistance."

It wasn't a simple question, because he was torn. He'd hoped, when he'd come home, that his sentiments would swing harder one way or the other while he was here, but that hadn't happened. And he was down to the wire now.

His partners wanted him back or they wanted his resignation so they could turn their temporary replacement for him in to a permanent member of the staff. And the medical practice here needed someone who could make the firm commitment. So, no, that wasn't a simple question at all. In fact, it was the hardest one he'd ever had to think over.

"Ideally, I could have both worlds—the one I have in New York and the one I'm trying to find here. That said, I know I can't, so my preference would be..." He shrugged. "That's what I'm trying to find out because I'm really straddling the fence."

"Like personal heart in one place and professional heart in another?"

"See, you do understand."

"The easy decision would be to flip a coin. Then you wouldn't have to buy me a new exam room and a surgical suite in Wyoming." She smiled. "Although getting that exam room and surgery would *so* uncomplicate my life right now. Save me half the work I brought with me to do."

"Which means you'll do it because you're about to have some spare time?"

"Which means I'll think about it. That's all I can say right now."

"Then how about you think about it over breakfast, and meet Brax?"

"I do have to eat, don't I? It's good for the..." She broke off her words and sighed as she glanced down the mountain then waved at the old man again, in case he was watching. "Good for me. It's good for *me*."

That's when Beau saw her drift away for a moment, thinking about something else, something profoundly sad and far away. It was perceptible in her eyes. In the way her shoulders slumped. He understood anger, and rage. He'd lived his entire life with an undertow of restlessness and discontent.

But sadness hadn't touched him, except for that one moment when he'd realized that his marriage had been about betrayal, not commitment. And even then that sadness had turned into intense distrust. But the sadness he saw in her…he didn't understand it. It was so deep, and so close.

"Before I meet him, will he be good with this, Beau? Your grandfather? Will he accept an outsider coming in and making suggestions as he's resisting *your* suggestions?"

"If you work for me, you won't be an outsider. And he's not an ogre. Just stubborn. But he'll listen to you because…"

"Because I don't share his stubbornness, like you do."

"You have a way with words," he said, standing up. "Very direct."

She laughed. "Very direct, and no partiality. As they say in today's vernacular, that's the way I roll."

Well, he was beginning to like the idea that Deanna had rolled into his life, even if it was only his professional life. Working with her for a while, whatever the reason, would be nice. For her nursing skills.

And maybe the pleasure of her company. Because he sure did like that as well.

Deanna refused yet another biscuit as she shoved away her plate. "That was amazing," she said, as Vera Holland, the Alexander housekeeper, tried ladling one last scoop of fresh fruit into Deanna's bowl. "But I can't eat another bite…for a week."

Brax laughed out loud. "You eat breakfast with us often enough and you'll see just how small your appetite is compared to the rest of us. Beau's slowed down, though, since he's been back."

"I like bagels," Beau defended. "Got used to them when I lived in New York. Give me a good, fresh poppyseed bagel, some cream cheese…"

Brax snorted. "City ways."

"Maybe, but your country ways will make me fat and lethargic. And, Deanna, we don't usually eat like this… eggs, bacon, biscuits, grits… It was going to be simple until I told Brax who you were and what you might do to help us, then he decided put on the spread to impress you because he wants to lure you over to his side."

"His side?" she asked setting down her glass of fresh orange juice. "How so?"

"My grandson doesn't think the way I ran my medical practice is good enough," Brax cut in.

Brax bit the inside of his cheek to stop himself from saying something he'd regret. Loving the old man was one thing, but too often lately tolerating him was difficult. Instead, he looked over at Deanna, who gave him a barely perceptible nod, like she understood. "What I think, Brax, is that I need to get out to the stables for a few minutes. If Deanna would care to join me…"

"You've avoiding the issue," the old man warned him.

"Not avoiding it. Just skirting around it until later."

"Now or later. We've got to deal with this, son."

"Which is why I'm here," Deanna chimed in. "To sort it out and hope you both listen to me."

"Then you've decided to do it?" Beau asked, glad and surprisingly excited. Holding the emotion in reserve, of course. "You've decided to work here for a while?"

"I think it's probably the best way to get up close and personal with the both of you. And stay impartial." She gave Brax a particularly pointed glance on that note. "So, yes, for a little while."

"Excellent. I think we'll have hotcakes for breakfast tomorrow morning," Brax said enthusiastically.

"I think I'll have yogurt, alone in my cabin tomorrow morning," Deanna countered as she scooted way from the table and gathered up her dishes. "Working here is one thing but fraternizing is another, if I want to be objective. And I want to be objective."

For the first time in weeks it felt like half the load had been lifted from his shoulders, and Beau was grateful for that. Grateful for Deanna stepping in. Honestly, he didn't know if there was anything she could really do about solving the problem here, but just having her understand and evaluate it made him feel ten times better. Gave him some hope.

Because on the surface, the problem looked pretty grave. The old man had practically raised him. Brax had turned his life inside out to always be there for a sad little boy who'd had an irresponsible father. And yet now, when his grandfather needed his patience and understanding, it seemed like he didn't have enough of it to give.

The compromises should have come easier, but they hadn't. The communication between them should have been better, but it wasn't. So, was this something Deanna, an outsider, could fix, or even nudge along in the right direction? Hell if he knew. But he was relieved more than he'd thought he would be because she just… He glanced at her walking into the kitchen with an armload of dishes, then noticed the twinkle in his grandfather's eyes. Deanna just fit. That's what it was. She just fit.

"You've got that look, Beau," Brax commented once Deanna was out of earshot.

"What look?"

"*That* look. One I used to see in you from time to time before you married the shrew."

"You mean admiration for a pretty girl? Hell, yes, I have it. Deanna's easy on the eyes."

Brax chuckled. "If that's what you want to tell yourself, fine. She's easy on the eyes. I'll agree. But that look…you're thinking of her in different terms, aren't you?"

"I'm thinking of her as the nurse who's going to drum some sense into that thick skull of yours, old man." He gave his grandfather an affectionate squeeze on the shoulder then headed for the door. "When she comes out of the kitchen, tell her I'm out on the porch, and I'd like her to join me."

"Like I said," Brax said.

"Like you said…nothing. Leave it alone, Brax. OK? Just leave it alone." Easier said than done. Because his grandfather did care, did want Beau to be happy.

No more than Beau himself did, though. Absolutely no more than Beau did.

"He's…" The word wasn't *stubborn*, even though Brax was stubborn. But she didn't want to be insulting because she liked the man. Saw a lot of Beau in him. "Formidable. Very strong-willed."

Beau chuckled. "You're trying to be nice."

"Maybe I am, but I like him, Beau. He's a lot like you. Or, should I say, you're a lot like him."

"I've been called worse."

Propped casually against the porch rail, leaning back against it yet not sitting, arms folded across his chest, feet crossed at the ankles...he was stunning. Especially with the way the morning sun kindled golden highlights in his otherwise dark brown hair.

He had a hard, chiseled look to him, and contrasted with Emily's softness, her pale skin and blonde hair, Deanna was sure the baby would be beautiful with the looks of either parent. Or both. "It's a compliment. And you're lucky to have him, Beau, stubborn or not."

"Don't know what I'd do without him," he admitted. "My mom died when I was a baby, and my dad spent most of my formative years trying to forget he had a kid. So Brax was the one who got me through the rough patches, especially when I was on the verge of turning into a juvenile delinquent."

"You were not!" she exclaimed.

"Worst kid in Sugar Creek. Ask anybody who remembers me. If there was trouble, I was either instigating it or in the middle of it." He smiled fondly. "I can remember maybe five or six times when Brax had to go down to the jail to get me out. And I'm not talking a hardened teenager getting thrown into jail. First time for me I was ten. I'd set one of the Founders' Day parade floats on fire."

So the baby would probably come with some feistiness. That was good to know.

"And they arrested you even though you were only ten?"

"More like locked me up until the parade was over so I didn't get into any more trouble. Then I got to wash Mr. Gentry's front window—he owned the bakery—once a week for a year because it was his float I burned down."

"And yet you didn't learn your lesson, did you?"

"About fires, yes. Didn't set another one. But there were other incidents. Mrs. Duncan's favorite porch rocker mysteriously ending up in the top of a tree. Mr. Baxter's car parked in Miss Monroe's front yard one morning…he was the very married school principal, she was the very single kindergarten teacher who was having an affair with him. Little town scandal revealed because I'd learned how to hotwire a car. Oh, and all the fire hydrants on Main Street being painted pink one night. To name a few incidents."

OK, so maybe feisty wasn't quite the best way to describe it. Creative. Yes, he was creative. A very appealing trait she would most definitely have to direct in the baby. "You terrorized the poor little town, yet look at you smile."

"I smiled then, too, until I got thrown into jail. Then it was all frowns and shaking because I knew what Brax would do when he came to get me out."

"What?"

"Hard physical labor. Mending fences, cutting back the brush line. Back-breaking work for anybody, and almost impossible for someone young and scrawny, like I was."

She had a hard time imagining him scrawny. "Yet you were a repeat offender."

"That I was."

"And if I were a psychologist, I'd say there was definitely a pattern there. Some kind of emotional process you were trying to work out."

"If you were a psychologist, you'd probably be right. But you're not. You're the nurse who's going to fix another of my problems."

"Who's going to *try* and fix another of your problems. No guarantees. I'll do the best I can, but I'm dealing with two very stubborn men who, I guess, have a long history of inflexibility. Am I right?"

He pushed away from the porch rail and glanced down toward the stables. "Care for a morning ride?"

OK, so he may not have answered her question, but his lack of an answer spoke volumes. No, it shouted. But she liked challenges. And the father of the baby she was carrying was definitely going to present her with a huge challenge.

"Sounds lovely, but no. I've got to get back to my cabin. You're not the only one who employs me, and I've got some calls to make." But a ride around the ranch might have been nice had she ever been on a horse before or had she not been pregnant. "And if you want me to work a few hours in your clinic every day, I've got to get a jump on everything else when I can. But I appreciate the offer. Oh, and so you'll know, I'll take on some house calls with you. That actually sounds fascinating. But not on horseback."

"I have an SUV, if that works for you? Or a truck, or my self-indulgent little sports car my grandfather calls an abomination to four wheels and a drive shaft. Take your pick."

"An SUV is just fine. Or walking, if it's not too far."

"Whatever you wish. But the horse option is always open."

What she wished for was a healthy baby. What she also wished for was getting to know the baby's father. Simple things. At least, she hoped they were simple.

Suddenly, nothing seemed simple. Not one blessed thing in her life.

CHAPTER FOUR

IF HE DIDN'T stop staring up at her cabin, he wasn't going to get anything done. Two of the horses still needed their morning workout, and there was a fence section out on the back forty he hadn't gotten to and probably wouldn't for a day or two. There was too much to do to kill time the way he'd been doing this morning.

Sure, it was all hands-on work he could have Joey or someone else do, but one of the reasons he liked being back here was that he got to flex different muscles. He'd done it when he'd been young, gotten himself all buff doing it. Then medical school and even during his short tenure as general surgeon in New York had changed all that. No more tough physical work. No more ripped muscles. He'd grown soft. Too soft, without the necessary hours to remedy the abdomen that was no longer a six-pack and the pecs that weren't quite as firm.

It hadn't mattered because he hadn't cared. Being on the margin of well toned had been good enough. Now he wanted to be toned and perfect again, the way he'd been a decade ago. No reasons or excuses necessary, and he sure as hell wasn't conceding the coincidence of Deanna's arrival. It was simply time, that was all.

So, after years of relying on his brain rather than his

brawn, he was being hit by this sudden urge to work himself back into shape, and this was where he could do that. But not if he kept standing here, staring up at her cabin.

"She's not up there, if that's what you're looking for. I saw her in town when I came through a while ago."

"I'm not looking for her," Beau said, even though that's exactly what he'd been doing. "Just…resting." At eleven in the morning. Like Joey was going to believe that.

"Well, looking or not, she's the prettiest woman I've seen around here in a long time. Sure glad the one you married the first time didn't ruin you for something else in the future." He glanced up the incline to the cabin and smiled. "Like the pretty little nurse you're *not* hoping to see."

Beau turned to face him. "Everybody knew Nancy was bad except me. Would have been nice if somebody had mentioned that to me before I married her."

"No, sir. You were staring cross-eyed at her, and it's not smart to come between a man and the woman he's looking at that way."

"Live and learn," Beau muttered, anxious to get off the subject. He didn't like talking about Nancy or thinking about her. "So let me get back to the horses. Onyx still needs a ride, so does Cashew, and I'm running out of time. I've got patients coming in early today."

"You're running out of time because you've been staring too long at her cabin." Joey chuckled. "And didn't she just leave here three hours ago?"

Beau dug deep for a comeback that would silence the man on the subject once and for all, but when nothing was forthcoming, Joey forged ahead. "Anyway, only because I think it's time you do more than stare, I'll exercise the horses and you can get yourself ready to see her when she comes to work later on. You know, get all primpy in front of the mirror…"

His chuckle turned into a belly laugh as he spun around and headed off in the opposite direction.

"I don't primp," Beau yelled after him.

"Neither do I," Deanna said, entering the stable from the other direction. "Decided a long time ago that with me it's the natural look or nothing."

Beau spun around to face her. "You're early."

"Actually, you never specified an exact time. So I'm neither early nor late. But I got everything done I needed to this morning, ran to the store in town, and decided to come here instead of going back up to the cabin for another hour or so."

Her gait was deliberately cautious and slow on the straw as she approached Beau. And so sexy he caught himself staring again.

"My first patient's due in about an hour, but you can work the hours that are best for your schedule. I'm grateful, not picky." His eyes darted to Joey, who popped back into the doorway behind Deanna, grinned, and gave him a thumbs-up. "But since you're here, I think it would be a good time to get yourself familiar with our medical set-up."

"Just point me to your fleams and blood-letting cups," she teased, referring to antique medical devices.

"We're a century or so past that," he said, laughing as he pulled a handful of sugar from his pocket then walking over to Nell's stall, where the heavily pregnant horse stretched her neck out to take it from his hand. "But sometimes I don't think so."

"Ah, that would be your attempt to sway me? Or, at least, prejudice me? And without the offer of future breakfasts?"

"How about the offer of dinner after our last house call this evening? Would that work for you?"

"We have a house call?"

"Five, if you want to go with me."

"I'll go, but not by horse. Remember?"

She walked up to Nell and stroked her muzzle, and moved in closer when she discovered the mare was as gentle as a kitten. Which put her in almost intimate proximity to Beau. He could smell her shampooed hair, feel the heat her body radiated. She was oblivious, standing there, making up to Nell. But he wasn't oblivious. In fact, he was so aware of her every nuance he had to take a step back. "Not by horse," he managed to say, hoping his voice didn't sound too adolescently squeaky.

"They're beautiful animals, though," she said, holding out her hand to him for some lumps of sugar. "I've always liked horses…in literature and movies. Never ridden one, being the city girl that I am, but I always thought I might like to learn someday. So, if I feed her this sugar she won't bite my hand, will she?"

He surrendered the sugar carefully, dropping each of the four lumps precisely, one by one, into her open palm so he didn't come into too much contact with her. "She's the soul of gentleness. Probably the sweetest horse I've ever known."

"And you've been around horses all your life, right?" Her first attempt to open her hand to Nell was met with skittishness, not by Nell but by Deanna, who pulled back before Nell could take the sugar. "Sorry, I'm a little nervous. This is as close as I've ever been to an animal this large. Will you show me how?"

He did. Placed four lumps in his own hand and gave the sugar to Nell, hand open and palm up. "It's easy," he said, handing another couple of cubes to Deanna. "Just relax and let Nell do the work."

Deanna smiled self-consciously, but still wasn't able to bring her hand all the way over to the mare's reach, so Beau took hold of her hand and guided it to the horse. And held it as the horse very gently lifted her lips and took the sugar lumps.

"That's amazing," she whispered, as the last of the sugar disappeared from her hand. "I can see why you love them."

"First time I was on horse was with Brax," he said, slowly pulling his hand away from hers, glad to break the contact. "I was three, I think. Probably too young for most contemporary parental thinking, but he took care of me. Put me up on the saddle with him, and we only went around the yard. Didn't get past the driveway. But I felt so…free. And invincible, like I could do anything.

"Of course, Brax inspired that confidence in me as much as the horse did. But I was having a rough life and I think that's the first time I ever truly understood that things would work out for me, no matter what was scaring me, because my grandfather would take care of me."

"I'm sorry," she said, wiping the horse slobber from her hand on a rag Beau had handed her. "It's a rough way to grow up, but you were lucky in ways so many kids aren't. I've seen them abandoned, left to fend for themselves, raise younger siblings, go to work when they're supposed to be going to school. I think we take a roof over our heads and a meal on our tables for granted too often."

"True colors," Beau commented, stepping away from Nell's stable, satisfied she wouldn't foal in the next twenty-four hours and anxious to get away from the spell Deanna was casting over him. And she wasn't even trying, unlike Nancy, who'd come at him with every flirtatious trick in the book. But Deanna was so...so unassuming, so unaware of what her closeness could do to a man.

"I'm sorry?"

"Brax always taught me that a person's true colors reflected the deep-down self that comes out naturally, when they're not trying to impress or intimidate someone. Your true colors are nice. Very compassionate."

"I didn't have parents either. They were killed when I was five, and my aunt and uncle took me in and gave me that roof and food. So I was lucky, like you were with Brax, but Brax wanted you, whereas my aunt and uncle didn't want me.

"I was an obligation for them to fulfill and I think that's where my true colors, as you call them, came from—from my need to fix situations that others can't, or don't want to, fix. Growing up, my situation was never truly fixed. Anyway, why don't you finish up what you're doing here, and I'll go wash my hands then take a look at your office, see what's there, and check out what I'm going to be dealing with?"

"It's the white building out at the side of the house. Two exam rooms, one room for emergencies, and one for minor procedures. Waiting room, small office and a supply room. It was the original house here, and Brax turned it into his clinic when he built the house he's in now…for my grandmother. She refused to live in the place where he worked."

He fished a set of keys from his pocket and tossed them to Deanna. "Make yourself at home. Today's schedule is on the computer…my addition to the practice because Brax prefers keeping everything on paper. Password to log on is Alexander."

"Trying to sway me again?" she teased.

"Maybe a little."

"Well, between us, I prefer the computer to pen and paper, so that's a point in your favor."

With that, she exited. Didn't look back. Didn't even hesitate like she wanted to look back. Just kept walking. Deliberately. Confidently.

"There something to be said for a filly that's reserved, the way she is," Joey said, coming out of the stable office.

"I thought you were exercising the horses."

"Can't do that without a horse, and I didn't want to interrupt you to walk through the stalls, so I…"

Beau waved him off before he could finish, then spun around and strode out the door. Truth was, Joey was hitting close to home with his comments. Too close, and it was getting to Beau in ways it shouldn't. "Not going near it," he muttered with iron resolve as he headed for the house. "Nope, not going near it." Then he caught sight of Deanna entering the clinic and stopped and simply stared again. "Not going near it," he muttered again, but this time the resolve wasn't quite there.

So far, the afternoon was going well. Easy work, all things considered, even though she was feeling the effects of it in her lower back. It had been a long time since she'd done any kind of consistent physical nursing duty and, so far, she was loving it. Three patients had already passed through the exam room she'd commandeered for herself—simple cases but rewarding.

And she'd assisted Beau with one sweet little lady, aged eighty, who traditionally should have been home knitting or baking cookies but who'd inhaled a few too many paint fumes, turning her kitchen from pale blue to sunny yellow. She was fine, a little light-headed, which was what had brought her to the clinic, and together Deanna and Beau had given her a complete exam, just to be on the safe side. Deanna had an idea that Mrs. Eloise Hightower probably marched right back home afterwards to finish her decorating and sniff more paint.

"Doing OK?" Beau asked, passing Deanna in the hall.

"Actually, I'm enjoying this. Is the pace always this laid back?"

He chuckled. "This is a vacation. I've had days where they're lined up outside. And I've just taken on another house call this evening."

"But not on horseback, right? Because expecting me to do anything more with a horse than give it sugar lumps will subtract countless points from your side." A sly smile crossed her lips. "Keep that in mind, Doctor."

"I am, which is why we're going by SUV, like I promised. Don't want to evoke the wrath of the medical-practice arbiter, do I?"

"No wrath in me," she said as she disappeared into the supply closet to fetch forceps and all the other necessities required to extract one very large splinter from one little toe. "At least, not yet," she called over her shoulder, then laid her hand across her belly.

"He wants to get me…which would be *us*…up on a horse. Which I'm not going to do because, well, you know the reasons. But you should probably also be aware that your daddy's a little bit of a cowboy. Very handsome, too, in the rugged cowboy sense. He's not ready to admit what he wants though, and stand by it, because it conflicts with everything he's planned for himself. I think we all face that at one time or another, don't we?"

Deanna assessed for a baby bump, a little disappointed she wasn't feeling it yet, although she did feel life, and a deep sense of contentment. "You're not what I had planned either, but I'm happy." Happier now that she had a better sense of Beau. She liked him and, truthfully, she could go home tomorrow assured that this baby had the best coming from both parents.

But what about Beau? That was the question still plaguing her. Did he need to know about the baby? Did he even want to know? It had been her decision to come and find him but, as far as she knew, it was still his decision to be anonymous. Which made this tough.

He's living in a backwoods area called Sugar Creek, Tennessee, Miss Lambert. Working as the area doctor, I believe. Words from the private investigator she'd hired to find Braxton Alexander, after her lawyer had obtained the information.

Sure, she could have bought more information, probably paid for a life history, including all the nuances. But that had seemed wrong to her. Seemed too intrusive, especially as Braxton Alexander—Beau—had been an unidentified donor prior to her search.

We're sorry, Miss Lambert. Those records are confidential. We informed Mrs. Braxton of the paternity error because of the legalities involved. But we do not divulge identities, even in cases such as this.

Cases such as this…one lawyer and one private investigator later and here she was, walking through a perfect, tidy little doctor's office, getting ready to treat one of that error's patients.

And, admittedly, she was a little excited to do so. This was nice. All of it. The waiting area was small but cozy. Both exam rooms basic but stocked with everything a GP would need.

And Beau's office… She stepped inside and looked around on her way to yank the splinter. To the left was a wooden shelf filled with medical texts, some very old, some much newer. Two generations of learning, she guessed. Then there was the wall of certificates and diplomas. All bearing the name Braxton Beauregard Alexander. Some yellowed through the glass, some more pristine.

It was all Emily's baby's heritage, she thought as she ran her fingers over the glass covering Beau's medical diploma. It was also something that made her feel even more…conflicted. "I'll figure it out," she told the baby. "Give me time, and I promise I'll figure out what I'm supposed to do."

"It's really pretty simple," Beau said from the doorway.

She spun to face him, and he almost took her breath away he was so handsome. Something she'd already known, something she still wasn't getting over. "Wh-what?"

"The splinter. Sterilize it, give it tug if it's visible. If it's not, come get me and I'll make a cut…"

She shook her head. "I know how to remove a splinter. I was just wondering…" She looked back at all the diplomas of the two Braxton Alexanders, M.D. "It's easier if I don't know the people involved. I'm great at the impersonal decisions, but this is going to get personal, which means it's going to get complicated. I like Brax. And you. And it's like I'm the referee in the ring, ready to call the winner the one who comes out hitting the hardest. I'm not sure I can do it."

"Then don't. Either way, I promised you the surgery and exam room in Wyoming, and you'll get them."

"Without doing anything? Because so far I've treated sniffles and a scraped knee."

He smiled. "I need help, Deanna. But not at the cost of making you uncomfortable. So if you can't work here, I'll understand. And if you can't make suggestions about how Brax and I can work out our differences, I'll understand that as well."

"I want to," she said. And she did. But how could she be objective when every time she looked at Beau her breath caught and every time she thought about him she remembered that he was the father of Emily's baby? It was crazy. Mixed up. Her pregnancy hormones weren't helping any by kicking in so often.

Yet she didn't want to leave. She knew what she needed to know, had seen what she needed to see, and still didn't to leave. "I'm not backing out of the agreement but just so you'll know, it's tough enough without you and Brax both trying to score points with me."

"Then I won't."

"As simple as that?" she asked.

"Simple as that." Rather than shaking hands with her when he extended his hand to hers, he held out a different set of forceps. "More precise than what you've got.

Those belong to my grandfather, these belong to me. And that's not meant to sway you but to put the best surgical instrument in your hand."

"Good thing," she said, taking the instrument then scooting around him, practically holding her breath until she was well out of his sight.

"I've got to get over this," she said to the baby as she opened the door and greeted ten-year-old Tommy Dodson, whose foot was propped up on the exam table, his hand firmly in the clutch of a very nervous-looking mother.

The mother-child bond, she thought as she commenced prepping Tommy's toe. *It was a strong one.* And she looked forward to its tug. She also felt guilty, and that's the part that held her back. No matter how much she wanted this baby, she wanted Emily to have it even more. But that wasn't going to happen, was it?

"So tell me again how you got the splinter in your little toe. Something about climbing barefoot on the wood pile...?"

"It's crazy, trying to do so many things all at once," Deanna said, shrugging out of her white coat and hanging it on a hook on the back of the supply-room door, only to miss the hook and watch it slither to the floor.

"How do you keep up with it? Actually, how did your grandfather keep up with it? And he didn't use a computer for the paperwork." She'd seen five scheduled patients and three who'd just walked in. Plus two telephone consults. And Beau had doubled that during his afternoon.

"It's not meant to sway you but I keep up with it by avoiding the personal things that can get in the way.

Like chitchat. I've found that if you ask Mrs. Milford how her cat's feeling today, or inquire about the status of Mr. Blanchard's latest carpentry undertaking, they'll tell you. At length. My grandfather did that, and I don't recall him ever seeming rushed. But it rushes me then I get grumpy, and all that shoots the day right out from under me. So, no chitchat."

Bending to pick up the lab coat, she felt a sharp jab in her back and gasped. "But he got through the day chitchatting and still delivered good medicine. So tell me how he did that, because I'd like to know." She grabbed the coat and straightened up, still fighting the kink that seemed to be becoming a permanent part of her back lately.

"You OK?" Beau asked, stepping up to her and grabbing hold as she finally made it back to fully upright.

"Nothing a nice long soak in a tub full of hot water wouldn't cure." Except, like horseback riding, that was off limits.

"Got a hot tub, if you're interested."

And it sounded so tempting, unfortunately... "Thanks, but there's one up at the cabin, if I want to use it." Which she wouldn't.

"Let me guess. You avoid hot tubs the way you do horseback rides?"

"What I avoid is wasting time, which is what we're doing, especially since I'd like to get your house calls done before tomorrow morning."

"And dinner," he reminded her. "There's a little roadside stop halfway back from our last house call, and it overlooks, well..." He pointed out the window to the mountains. "More of that, only closer."

More of that was exactly what she needed. After

such a short time here, she was already becoming addicted to the area—the mountains and trees, the lovely little stream that ran through the valley. Even the birds.

Except for the isolation, it was everything she wanted, not just for herself but for Emily's baby. It crossed her mind that if she did tell Beau this baby was his, he might want shared custody. Which meant Emily's baby would have all this, provided Beau stayed here. It was something to consider, one thing amongst so many.

"It sounds lovely," she said, heading to the door. "I'm going to run back to my cabin, change my shoes, splash some water on my face, and I'll be good to go. And maybe by the time we're on our way I'll have an idea of what to do about the patients who stop in without appointments, because you'd have been in the clinic for hours still if I hadn't been there to help."

"I think a few people came out just to see you. Normally I don't have so many minor casualties."

"But today you did, and that's the problem. What if I hadn't been here and you'd had that many people waiting, plus your house calls?

"And, Beau, you're using the computer, which is good, but the problem is it takes ten minutes to get a patient checked in and out, and you're doing that yourself. It's something a medical receptionist could do, if you had one." Which really did sway her to his side, she had to admit.

Beau held up his hands in mock surrender, smiled, and said nothing.

"OK, point taken. You're not going to comment. I get it."

"You're right. No comment. I'll just say go get ready

for house calls, and I'll pick you up in thirty minutes. OK? And, Deanna…thanks. I'm not sure everything here is solvable, but I appreciate having someone who can see what frustrates me. And, no, that's not meant to sway you either. It's just a statement of fact and a hope that you can stay and figure out how to fix it because I know what I want, but I may be a little too involved to be as objective as I should be."

"You're not old-school medicine the way Brax is. Country GP has taken on a new definition, and Brax just hasn't come round to that. Which is fine because it works for him. But you're the new breed and that's good in so far as medical advances go, although I think in ways it's also a limiting on the personal level. The problem's easy enough to spot, although I'm not sure how easy it's going to be to fix. But medical solutions are what I do, so we'll see."

"Medical solutions, and making my day better. I'm probably going to thank you a thousand times over the next few weeks for doing this."

She smiled then waved him a quick goodbye and sprinted out the door. For what it was worth, he'd made her day better, too. Not just because he'd let her work in a different aspect of medicine than she was accustomed to but because he'd allowed her to see things she needed to see.

"I like your daddy," she said to the baby as she sped up the road to the cabin. "Now all we have to do is figure out if you'll ever have the opportunity to like him as well."

Late afternoon had taken on a cool edge, and Beau inhaled the pure mountain air deeply. It was good being home. He wasn't sure he could live up to the expectations of being the area's doctor but he didn't regret his temporary change of life.

He had big shoes to fill, though. Huge shoes, and most of the time people simply thought of him as the kid. Brax's grandson. Juvenile delinquent. So maybe his youthful reputation here hadn't been stellar, but Brax had handled it…had handled him. And he owed the old man more than he could repay.

He just wasn't sure, though, he could replace him. And that was the problem. If he stayed, new ways would have to replace the old. Deanna was seeing that, working directly in the middle of it. And he trusted her to make the right decisions.

But his grandfather was so resistant. Probably resentful that what had worked perfectly for him was being pushed aside. And there was no way in hell he would hurt his grandfather. That was the bottom line. In which case, maybe it would be easier to simply hire a doctor to come in and do the job at hand, and work with what was there, what was already established.

Someone else wouldn't be so…restless. And he was restless. Since his marriage and divorce, since his near—and fake—brush with fatherhood, it was like his world had turned upside down and had never quite righted itself. He wanted this life, he wanted his life back in New York. Wanted to be a country GP, wanted to be a surgeon. At the same time he didn't have a clue what he wanted.

So much indecision, all a year or more in the making, and he was no closer to figuring out what he was going to do now than he'd been a year ago when he'd come home.

And Deanna? He wasn't sure what he expected from her. Maybe someone who would support some tough changes that would have to happen if he stayed. Or support his decision to leave, if that's what it came to.

Maybe, though, she was a distraction. Something to take his mind off the things he didn't want to think about.

Whatever the case, Brax was on his way to town for the evening, and as he helped his grandfather out to the pick-up truck, Beau's gaze inadvertently went up to the ridge where Deanna's cabin loomed over the back acreage. Rather than looking away, he let himself stare for a moment—stare and wonder about the woman up there. She wasn't here to do what she claimed. He knew that and he believed she knew he knew. For now the illusion would stand, but he was curious.

"I can see why you'd enjoy coming out here to make house calls," Deanna said. She was seated next to Beau in his four-wheel-drive SUV, glad they were in something woods-worthy. "I'm not a deep-woods kind of a girl, but this is lovely."

Trees were so dense that the fading daylight trickled in only in ribbons. The undergrowth of rhododendrons with their lush purple flowers grew expansively under the thick green canopy. And there was a richness to the air that she'd never known could exist. These were the areas she cared about in her work yet they were areas she rarely ever saw, and being out in the thick of it made her feel very limited by her academic focus.

Deanna was gaining, first hand, a totally new understanding of what medical life in these isolated areas was like, and it made her wonder how much she was missing, both professionally and personally.

"It's a different way of life," Beau said. "When I was a kid, I couldn't wait to get out of here. But now it's nice to be back. Makes me realize just how hectic it is in the city."

"You thrive on hectic, though, don't you?"

"I thrive on work. If it's hectic, that's fine because it keeps me away from…"

"A personal life?" she ventured.

"I excel in medicine, but I don't excel in the personal. When I was a kid I was…let's call it antisocial. Found a certain confidence in it, I think."

"Yes, you did mention you were a troublemaker."

He chuckled. "I like to think of it as being a result of my father, but the reality is I was just a brat. That was my nature. But Brax taught me how to turn that into hard work, and showed me how hard work paid off. It was a better way."

"Then being at odds with him the way you are now makes you feel, what? Guilty?"

"Very perceptive, Nurse Lambert."

"Doesn't take a lot of perception to see it. But what I also see is two very stubborn men who are fighting *not* to meet in the middle." Would that stubbornness pass along to the baby?

"I've practiced medicine outside Sugar Creek, he hasn't."

"Which makes you right…in your opinion."

"Which makes me right as far as the way I want to work here. If I stay."

"So what it boils down to is your way or you leave. And you're hoping that my presence, and my professional recommendations, will substantiate your way."

Yes, *very* stubborn. But it was laced with determination and dedication, and she liked that quality in him. She hoped that, more than the stubbornness, would carry through to the baby.

"When you put it that way, it sounds pretty confrontational, doesn't it?" He slowed the SUV where the road turned into a barely passable path, then killed the engine. "Oh, and from here we walk. But it's only about a quarter-mile."

"Seriously, people live out here? How do they get in and out?"

"Back road. It's shorter, and steeper, and hell on a vehicle's suspension, so I prefer the longer, slower, easier road. And it's a pleasant walk, by the way."

"It had better be," she grumbled good-naturedly, grabbing her medical bag then sliding down to the ground. "Because this wasn't in my job description." Although, truth be told, she was looking forward to the hike. Working on her feet all day had only made her crave more and, for someone who spent a good part of her days at a computer, this was just what she and the baby needed.

"And, yes, it does sound confrontational. But sometimes we have to draw our line in the sand and stick to it, don't we? Even if the person on the other side is someone you love. Makes life interesting, I think."

"You're very cagey," he said, taking her medical kit and strapping it onto the backpack he'd slung over his shoulder. "And I have an idea if Brax had gotten to you first, you'd be wholeheartedly on his side."

"I don't take sides in my work. I do have opinions… objective opinions I offer the people who need my ideas.

And subjective opinions, which I keep to myself. But it's always about what's best for the medical community as a whole."

"But you favor Brax." Statement, not question.

"I favor whatever works best for Sugar Creek. I haven't seen enough yet to decide what I think it is. But I'll warn you it's going to involve compromises on both sides. Experience has taught me the best solution always does."

He laughed. "Like I said, cagey."

"Been called worse," she said, taking hold of the hand he extended her at the trail head and stepping lightly over the trunk of a fallen tree on which countless people had carved initials. She studied it for a moment. Smiled. Thought about all the people who'd hiked this trail before. Wondered about their names.

"Are your initials there?" she asked, once they cleared the spot and he'd let go of her.

"Nope. You carve your initials and that's…permanence. Not sure I'm ready for that yet."

"Does that have to do with your bad marriage?" she asked, fully realizing it was none of her business. But she wanted to take the liberty anyway, to find out more about this man. "Because the walk down that aisle means permanence, and you took that walk."

"In a weak moment. She was pretty."

"So beauty turned your head, but couldn't keep it turned?"

"Beauty married me for my money, as it turned out."

"And broke your heart?"

"Not that so much as embarrassed the hell out of

me. Look out for that root," he warned, reaching out to take her hand again.

She was glad to hold onto him, and it wasn't because of the trail. She liked his touch. Soft hands, but strong. Protective. Something she'd never really had in her life. "This is the first of six house calls?" she asked, stepping a little closer to him.

"The others aren't so isolated. Diabetes check, blood-pressure check, short procedures. Thought we'd get the most interesting case, and longest visit, out of the way first."

"Sounds like you look forward to this part of your grandfather's practice."

"Do I detect that you might be trying to trap me into some kind of confession?"

She laughed. "Just trying to point out that you like parts of his practice. That's all."

"What I like is simplicity in a system that works for me. That's the way I was in New York, and it's the way I am here. It's part of who I am. It became a bigger part, I think, after my marriage ended and I was trying to put back the pieces of me she'd taken away." He turned to look at her. "Have you ever been married?"

"No."

"Ever come close?"

"Not really. Haven't ever met someone I'd want to be that serious with."

"Maybe that's smart. Live your life for yourself, keep any involvement at arm's length. Because once you open that door and let it in…" He shrugged. Cringed. "Sometimes you can't stop the momentum. If it's what you want, that's fine. But if it's not, you're in more trouble than you ever knew could happen, and there's not always an easy way out of it."

"So, you're anti-marriage? Anti-relationship? Which one?"

"Neither, and both. I did it so badly the first time I'm not sure I'd trust myself to try it again."

"Which is why you need help with the decision on whether to stay here or go back to New York? You choose badly. Is that it?" He was insightful into his own process, but she wasn't thrilled about his conclusions because if she did decide to tell him about his baby, she wasn't sure how he'd take the news. There were moments when she thought he'd be thrilled, but now, hearing all this, she doubted he'd even want to know.

And his view on relationships as a whole was pretty discouraging. Maybe that's what bothered her most.

"I made a bad choice once and I'm trying to stop myself from doing it again."

"But you can't equate marriage to a medical practice."

"What I can equate, though, is blindness to blindness. I was blinded by Nancy. And I'm also blinded by my own likes and especially dislikes as a doctor. They're not that different from each other. I see what I want to see and put on blinkers to the rest. That's what I'm trying to overcome right now. With your help."

"With my help." She admired his openness. In her experience, most people either wouldn't admit their weaknesses or couldn't see them. Beau was extraordinary in this, though, and it was another nice trait she hoped would be passed to the baby. It also made her wish Beau could be the one to actually teach or nurture that strength in his child.

In fact, she wished for it so much she could almost picture Beau walking through these very woods hand in hand with a toddler, teaching him or her about life in general. Pointing out trees and birds and flowers. Stopping to examine a shiny rock or look at an ant scurrying its way home to its colony. It was such a nice image, it elicited a sigh from her.

"Tired?" he asked.

"A little bit. But I'm also wondering what's going to be interesting about this first house call."

Beau chuckled. "You'll see, in about five minutes."

And she did. After five minutes of idle chitchat and watching out for other tree roots and rocks hidden by vegetation, they came to a little cottage. A well-kept cottage, actually. It looked freshly painted. White. With green shutters. And totally out of place here, in the middle of the woods. No one around for miles. "So, who's our patient?"

"Arthur Jeremiah Handler."

"*The* Arthur Jeremiah Handler?" His paintings were legendary. And very, very expensive, as he only did one or two a year.

"He found this place when he was scouting a location to paint, and that was thirty-five years ago. I remember Brax bringing me up here, and it always seemed like such an adventure. Sometimes we'd camp out in Arthur's front yard for a night, build a huge bonfire, cook our dinner, sleep in a tent. Although I think Brax usually sneaked out after I went to sleep and stayed in Arthur's guest room."

"Then he's a recluse?"

"Not at all. He just likes separation when he's painting. When he's not painting, he lives in Paris."

"So I take it he's painting."

Beau nodded as he knocked on the door. "Chronic diabetes, by the way. He maintains it well here, but when he's in Paris…"

"When I'm in Paris the magnificent pastries are my comeuppance," Arthur Jeremiah Handler said, opening the door to them. "Beau, thanks for coming. Have you gotten yourself married again?" Arthur asked, first giving Deanna a very deliberate head-to-toe appraisal then pulling her into his ample embrace.

"Because this one is much better than the last one. Prettier. More intelligence in her eyes. Doesn't radiate distrust and manipulation the way your Nancy did."

"Not married," Deanne managed to squeeze out while still enfolded in his meaty arms. "Just working as his nurse."

"A nurse?" Arthur bellowed. He finally loosened his hug. "How's Brax handling that? Not good, I imagine."

"No, not good," Beau said, stepping inside then taking hold of Deanna's hand and pulling her well past Arthur. "And this is Deanna Lambert, by the way. She's a consultant for medical practices, and she's agreed to help me for the next month."

"Nice to meet you," Deanna said, looking around at the cottage. It was lush. Huge leather furniture. Antique brass figures everywhere. Rich-colored paintings she took to be Arthur's own work. All of it a man's world.

"Not as nice as it is to meet you," Arthur replied, wiggling very bushy white eyebrows at her. "Rare beauty such as yours is welcome in this home any time it presents itself on my doorstep."

"Knock off the charm, Arthur. Deanna's all business. Probably rather stick you with a lancet than listen to you."

She liked the fondness between the two men. Arthur, who was probably Brax's age, looked like Santa Claus, with a round belly and a white beard. And the most amazing, astute eyes. So much so they almost scared her. But he was an artist so he saw the world through an artist's eyes. Still, the way he was staring at her right now...

"If you insist on using the lancet, my dear, you may have any finger I possess," he said, holding out his right hand and turning it palm up for her. "In fact, you may have all of them, if you wish. But before you make me bleed, I think it's fair to warn you that I have indulged on the finest Paris has to offer and my test results here will reflect that I haven't eaten as wisely as I should."

"An A1C blood test will tell us everything we need to know about your eating, Mr. Handler," she said, pulling an alcohol swab from her kit, ripping it open then cleaning the tip of his index finger. "Unfortunately, I'm not prepared to do that kind of a blood draw here, so I may have to schedule you into the clinic in the very near future."

Pulling the lancet device from her kit, she anchored a fresh lancet in it then warned him, "Little stick." Said after the stick, actually. She waited five seconds for the results then said, "Normal."

"Of course it's normal. I'm always a good boy when I'm in Sugar Creek. By the way, Beau, does your nurse know I avoid doctors' offices?" Arthur asked. "Absolutely abhor those dismal little places. They're for sick people who have infectious coughs and other disgusting symptoms."

Beau chuckled. "But Deanna is pretty formidable, Arthur. If she schedules you an appointment, I wouldn't go up against her if I were you.

Arthur turned to regard Deanna and opened his mouth to protest, but she beat him to it. "A full panel of blood tests, Mr. Handler. And a routine EKG as well to rule out any heart problems that might result from those Paris indulgences. Things that can't be done on a house call. I have an opening for you next Monday. First thing in the afternoon, say, one o'clock. Shouldn't take more than an hour. So, may I count on you being there?"

"Miserable things those damned office appointments," he grumbled. "Besides, Brax and young Beau do a respectable job here so why drag me out for something I don't need?"

"But I've told you it was time you came in and had a proper physical," Beau interjected.

"To no avail, young man." He turned a pointed glance at Deanna. "And young woman. Because I will not cross the threshold to your clinic. Not next Monday. Not any Monday."

"And you thought Brax was stubborn," Beau commented to Deanna.

"Your grandfather is a mere amateur," Arthur said, "but I have perfected stubbornness to an art form."

"So, are you and your stubbornness ready for an exam, Arthur?" Beau asked.

"By an exam you mean…"

"An exam." Beau grinned. "Everything I can do on a house call."

"Then I'm going to have to ask your nurse to please go fix us a pot of tea because there are parts of myself I've never exposed to a woman, and never intend on exposing to a woman. And I'm not being a chauvinist, Miss Lambert. I'm merely trying to cling to the last shred of dignity a man my age has."

She liked him. Liked his manners, his charm. Especially liked his wit. "With cream, sugar, lemon?"

"Civilized, my dear. Cream, light sugar. Oh, and I've just pulled some fresh bread from the oven...yes, I do bake. It's a pity some woman didn't latch onto me in my prime.

"Anyway, please help yourself to whatever you want. Jam is in the fridge, along with an assortment of fresh vegetables and fruits. I'm sure a woman in your condition could use a healthy snack after the ordeal Beau has put you through working with him."

"My condition?" she sputtered, not sure what he meant.

"With child, of course."

"But..." No, she wouldn't deny it. In fact, back home nothing about her pregnancy had been a secret. But here, in front of Beau... "I mean..."

"It's in your glow, my dear. I've painted dozens of ladies with the same glow. Did a portrait series of the various stages of pregnancy so I recognize it the instant I see it."

"You didn't tell me," Beau murmured, clearly shocked.

"You're not my doctor. And I'm barely started." As if to prove her point, she ran her hand over her perfectly flat belly, only...was it larger today than it had been yesterday? Or was her imagination getting the better of her? "And healthy. Capable of fixing a pot of tea, too," she said, then scooted into the kitchen and leaned heavily against the first available wall she could find.

Now what? Stay here and keep on doing what she was doing? Or leave, convinced that Beau was a good man?

And still wonder why he'd become a donor. That was the biggest question that remained. By all observations, he wasn't social, didn't want involvement. Yet agreeing to father an anonymous child somewhere was about as social and involved as it got without true involvement. She didn't understand it. The thing was, even if she knew all the nuances, all the details, it wouldn't make a difference. She was carrying his baby, and she was going to raise it. Nothing about that would change.

Yet she didn't want to leave. Not yet. "So we're right back to the place where I don't know what to do," she whispered to the baby. Then shut her eyes. Tried to wipe everything from her mind but the life inside her. Which, in her mind's eye, right now was a little boy who looked just like his daddy.

"You OK?" Beau asked from the kitchen doorway.

"Where's Arthur?"

"Getting ready to be examined. So, how far along are you?"

"Nine weeks. Sailing through it like a champ."

"And keeping it a secret?" he asked.

She shook her head. "Not really. Just didn't have too many opportunities to insert it into our conversations." She shrugged. "No big deal."

"What about the father? Is it a big deal to him?"

"Nope. He made a one-time deposit in the sperm bank, I benefitted. Good for him, I suppose. Wonderful for me."

Beau raised questioning eyebrows. "But you don't seem happy."

"Quite the contrary. There's nothing I want to do more than bring this baby into the world and be the best mom I can possibly be."

"Then smile when you say that, Deanna, because I'm not convinced."

"You don't have to be," she said, stepping away from the wall and heading to the old-fashioned gas stove to fetch the tea kettle. "For what it's worth, though, I wanted to do this. From the very first moment Em...I thought about it, it's all I wanted. So if you're not seeing happiness, it's because you're not looking. Arthur saw it right off. You know, that pregnancy glow. And I'm sure, by now, he's ready to get your poking and prodding over with."

He studied her for a moment then nodded. "And for what it's worth, good decision about the horseback riding. I just wonder why you didn't tell me that was the reason." Then he left the kitchen.

"You didn't know?" Arthur asked. "From the way you look at her...I thought the baby might be yours. Miss Lambert is a far sight better than what you ended up with the first time."

"I've only known her a couple of days. And she's *only* my consultant. That's all."

"With that look I saw in your eyes, Beau, I think you've known her a lifetime. Or wanted to know her." He grinned. "Now, tell me what you want me to do because I'd like to get this whole mess over with and go have tea with that lovely *consultant* of yours."

Beau snapped on a glove. "Guess what comes next," he said.

He'd thought she was reserved, and now he knew why. Still, she didn't seem happy enough. Especially for someone who'd made the choice to bring a baby into the world on her own. It was a tough decision but an exciting one. In Deanna, though, he saw confusion where he should have been seeing joy. There was something else, he decided. But he couldn't imagine what. More than that, he couldn't imagine why he cared. He did, though. He cared, and he didn't want to explore the reasons why. In fact, he didn't even want to think that there might *be* a reason.

CHAPTER FIVE

"I LIKE YOUR FRIEND," Deanna said. She was settling into a chair at an outside table that sat, quite literally, over the mountain stream running directly beneath the little restaurant where they were about to dine. It was a cozy place, its ambience more like an elevated patio, enclosed by screens rather than walls, with casual outdoor furniture and low lighting in the form of muted Japanese lanterns. While it wasn't elegant, and in the full light of day might have looked a bit tacky, Beau's choice was a comfortable one. And tonight all she wanted was comfort.

It had turned into a very long day for her. And a hard one as well, since the physicality of the day had finally caught up to her.

Still now, at day's end, she was beginning to realize how much she missed real nursing duties, the kind where you spent your day with people, not research, phones and computers. "He's quite charming. Very direct."

"Arthur? He was my port in the storm several times when I was growing up. You know, that adult figure with a voice of reason who just seemed to understand you better than your parents did. Or, in my case, Brax.

That's what I thought, anyway. And you're right. He is very direct."

"I saw one of his paintings once, years ago, in a museum. And I thought he must be a serene man, the way he captured the essence of the mountainscape. I mean, how many people have painted mountains and trees and done so adequately but unremarkably? Yet in that painting it was like I was there, and I could feel that same peacefulness he must have felt when he was painting it.

"In fact, that painting is what inspired me into rural nursing research. When I discovered that places like he painted struggled for the medical care most people are accustomed to...I guess it bothered me that just off the edge of the canvas there were hard realities to deal with.

"Anyway, here I am, and I just fixed him a pot of tea, Beau! The man makes a difference in the world, and I fixed him a pot of tea."

She was perplexed, though, why someone like A. J. Handler would isolate himself the way he did. He belonged to the world, and the world was a better place when he was in it and not hiding out in a secluded mountain cabin.

"I have an idea you could stop by and fix him a pot of tea any time you wanted. He loves having visitors. And I noticed that he said he *might* stop by the office for an exam. That's the one thing I never expected from him."

"He's an old sweetie. Just needs a little nudging, that's all. But why does he live so far away from everything? Especially if he loves having people stop by?"

"I don't believe he thinks he's far from everything. In fact, I'm pretty sure Arthur believes he's living in the center of his universe. Guess it depends on your perspective, doesn't it?"

"And on what makes you happy." She glanced at the menu, ordered a dinner-sized salad and green tea, along with a basket of home-made rolls, then shut her eyes for a moment to concentrate on the sound of the stream coming in through the screened walls. So peaceful, so relaxing…it almost made her forget New York for a moment. Almost made her forget she really didn't belong here.

"Sometimes happy is hard to figure out," Beau said, after his order for mountain trout was placed. "When I was a kid, happy was the new bicycle I wanted more than anything I'd ever wanted in my entire life. I worked hard for it, took on extra chores, saved my money and on the day I went to buy it, there was another bike in the shop, a lot nicer, and a lot more expensive.

"It would have been weeks before I could afford it, so I bought the one I'd originally had my heart set on but I was never happy with it. Essentially, what made me happy one moment turned into a reminder of what I wasn't happy with for a long time afterwards."

"I learned early on that you're responsible for your own happiness. It's what you create for yourself, or nurture in yourself."

"Then that would preclude finding happiness in someone else, or loving someone who makes you happy."

"You said you were divorced, so do you still believe in that?" she asked, as she picked up the iced tea the server had just brought over. "I mean, I think anybody who marries expects to find happiness, but you went through it and got out. And look at you now. You're trying to find some kind of life right here, which I suppose could be translated into happiness. But it doesn't include someone else. It's what you're trying to create for yourself, and I'm not sure it was in your plan when you married…"

"Nancy. Her name is Nancy. And, no, what I'm going through right now wasn't part of *that* plan. But I'd hate to go through life believing that the only person who can make me happy is me. That my happiness is dependent only on something of my creation."

He was an optimist, she decided. A believer in things greater than himself. She liked that, actually. She didn't have the same kind of optimistic outlook herself, but she liked it that the baby's father had that in him.

"I'm not saying that happiness can't happen *because of* somebody else, or even *with* somebody else." She was certainly happy because of the baby. "But you shouldn't depend on it because if you sit around and wait for it to happen, you might miss out on something good."

"Like being a mother?"

"Like being a mother," she said, almost reverently. "But I wasn't supposed to be this baby's mother. It was never my intention to have a baby for myself."

"Then you're…"

"Carrying this baby for my cousin. Her embryo, actually. But she died, and I wasn't left with many options. There was a mix-up. Somehow sperm samples got switched, and Emily's baby…the baby I'm carrying didn't belong to her husband. After she died, he signed all the choices over to me and walked away…"

Beau tilted his head with concern.

"I was deriving my happiness from helping her find hers. But things change. Certainly my direction did, yet I'm still creating my own happiness by knowing that

I'm bringing Emily's baby into the world the way she wanted, and I'll be the best possible mother I can be."

"But happiness doesn't have to be something you create. It should be something you simply have. Something that flows in and out naturally. I wanted to be happy in my marriage. I expected to be, and it didn't work out. But I never, once, thought that I had to somehow build or create that happiness. It should have come as part of having everything I wanted. The fact that it didn't is unfortunate, but it doesn't take away from my basic faith that when the pieces of your life fall into the right place, happiness is what happens."

"Or should happen."

He smiled. "Be patient with yourself. Maybe you haven't found it yet, but that doesn't mean you won't. Your baby is where you start, I think."

"Not my baby," she said, almost to herself. Because it wasn't. It was Beau's baby, and Emily's. And maybe that's what washed the melancholy mood over her, thinking that her cousin had created something with Beau—that happiness—she never would. "Anyway, enough of that. I'm really tired, and as soon as we've eaten, I'd like to go back to my cabin, because I've got another couple of hours of research ahead of me tonight."

"What you've got ahead of you is resting. As in going to bed. Or reading a romance novel or listening to whatever kind of music you like to listen to."

"Classical."

"Then classical it is, because your working day is over. Doctor's orders, and if he as to, Doctor's going to hang around for a while to make sure you do what you're supposed to. Oh, and while we're on the subject, I think we'll skip the house calls now that I know—"

She thrust out her hand to stop him. "I know my limits, Beau. I appreciate your concern but, please, let me be the one to tell you when I'm not able to make a house call. OK?"

He reached over and took hold of her hand. "I'm sorry for your loss, Deanna. In everything we were talking about, I think that aspect got misplaced. But you must have loved her very much to want to carry her child, and I'm sorry she died."

"So am I," she whispered, batting back a sudden tear. "I try not to think about it because it's not good for the baby. But she was my best friend. My only friend. And sometimes I feel so…" She shook her head. "Hormones flipping over, making me weepy. Sorry."

"'Tis a far nobler thing…"

She sniffed away the last of her tears and smiled. "I appreciate the compliment, but taking care of someone you love isn't noble. It's what life's supposed to be about. You take care of Brax, I take care of Emily's baby. It's the way the universe is suppose to work."

"Are you going to be OK? I don't want to take you back to the cabin and leave you there alone. Let's just say hormonal, weepy, pregnant women should have a shoulder to cry on. That's the way the universe is supposed to work, too."

"You're kind," she said. "But the problem with pregnancy is you never know what's going to make you cry or when it's going to happen. So for me to have your shoulder, you'd have to stay with me twenty-four hours a day."

"I've stayed in worse places," he said.

Why did he have to be so nice? Why did he have to be the kind of man it would be so easy to fall in love with? The kind of man she'd fall in love with if she were the falling kind? "Is that a compliment?"

"I'm not sure you'd be easy with a personal compliment, would you?"

Before she had a chance to answer, the server brought their dinners to the table. Her salad, his mountain trout. As soon as the plates were on the table, Beau switched them. Took the salad himself, and moved the plate with broiled trout, fresh asparagus and brown rice in front of her. "No arguments," he warned. "Your baby needs more than lettuce and tomatoes after the day you've given him, or her."

"I'm too tired to eat," she protested.

"Tell that to your baby, who's probably craving protein."

"The baby's two months along," she said, grabbing back her salad. "And I'm on good prenatal vitamins for nights like this when I don't eat as well as I should. But thanks for fussing. I haven't had anyone to support me in this pregnancy, and it's nice to think someone cares."

"Someone does care."

"Why, Beau? We've known each other a few days, so why would you care? You're not my doctor, not even my friend, really. So I don't understand it."

Rather than answering, Beau forked up a bite of flaky fish and reached across the table with it. Headed directly for her lips. "Open up," he said. "One bite, and I'll tell you why I care."

She did have to admit the fish smelled divine. And it tasted as good as it smelled as it passed between her lips. Savoring the moment, the food, the pure sensual feel of being fed by him, she lingered as long as she could before she had to swallow, almost regretting that the moment had ended. Another place, another time, it could have been so romantic… "OK, tell me."

"I like you."

"That's it? You like me?"

He forked up another bite of fish and held it out for her. "One more bite and I'll tell you."

It was all she could do to keep from melting under the table as the second bite passed her lips and she watched his hand slip back over to his side of the table and break off yet another piece of fish. Meaning another bite… "Two bites down, now tell me."

"You're smart. You're efficient. Most of all you're independent, which, since my divorce, I value more than almost anything else in a woman."

Well, not the compliments she would have liked, but they were honest. And this wasn't a romantic scenario after all.

A sly grin slid across his face. "Oh, and you're easy on the eye."

Now, that pleased her. "Did you forget that I'm pregnant?"

He held up the third bite and she took it. When she'd finished, he said, "Pregnant is beautiful. Nancy, when she was thinking about getting pregnant, was having fits about gaining the weight, getting swollen ankles, looking frumpy. She was willing to put up with it to get my money, but she wouldn't have been pleasant to live with."

"Before I say anything, no more bites, please. I really do want to eat my salad, and I've already eaten too much of your meal."

"You sure?"

She smiled. "Sure. And I do worry about the weight

gain and the swollen ankles, but not in terms of how I'll look so much as my overall condition. I have to stay healthy for this baby. But as far as looking frumpy… who cares?"

"Which gets back to my original statement. I like you, and that's just another of the reasons why."

"But you didn't know that about me until just now."

"It's an assumption I could make, though. One, among many."

"So now you're making assumptions about me?"

"A few."

She stabbed a cherry tomato with her fork and poised it halfway across the table, feeling bolder than she'd ever felt before. "So, can I tempt you with my tomato, Doctor? You tell me your assumption, I'll give you my tomato."

"Sounds like a bribe to me," he said, his voice a little rougher than usual.

"Maybe it is, maybe it's just a simple offer of salad. But only if you tell me one of those assumptions."

"You're practical."

"Not enough to get my tomato."

"Caring."

"That should be a given considering I'm a nurse."

"But you're a nurse researcher, which could lead me to a different direction with my assumptions."

"Such as?"

"People frighten you in the personal sense. Or, you don't understand them. Or you're afraid they'll hurt you."

This was going much deeper than she wanted it to, because he was right about all of it. And she didn't know what kind of answer to give him and still keep the distance she wanted. But as it turned out, she didn't have to answer him because he plunged ahead. "And you're a good kisser?"

"A good kisser?" she sputtered.

He nodded. "Beautiful lips. Nice and full. They look very soft. And you don't wear lipstick… I hate lipstick. Prefer the natural look. Which leads me to the assumption that you're a good kisser." With that, he took the fork from her hand, ate the tomato, then handed her back an empty fork. "Am I right?"

"Don't know," she said, spearing a cucumber slice for herself. "Don't rightly recall that anyone's ever critiqued my kissing."

"Pity," he said. "I'd like to read the review. Anyway, I deserve another cherry tomato for baring practically my entire soul to you."

"Your soul?"

"Well, maybe not my soul but my fondest wish."

"Which is?"

"Nancy wore hideous, fire-engine red lipstick. All the time. Day, night, to bed. My fondest wish is that if I ever do get involved again, I want the lady in question to have natural lips. Like yours." With that, he turned his attention to his dinner and she dove right into hers, and the conversation went medical for the rest of the evening.

Which was for the best, she decided a little later as she entered her cabin and he went to do the gentlemanly thing by putting on a pot of tea. Yes, it was definitely for the best they stay on safe territory because, given the chance, and one more cherry tomato or bite of mountain trout, she might have shown him what it felt like to be kissed *au naturel*.

CHAPTER SIX

"PART OF ME really believes he should know," Deanna whispered to the baby. "But only if he wants to, and that's the problem. I don't know what he wants. So we just do what we're already doing, and keep taking it one day at a time."

She went into the great room, where she turned on the large-screen TV, popped on an old Kathryn Hepburn movie she'd found in the cabin's collection, settled down onto the sofa, hoping it would agree with the growing ache in her lower back, and promptly started relaxing to the raspy-voiced Kathryn having her way with her on-screen hero.

"I'm settled in," she called to Beau. "Doing what the doctor ordered."

"Not working on a report, are you? Or doing some research? Hiding it under the covers so you won't get caught?"

She laughed. "No. I'm getting ready to relax with a movie."

"And the world didn't come to an end because you're taking the rest of the evening off, did it?"

It unnerved her how well he knew her. Especially in such a short time. Was she that transparent? Could he see her confusion, or the intent on her face every time he looked at her? "I'm really not that obsessed."

"Yes, you are," he shouted over the screech of the tea kettle's whistle. "And stubborn, too. Sort of like the pot calling the kettle black when you call me stubborn."

This was nice, she had to admit. Cozy on the couch, Beau standing watch for a little while. And Hepburn... Hepburn was always strong, the way Deanna wanted to always be strong. "The way I'm going to teach you to be strong," she said to the baby, as she pulled a blanket from the back of the sofa down over her.

"But you're going to have real role models in your life, not images on screens the way I did. Me, maybe even your da..." On a sigh, her day drifted away for a little while, even before her tea had completely steeped.

Beau set the tea aside and simply stood in the doorway, watching her. She slept with a smile on her face. He'd never really seen that before. He'd read about it in books, seen it portrayed in movies, but had never witnessed it. But yes, Deanna slept with a smile on her face. Beautiful face, he thought. Not angelic. Not even soft. Beautiful in character and determination. Especially beautiful in strength. A face he could get used to looking at, though.

Exhausted, Beau slumped down into the chair across from her and kicked off his boots. He promised himself he'd rest for five minutes, then drag himself out and go home. So, propping his feet up on a footstool, he leaned back, cupped his hands behind his head, and simply existed there, listening to the gentle in and out of Deanna's breathing, wondering about the way she faced the world.

There wasn't really a way to define it. Maybe head on. Or combatively. Yet there were these moments, these off-guard moments, when he'd see such vulnerability in her eyes. And sadness. Maybe that's what pulled him in the most. And now he understood why. She was having someone else's baby, a very altruistic thing to do. Also something that had turned out so tragically.

It couldn't be easy, having everything change like that. Like the way everything had changed in his life. *How do you expect me to get pregnant when you're never home? It's not like that window of opportunity is open every day of every week of every month, Beau.* OK, so Nancy had made him feel guilty. But in his defense those had been busy days, fighting for his place in the hospital hierarchy, being saddled with more responsibility than someone in his upwardly mobile position needed.

Then life had changed for him as well. And with him, like it was with Deanna, it could never change back. But it could get more complicated, he thought as he watched her sleep.

This was complicated, sitting here, watching her sleep. It's because she's pregnant, he tried to convince himself. That's all. It was the right thing to do, trying to help her.

"Beau?"

He resisted opening his eyes. His five minutes weren't up yet and he was too tired to move.

"Beau, it's seven o'clock."

Couldn't be. He hadn't gone home yet.

"I've made a pot of coffee."

Yes, he could smell it. "Five minutes," he protested,

slowly becoming aware that he'd spent the entire night in the chair.

"Brax called and…"

Instantly alert, Beau opened his eyes and pushed himself from slumped to straight up. "Brax? Is he OK?"

Deanna laid a reassuring hand on his shoulder. "He's fine. Just wondering where you were. I told him you'd stayed over and that you were sleeping like a baby. He wanted you to know that Nell's on the verge of giving birth. Your pregnant horse, right?"

Nodding, Beau ran his fingers through his hair and forced himself to wake up. "One of my horses. Ran a few races, won, then pulled up lame. So we bred her with another champ, hoping to produce a champion."

"It sounds so clinical."

"It *is* clinical. I found what I thought would be a good genetic match for her, bought the frozen semen…"

He looked up, saw that her face had gone ashen. "What?" he asked, pushing himself out of the chair. "What's wrong?"

"Nothing. Nothing's wrong. I just need to…take a shower…" She swallowed hard. Looked up at him. "Why wouldn't you have simply put her out in a pasture with one of your stallions and let nature take its course?"

"Because nature's course in the case of my two stallions wasn't good enough. If the best was out there to be had, that's what I wanted. Because…" He shrugged. "Because I wanted to produce championship offspring. Or, at least, take my best shot at producing a champ. It's done all the time, Deanna. People want—"

"Champions," she said.

"What just happened?" he asked, stepping forward, only to have her step back. "You went from friendly to…I guess the best way to describe it would be stricken."

"Backache. Comes and goes."

She wasn't telling the truth. It was obvious. In fact, the expression on her face was a dead giveaway when she was trying to be evasive. It had all started when he'd mentioned inseminating his horse, which had probably reminded her of… Damn, he was stupid!

"Look, I'm sorry. I know it sounded like a cold, calculating thing, having my horse inseminated, but in the animal world it's a big business."

"In the people world, too. Choose a pretty face from a book, check their IQ, their profession, their background. What's not big business about that?"

Hormonal swing? Maybe he'd just touched a raw nerve. The problem was, with Deanna he wasn't sure how to untouch it. "It was a choice, Deanna. You, Emily and her husband…a choice from your heart to help them. That's not big business. In fact, it's about as personal as it gets."

"It's just too close," she said, shrugging. "Especially when I'm still not used to…to any of it."

"For what it's worth, you're going to make a sensational mother." He reached for his boots and regretted having to put them on, but he was already an hour late starting his day and he did want to get down to Nell to see how the birthing was progressing.

"I see it in you, Deanna. And that's not the doctor observing the nurse but me observing you. Even if your situation isn't what you might have chosen for yourself, that baby you're carrying is one lucky little kid to be getting you."

She walked over to the rear window and looked out at Brax's pasture for a moment. Then drew in a deep breath and let it out.

"I'm not a nurturer the way you're supposed to be when you have children, Beau. I rely on judgement, knowledge and skill, but I don't have that natural instinct good mothers have. For this baby, there are things I know I have to do—eat properly, get good rest, avoid certain activities.

"But that's all knowledge from a book, not knowledge from inside me. And I think getting myself so deeply entrenched in Sugar Creek almost from the moment I arrived is a distraction I probably, subconsciously, want because it puts off the inevitable."

"Which is?"

"Wondering if I can be a good mother to this baby." She swiped at tears she didn't want to shed, especially so early in the day. "It's all I worry about now, and I'm sure some of this is a hormonal swing. That, plus my back hurts and I'm not even..." She gestured a big belly.

"I can't help you with the hormonal swings, and other than telling you I think you're going to be a fantastic mother there's nothing I can do about that. But I can do something for your back, if you let me." he said. Standing, he walked over to the window, stood behind her, but kept his distance. "You have to be willing to let someone help you, rather than pushing them away."

"I don't really do that, do I?"

He chuckled. "You've got more ways to push people aside than anyone I've ever seen."

"But you're the persistent one, right? The one who wants to conquer that in me?"

"Not conquer it. Just prove to you that you can let people in and not get hurt all the time."

"But get hurt some of the time."

"We all get hurt, Deanna. You can't avoid it. It's called life, and sometimes life just knocks you down."

"Like your divorce?"

"Not the divorce. It stung, but it had to be done. But I had other expectations in that marriage, things that I wanted as badly as you wanted to help Emily, and they were taken away from me the way Emily was taken from you.

"And while I'm not equating your tragedy with mine, I just want you to know that I did get hurt, and if it hadn't been for the people I let in, I'd probably still be wallowing in it."

"What?" She asked, turning to face him. "What hurt you that deeply?"

"The betrayal, for starters. And the knowledge that I'd been so oblivious to something everyone around me saw. But most of all…we were in the pre-baby planning stages. At least, I thought we were. But it wasn't working out, she wasn't getting pregnant, and that's when it started to fall apart between us. Or, at least, that's what I tell myself to keep from sounding so utterly stupid. Because we were never, truly together."

"But you wanted a child?"

"Not when she did, but yes. Then when she told me she was…"

"She was pregnant?"

He shook his head. "That's what she said but it was another one of her lies to hold onto me. Or shall I say my wealth."

"But you can't fake a pregnancy. Maybe for a little while, but…"

"She never planned past the first part of it. You know, tell your husband whatever you have to then figure out how to deal with it. Well, when I didn't see symptoms, like morning sickness…"

"I don't get morning sickness."

"Yes, but you don't consume wine either. Or spend time in a hot tub, or tell me you're going to visit your mother when, in fact, you've gone off for some tweaking on your eyelids. She had an elective cosmetic procedure done, and when I found about it, I knew she wasn't pregnant because no reputable plastic surgeon would do that on a pregnant woman."

"I'm so sorry, Beau. It must have been awful."

"Finding out my whole marriage was a lie? Yes, it was awful. But the thing is Brax was there to help me through it. And Joey. I had to let them in, though."

"Which is what I don't do."

"It's not easy."

"But it shouldn't be so hard either. I just don't have much experience."

"Stay here long enough and the whole town of Sugar Creek will embrace you and your baby, Deanna. That's the way the people here are."

"And you're one of those people." She reached over and gave his arm an affectionate squeeze. Then swiped at one stray tear that had held back for a solo journey down her cheek, and sniffled. "Starting with that back massage, I hope."

Beau held up his hands and wiggled his fingers again. "Any time."

"If you have time, how about I grab a quick shower first, then…?" She wiggled her own fingers back at him.

"Sounds good to me." To heck with the time of day, to heck with all the things he had to get done. Giving Deanna a massage suddenly topped his list of things he wanted to do, and that's all that mattered. So he went back to his chair, kicked off his boots again, settled in and listened to the sound of the water hitting the sides of the shower.

Tried hard not to imagine that same water hitting Deanna. She was pregnant, after all. And while he was a man, and *those* thoughts came naturally, he shouldn't be having them. Not now, and especially not about a pregnant woman. But, damn, they wouldn't go away!

"It's getting complicated," she said to the baby as she adjusted the shower spray so she could feel the sting of the water pellets. They invigorated her, would hopefully knock some sense back into her. Whatever was she thinking, melting down in front of him that way? But he'd been so clinical, talking about picking out the perfect *sample* for his horse, talking about wanting to breed a champion. She understood that in the animal world, especially for someone like Beau who loved his horses.

But his clinical example had turned into her personal example when she'd started to wonder if he considered himself the *champion* women would want to father their children. Had that been his reason to donate sperm? If it was, it didn't make sense after how he'd described what he'd gone through after discovering his wife's lie about her pregnancy.

Yes, it was definitely getting complicated. "But I don't think he's like that," she said, laying both hands across her belly. Still, the proof might be in the life she was carrying. Did it really matter why he'd donated? For curiosity's sake, it mattered now more than it had before because…

"Because I know him now. And don't get me wrong," she continued, "you have an amazing daddy. He's someone…" Someone she might have picked for herself. Beau himself. Not his sperm. She liked his devotion to a cantankerous old man. Liked the way he took care of the people in Sugar Creek. Even liked his connection to nature.

Most of all, she liked his sense of duty. Beau tried harder than most people to make his life work in a place he didn't necessarily want to spend his life. Giving up a surgical practice to take on GP duties. Giving up the whole New York experience for quiet little Sugar Creek. All because he was a dedicated man who had a higher sense of obligation that she'd ever seen in anybody else.

"I'm glad he's your daddy, and not…" She bit off her words. No, she didn't have the right to say them out loud. Or even think them. Because that would be disloyal to Emily, and she'd never, ever do that. Emily had wanted her husband's baby. This was supposed to be Alex's baby. If it had been…

Bad thoughts. Horrible thoughts, and she didn't want them anywhere near her, or the baby. So she turned the shower spray to cold and let the icy water shock her back into reality. "It's going to be fine," she said moments later, while stepping out of the shower. "We're going to figure out how to deal with everything."

But everything was a mess. And the mess was getting bigger. Getting close to Beau had been a mistake. Letting him get close to her was just as big a mistake.

She knew that as well. Then working for him on top of everything else?

That's what was on her mind as she pulled on some jersey knit pants and a T-shirt and headed down the stairs, fully aware she was only compounding the mistakes by allowing his fingers to travel the length of her spine. Yet, for now, she didn't care. This wasn't about the baby, it wasn't about anything except…her. God help her, this was what she wanted to do no matter how much she knew she shouldn't.

"If you want my unprofessional opinion, I think you should quit being a doctor and become a masseur." Five minutes and she was already feeling better. For some reason he knew exactly where she hurt. "You've got a fortune in those fingers. I could almost guarantee you instant success, even in a place like Sugar Creek."

He chuckled. "And wouldn't that just give everybody here something to talk about?"

"Until they experienced your fingers. Then they'd know." Yes, they would know. The way they probably knew that she was fixing dinner for Arthur Handler tonight. She'd invited him, he'd accepted, with the stipulation that he'd bring the wine…for himself. And a very pleasing local fruit juice for her. He'd also told her to include Beau in that invitation but so far she hadn't because up until now she'd managed to keep everything just about professional between them. Including this massage: it was necessary for her best performance later on, in the clinic. That's what she was telling herself, at any rate.

"Massages first, then what? A day spa?"

"Nothing wrong with a day spa. I treat myself to one

a couple of times a month. It's nice to have somebody pamper you for a few hours." His fingers pressed deeply along the right of her spine and she sucked in her breath then released it slowly. "Lets you… Oh, my…you're on it." Perfectly on it. "That's not going to give me trouble throughout my pregnancy, is it? When I'm bigger?"

"It could. The strain isn't bad, but the more weight you put on your front, the more it's going to pull on your back."

She'd escaped morning sickness, so maybe this was the trade-off. "How long will I be able to have massages?"

"For as long as you want them, provided you find someone who's willing to do them while you're on your side, or even sitting up."

She wanted to ask him if he'd continue with this while she was here, but that was out of line. This was a one-off massage, and anything else turned it into a personal situation. If she wasn't comfortable inviting him to dinner, even with another person there, asking him to work on her back a couple times a week was as far out of the question as it was her comfort zone. But she wanted to. Oh, how she wanted to.

"I'll give my grandson credit where it's due. He was smart to bring you in."

It had been a nice morning, the first part spent with Beau, the second part reading, and now she was on her way to work, walking across the front yard on her way to the clinic. With Brax tagging along, keeping better pace than she might have expected from a man recovering from a stroke.

"So you weren't against it? Beau led me to believe you don't want anything changing around here."

"In theory, that's right. I don't. It's still my medical practice but nobody seems to remember that. But in practice…" He shrugged. "I can see that some changes might help things. You being one of those changes."

"You do know I'm not here permanently, don't you? I'll be leaving in a month, and Beau's going to have to find someone else to replace me if the two of you can come to an agreement about bringing in outside help."

She'd leave sooner, if she could force herself to leave. It was getting too cozy, too easy, and while she kept telling herself it was temporary, something in her heart was telling her she wanted it to be permanent, that she was in a settling-down kind of mood.

"Maybe even a couple of people because the catchment area of this practice is huge. What happens when he's either up in the mountains seeing Arthur Handler or en route to the hospital? What happens if there's an emergency in Sugar Creek where he's needed, and he's not here?"

"We've always managed."

"You've managed and from everything I hear, you're an excellent doctor. But Beau wasn't educated in your medical system and his first choice in what he wants to practice is not what you've set up here." She opened the front door and held it open as Brax passed through.

"That's not saying that you have to agree with him on everything, or he with you, but you've got to come to some sort of an understanding about who's in charge and who's making the decisions, or Beau will go back to New York and you'll either have to close the practice altogether or bring in a complete stranger. And somehow I don't see that working for you so well."

"So nothing I've done before my grandson took over matters? Is that what you're telling me?"

She went to the blinds and opened them to the view of the mountain, then turned on the light. "Everything you've done here matters. But what Beau's trying to do here matters, too, and you've got to take that into consideration if he decides to stay.

"Honestly, I think he wants to stay, but with the way you keep going at him, that means turning himself into something he never set out to be. You're not making it easy on him by demanding he keep everything the same as it was then fighting him when he makes a change."

"Then he should be the one telling me. *Not you!*"

This wasn't her crisis to solve. But she cared. Deep down, she wanted it to work out for both men because... they were kin to the baby she was carrying, and something about that mattered.

"Maybe he has tried to tell you and you weren't listening." Walking over to alcove where the coffee pot sat empty, she picked it up and went to fill it. "I know your life is disrupted," she said, returning to the waiting area, "and you don't like things the way they are now. But Beau's life is just as disrupted as yours, and none of this is what he wants either."

"Then he should get the hell out and go back where he belongs!" Brax snapped, taking the coffee pot out of her hands and finishing the task of making coffee.

"It's an option, and your attitude is pushing him in that direction. But that's not what you want, is it?"

He stopped for a moment, looked at the loose coffee

he was about to pour into the filter, then sighed. "What I want doesn't matter. Not any more."

"I think Beau giving up his life in New York to be here with you says otherwise. Or *would* say otherwise if the two of you would quit knocking heads. And you're equally guilty on that account, Brax."

"I take it back. He should have never brought you in."

She laughed. "Because I tell the truth, and the truth hurts?"

Plopping the filter into place, he put the pot on the hot plate then stepped away. "Because you're too damned perceptive."

"And women should be seen, not heard, right? And their place is in the kitchen, fixing waffles."

He grudgingly gave in to a smile. "You've got a sharp tongue, young lady."

"And I know how to use it." She arched playful eyebrows back at him

"So you do. Now, what can I do to help you? I've got a free afternoon, and if you really think this clinic needs someone else, I'm the one."

"Is Beau going to go for this?"

"Hell, no. But you'll go to bat for me, won't you?"

Now she was trapped between Beau and Brax. More involvement, more personal conflict to deal with.

"In a limited way, maybe. And that's very limited, Brax, because you still have a way to go before you're ready to step back in fully."

"You mean the cane?" he asked, holding it up.

"Yes, the cane. But also the attitude, the stubbornness. And right now I don't think the two of you could work together. Not without some pretty close..." Deanna smiled sympathetically. "Let's just call it supervision."

"More like refereeing," Beau said from the doorway. "And, no, he's not working. Do you hear me, Brax?" He raised his voice for emphasis. "You're not working."

She glanced up to see Beau filling the doorframe, and her heart clutched. For a moment she wondered what it would be like to simply stay here and be part of all this. Would she be able to keep the secret and still live her life? That was pure fantasy, pregnancy nesting hormones kicking in.

Still, that's why she'd gotten herself involved in a family struggle that really wasn't any of her business. She wanted to nest. Or settle in. Or sit in front of that massive stone fireplace in the great room up in Brax's house and knit baby booties for the next seven months... even though she didn't know how to knit.

"Is this where the argument begins?" she asked. "Because I may side with your grandfather on this one."

"No arguments right now. Not enough time. Nell's giving birth *right now* and I thought you might want to come and see," Beau said, backing out the door. "Don't have patients coming for an hour yet, so..." He shrugged. "Either of you care to join me?"

"I'd love to watch," Deanna said, turning off the coffee pot and heading out the door behind Beau. With Brax right behind her.

"It's best to watch her quietly from a place where she can't hear or see you," Beau explained, as they entered the next stall over. "A mare gets nervous when too many people hover around, watching. They'd rather give birth where it's secluded and peaceful."

"That's the way I want to do it," Deanna commented, then realized that Beau, Brax and Joey were all staring at her. "It makes sense. Mozart playing in the background, dimmed lights…"

Beau studied her for a moment then smiled. "Nancy always said she wanted to be drugged so hard she wouldn't wake up for a couple of days."

"She wanted designer hospital gowns, too," Brax snorted. "And her beautician on standby. So…" He directed his stare at Deanna. "It's true what they're saying about you?"

"Yes, it's true. I'm pregnant. And just so you'll know right up front, there's no father in the picture."

"Unfortunate," Brax said. "But people are making their various choices these days, aren't they? And single parenting is one of them."

"Single parenting means that when I give birth I'll have the *only* say. Same goes for raising the child as well. That's the beauty part about doing it *without* a significant other. There's no conflict. No one to get in the way."

"Or to hold your hand when you're giving birth or going through a rough patch," Beau said, quietly. "And share the joy."

"Life's always about trade-offs, isn't it?" she said as the miracle of life unfolded quickly in the next stable. It had only been five minutes, and mama was on her side now, with her baby emerging into the world, kicking its way out of its placenta. All so quickly, all so beautifully. And this was going to happen to her.

It was hard to believe that very soon she'd be doing what Nell had just done. Instinctively, her hand slid to her belly. She felt so close to Emily's baby right now. And Beau's baby. That was something she couldn't forget.

"Baby's breathing fine," Joey called over the stall railing. "Everything's looks good. I think we need to give them some bonding time…*alone*."

Maybe that was true, but Deanna didn't want to leave. Watching something so simple yet so magical caused unexpected emotions to well up inside her. This was a horse…an animal. And she was already bonding with her baby. Such a natural thing, and it gave Deanna hope that the same kind of instinct would soon take over in her. If not during the pregnancy then at birth, the way it was unfolding with Nell, who was already nuzzling her baby, already being a mother in every way that mattered.

"I'll come back in a little while to make sure everything is going the way it should," Joey said, shooing them out of the stable.

"So, back to the clinic," Brax said, staring Beau straight in the eye.

"What did you say to him?" Beau asked, as Brax set off toward the clinic like a man with a purpose, and they lingered behind.

"Well, for starters, I told him I'm on his side about working. Not a full schedule but something abbreviated. And I told him he's stubborn, and grumpy, and some other things that don't matter."

"Well, you've got the touch. That's all I can say. Something about you has the charm to soothe a savage old doctor."

"I listened to him. It's a simple thing, really. You just put aside your point of view and hear what the other person is saying."

"When you say *you*, you mean…"

"You. Your grandfather is scared of becoming irrelevant. What he sees happening is that you're telling him his clinic already is. Then when you refuse to let him come back to work…"

"But the man has worked all his life. He's got a lot of good years left, and he should be enjoying them, not working through them."

"Unless enjoying them and working through them are the same things for him. But you've never asked him about that, have you?"

"I don't have to. I inherited his obsession with work, and I'm fighting like hell to get away from some of it because it will destroy everything. I mean, I never even noticed what kind of woman I married. Didn't take enough time to get to know her before the wedding, hardly ever saw her afterwards because I was working damned hard to establish my career.

"My examples in life were Brax and my father, and I turned out to be like Brax, either by heredity or choice. Or a little of both. Either way, I'm fighting against that kind of obsession because I don't want to end up alone and bitter like him."

"Except he's not alone. You're here, and I think that's what he wants."

"Yeah, right. By trying to push me away."

"Or by trying to force you to fit into a system of medical practice he believes won't make him irrelevant." She shrugged. "It's hard being pushed aside. I was raised by good people who took care of my basic needs, but I was an obligation to their family, not a welcomed addition, and I got pushed aside all the time. So I understand where Brax is coming from."

Walking over the grass, she stubbed her toe on a small tree root sticking out of the ground and pitched forward slightly. Before she could right herself, she felt his protective arm slide around her waist then tighten, indicating he wasn't going to let go of her.

And she liked it. Too much. She also wished they could walk much further together like this, rather than the few hundred yards left to them. A little was a lot, though. She was grateful for it. Scared as well.

Mostly, though, she was just enjoying the moment.

CHAPTER SEVEN

"Brax and Joey are staying in for the evening. Brax is sharpening up his scalpel or something, getting ready to go back to work tomorrow after an hour in the clinic learning, or should I say fighting, the computer system, and Joey isn't going too far away from the stables. But I do appreciate the dinner invitation." Beau placed a bottle of sparkling grape juice on the counter then added, "And fifteen minutes is ample notice."

"I thought about inviting you earlier, but then…"

She didn't blame him for being peevish. Letting someone know they were an afterthought would make most people peevish. Except Beau hadn't been an afterthought. In fact, she'd spent the entire day going back and forth on whether or not to invite him, and she'd come close at least a dozen times as they'd brushed shoulders in the clinic.

The only reason he was here now was that Arthur had guilted her into picking up the phone.

"Then I wondered if it was wise to turn a professional relationship into something else."

"Something else? In only a few days you've slipped into my life like nobody ever has before. And not just my professional life. So what the hell do you call that?"

"Making the best of a difficult situation," she responded, much too quickly. "I'm working for you, Beau, and something I never recommend when I consult is fraternization. It makes things…unmanageable when professional turns to personal."

"Good show, Deanna," Arthur quipped from his stool at the kitchen counter. "I'd say you're spot on with that point."

"And this is Sugar Creek, Tennessee. Personal and professional is all one and the same."

"I will say Beau has a point," Arthur commented.

"Which is why the people here in town think you're too stand-offish? Because it's all one and the same?"

"She's got you there, my boy." Arthur twisted to watch them spar.

"That's different. They're patients, and it's always wise to keep a professional distance from your patients."

"Like your grandfather never did?" Arthur asked.

"My grandfather grew up in a different medical era," Beau retorted, but to Arthur, not Deanna. "Back in the day when the good old GP was like part of the family."

"Which doesn't seem bad to me. In fact, I used to look forward to his house calls because I enjoyed a good game of chess and a pleasant hour of stimulating conversation. Which, by the way, I don't get from you. All you do is lecture me about my blood pressure and tell me to cut back on salt or butter. That lecturing is probably why my blood pressure shoots up the moment you walk in the door. You stress me out with your professionalism, son. Which means you're part of my medical problem, not my medical solution."

A huge grin crossed Arthur's face, and to emphasize

the rightness of what he'd just said he folded his arms across his chest and simply stared.

It was Deanna who took up the cause, but not by coming to Beau's defense. "Brax put in his first hour today and, with any luck, he'll be able to increase that gradually. Not sure in what capacity, as I think that's something Brax and Beau have to work out between them. But don't give up on those house calls with chess and lively conversation because they might just happen again."

"Or not," Beau argued.

"Can't you sympathize with your grandfather for a minute? All his years of experience should count for more than struggling with a computer for an hour."

"I sympathize. But can't you also understand that I'm worried?"

"And quite rigid," Arthur interjected. "Which is why Deanna had qualms about inviting you for dinner this evening. You positively emanate stress, which can't be good for her baby."

"Then I should go," Beau said, and immediately headed for the door. But Deanna caught up to him just as he stepped outside.

"That's not what it's about," she said before he reached the steps leading down to the walkway. "Arthur's only trying to protect me, and I appreciate it. But it's not about stress you're causing me. I really did want to invite you, but I do wonder about crossing over the professional line, Beau. I know I've already done that here and…" she shrugged "…it's confusing."

"Why?" He turned to face her. "Why is it confusing?"

"Because I don't get involved that way. When you put

yourself into the middle of some kind of personal relationship, expectations start to build. Before you know it, those expectations take root, and they become part of the real you and not just the you who processes them in and out of her life as fast as she can so she won't get hurt. And when I say *you*, I mean me."

"Have you been hurt that much, Deanna?" he asked, his momentary anger already gone. "Hurt so much or so badly you'd rather be alone?"

"Nobody would rather be alone. That's not how we're made. But…" She glanced in at Arthur, who was making merry with a bottle of wine. He might be a party of one in the world, but nothing about that man smacked of aloneness because he was simply part of the universe and it showed in everything he did.

"But that's how life turns out sometimes, and you can either let it wear you down or make the most of it. The thing is, you've got Brax and all he wants is for you to be there. And you can't see that because you're too busy pushing him aside, like I told you earlier, and convincing yourself it's for your own good."

"I'm not pushing him aside. Just letting him recover. There's a difference."

"Not to Brax there's not. Can you imagine what it feels like to wake up one day with everything ahead of you, and find it all gone the next time you wake up? I know you had a rocky childhood with the way your dad was, but there wasn't a day of it you didn't have that man who's down there, sharpening his scalpels. It doesn't matter who we have. What matters is that we have someone. And you're throwing that away because you're both so much alike.

"What is it about him that you detest or loathe or despise so much that you're not willing to concede even an inch?"

"I don't detest, loathe or despise anyone, Deanna. I love that old man." He swallowed hard. "And I almost lost him. When they called me and told me he'd had a stroke and was in Intensive Care… I had a dad who came and went, did what he wanted whenever he wanted, and I never figured into his life. But Brax, he was…larger than life. Strong. Then he had a stroke and…"

She laid a hand on his arm. "He still is larger than life, Beau. And strong. You can't protect him from the life he wants, though, and I'm not sure you should. Medicine is what he loves, and all he can see is that you're trying to deprive him of it. Reasons don't matter, and when the emotions are as strong as his, and yours, I'm not even sure the reasons are getting heard."

Her stomach churned over her own words, because Beau had wanted children. She knew that now. And she was having his baby yet depriving him of it. So maybe it was time to tell him and let it be what it was meant to be. Take her own advice and include him. "Um, Beau, while we're on the subject…"

"My blood sugar is getting low," Arthur called through the door. "Wasn't the invitation to include dinner? Or did you two out there forget that I'm in here, practically starving?"

Deanna smiled, partly relieved, partly annoyed.

"Five minutes to get it on the table," she called back, then shrugged apologetically at Beau. But it wasn't a silent apology that he understood, maybe not one he even saw. No matter. There'd be another time. A better time. Or maybe she'd talk herself out of the whole folly and go back to the notion that he'd made an anonymous donation because he'd wanted to be anonymous.

"I did sort of forget he was here," she whispered before they went back into the cabin.

"Of course you did," Arthur quipped. "Parts of me may be going, but my eyes and ears are still very good, my dear. Keep that in mind if you two want to wander off and whisper sweet nothings."

"Not us," Deanna said, swooping past him to grab the salad from the fridge. "We're colleagues and…" She glanced at Beau and smiled. "Just friends."

"Anything you say," Arthur retorted, grabbing a breadstick and giving her a smug grin. "As long as you believe it, that's all that matters, isn't it? But I suppose, as they say, for a tree to become tall it must grow tough roots among the rocks. Your roots will grow tough enough to accept what you need to, my dear."

"Friedrich Nietzsche," she said. "Smart man. But put away your imagination for a while and take this bowl of salad over to the table." She pushed it into his hands and winked at Beau, who was standing in the doorway, simply watching.

"Ah, the course of young love seldom runs smooth," Arthur said, as he turned his back on her and headed to the table. "I dabbled there a time or two in my misspent youth, maybe a few times since in the subsequent years. Wouldn't have missed it for the world. In hindsight might have even done a few things differently. And just for future reference, I don't like being in the middle of a quarrel among my friends so, please, make love, not war."

He wiggled bushy eyebrows at them as he placed the salad on the table, then chuckled as he raised his wine glass to his lips and mumbled his next words into the Cabernet Sauvignon. "*Just friends*, my wrinkled old ass."

"Up for a walk?" Beau asked.

From the kitchen window, they were watching Arthur's tail lights descend the mountain road. Amazingly, he was stone sober. Not even sporting a buzz from the glasses of wine he'd consumed over the past couple of hours.

In fact, he'd left earlier than they'd anticipated, claiming he was inspired to go and paint night life, whatever that would turn out to be. Maybe fireflies. Or maybe the late-night customers trickling into the café in town. Most likely, though, he was leaving early to give them the rest of the evening alone.

Which actually sounded nice to her, relaxing with Beau for a while or even taking that walk. But not for whatever Arthur thought might happen. "Maybe. I did eat an awful lot, didn't I? Seriously, two pieces of that strawberry cheesecake Arthur brought with him?" She patted her belly. "I'm blaming it on the mountain air. So, yes, let's go so I can walk off some of the calories."

"In your defense, those pieces of cheesecake were small. And you are—"

She laughed. "Eating for two. I know it and, trust me, I rely on that excuse a lot. But tonight it was pure gluttony. It's nice having friends to share a meal with. Something I rarely ever did back home, unless it was with business associates. And what surprised me about this evening is that you didn't have any house calls or emergencies."

He put the last of the plates in the cabinet and shut

the door. "Sometimes that's the way it works out. Or maybe I did some last-minute arranging so I could have dinner with you."

"I really am sorry for the late invitation, but—"

He thrust out his hand to stop her. "I understand. You were applying New York City ways to Sugar Creek. Back in New York I would have done the same thing because you're right, business and personal pursuits don't mix. But it's different here."

"Which is kind of nice, isn't it?"

He smiled. "Most of the time, yes. So, about that walk. There's a place I want to show you. I used to camp there when I was a kid. Actually, I called it running away from home. Brax always knew where I was because he could see my campfire from the house, but I didn't know that. And sometimes, if I didn't build a fire, he'd sneak up to an adjacent ridge just to make sure I was OK."

"You really thought you were getting away with it?"

"In the simple thinking of a child, I *knew* I was getting away with it."

"How long did it take until you went home?"

"Always the next morning. I suppose I thought if I showed up at the breakfast table like I did every morning, Brax would never know I'd run away the night before. And he never mentioned it. Every single time I came back, there he was, sitting at the table, reading his morning paper, drinking his orange juice."

"So, how was the secret revealed? Or was it?"

"I was getting ready to go away for college, going through all the obnoxious things boys do at that age. But things were changing. I was with Brax full time by then, and I knew I'd never see my old man again.

"He wasn't dead, but I just had this sense that it was over and he'd moved entirely into whatever kind of life he wanted. Turned out that was exactly what happened. But at the time, even though I was relieved overall, I was still feeling…abandoned. And dealing with moving away, starting college…rough times.

"Anyway, I went on a little bender, shall we call it. Got myself pretty drunk the night I graduated from high school, ended up in jail. Then, instead of coming to my rescue, the way Brax always had, he left me there. Three days! Thought it might teach me a lesson."

Beau winced at the memory. "Oh, yeah. The food was awful, the cot was awful, there was nothing to do but stare at the walls. Three days of it was all I needed, and when Brax finally came and got me I was angry. Decided to avoid him for a day or two, and went camping at my spot.

"But Brax followed me up this time, said he didn't want to miss the opportunity of running away with me, maybe for the last time. Then he told me how he'd spent nights watching me from the house below, and as often as not from the next ridge over. Said he'd thought about telling me he knew my *secret*, but that sometimes secrets served real purposes."

"How'd you feel about that?"

"A little angry at first that he'd kept it a secret, but overall glad he finally told me because I was mature enough to realize that he had simply been taking care of me the best way he could. When he told me, it became a turning point in our relationship, I think. We went from adult-child to equals, and it was nice."

Hurt, then relieved? Maybe that's the way he'd feel if she revealed the truth about the baby. But deep down she knew that was over-simplifying a matter that was much more complicated than a grandfather looking after his grandson. "Do you believe that secrets can serve real purposes?"

"Only if they're meant to help. Not hurt."

The weight of her secret was getting heavier all the time now, and she wondered about its purpose. Was it changing now that she knew Beau, even had feelings for him? Because right now all she could think about was who would be helped if she told him, and who would be hurt.

Suddenly, Deanna felt emotionally drained, which brought on physical lethargy. "Could we go to your run-away place another time, Beau? It's been a long day, and I'm only now realizing how tired I am. So all I'd like to do is crawl into bed."

"Are you feeling OK?" he asked, instantly concerned.

She shrugged. "Mostly tired." She turned, started to head for the stairs, but as she walked past Beau, he reached out and took her by the hand, and there was nothing in her that could make her pull away from him.

"I do want to be your friend," he said, stepping closer to her. "Not your colleague but your friend. Someone you can trust, or turn to, because I get the sense that you're lost, Deanna, and struggling with something that's bothering you. But I want to help, if you'll let me."

"I appreciate that, Beau. I really do. But it's complicated."

"Any more complicated than asking you to step into the middle of this mess I call my life and fix it?"

She sighed. "That's what I do, though. I fix things."

"You fix everybody else's things. But why won't you let someone help you fix whatever needs fixing in your life? Because I do care, Deanna. Maybe even more than you're comfortable with."

With that, he pulled her into his arms and simply held her. Nothing else. Just wrapped his arms around her and let her lean there, feeling safe and protected. Most of all, feeling cared for. She knew she couldn't have it for ever yet for a few moments she simply wanted to linger and pretend that this was what her for ever could be about. Being held, enjoying the feel of being pressed tight to him. The feel of his muscles, his strength.

It was only when comfort turned to sexual tingling that she pulled back, quite surprised to be having that reaction. Looking up at him, at his face, she saw his smile, and what else? She looked again, wondering if his eyes might be betraying some of that same sexual awareness. Or was she simply misreading a kind act from a kind man? Was she seeing what she hoped to see and not what was there? "I appreciate you wanting to help me but—"

"Try me, Deanna. Just trust me, and try me. You keep telling me that Brax and I need to meet in the middle, but I think you and I need to do that too."

She wanted to. But this was so hard for her. Opening up was so very difficult because no one besides Emily had ever wanted to care, or even listen. She had become proficient in locking it all inside herself.

Beau was genuine, though, and he did want to help her. How far could she go with Beau and not become so overwhelmed with guilt that it affected the baby? Or hurt Beau, if she decided to tell him?

She'd come so close to telling him once, and the longer she put it off, the more difficult it would be. Now it wasn't just about what was best for the baby. It was also about what was best for Beau. It was time to take that first step.

"Look, I owe you some honesty here. What's going on with me isn't about friendship or professionalism, or where or how to draw the line. You're not looking for a relationship and neither am I. So why get ourselves involved in anything other than the ways we're already involved? And I think it would be very easy to get involved, Beau. I'm attracted to you. I won't lie about that. If I were looking for a man in my life, I'd be looking for someone like you. But I'm not in a place yet where I want that kind of involvement because I have…other priorities."

"Wow. When you said you'd be honest, you meant it, didn't you?"

"It's all I have. And I'm sorry. But neither of us is ready for what could happen here. Especially when I tell you the second part of all this."

"Where it gets even more complicated?" he asked. "Because I'd like to respond to the first part before we move on, if I may."

She reached out and gave his hand a squeeze. "You don't have to. I understand that you may be feeling responsible for me because I'm…pregnant. And maybe a little sorry because my life's in an obvious mess. But you don't have to worry about me because I can take care of myself. And I'm sure some of this is about my hormones. Which is why I want to be honest with you about everything. Because there's more to it, Beau. The baby I'm carrying…"

He stopped her confession when he pulled her hand to his lips and kissed the back of it. Then stepped forward, tilted her face to his and kissed her very gently on the lips. Amazingly, she didn't resist. In fact, she rose up on tiptoe as the kiss lingered on, and twined her arms around his neck. Then thought better of it and pushed back from him.

"I think maybe your hormones might be affecting me too, causing me to have thoughts your hormones might want but I'm not sure you do. Which means it's time for me to go," he said with a wink, as he headed out the door.

"So much for telling him the truth," she said, as her hand slid across her belly. "The thing is, I told him the wrong part of it." The very worst of the wrong part, that she was attracted to him. "So next time kick me," she said to the baby. "When I open my mouth and the wrong things start to come out, kick me as hard as you can. *Please*."

"When?" Deanna asked. She was too groggy to be coherent, but the shrill voice on the phone was quick to cut through her stupor. She glanced at the clock. Ten after *three*? Seriously? She'd been tossing and turning for hours, thinking about that kiss, the lead-up, its aftermath, and all the things it might or might not imply, trying hard to convince herself it really hadn't meant a thing. So, by her calculation, she'd been asleep only about an hour.

"Did you call Dr. Alexander?"

Somewhere in Janice Parsons's panic what she thought she heard was that Beau wasn't available, and Deanna didn't know what that meant.

"OK, Janice. Listen to me. I don't suppose you know if Lucas has ever done this before." Janice didn't know, and the social workers still hadn't found any relatives to look after him. "OK, I'm on my way. But by any chance, does someone in your family have an inhaler?" No such luck.

"Look, I'm going to run by the clinic, grab some medicine, and I'll be there as fast as I can. In the mean time, have Lucas sit up then try doing something that calms him down, like reading him a story. And call me back...*for anything*."

By the time she'd clicked off with Janice, she'd pulled on a pair of jeans and a T-shirt, and was on her way to her car, shoes in hand. Once in the car, she dialed Beau and waited until the phone flipped over to voicemail, then left a message. "We have an emergency at Janice Parsons's. Lucas seems to be having an asthma attack. I'm going to grab meds from the clinic and go on out to see him. If you get this, I'll meet you at her place. It's number eleven on Old Mill Road."

She clicked off, curious why Beau wasn't answering. On impulse, she dialed Brax's number. The old man picked up on the second ring.

"Is Beau there?" she asked him.

"He went out on a house call earlier. Horseback. Why?"

"I have a three-year-old having an asthma attack, and I'm on my way to make a house call myself. I'm going to have to stop by the clinic and grab an inhaler or whatever you've got, and I was hoping Beau could go out there with me."

"I'll leave him a message, and in the meantime I'll go on over and get what you'll be needing rounded up," Brax said, then hung up.

Minutes later, after what seemed like the longest drive down the mountain road ever, Deanna pulled up at the clinic and was greeted by Brax and Joey stand-ing at the clinic's front door with supplies—meds, in-halers, portable oxygen. And Brax had his medical bag in his hand as well.

"You don't have to come," she protested, as Joey loaded the supplies into her back seat.

"You don't know the roads, so Joey's going to drive," Brax stated.

"And you?"

"Along for the ride."

"Carrying your medical bag?"

"You've got yours, I've got mine. If Beau shows up, he'll probably bring his. What's the big deal who has what?"

"You're an impossible old man, you know that?" she said, moving over into the passenger's seat as Joey climbed behind the wheel and Brax took his place in the rear. "I can see why Beau gets frustrated. And you know he's likely to kill one, or all three of us, when he finds out you're making a house call at this time of the night."

"Then we won't tell him if he doesn't show up," the old man retorted.

"OK, if you're going to come along, then you've got to listen to me tell you why Beau needs help here. He can't handle it all alone, Brax. He needs someone to run the office. A nurse or medical assistant to help with the medical end of things. And I'm even thinking he could use another doctor. Maybe a specialist like a pe-diatrician.

"None of this means you won't be able to practice again. But if he keeps up the practice of making house calls, it's not going to be you making these middle-of-the-night runs. So think about the alternatives because something's got to happen, and soon. Even with his mornings off he's working at a crazy, unhealthy pace."

"But I managed all those years and—"

"And you didn't have a life," Joey interrupted. "You worked twenty hours a day and slept four. Which got you where you are now. But Beau's got more sense than that."

"Everybody's ganging up on me," Brax snorted. Then he went silent for the rest of the trip to Old Mill Road, and Deanna hoped he was considering all sides of Beau's dilemma. Because if he wasn't, and he truly couldn't see the value in bringing in others to work with Beau, this wasn't going to be a solvable situation. Which meant that Beau *would* return to New York and Brax would have to sell his practice to someone else.

It wouldn't make anybody happy. Not Brax, not Beau. And, for some strange reason, not even her. To see it end would be sad.

CHAPTER EIGHT

JANICE PARSONS'S HOUSE, where every single light was on, was shining like a beacon on a very dark, secluded road. "He's breathing better," Janice said, running up to the car before Deanna had a chance to get out. "But I can't do this. I have my own kids to take care of, and this scared them to death."

"Where is he?" Deanna asked, trying to ignore the woman's panic.

"Upstairs, second door on the right. My husband's with him."

Her husband, a huge lumberjack-looking man, was sitting in a rocking chair with Lucas, who was audibly wheezing but not in the throes of a very bad attack. When Deanna approached them, the man said nothing but simply stood and handed over the boy then exited the room.

"Lucas," Deanna said, setting him down on the bed. "Are you feeling better?"

Huge tears welled in his eyes and he sniffled in a ragged breath but didn't say a word.

"He doesn't talk," Janice said from the doorway. "Doesn't eat. Doesn't interact with my children. And now this…I don't know what to do for him." Her panic had given way to discouragement. "I can't keep him any longer, Miss Lambert. He's taking too much time away from my children, and…"

Deanna nodded then waved Janice off, not to be rude but to be silent while she listened to Lucas's chest. There was definitely some pronounced wheezing going on bilaterally, but nothing as bad as she'd expected, and she wondered if Janice had overreacted or exaggerated simply because she was at her wits' end.

"Lucas," she said, pulling her stethoscope out of her ears, "do you know what this is?" She pulled an inhaler out of her pocket and showed it to the boy, but he neither looked at it nor did he respond. So she forged on. "It's going to help you breathe better. When I put the white part in your mouth, I'd like you to take a deep breath. Can you do that for me?"

Again there was no response. But she needed him to acknowledge, in some way, that he knew what she was about to do. "Lucas, look at me. This is very important. I want to give you something to help you breathe, but I need to know if you understand what to do. Can you take that deep breath for me when I put the white part in your mouth? You don't have to swallow it or anything. Just wrap your lips around it. Can you do that for me?"

Again there was no real response except a quick glance at her. One fast look then his eyes were cast downward again. But that's all she needed. Her opening. He was listening and he did understand. The rest of it was about one very sad little boy who missed his mommy and daddy, and while her memories were dim, she did recall feeling the way Lucas had to be feeling. "OK, just open your mouth a little for me, and…" When he did, she slipped the inhaler mouthpiece just past his lips. "Take a deep breath for me, Lucas. A very deep breath."

The boy obeyed, and on cue Deanna pumped the bronchodilator into him. "Now, let me count to twenty for you, and when I get to twenty, that's when your breathing will start to get better. OK?" Of course, it didn't work that quickly, or that easily, but if he believed it did, she was home free.

He nodded, so she started to count. "One...two... three..."

"And you said you were afraid you might not have the right natural instincts to be a mother," Beau said from the doorway.

"Thirteen...fourteen...fifteen..."

"I think you've got it all," he continued.

"Nineteen...twenty. Now, is your breathing better?" she asked.

Lucas didn't look up but he did nod in the affirmative.

"Good, now I want you to scoot back and lean against the pillows, and just rest there for a few minutes. Can you do that for me, Lucas? Rest against the pillows, sitting up. It's important that you stay sitting up."

"His vital signs?" Beau asked, stepping into the room.

"Blood pressure a little up, respirations and pulse a little up. Nothing critical. And your grandfather was the one who technically prescribed the bronchodilator, if that's what you're worried about."

"My grandfather is engaged in a game of checkers with one of the kids downstairs, trying to keep Janice from having an asthma attack herself she's so stressed. And, no, I wasn't worried about you using an asthma drug. I'm glad you took the call. I was out seeing Mrs. Gardner. She's close to seventy, her husband died recently, and she occasionally has rough nights being alone...panic attacks. Apparently she's in a dead zone for cell reception."

"But she's better?"

Beau nodded. "For tonight. And Lucas?"

She glanced at Lucas, who was staring out the window next to the bed. "It wasn't a serious attack but Janice wasn't going to take no for an answer."

Beau motioned Deanna into the hall. Lowering his voice, he said, "And she's not going to let Lucas stay here any longer."

"I guessed that's where this was leading so somebody will have to call Social Services."

"No, that's not what I'm saying. When we leave here in a little while, Lucas is going with us. Janice won't keep him, not even for the rest of the night."

"What will we do with him?"

Beau shrugged. "I'm hoping you'll take him until morning."

"Me?" She didn't know how to take care of a child outside her capacity as a nurse. She had no idea what a three-year-old was about, unless someone wanted a dissertation on the anatomical structure of a three-year-old. But surrogate mother duties? They were coming soon enough to her and she didn't want to bring that deadline forward until she'd learned more, read more, watched more videos. "I think he'd be better off with you."

"He's responding to you. Look at him, he's watching you, not me."

It was true. He was. "But, Beau, I..." She shook her head. "I can't..."

"Sure you can. Just pretend it's three years from now and this is your child who needs to be cared for."

Caring for Emily's baby three years in the future... that's the thought that calmed her down, made her realize that motherhood was going to be thrust upon her one way or another, and very soon. So why not get some pre-mothering in now? "The cabin does have one bedroom for kids. I suppose I could manage it for the rest of the night."

"Possibly part of tomorrow."

She looked back in at Lucas, who was still staring at her. Big blue eyes so lost it broke her heart, curly blond hair so cute she wanted to tousle it. As she watched him for few moments, something stirred in her, something profound and unexpected because, suddenly, all she wanted to do was take him back to the cabin and tuck him into bed. No more hesitation, no more worry.

The mothering instinct welling in her was turning fierce, and doing so very quickly. Sure, it was the batting back and forth of her hormones but that didn't change what she wanted, which was having that little boy in her arms. "How can that happen so fast?" She asked, not meaning to say it out loud.

"What?" Beau asked.

"The way my switch turns on and off. One minute I can't take him home, the next minute I want to so badly I'm about ready to knock you over to get to him."

He chuckled. "One of the beautiful things about pregnancy is it's unpredictable."

"Guess that's good because I do want to take him. But they've got to find his family, Beau, because he needs to be settled in." A feeling she remembered having about something she'd never had when she'd been a child. Still didn't, even now.

"Then I'll make sure the proper authorities know where he is."

"How did you know we were here?" she asked, before she went back to gather up Lucas and his few belongs that had been salvaged from the car wreck.

"Got myself out of the dead zone."

"Well, you need a better way to communicate if you're going to wander around the mountains at night, or any other time. I was worried. Oh, and by the way, I had a little talk with your grandfather about some practical matters regarding the medical practice."

"And?"

"He's not talking to me right now, but he didn't thump me with his cane either, so I guess that's a good sign."

Beau reached across, brushed her cheek with his thumb and smiled. But he didn't respond so to fill in the awkward silence between them, she continued, "Anyway, let me go grab Lucas and get him out to the car. And round up Joey and your grandpa, too."

"Joey's already taken the horse back to the stables… short cut through the woods. So you're stuck with me."

Stuck with Beau…there were times that didn't sound so bad. But that didn't block out the fact that she'd tossed and turned for three hours because the only thing looping through her mind had been one terrifying question: what would it be like to stay here and be close to Beau? Or even, in some distant part of the wildest of imaginations, be *with* Beau.

Because, yes, she was falling for him. Which was giving way to senseless notions and absurd schemes as there was still one huge obstacle to overcome—telling him that the baby she was having was his. However was that going to work out?

Right now, she just didn't know.

"OK, Brax is settled back at the house and Lucas is tucked in upstairs. So what about you? Are you ready to be tucked in?"

"Again. Tucked in again," she said. Too tired to trudge into the bedroom, she slumped into the over-stuffed sofa in front of the fireplace. "I was tucked in before."

"No doubt sleeping like a baby."

"No doubt," she said, yawning. "But I'm going to stay up for a while, in case Lucas wakes up. He's in a strange bed, in a strange house, staying with people he doesn't know, and he doesn't understand it because his world has changed into a big, scary place. So I want to stay close by." She smiled. "Be a little over-protective."

"That's the natural instinct you were afraid you didn't have," he said, smiling.

She stifled a yawn and laughed. "I hope you're right. Especially for Lucas right now. I mean, I know what's it like to wake up in the middle of the night and be so scared you don't know what to do, and you don't have anybody to turn to. Which is why I'll stay up, in case Lucas wakes up."

"Which is why *I'll* stay up," Beau corrected. "You're exhausted, and you need the rest. And before you think you can win this argument, you're sleeping for two."

"Not fair," she said.

He smiled as he extended a hand to help her up off the sofa. "All's very fair. You came to Sugar Creek for one reason, and I'm taking up all your time with things I'm supposed to be doing. The least I can do is let you sleep the rest of the night, uninterrupted. Oh, and sleep late in the morning as well. Doctor's orders."

The feel of his hand was so…so comforting. Smooth. Strong. His kiss, his touch… This was getting serious now. And she was too confused to figure out how to handle it. So, for the moment, she wouldn't. "Well, if the doctor insists," she forced herself to say as she moved past him, refusing to do so much as even look up at him.

"The doctor insists. And, Deanna…"

"Yes?" Approaching the stairs, she stopped and finally looked into his eyes. But he didn't say anything. He simply smiled, then nodded.

And what she'd known only moments earlier was now confirmed. She'd gone and done the wrong thing. The worst thing. The most stupid thing. Yet the most wonderful… Except now she had to figure out a way to undo it. "I'll see you in a few hours," she said, then turned, practically flew up the stairs and shut the bedroom door behind her. Locked it. Yet still felt more vulnerable than she'd ever felt in her entire life.

Yes, she had to figure out a way to undo the mess. And undo it fast.

Beau watched Lucas, who sat at the breakfast table much too quietly for a toddler. His heart ached for the little boy but physically there was nothing wrong with him and emotionally nothing he could do for him. He felt powerless and discouraged. He hated seeing anyone suffer this way, but watching a child going through this was the worst.

He'd known abandonment himself—the death of his

mother, a father who had wandered in and out, a wife who'd had her own agenda. In an adult way he understood these things, understood the pain they'd caused him. But Lucas had no basis for understanding, no basis for knowing what the awful pain meant.

"At that age you loved to ride with me," Brax commented. He'd come up to the cabin for breakfast earlier, at Beau's invitation. "In fact, every time I walked out the door, you were hanging on my leg, begging me to take you on a horsey ride."

Beau remembered that. "And that little *horsey* song you'd sing to me." *If I had a horsey, you know what I'd do?* It had been a purely a made-up little song to soothe a distressed child, but it had been Brax's cure for all those times Beau's dad had dropped him off for an hour or two and hadn't come back to get him for a week or two.

"The horses cured so many things for me. Made things seem better. And you always saw that, didn't you?" They'd given him the confidence his dad had taken from him. Confidence and purpose. But all that had really come from Brax.

"Well, I saw how you always lit up when you saw them so I used some common sense."

"More than common sense, Brax. Way more than common sense." Impulsively, he crossed the room to his grandfather and gave the man a hug, then a kiss on the cheek. No words. Just the loving gesture. "I don't know if Lucas has ever seen a horse. According to his parents' identification, they were from Chicago, and the last time I was there, I don't recall seeing any horses within city limits, so maybe this will be a good experience for him."

The way it had been a good experience for Beau. "But maybe you could take him down to the stables later, like you used to do for me?"

"Me? Are you sure about that?"

Beau chuckled. "You have a way with children, old man, so don't push it, OK?"

"Me, push anything? Not a chance, but you'd better watch it because that nurse you hired is the pushy one. Damned pushy."

Beau simply shook his head then grabbed two glasses of orange juice and carried them over to the table.

"So, does anybody know what the boy's parents were doing here?" Brax asked.

"According to the police report, they'd rented a cabin for a couple of weeks, but somewhere closer to the North Carolina border."

"Damn shame what happened. And you said the authorities haven't turned up any relatives yet?"

Beau shook his head on his way back to the stove to grab the platter of fresh pancakes he'd just cooked and carry them over to the table. "Not yet. But they're still looking." Then, under his breath, he said, "Hope they find someone soon. I don't like the idea of him having to go into foster-care, but that's what might happen."

"No way in hell!" Brax snapped, also under his breath. "That boy needs family who care about him. And if they think they're going to put him in the guardian home or with a foster-family…no way in hell!" he snapped again. "I've got a big house and he's welcome there."

He picked up the maple syrup container, took it to the table, sat down then slathered more maple syrup on his stack of pancakes than one human being had a right to eat at any one sitting.

"I mean it, Beau. I'm not too old to take care of him, if that's what it comes down to." Then he scooted a plate with one pancake on it towards Lucas and placed the syrup bottle next to it. "Losing a parent is a tragedy, but being all alone..." He shook his head. "I'm not going to allow the boy to face that with strangers."

"Seriously, you'd let him stay with you?" he asked, thinking back to all those times he'd been the little boy abandoned on the side of the road with his blanket and told to walk down the driveway until he got to his grandfather's house.

It had been a short walk, maybe just a quarter of a mile, but to a scared five-year-old dragging his blanket down that dusty drive it had turned into the longest walk in the world. And he'd been dumped out of his father's car to take that walk so many times. But Brax had always been there to take him in.

"I'd let him stay with us, Beau. *Us*, because we both understand..."

Both men watched quietly for a moment as Lucas looked at the pancake then tentatively picked up the syrup bottle and mimicked Brax by pouring on way too much. But that's all he did. Once the syrup was dripping over the edges of the plate, Lucas put the syrup bottle back on the table and simply stared at the drippy, sticky mess. Didn't attempt to eat it, didn't even attempt to play in it, which caused Beau even more worry. At that age what child could, or would, resist playing in such a puddle of goop?

"If they were looking for *my* relatives," Deanna said on her way down the stairs, "they wouldn't turn up anybody, because I don't have anybody. Maybe some very distant cousins but nobody close enough to be considered real family. I wondering if that could be the case here. Hope it isn't, though."

"Thought you were going to sleep late," Beau said, diverting his attention to Deanna for a moment and noticing the way the morning sun streamed in through the window and framed her every step down the stairs. She was the picture of perfect grace and beauty, and he couldn't help but stare.

Feelings for the little boy, feelings for the pregnant nurse…domesticity was practically strangling him this morning. The implication of it made the first few bites of pancakes turn into lumps of cement in his gut. What the hell was he doing, anyway?

"For me, this is late. Besides, I smelled some mighty fine aromas floating up the stairs, and it's not every day I find someone in my kitchen cooking for me." She acknowledged Brax with a smile then looked at Lucas, who was simply staring at his pancake.

"Someday, Lucas," she said, as she approached the massive, hand-carved pine log table, "you're going to want to impress a lady, and cooking for her is a nice way to do that. But not with so much syrup."

She reached over to take away his plate but he grabbed it out of her hands and moved it right back to the spot in front of him. He didn't say a word but the angry look he gave her spoke volumes.

"Our guest seems to have a temper," Beau commented, setting another plate with a stack of pancakes on the table and gesturing for Deanna to sit.

"Well, if he insists on keeping that pancake, he's going to have to eat it. So, can you cut it up yourself,

Lucas, or do you want me to do that for you?" Before the boy had a chance to answer, if he'd even been inclined to answer, Deanna took his fork and cut several bite-sized pieces then paused to see if he had any reaction. None, outside of watching, so she handed him the fork to see what he'd do.

The answer to that came in about two seconds when he hurled the fork across the room. Two seconds later the plate followed, spilling pancake and syrup and shattering the plate into thousands of tiny glass shards. Which left Beau and Deanna staring at each other, clearly wondering what to do, while Brax ignored the whole thing and simply continued to eat.

And Lucas…again there was no response, except for the huge tears rolling down his face.

Instinctively, Deanna scooped him up into her arms, cradled him and rocked him as his silent tears turned into sobs that racked his tiny body.

Nobody in the kitchen said a word. Beau simply stood there, feeling more helpless than he could ever remember feeling, and even Brax quit eating when the lump in his own throat grew so large he couldn't swallow.

"Shh," Deanna whispered to Lucas as she stroked his hair. "It's going to be all right, sweetheart. Everything's going to be all right."

No, it wasn't. Beau knew that for Lucas Dempsey nothing was going to be right for a long, long time, and there wasn't a thing he could do about it. But bless Deanna for stepping in the way she was. He was holding onto her for dear life. And somehow he didn't think Lucas was going to have to come and stay with him and

Brax. He was already where he was going to stay for the next little while.

"You're safe here, Lucas," she continued. "Beau and Brax and I are going to take good care of you."

"Or just Deanna," Beau said.

"Why just me?"

"Because he's responding to you and you're responding to him. Because you're turning into a nurturer, and he needs nurturing. Because doing the family thing isn't for me. Take your pick."

Because it all scared him to death—getting attached, having it ripped away. He wanted what was best for Lucas and he'd absolutely take him in, if that's what it came down to, but the noose of domesticity was getting even tighter and Deanna's affection for the boy was the solution. So why not take advantage of it? It was good for her, good for the boy...perfect situation that would let him breathe freely again.

Deanna gave him a curious look but didn't say anything. She simply stared at him like she was staring at a stranger.

"What?" he finally asked.

"Nothing. Just..." She shrugged. "Nothing."

Was it his imagination or did Deanna look...sad? Maybe even a little angry, although she was trying hard to hide it. "It's best for Lucas," he finally said.

She nodded, didn't speak.

"And you know Brax and I will do whatever we can to help you."

Again a nod but no words.

"Better not open your mouth again, son," Brax warned. "You've already got both feet in it, don't think there's room for anything else, like that crow I think you're about to have to eat."

"I was just saying—"

"That's the problem," Brax continued, "So quit *just saying* while you're ahead. Actually, you're not ahead, so quit saying it before you fall any further behind."

"No, it's fine," Deanna interjected. "If Beau doesn't want to do the family thing…"

"Big crow to eat," Brax mumbled. "Big, *big* crow."

"How about I let you two men stay here and talk it out, fight it out or do whatever you do while Lucas and I go down to the town and start over with breakfast?" She deliberately turned away from them to devote her full attention to the boy. "What would you like for breakfast, young man?" she asked him. "What's your favorite thing to eat in the morning?"

"Cereal," he said, his voice muffled into her chest.

"Then I think we need to go to the café and buy you some cereal. After that, we'll go to the store and you can pick out a box of your favorite. Will you do that with me, Lucas?"

"Uh-uh," he said.

"And maybe we can find a game you'd like to play. And some books we can read. Does that sound like fun?"

"Uh-uh."

She glanced at Beau. "I'd invite you to come along but what we're going to do is pretty much one of those *family things*."

It was said with so much ice it immediately chilled him to the bone. It was obvious he'd said the wrong thing, but in his defense it was his reaction to feelings he didn't want to have, feelings that were pushing their way in despite his best effort to push them away.

"You got that crow handy," he said to Brax as Deanna and Lucas headed out to the car, "because I think I'm going to be gnawing on it for a while."

"Or just admit what you're feeling?" Brax suggested.

"You mean confused?"

"What's confusing? You're falling in love with her, aren't you?"

Beau shrugged. "I don't know what I'm doing."

"And the fact that she's pregnant doesn't matter?"

"It does, but not the way you think." The facts of her pregnancy were for her to divulge if she wanted to. As far as he was aware, Brax didn't know. "More than anything, I admire her for what she's doing."

"Look, son, I know that Nancy really messed you up with her motives and pretending to be pregnant. But that's the past. You need to put it behind you or, mark my words, you'll regret letting someone like Deanna get by you. Don't you think you owe it to yourself to get just a little involved with her? Or even see if there's a reason to think about getting involved?"

"I'm not shopping for women," Beau snapped.

"Didn't say you were. But let's just say that you never were very good keeping secrets from me. It was always in your eyes, son. And what I'm seeing there when you look at her..." He shrugged. "Never saw it there for Nancy. That's all I'm saying."

Beau shut his eyes. "I'm not ready. I just can't do it again," he said, fighting back the images of Deanna that kept popping into his head. "Deanna may be the best thing I'll never know, but..." Opening his eyes, he shrugged. "She deserves more than someone who doesn't remember how to trust. And I just can't remember what it was like before Nancy happened to me. Besides that, Deanna's not interested. She told me so."

"That's what you're saying, too, but look how interested you *really* are. Could be the same with her. Either way, you'll remember what you need when you need it. Until then, one step at a time, and that first step is out the door. Go fix what you broke with Deanna, even if you aren't going to take a step closer than that, because you're not the kind of man who'd let it slide by.

"She's quality through and through, son, and pretty damned tolerant of putting up with everything we've thrown at her since she got here. So go set it straight with her, and let me finish my breakfast in peace. Will you?"

"One step," Beau said.

"But you'd better make it a pretty damned fast one, because she's already halfway off the mountain. Deanna's the real deal. Nancy was only a cheap imitation."

Deanna was more than just the real deal, he was coming to realize. She was the *only* deal. But as clear as that was to him, he still didn't know what to do about it. One way or another, though, everything in his life was about to turn over in ways he couldn't anticipate. Given his present confused state of mind, he wasn't sure he wanted to.

Although in his true heart, he knew. He absolutely knew.

CHAPTER NINE

IT HAD TO be the hormones, because now she was embarrassed about the way she'd reacted to Beau's pronouncement that he didn't want to do the family thing. It was his choice, probably for very good reasons. And it was none of her business. Still, hearing those words from the father of the baby inside her had evoked a strong, fast emotion she hadn't expected. He'd hurt her feelings. Granted, the circumstances weren't normal. Not anywhere close to normal. But she'd reacted the way she might have if they were in a relationship, which was just plain senseless.

"I could ask around and see if someone else could keep him until the social workers figure out what to do," Kelli Dawson suggested. She'd slid into the booth across from Deanna the instant Deanna and Lucas had ordered breakfast cereal, and right now Lucas was pressed so tightly into Deanna's side it was hard for her to move.

"No, we're fine. I don't think shuffling him off to yet another situation is a good idea. And I've got Beau, Brax and even Joey to help me. And Lucas...well, we get along. We understand each other, I think. I want to keep him if I can until his permanent situation is arranged."

Funny how she was almost picturing Lucas as part of her little family. Her, Emily's baby and Lucas. And… No! She wasn't inserting Beau into that scenario. That was too much of a family thing to do. "We're good," she said, holding a little tighter to the boy.

"Strange how life works out, isn't it? A few days ago you didn't know any of them, and now look at you, all involved."

Yes, just look at her. *All* involved. "Just going with the flow," she said, as the server brought Lucas's cereal to the table.

"Sure I can't get you something?" the server asked her.

A little unexpected queasiness had set in, just when she'd thought she'd escaped the whole morning sickness process. Nothing substantial. Not even in proportions she'd attribute to what she'd always believed morning sickness would be. But what she was feeling right now didn't seem like it would connect so well to food, so she opted for a cup of hot tea with a single slice of toast, with the hope she could force herself to eat it.

"Just the tea and toast," she said, picking up the small pitcher of milk on the table and pouring it over Lucas's cereal.

"I got that way with my first two," the server said. "Didn't want to eat a thing. Lost a few pounds in my first three months, then went on to make up for that after the morning sickness was over. Toast works. And when you leave here, I'm going to send some saltine crackers with you because they're good for morning sickness, too."

"You're pregnant?" Kelli asked, sounding surprised.

Well, the cat was certainly out of the bag now. "Right

at two months." She tried forcing a smile, wondering how fast the news would spread.

"Is it good for you, or bad?" she asked, as the waitress, whose name was Jane, stepped in a little closer to hear the details.

"Good. Very good. I made the decision to do it..." She shrugged then took a deep breath. "Do it the way I'm doing it."

"All alone?" Kelli asked, sounding like she couldn't bring herself to believe that someone would make the choice to be a single parent.

"All alone. Single mom." She glanced down at Lucas, who was simply staring at his cereal. He was holding onto the spoon with a grip so tight his little knuckles were turning white, but there was nothing in his eyes to suggest he even knew the bowl of cereal was sitting in front of him. "And very happy about it."

"Well, good for you," Jane said, giving Deanna a squeeze on the shoulder. "You're going to be a terrific mother. And you can count on the people in Sugar Creek to help you out when the times comes."

Apparently Jane didn't know she was a temp here. The offer of help and support sounded wonderful, though. And very tempting. "I think the help I need most right now is trying to find a way to get Lucas to eat. Beau made pancakes for breakfast this morning but Lucas wouldn't touch them. So I brought him here for cereal because he said it's what he wanted, and now..."

Kelli and Jane turned their attention to the boy, who'd twisted around to stare out the window. "My son is about his age," Kelli said. "Maybe a little older. Do you think he'd like to come over and play this afternoon?

"My husband's built a play fort, which Max dearly

loves, and we'd planned on lunch and games in the fort later on. We turn it into a scavenger hunt, hide little things around the yard for Max to find, then when he does he has to tell us what they're used for. It's a teaching game, actually. My husband is an elementary school teacher, so we're all about education."

"I don't know if Lucas is up to it," Deanna said. "But that might work out as I need to go on duty at one. At least it would give him a chance to be around someone closer to his own age, which will probably be good for him because he's surrounded by adults right now. That can't be much fun, can it, Lucas?" she asked. "Not having somebody your own age to play with."

Lucas responded with a shrug then leaned his head against the back of the bench seat and closed his eyes. She knew he was past most of the crying now. This was despondency. He was sinking into a well of depression and for someone so young, that was dangerous.

She understood it better than anybody but Lucas could know. And what she also understood was that he did need some normalcy in his life, because at his age that would distract him for a little while. And even the smallest distractions counted. "What time do you want me to drop him off?" she asked.

"On your way to work is fine. I've got one appointment this morning then I'll be home for the rest of the day, and since this is summer holiday, David's there all day."

"Chocolate milk," Jane piped up. "I think Lucas needs a big glass of chocolate milk. Don't you, Lucas?"

Surprisingly, Lucas turned his head, looked at her for a moment then very quietly, said, "Yes, please."

"Amazing," Deanna said.

"Not amazing. Just years of experience, three children and five grandchildren." She bent down closer to Deanna and whispered, "And it's not really chocolate milk. One of my grandchildren is a picky eater so I keep a childhood supplement on hand. It's full of essential vitamins and it fools her every time. So let me run home and get a can…"

"You don't have to do that," Deanna said.

"It's just down the street. Be right back." She pulled off her apron and tossed it across the food counter to a perky, fiftyish redhead with a name tag that read "Cathy", then bounded out the door.

"She can just leave like that?" Deanna asked Kelli.

But her answer came from Beau, who'd walked in at the same time Jane had exited. "One of the advantages of living in a town like Sugar Creek is that you don't have the same rules. Nice place to raise a child, actually."

He'd followed her to town, and seeing him standing at the end of the booth, knowing that he'd come there for her, caused her pulse to speed up. "Shouldn't you be out at the stables?" she said, as Cathy brought over the cup of hot tea and the toast she'd ordered. Problem was, it seemed even more unappetizing to her now than it had been when she'd ordered it just a couple of minutes ago.

"I was, but I think I gave you a wrong impression and I wanted to clear it up." He glanced at Kelli and smiled. "By the way, I may have someone who's interested in buying the cabin overlooking my grandfather's place. The one where Deanna's staying. It comes with all the acreage all the way down the side of the mountain, doesn't it?"

"About seventy-five acres, total. Adjoining your

property." She fished a business card from her purse and handed it to him. "Please, have him or her call me. I've got a motivated seller." She glanced at Deanna. "Not you, is it?"

"Afraid not. In fact, as we speak, I've got an agent back in New York who's looking for a new apartment for me. Sorry."

"I was really hoping you'd stay. Doc Beau is right," Kelli said as she scooted off the bench. "This is a nice place to raise a kid. Look, I'll see you around one. And, Lucas, think of some things you'd like to do this afternoon. Maybe go wade in the creek? Or take a hike in the woods?"

"Lucas has an outing planned?" Beau asked, as Kelli took her leave and Jane re-entered the diner with the fortified chocolate children's beverage she was calling milk.

"While I'm working."

"You don't have to work, Deanna. Brax is ready to manage the office."

"And Brax isn't a nurse. You need medical help, which he's not ready to do yet, except in very minor cases."

"And you need to get back to what you came here to do in the first place."

Outside the actual work she'd brought along, everything important she'd come to do had already been done. She knew as much as she needed to know about the baby's father, including that he didn't want children.

Should she tell him the baby was his or not? Somehow she'd been wandering around in a fuzzy fantasy where she would tell him, he'd be thrilled, and their lives would forever intertwine. That wasn't going to happen, though. Her life was going to be wrapped up in something he didn't want, and there was nothing she could do about it. Not on her side of it, not on his.

So while she might have convinced herself into believing she had some feelings for Beau, she'd have to convince herself right back out of it.

"My client came to a conclusion on how to proceed with the problem, so nothing else is required except to implement the plan." And that was the hard part. For, as much as she knew what she had to do, nothing in her was pushing in that direction. Not yet, anyway. "So except for a few loose ends to tie up, I'm…free." She looked at Lucas.

"But I'm going to hang around for a while until we get *this* situation taken care of because I'm discovering I like doing the family thing."

"We need to talk about that. *I* need to talk about that because—"

"Chocolate milk," Jane interrupted, setting the cup down in front of Lucas, who came to life long enough to pick it up and take a few sips.

"Good?" Deanna asked.

He answered with a nod. Then went back to staring out the window. But this time he continued drinking.

"It's a miracle," Jane pronounced. "And if you don't get some of that toast in you, I'm going to go home and get *you* a can of my special chocolate milk."

Chocolate didn't sound good at all. In fact, the mere thought of it forced Deanna to break a corner off the piece of toast and stuff it in her mouth, hoping it would dissolve before she actually had to chew it.

"Nausea?" Beau asked.

"A little. Probably a hormonal swing."

"Or a vitamin B deficiency, or stress. Carrying twins or triplets might cause more nausea than normal."

"Twins?" Deanna asked.

"Or triplets?" Jane interjected. "Don't recall knowing anybody who's had triplets."

Deanna shook her head. "Not twins." Although the doctor who'd done the implant procedure had mentioned the possibility. But she'd never thought in terms of having twins. Emily had wanted a child, and in Deanna's mind that's what the outcome had been. Still…

"How long since you've had an exam?" Beau asked her.

"Not so long that you're going to do one on me," Deanna said, forcing herself to take a second bite of the toast while forcing herself to *not* think about twins.

"You haven't had an ultrasound yet, have you?"

"It's scheduled for when I go back to New York."

"In a month."

"A month. But I think you should find out sooner, considering…" He glanced at Jane, who had wedged herself in even closer, trying her discreet utmost to hear every word. "Considering," he repeated, and didn't qualify it further.

"He's a good doctor," Jane said. "Almost as good as his grandpa is. I know you're a nurse, but if I were you I'd do what he says."

"Except there's no convenient way to have that done around here, is there?" she said, feeling like she was being put under a microscope, with all the attention she was getting.

"My helicopter will get us to a real medical center in no time at all. And all I have to do is make a phone call to get you a referral to an obstetrician."

"If that's what I want to do. But it isn't, Beau. I'm capable of handling my situation very well on my own. And the nausea is a passing thing." She popped a large piece of toast into her mouth like that was going to prove something then fought to swallow it.

But the gag reflex got her and by the time she'd slid from the booth she knew she'd made a big mistake. "Watch Lucas," was all she managed to get out before she dashed to the restroom.

"Brave young lady," Jane said as she finally went to wait on another customer. "Too bad she's alone, going through this. But we all make our choices, don't we?"

"Yes, we do," Beau said, his focus clearly on something that wasn't visible. "We all make our choices. Then, good or bad, we have to live with them."

As far as patient care went, the afternoon was light, although there were a few scattered people to see this evening. No one too far away, though, and Beau was definitely beginning to see some advantages to encouraging a few more of his patients to come to the clinic rather than him going to them.

House calls were taking up a lot of his time, especially on an evening like this where he'd rather spend his time relaxing with Deanna here on the porch. Making things right between them again. But he had an hour then he was off to tend a case of bronchitis, a suspected bout of gout, and a chronic bellyache that was always caused by greasy food. Would have been a perfect night to settle in, though.

"So tomorrow morning we'll fly in early, you'll have your exam, and we'll be back before noon." Beau handed Deanna a glass of lemonade, and sat down on the porch swing next to her. "Brax will look after Lucas and—"

"And you'll be the pilot?" she asked.

"Unless you want to be."

"Why are you doing this?" Deanna asked him. "Not just getting me to an obstetrician for an ultrasound but everything? It's like you're settling into that family thing you don't want to be part of."

"I really misspoke. That was some of the ugly sentiment lingering from my marriage, which always seems to pop up at the worst times. But it was hell, Deanna. And I was so damned blind to it all…" He gave a deep sigh. "What does that say about me? What does it say about my ability to have the kind of perception and strength a family would need from me?"

"It's not about your perception or strength, Beau. It's about your trusting nature, which is a good thing. It's about the way she hurt you because you trusted her."

"Trusted her… On the days she was ovulating, she'd call me, beg me to come home. If I couldn't she'd come to the hospital and just barge in. I felt guilty because I knew I was leaving her alone too much, and I thought she was reacting to that loneliness as much as anything else. But what she did… I was just, plain stupid."

"We all see what we want to in various situations. You were busy and ambitious, and you believed that was what made her so needy. I can understand that."

"So it's not the family thing I don't want. Even though I wasn't sure I was ready for a family at the time she was trying to get pregnant, I was ecstatic when I thought she *was* pregnant. What I said about not wanting to do the family thing was reactive, but it was also a reflection of where I'm afraid I'll fit into a family situation."

"What if a family situation came at you from out of the blue? One day you're free of it and the next day..." she shrugged "...you're a daddy, or about to become one?"

"Do you mean Lucas?"

"No, I mean...your flesh-and-blood baby."

"Can't happen. Since Nancy, there hasn't been anyone. Before her I was careful. And anyone else claiming I'm the father of their baby..." He shook his head. "Not falling for it this time. You know, fool me once..."

"And that's your final word?" she snapped.

"Deanna, what's going on here? I came to apologize for what I said, for the impression I gave you, but you're angrier than you were when I said it. So what just happened?"

"Common sense, Beau. A great big dose of common sense."

"And I'm supposed to understand that?"

"You don't have to because I finally do. Anonymous means anonymous, Beau. I should have realized that from the beginning and let it go. But now I know."

That clearly made no sense to him. Had he said something else to anger her this way? If so, he didn't know what. And even a quick rethink of his words didn't reveal anything. So now what? Chalk it up to a hormone fluctuation and let it go? Or actually consider that there were aspects to Deanna's personality that were a little off? "And you're not going to tell me?"

She laughed bitterly. "Tell you? Why would I tell you, of all people?"

"Because I thought we were friends. Even more."

Deanna drew in a steadying breath then squared her shoulders. "We are," she said. "And I'm sorry. I didn't mean…"

"Yes, you did. I don't know what that was about, or why. But you meant it, and I'm hoping it was a hormone rage." Hoping for that more than he'd hoped for anything in a long, long time.

She laid her hand across her belly protectively. "Me, too. But I know it's not. And, no, I'm not crazy, which is probably what you're thinking. I'm just coming to terms with the way I'm going to live my life, and you're in the proverbial cross-hairs as I'm working it out. It scares me. All of it scares me.

"And on top of what I already have, I've been thinking about keeping Lucas if Social Services can't find his family. I mean, I'm not even sure I can manage one child, and here I am practically on the verge of making an emotional commitment to another one. So, these questions are boiling up in me and, yes, while I may tell you I'm not crazy I'm wondering if I am. I'm also angry for things that don't make any difference to you, and it's hard to control. But that's what I'm working though right now."

"You won't let me help?"

"You can't."

He reached over and took her hand. Gave it an encouraging squeeze, which was all he meant to do. But he tried letting go, and couldn't. Her hand was a nice fit in his. It felt so natural holding it. And she wasn't resisting. Wasn't pulling away or getting restless. In fact, she seemed to be relaxing…differently. "I know how it feels being that confused. Been there a few times."

She laughed, but it was a melancholy laugh. "I think

confusion is an understatement for the way I'm feeling right now. And for the way I'm going back and forth with some of the major decisions in my life."

"I hope one of those decisions is about staying here. I know I've mentioned it before, or should have if I didn't, but have you given it any serious thought?"

She went rigid and yanked her hand out of his. "I have another year on my contract, with an option to extend it a further year, with a substantial bonus. Or rather substantial penalties if I don't fulfill my obligations."

Back to square one. This was Deanna doing what Deanna did best—pulling away. His advance, her retreat. He knew better, but with her he couldn't help himself. It always slipped out.

"OK, I'm going to ask you again and hope this time you'll tell me. What's this really about?" he asked.

"I don't know what you mean."

"Yes, you do. There's something else going on. It's either about why you're really here or maybe it's about your pregnancy. I don't know, can't even venture a guess. But I know you like it here and I have an idea you've even thought about staying here and raising your baby. Yet look what you do when I mentioned that this might be a life change to consider."

"Is that how you see my staying here, as a simple life change?"

"You can stay on as my nurse, if that's what's worrying you. I've already seen how much I need help."

"Oh, right, like that's going to solve everything. I decide to stay then you decide to go."

"I haven't decided what I'm going to do."

"But it's easy for you to suggest what I should decide?"

"Deanna, please…" he cried in exasperation. "Just talk to me about it. Maybe I can help you."

"Or hurt me," she muttered. "Look, I appreciate you coming up here to explain what you meant. And I'm sorry for the way I've been acting. But…I don't know anything right now, and that's the problem. And I can't figure it out around you because…"

"Because I'm part of it?"

She nodded, brushing back tears. "Look, you've got house calls to make, and I've got a little boy to take back up to my cabin and get ready for bed. So unless you need some help with your house calls…"

"Take a walk with me, Deanna," he said, standing up. "If I can't fix what's wrong with you, at least let me try to help you relax. Help get you into a place where you can make sense of what's going on with you. Let's take that walk I offered the other night. But to a different place. A place I think you need."

She shook her head, still dazed by all the craziness coming out of her. It was like she could hear it pouring out, and she wanted to shut the dam gate but couldn't. How could she ever tell him that not only was she carrying his baby but that she'd fallen in love with him?

He might believe the love part, but he'd never believe her about the baby, which would then make her look just like Nancy to him. Someone who'd faked a baby, or a baby's paternity, just to get whatever they wanted from him.

So, no, she couldn't let herself get any closer. This wasn't a game. Wasn't some innocent flirtation, where they might spend some time together, maybe even have a brief fling. This man was the father of a baby he didn't want and didn't even know existed, and as easily as she'd told him the first part of the truth, there was no way she could be around him and not tell him the rest of it. Maybe not now, not at this very moment, but someday it would happen. That was the only thing about which she was sure.

"I, um…I'm really tired, Beau. I just want to settle in with Lucas, if you don't mind."

She glanced in the window and saw Lucas and Brax sitting on the floor, playing a game, and a lump rose in her throat. She'd made such a mess of this, starting with getting too close to Beau. Then developing feelings for him. Then, for a moment or two, actually thinking there might be a way she could settle down here, live a happy life, keep her secrets to herself.

"Half an hour. That's all I'm asking. Just thirty minutes, then you can have your evening back and I can go do my house calls."

Thirty minutes in which to dig a deeper hole. Of course, she could always crawl into it once she'd dug some more, couldn't she? "I'm not wearing hiking shoes," she argued, hoping he would just leave it alone.

But, he didn't. "You don't need hiking shoes. It's a flat walk, down to the creek." He grinned. "And I'll carry you, if I have to."

"And Lucas…"

"He's in good hands. Besides, he loves the old man. Just look at them."

She didn't have to. She'd already seen the way Lucas responded to Brax. "You're not going to give up, are you?"

"Not a chance. Even if you won't tell me about the demon you're fighting, I can still stand there to fight it with you because no one should have to tackle their demons alone."

He was just too good to be true, which made her ache all the more for what she couldn't have. But she would tell him the truth. Even with all her vacillating, she'd always known she would.

Although now she had to wait until the situation was resolved with Lucas. If she told Beau the truth *now*, the wall that would immediately go up between her and Beau could also shut out Lucas in some way. She couldn't allow that. Lucas needed the three of them united, not separated, in order to get through what he had to get through.

Funny how that worked out. She'd come here wanting to protect one baby and not sure she had the instincts to do so. But her instincts had taken on a razor-sharp precision because she was fighting to protect Lucas now as well. She didn't yet know the ending to his story, but she knew this part of it and he wasn't going to be drawn in into the mess she'd made.

Taking one more look through the window at Brax and Lucas, this was the first time she'd felt on solid ground in a while. Sad, but solid. And she was doing the right thing.

"Look, let me go and make sure Lucas is OK, then I'll be right back." Truth was, she needed a moment away from Beau to gather her wits and move forward with her plan. "Lucas," she said, stepping through the door, "Beau and I are going to go for a walk before we go back to the cabin. Is that OK with you, or would you rather go back to the cabin and get ready for bed?" Like she didn't already know the answer to that.

The boy looked up at her, clearly not happy to be interrupted in what seemed to be a very old board game—the one where you advanced your game piece until you found the lost king of candy.

Had it been Beau's game when he'd been a child? She could picture a very young Beau sprawled on the floor with his grandfather, going after that lost king in earnest. He had probably been a very serious child, much the way Lucas was. And bright. She couldn't picture him any other way. Couldn't picture Emily's baby any other way either.

"Stay here with Grandpa Brax," Lucas said. Only Brax came out more like Bwax.

"*Grandpa* Brax?" she questioned.

"He had to call me something," Brax explained, grinning a bit sheepishly.

"I suppose he did," she said, even though she knew emotions here were tugging much harder than they should. "Anyway, I'll be back in a little while. Got my phone if you need me…or Beau."

"Take your time," Brax said. "Young Mr. Lucas here is beating me royally, and I need some time to reclaim my game-board dignity"

"I'll bet," she said, then returned to the porch.

As they set off across the meadow, Deanna purposely lagged a couple of steps behind Beau, nothing obvious she hoped. Right now, close proximity was her enemy, and she wasn't walking into a battle she couldn't win.

"Is this another one of your special places?" she asked, as they approached a wooded copse.

He slowed but didn't turn to face her, so he must have sensed she didn't want to be too close to him.

"No, not really. But I thought it could be yours. It's so quiet here, it's soothing to the soul, which is what you need, Deanna. I may not understand why, and you may never tell me, but I do know it's what you need."

He was so perceptive. So caring. And this was so painful. "You're bringing me here to listen to a sound that will soothe my soul?"

"Yes. For you, and your baby." Stepping out of the meadow onto a path, he finally stopped and waited for her to catch up. Then took her by the arm. "Just so you don't trip over a tree root," he said.

"Beau, it's not that I don't want to be close to you, but with having Emily's baby and—"

"No explanations, Deanna. You don't want to be too close to me, and I accept that. But now this is for your safety. I don't want you falling."

Except she'd already fallen. And she wasn't sure she'd ever truly be able to get up again.

"Do you realize you've never once called that baby yours? It's always Emily's baby, or the baby, but not *your* baby."

"Because it is Emily's baby."

"It's your baby now, Deanna. And I don't understand what's holding you back from thinking about her or him like that. But you don't. I think you may have accepted Emily's loss but you've never let yourself accept Emily's gift. And you have to do that, Deanna. Because when you do, that's when you'll start feeling the joy you've been missing in this pregnancy. The baby is yours now. Nobody's but yours."

Glancing up to see his face, she found she couldn't because the darkness was beginning to settle in all around him. But he was so handsome even in the dimming silhouette. "I want this baby, Beau, and I want to find joy in the whole process. But sometimes life just turns into a big struggle that you can't figure out, so you simply go along and discover later on that you've gone the wrong way."

"Like I did with my wife. But I forced myself into the resolution."

"By divorcing her. I don't mean to sound trite about this, but sometimes that's the simple solution—just walk away from what doesn't work out."

"Or ignore it, which was what I did for two years. I knew exactly what I was doing but I just didn't want to go to the effort of fixing it. Then when I came here, to stay with Brax after his stroke, nothing was that good either. But after a long time of dealing with whatever I had to in order to get to the next day, I realized that one day at a time isn't enough. It doesn't make me happy because it doesn't allow me any room to hope and dream and work toward something that will make me happy.

"Which is why I asked you to help me. I'm working really hard to figure out what it is I'm going to have to do to find a life that doesn't simply exist from day to day. I think you believe that if you start thinking of Emily's baby as your baby, that gives you a life you don't think you deserve. Something more than that one-day-at-a-time existence."

There was nothing to argue because he was right. As much as it hurt, moving away from her own day-to-day existence scared her to death. Doing it without Beau scared her even more. "I don't know what I deserve," she finally said.

"But do you know what you want?"

"Pristine silence," she said. "Thirty minutes of pristine silence."

He held out his hand to her and she took it, and for

the next couple of minutes as they walked along the trail neither of them spoke. At the end of the trail, save for the noise of the stream trickling over its rocky bed there was silence, and she almost believed she could clear her head here. At least, she wanted to believe it.

"Now, take off your shoes and after that you'll have a couple of options. The water is knee deep so you can roll up your pants, wade out with them down and get soaked, or take them off altogether, with the knowledge that I am a doctor and I've seen beautiful legs before."

"You've never seen my legs," she said, stepping back as his own choice was made clear. Off with his jeans.

"You've never seen mine either, but that's about to change."

He kicked off his boots, bent down and pulled off his socks, then stood back up, unzipped then started to slide his jeans down over his hips. And while she should have turned her back, she couldn't. She wanted to imagine this was going to be something more than wading out into the creek so, like Beau, she undressed down to her panties, then took the hand he extended and waded out into the middle of the stream, where he led her to a large rock.

"This is it," he said.

"It?"

"Your thirty minutes of pristine silence. Make yourself comfortable, dangle your feet in the water if you're OK with that, and enjoy."

Then Beau sat down, and Deanna sat next to him and they both dangled their feet. And sat quietly, holding hands, for the next thirty minutes. But it was mere moments before sadness overwhelmed her again.

This was where she wanted to be. With Beau. Just like this. With pristine silence in her soul.

"We're on our way," Beau said. Their thirty minutes had expired and they were halfway through a second course when reality came crashing down. "Don't let him move, even if you have to have Joey tie him to the bed."

"Really? You brought your cellphone into the pristine silence?" She thought about it for a moment, wondered where he'd tucked it, then shoved that thought completely out of her mind.

"Doctor on call," he said, sliding down off the rock and extending her his hand. "This is the escape but that's the world I live in here. No getting away from it."

She took his hand and followed him back through the water then tugged on her clothes and shoes as fast as she could. "Who is it?"

"Arthur. Brax and Joey and Lucas are up at his house. It's a heart attack."

"No," she whispered, as they set off down the trail. "How far out are we?"

"Twenty minutes, if we hurry. But I don't want you running. Not out here, in the dark."

"Then go on without me. You get to him as fast as you can and I'll go to the clinic to get things set to receive him. I'm assuming we'll transport him somewhere else but we can get the preliminaries taken care of at the clinic first."

"We'll transport him if he's stable enough. And if he lets us. Arthur isn't always…co-operative."

"You just go take care of him, OK?"

"I don't like leaving you out here."

"I'm a big girl, Beau. If I can take care of myself in New York, I sure as heck can do it here. So, please…"

"Stay on the trail. And call me if—"

"No ifs. Just go. *Please*. Take care of him!"

He turned away from her but didn't move. Instead, he turned back around to face her, took two giant steps forward, pulled her into his arms and kissed her. It was a short kiss but powerful. A kiss she wanted, at another time, another place. Where there was less confusion. But she didn't have any time for that as she was still reeling from the shock of it, trying to make sense of it, when Beau pulled back and let out a deep breath.

"The first kiss was to see if there would be a second one. The second one gives us something to talk about," he said, then didn't wait for Deanna to respond. Rather, he bypassed the laid-out trail and went crashing through the trees and undergrowth in a direction she didn't know. But she heard him for several seconds, and felt him for even longer than that.

When the full realization of what had just happened sank in, she laid her hand on her belly and sighed. "Your daddy just kissed me again," she said. Then smiled. "And I liked it. So now let's you and me talk some things out on the way back to the clinic, and see if we can figure out where to go from here. Because it won't work. And my heart is breaking. And I want you to get to know him. And I'm so…scared."

CHAPTER TEN

BIG MAN BROUGHT down by an arrhythmia. As Deanna inserted an IV into Arthur Handler's arm, she realized that she couldn't go back to research and organization. Not on a full-time basis. What she did was important because it made medical services in areas like this possible, but after being part of those medical services and making a different kind of difference, her world had to be about both, and she was going to have to figure out a way to make that work. That, among so many other things.

"You're going to feel a stick," she said, noticing the man was looking away, squeezing his eyes shut as tightly as he could.

"Don't need an IV," he grumbled.

"Maybe you wouldn't have if you'd mentioned to any of us that you've been getting these chest twinges for a few weeks. But you didn't. So now it's an IV…" She poked it into his arm carefully then taped it in place.

"You're not very sympathetic," he snapped. "Good thing you do research and not patient care, because there's not a sane doctor in the country who'd have you as his nurse."

Words spoken in fear. Deanna knew that and didn't

take them personally. In fact, her reaction was to take hold of Arthur's hand and simply hold it. "You're going to be fine, Arthur. I doubt you'll be in the hospital more than a couple of days, and after that you'll be recuperating…" He couldn't go home, because it was too isolated, and there was no way he should be alone. "Recuperating in the cabin, with your least favorite nurse taking care of you for a while."

Yet another commitment to keep her here a while longer. It was amazing how her life was expanding in so many directions, and all of it felt so right and so wrong at the same time.

"Will you stick needles in me then?" He tried to grumble, but the best he could muster was something that sounded more like a scratchy throat.

"Probably," she teased. "Because I'm very good at it. Rather enjoy torturing people like you."

In response he squeezed her hand but still refused to look at her. "So, who's flying me?"

"Joey's the pilot, and Beau and I thought we'd hop a ride in just to annoy you." Adjusting the IV bag to a slow drip, she didn't attach any medication to it as Beau had already given Arthur a nitroglycerine pill, which had relieved his symptoms almost immediately. The IV was precautionary, in the event they had to get other meds in fast.

"You shouldn't go," Arthur said.

"Because I'm pregnant?"

"Too much stress. You should stay here and rest."

"I'm going to have some tests run in the morning so whether it's now or then, I've got to take a ride." It was time to move forward differently with her life. She wasn't sure yet what that meant, but getting the proper tests, especially with her better than average chance of a multiple birth, was the first step.

"And the ride's ready," Beau said, coming up behind her and slipping an arm around her waist. "Brax will be fine with Lucas, so we're good to go."

Good to go. Airplanes were fine, but helicopters... Deanna drew in a deep breath and braced herself. The ride was going to be bumpy in more ways than one.

OK, maybe the kiss hadn't been the best idea he'd ever had but, damn it, how could he *not* have kissed her? Sure, there were complications. Her emotions, the fact she wouldn't let him in. And if she went back to New York...well, he could go back there with her. His job was certainly still open. And maybe that's what he'd do, even after all the fuss of trying to figure out how to make his life work here. The truth of the matter was it would work perfectly right here in Sugar Creek, Tennessee, if Deanna stayed. So far, she didn't seem inclined to.

"You comfortable?" he asked her. She was strapped into one of the two passenger seats across from him, while he was in the jump seat next to the stretcher.

"Not sure. I've never been in a helicopter before, so I don't know what comfortable's supposed to feel like. But I'm OK."

"You look..."

"Worried? I am. Not about the flight. But I've decided to go through with the tests tomorrow, since we'll be at the hospital anyway. And I've been thinking, what if...?"

Beau shook his head and reached across Arthur to

take hold of Deanna's hand. "No what-ifs, OK? Everything is going to be fine."

"But it could be twins, or more."

"Or it could be one, perfectly healthy, beautiful baby. Although twins are good."

Deanna leaned back in her seat, shut her eyes and moaned. Out loud.

"Motion sickness?" Beau asked, as Deanna's hand slipped out of his.

She shook her head but didn't say a word. So Beau chalked it up to flight jitters and didn't bother her. Just let her sit there, looking a bit miserable. Until…

Her eyes shot open. A pain was ripping through her side. Hot knife. Searing. Fast. Complete. Then gone.

"What?" he asked.

She didn't know what. It had come and gone in a second. "Nothing. Just not liking the ride so much." Probably a touch of indigestion. Yes, that's what it was. Indigestion, foe of many a mom-to-be.

"That wasn't a 'nothing' expression on your face, Deanna."

"It was a totally 'nothing' expression," Deanna said defensively, clamping her arm against her side to splint herself in case the pain hit again.

"She's a very self-sacrificing young lady, Beau. If she was in pain, I don't believe she'd tell you," Arthur interjected.

"I *said* I'm fine," she snapped.

"There's my proof, Beau. Deanna's being snappy. Better take heed."

"OK, indigestion," Deanna admitted. "I don't always eat the way I should." Another shooting pain hit her, only this time it went from her lower right abdomen and wrapped round to her back. Beau was immediately at her side. He stepped over Arthur and planted himself in the seat next to Deanna.

"Describe the pain."

She nodded. "Sharp, intermittent." She showed him where. "And it just started. I'm not like Arthur..." she glanced down at the man, and forced a smile "...who had *twinges* for weeks."

After a quick assessment of Deanna's vital signs, Beau prodded her lower right abdomen, which elicited a moan. "You've had those back spasms. And you were nauseated earlier," he said. "Was it morning sickness or something else?"

"I haven't had morning sickness, and this far along I was surprised it would start. So maybe it wasn't..." A pain grabbed her so hard she gasped. "It's risky, having my appendix out while I'm pregnant, but I think..."

He took hold of her left hand. "Not as risky as you'd think. Medical technology has come a long way in protecting both mother and baby during something like this. The bigger risk is not having it fixed, and taking a chance at a rupture."

"Am I in trouble?" she asked him. "I didn't know anything was wrong."

"If it's appendicitis, the longer you wait the more likely it is you'll have complications. As the uterus gets bigger, it basically pushes the appendix up towards the right kidney. That causes the pain you'd expect with appendicitis, but because of the shifting around going on, back pain is common. Which you've been having. Also, appendicitis can mimic other things, like a kidney infection. Then there would be the typical symptoms of appendicitis—nausea, vomiting, loss of appetite, which you've been experiencing as well."

"So, I've been having appendicitis for a while. And I've put my baby at risk?"

"It's early, Deanna. Everything's going to be fine."

"And in my defense," Arthur said from his stretcher, "there was nothing differentiating my twinges from the indigestion I suffer after eating a fine French meal. *Foie gras...*" He raised his hand to his mouth and kissed his fingertips, even though they were impeded by his oxygen mask. "Food of the gods."

"And food of your past," Beau said.

"The indignities we must endure," the old man said, then reached up and took hold of Deanna's right hand. "After we land, I'm sure we'll be parted, Deanna. But I want you to know that after your surgery I'd be delighted to spend my convalescence with you convalescing at my side. Helping each other as we are able to. And your surgery will go splendidly, my dear. Simply splendidly. For both you and the unborn Lambert."

She hoped so. Shutting her eyes and leaning her head against the helicopter's cabin wall, she discovered she was too numb to think. The pain didn't matter. It came and went, and as soon as they operated, it would be gone permanently. But she was so frightened for the baby. It was an indescribable feeling...something that came from a place she didn't fully understand.

Part of the feeling was the possibility of losing Emily altogether. She knew that. But there was something else...the possibility of her own loss. She wanted this baby. Not just for Emily. She wanted it for herself because...because she loved it. Truly loved it. Because it was her baby. Her baby.

"My baby," she whispered, as tears slid from behind her closed eyes. "It's my baby."

"Arthur's squared away in Cardiac Care, and mad as hell because he can't be down here to support you," Beau said.

He looked so good in surgical scrubs. Even through the pain and the first round of IV drugs, that's the first thing she thought when Beau entered the ER room. So handsome. "How long before I go in?"

"About ten minutes."

"Are you going to be in there?"

"I can't," he whispered, pulling a chrome stool up to the side of her bed and sitting down. "They'll let me observe from the window but I'm too...involved to scrub in."

"I wish you could," she said, reaching through the rungs of the bed rails to take hold of his hand. It was time. She knew it. Everything inside her knew it was finally time. Because his baby was at risk, and he did have the right to know. His baby, her baby... "Am I approved for the laparoscopic procedure?"

That meant the surgeon would make several tiny cuts in her abdomen and insert a miniature camera and surgical instruments, then watch the image of the procedure on the screen as he removed the appendix. Totally unlike traditional surgery with general anesthesia, a large incision and direct observation of the appendix, this was less invasive, required less anesthesia and recovery time was much faster.

"The obstetrics team thinks you're a good candidate. Your uterus hasn't expanded so much that your appendix won't be seen through the camera, and you're in good health. So it's a go, and they're scrubbing in too, just to be there."

"Good hands," she murmured.

"Very good hands. It's an excellent hospital."

"I mean yours," she said, as she fought back the pre-anesthetic grogginess overtaking her.

"Look, Deanna. Before they take you, there's something I want you to know. About that kiss…"

"You didn't like it?" she interrupted.

"No. I loved it. It wasn't a mistake. Neither time."

"Could have been longer," she said. Her words were slurring now. She could hear them and they came out with such effort… *Have to tell him. Now. He has to know.*

"It will be longer next time," he said. "If that's what you want. I've done a lot of thinking, but now's not the time to talk about this. So…"

"Shh," she said, raising her finger to her lips to silence him and totally missing her face. "I have to talk now."

He chuckled. "You won't be talking for long."

"Which is why I have to say this now. The baby—"

"Will be fine," he interrupted. "I know that's your biggest fear. But the baby will be fine."

"My baby," she said, fighting to stay awake.

"Of course it's your baby." He lowered his face to her hand and kissed the back of it. "And you're going to be the best mother—"

"Your baby," she said.

"Yes, I'll love it like it's my baby."

"It *is* your baby," she said, as her eyes started to flutter shut. "Emily's egg, your sperm. Your baby…"

"No way."

"Your baby," she said one final time, then drifted off.

* * *

"How's she doing?" Brax asked. He was strolling down the hall like he belonged there. No cane, no limp. A totally revitalized man.

Beau nodded. "They just took her in. I'm going to go…" He looked at his grandfather. "Where's Lucas?"

"With Kelli Dawson. She's looking after him for the day."

"She said something, Brax. Deanna said something I don't understand, and maybe it's because she was most of the way under, but…" He thought about her words again. Put together, they made sense. But in the whole context of his life they didn't.

"Judging from they way you're as white as a ghost, I'd say whatever she told you was pretty earth-shaking."

"To put it mildly. She told me the baby she's carrying is mine. To cut a long story short, she was carrying her cousin's baby, and her cousin died. Deanna said her cousin's egg was impregnated with my sperm. Earlier she told me that the reason her cousin's husband didn't want the baby was that the insemination had been done with the wrong sperm. But—"

"Maybe it's true. Mistakes happen…" Brax shrugged. "Or maybe what she said was simply the anesthetic ramblings of a woman in love who wants the man she loves to be the father of her baby. That's been known to happen, too."

"She loves me?"

"Are you blind, son? That woman turned her life upside down, and it wasn't because she's clamoring for a future here in Sugar Creek. She's been clamoring for you. You're in love with her, aren't you?"

"Maybe I am."

"Maybe, my ass." Brax squared his shoulders. "Deanna Lambert's the finest woman you're ever going to have in your life. If you let her into your life. And if you want my opinion—"

"Like I could stop you," Beau interrupted.

Not to be dissuaded, Brax continued, "If you want my opinion, you'd be a damned fool to let her get away. Unless it's her baby that's stopping you. Is that why you're out here with me rather than barging your way into surgery and letting her know you're with her every step of the way?"

Was it the baby that was causing him to hesitate? Or his fear that when she was better she'd go back to being the Deanna Lambert who wanted to go it alone? "I don't know," he admitted.

"Then I'd suggest you find out, son. Instead of complicating the thing, simplify it. If you love her, tell her, then find a way to make it work."

"Easy for you to say," Beau said, then he headed down the surgical hall and straight into the scrub room. The thing was, it was easy for him to say, too.

"I love Deanna Lambert," he said, as he tapped the faucet on with his foot and began the scrubbing routine. "I love Deanna Lambert." So now it was time to step up to that love and find out if she loved him back. Or be miserable in silence for a long, long time. Maybe for ever.

Oh, how she didn't want to wake up, but that's what the voices were telling her to do. Cloudy voices, distant voices. And…she could hear Beau.

"Wake up, Deanna. It's over now. Baby's doing fine, and you're doing fine."

Baby's doing fine. Beautiful words that made her feel so much better. "Your baby," she murmured.

"We'll talk about that later. Right now, you just need to concentrate on opening your eyes."

Other voices she didn't recognize chimed in. They wanted her eyes open, too. "Don't want to," she shouted, or was she just whispering? In her head it all sounded the same.

"Sure you do. You want to wake up and open your eyes."

Beau's voice again. For him, she did want to wake up and open her eyes. Only for him. "Love him," she murmured. "I love him."

"I think that was meant for you," Brax said.

Brax, what was he doing here? He shouldn't be here, too. "Lucas?" she forced herself to say.

"He's fine. Don't worry. Kelli Dawson is keeping him until one of us gets back to Sugar Creek." Beau brushed his fingers across her cheek. "And if you ever even hint that you don't have maternal instincts, Deanna Lambert, I'm going remind you of your first two concerns coming out of anesthesia. "

"But he's OK," she said, sighing. "That's good, because I'm going to keep him if I can." Now she felt better. Lucas was fine. Her baby was fine. Beau was here. "All good," she said, then let the clouds roll over her consciousness for a while longer.

"It's about time," Beau said, only a moment later.

This time she did open her eyes, and the only person she saw was Beau. "How long was I…?"

"We tried waking you a couple of hours ago, but you weren't ready. Once you knew that Lucas and your baby were fine, you drifted off with a smile on your face. A beautiful smile."

"Hope I didn't say anything I shouldn't."

"Nothing you shouldn't, but…" He paused then walked over to the window. It was a small hospital in a beautiful area, and Deanna's view for the next couple of days would be a mountain. "But some of the things you were trying to tell me were…well, pretty crazy. About the baby being…"

"Yours?"

"It's not an easy subject for me, Deanna." He turned to face her. "I know you were in a lot of pain then under anesthesia, so I understand that some of the things you said might be a little off. But there's something you have to know. Back when I was married, my wife drove me crazy with her obsession with getting pregnant. Every day, every night she came at me with it and I gave in to something I shouldn't have done.

"Like I told you, she'd come to the hospital, and it was embarrassing me. She asked me to bank my sperm so if I wasn't available when she was ovulating… I did, because I was feeling so guilty and so pressured. Then when you told me the baby you're carrying is mine, and you said there was a mix-up with the sperm used in fertilizing Emily's egg…"

He drew in a ragged breath. "To cut a long story short, I found an e-mail from Nancy to her lawyer, asking him approximately how much she'd be entitled to if she had my baby as opposed to how much she'd get if she simply walked away.

"I'd had this inheritance from my mother and she wanted as much as she could get. So I had the sperm destroyed, gave her a settlement just to be done with it, and…and that's about it. Until you said…"

"I'm having your baby. I'm so sorry, but it's the truth. My cousin Emily—her husband's name is Alexander Braxton and it seems *his* sperm was destroyed accidentally. Maybe in place of yours, I don't know. But Emily's egg was fertilized with your sperm. My lawyers had to fight to get the information, but that's what happened.

"And when Emily found out, she told Alex, who said he wasn't going to raise another man's child. He gave Emily a choice—him or her baby. She chose her baby, and she was leaving him when…" She shut her eyes. "It was raining that night, she missed a turn. And I became a real mother to her child. My child. Your child. Except with the things you've said…"

"Damn," he muttered.

"You have a right to question me, Beau. I understand. Especially after what Nancy—"

"No. I don't question what you're saying, Deanna. You're not lying to me. But that's what your conflicts have been about, isn't it? Telling me."

"I tried, Beau. So many times I tried. But I was scared, because I was falling in love with you and I didn't know…"

"You didn't know what I would do because of all the stupid things I said. Deanna, I'm so sorry. You were hearing my anger, because I've never completely put it behind me. Brax keeps telling me I need to move on, but it's like so many things in my life were frozen in place. Until I met you. Then I wanted that change to happen, but you never let me in completely, so, instead of risking being hurt again, I put up my defenses. And I'm so sorry."

"But you didn't know. How could you? I'm the one who should be apologizing because I never meant to hurt you, Beau."

"Would you have told me if the baby's life hadn't been in danger?"

"I would have. But I thought that would put up a wall between us that would never come down, and because Lucas and Brax… I really do want to adopt Lucas if I can, so I had to consider what was best for him, and that was being around you and Brax. He needs you both right now, and I didn't want my situation to pull him away from you. After his situation was resolved, I would have told you about the baby. I promise, I would have told you."

"And now I'm going to be a father," he said somberly.

"Any way you want to do it, Beau. You do have a choice in this, and I'll respect it."

"Did you come to Sugar Creek to spy on me?" he asked, a twinkle popping into his eyes.

"Spying was all I meant to do. I knew what kind of person Emily was, but I wanted to know what kind of person my baby's father was. I think it was part of my need to put off accepting how my life was changing, the real pain of missing my cousin, maybe a whole lot of other things I haven't figured out yet. But I wanted to know, wanted to see for myself."

"Then look what happened."

"Just look," she murmured, as her eyelids started to flutter down.

"Before you go back to sleep, would you answer one more question for me?" he asked, leaning over the bed rail.

"I'll try," she said, her eyes not opening again.

"Will you marry me, Deanna? Stay here in Sugar Creek with me? Raise our baby together, adopt Lucas, put up with my hectic lifestyle and deal with my cantankerous old grandfather? Or do it in New York and start a new life together there. Any way you want to do it, because I love you."

"With you," she said. "I want to do it with…" Sigh. Over and out.

"Well, it wasn't the most romantic proposal, but I'll do it again, Deanna. When you'll remember it." He bent over and kissed her on the forehead, then pulled aside her gown, looked at her belly, bandaged as it was, and smiled. "Our baby."

"Emily Rose Alexander," Deanna said, cradling her daughter in her arms. "Do you know how much your mommy and daddy love you?" They were living in the ranch house now, and Brax had bought and moved to the cabin up on the ridge, happy to be someplace with a better view. He was practicing medicine again in a limited capacity, mornings only, while Beau and Lucas tended the horses. And Deanna was continuing her consultant work, but only part time, and always with her daughter close by.

In their efforts to expand medical services, Beau and Deanna had even brought in a pediatrician to take care of the increasing kiddie population in the area. The clinic was expanding, life was expanding, and it was everything Emily would have wanted for her daughter. Everything Deanna wanted for *her* daughter and son.

"When can she come outside and play with me?" Lucas asked impatiently. The same question he'd been asking for weeks.

"Not for a few years," Beau said, settling down on the couch next to Deanna. "And, Lucas, you'd better put on your boots because your grandpa is on his way here to give you a riding lesson."

"Grandpa's more fun than Emily," Lucas said. "She can't do anything."

Beau and Deanna looked at each other, smiling. Lucas was legally their son now. There hadn't been much of a legal ordeal since there was no family to be found. And he was turning into a grandpa's boy. Great-grandpa, actually. Of course Brax was spoiling him rotten. "And Grandpa's going to teach Emily to ride when she's old enough," Beau said.

As Lucas scampered off in pursuit of his riding boots, Deanna handed Emily over to Beau then started to stand up. But he grabbed her hand and pulled her back down to the sofa next to him.

"As much as I'd love staying here with the two of you, I've got a couple of patients coming in this afternoon."

"But I'm the doctor," Beau said, as he made faces at his daughter.

"And I'm the nurse who shares her husband's practice, and handles minor cases so he can have more time with his family." She smiled. "Remember the plan to keep you less obsessed?"

"I've got a house call later on. And I promised Arthur I'd stop by for a few minutes. He's writing a book on his journey from heart attack to fitness guru and he wants me to check a couple of his medical facts."

"And I've got to take Lucas for pizza while you're gone. It's a date for just the two of us, and Brax is going to have an evening alone with Emily, which he's been pestering me about for days."

"What about us?" Beau said, feigning a hurt expression. "When do we get some time alone?"

"Trust me, I've got you penciled in. Tonight. Champagne. Dim lights. Soft music. Hot tub for starters."

"Then what?" he asked, his attention now fully diverted from Emily to Deanna.

"Everything," Deanna said, scooting in closer to him, then laying her head on his shoulder. "Absolutely everything."

* * * * *

A sneaky peek at next month...

CAPTIVATING MEDICAL DRAMA—WITH HEART

My wish list for next month's titles...

In stores from 7th June 2013:

Available at WHSmith, Tesco, Asda, Eason, Amazon and Apple

Just can't wait?